SHORTS

New Writing
from Granta Books

Granta Books
London

Granta Publications, 2/3 Hanover Yard, London N1 8BE

This collection first published in Great Britain by
Granta Books 1998. This collection copyright © 1998 Granta Books.

Typeset in Berkeley by M Rules
Printed and bound in Great Britain by
Mackays of Chatham PLC

Since its relaunch as an independent literary publishing house in January 1997, Granta Books has built a reputation for its commitment to discovering and introducing new fiction.

Shorts brings together twenty-one stories by such diverse and well-established writers as Louis de Bernières, A.L. Kennedy, Hanif Kureishi and Romesh Gunesekera, as well as the newer voices of Michelle Huneven, David Treuer and Kamila Shamsie, who is published here for the first time.

We hope *Shorts* will be enjoyed both by long-time fans of the short story, and readers new to the experience. If you enjoy *Shorts*, look out for new Granta Books collections from Kirsty Gunn and Ali Smith in the near future.

Contents

A Drive

Philip MacCann

I came down our drive and on to the footpath but my old man was still polishing the aerial of the Toyota. The sky was dark, for summer. At the top of our road two of my friends were climbing into the waste ground. I went round the back of our car and I put my Gameboy in the boot. But then I heard, 'Dear, dear.' I looked up at my old man. He was making a big thing of it, letting on to be completely baffled. Inside my head I said, 'Fat bastard'. A black woman squeezed past us with a trolley and I went back in through the front door to get my Lego robot.

Only months ago my old man got the car he had been saving up for with alloy wheels and all. It is a good sporty one but it is only second-hand. I thought he was going to go mad taking me on trips, but then he had a stroke. He was sad about that but it is kind of funny too with the invalid sticker in the back window and all. I came back on to the road now with MegaMan, ready to go. My old man's face was cross. Something was up with him again. He leaned more of his weight on his walking stick and looked right in my eyes. 'Where are you going?' he asked as though he was a bit puzzled.

I had to think about that. The footpath was going kind of sharp and then blurry from a cloud. I clashed the boot shut for him and answered, 'On a drive.'

He lifted his eyebrows and said, 'Oh?' he said. 'Well.' He pressed the lid back on his tin of polish. 'Off you go then.' His eyes were right on mine.

I said, 'What?'

'Bye bye then.' He kept looking. I could feel my heart begin to thud slowly. I looked up and down the road. Then I started walking down the footpath, still holding my robot. I did not know where I was going yet because the waste ground was the other way. I walked slowly and my body felt very light. When I reached the corner on our road he called down after me, 'Hey!' I stopped and looked back at him. 'What about our drive?'

I stood for a few seconds scratching my ear. Then I walked back up, bobbing my head so he would think I was not fussed. I only climbed into the passenger seat against my consent.

He limped along the side of the car mumbling to himself, 'Squeaky boxes. And robots.' He turned in our garden. I hate his car. It is flashy but there is lots wrong with it. It smells of sweat and the window is too stiff to roll down. I knocked the seat back a notch and waited for him. Kids were shouting in the distance, their voices kind of muffled. Only my friends and I play on the waste ground. Our area has a lot of black families and my old man says, don't play with those monkeys. But I do not care because I am only boarding out with my old man while I am waiting to be adopted.

In a few minutes he came out again. He managed to squeeze into his seat. He got his breath. He was in a better mood now. He twiddled the gear stick before trying the engine. It would not start at first but after twisting the key a few times the engine revved up. He took the car carefully off the kerb and peered up at the sky and went, 'Not so bad.' I looked out my window. Everything was dark and white at the same time. The car stuttered as it gathered speed. We drove past the big poster of the little kid sucking the big ice lolly. My dad started to tut and he shook his head again. I knew he was going to start on about my playing on the waste ground. He said, 'That ground is only a place for queer people. Perverts.'

I was right.

As we passed the demolished shop the car started to judder. There was reggae coming from a bar and I spotted some of my friends in a gang at the corner. Delmar leered at us. My dad opened his collar button. I turned to see them through the back window. Then, just like that, the car cut out. 'What in hell's blazes!' he hissed. I grinned at my friends and throttled my neck in a jokey way. We rolled for a bit until we came to a halt. There was a big cardboard box sitting on the main road. 'Well, that's nice,' said my dad winding down his window. His voice got steadily louder. 'That's those bloody bastard friends of yours, I can't keep my car outside my own house!' I could not think what to do with my face. He started laughing and I jumped. 'If you think I'll be defeated by the likes of that ignorant rubbish,' he went on. 'No sir. On no account.' His cheek was twitching.

The following afternoon he worked at the engine. He had pieces of it all over the footpath and the car was cranked up. There was a blotch of oil on his face. My eyes kept avoiding it. 'See those spark plugs?' he said. I said, 'Those?' but I was really watching Delmar up ahead. He had climbed into the skip on our side of the road and was trampolining on all the rubbish. I could see him clearly because the light looked sort of very washed after the rain. A skinny kid was with him. 'Never mind them,' said my old man quietly. 'Always keep your spark plugs well filed.' He

3

unscrewed one slowly. He slipped it out. He began filing the tip. 'It's the sort of thing shows you know better. That you aren't just a complete Yahoo.' The kids started towards us with long slow movements. 'Take it,' said my dad. Delmar was flashing his teeth. 'You do it.'

'What's happening?' asked Delmar with his head lolling on one side.

'Dunno,' I said.

I sneaked a glance at my dad. His hand was going up and down on the plug again.

'You coming down the dump?' Delmar wanted to know. On his T-shirt was a pop star.

'I can't,' I told him. 'I have to do this.' My old man did not stop filing. He was breathing through his nose.

'Don't worry, mister, we won't get in no trouble.'

'Are you watching me do this?' my dad rasped.

I answered, 'Yes.'

My friends sauntered away. Delmar shouted back, 'Is that your brain you're fixing, mister?' I looked at the spark plug being filed.

'Is that . . . filed down?' I said quickly.

He twisted it back into the engine. He straightened up and rested on his stick. His eyes were closed like he was taking another dizzy spell. He wiped his fingers on a cloth. There was a small bubble between his lips.

A bit later I got away and I went after Delmar. At the top of the road I turned in behind the hoarding with the poster of the kid sucking the big lolly. I could see the both of them in the distance tugging at a rubber belt or something. The sky was very low and white. When I got close I hauled up some plasterboard. 'Watch out,' I called and slugged it towards them into a ditch of brown water in front of me. It splashed softly. Then I felt a bit stupid.

'Watch my 501s!' his friend called across. 'Or I will sue you.'

We kicked through loads of rubbish and newspapers. I could hear a tiny ice-cream van tinkling in the distance, but clear as though it was tiny and up against my ear. The other kid's name was Ancel. 'What, pencil?' I said.

'Shut up, right?' His teeth were a bright crescent shape. 'You were born to die. And we were born to kill you.'

I mumbled, 'Kiss my ass, Dairy Milk.'

We chased through brambles down a wild slope. There was more ground at the bottom which stretched across to the rear of some disused shops. We stayed in the grass and they laughed at my dad, calling him a nutter. I said his name was Gerry Atric. I made them giggle.

'Why won't he let you play down the dump?' asked Delmar.

'Cause there are perverts down here,' I told them.

We lay on our bellies chatting like that for a long while.

The next day my old man was eating his dinner in front of the TV and I was in our hall messing with my cars. I could hear men loading the skip outside on the road. We are the only ones in the terrace who own our own home and he makes it look good with peacock feathers in a vase and things like that. You have to be quiet in our house and keep it nice and treat the carpets with respect. Every morning I take down all the toys I wanted for the day so as not to keep running up and down the stairs and wear them out.

I got bored with my cars so I stood in the doorway of the front room with nothing to do.

'I suppose you know nothing about your own history,' said my dad with his mouth full. 'Exhibitions. Where you can learn things.' I peered at the TV. There were black and white photographs on it. 'I could drive you somewhere like that. A whole different world.'

I sat down on the settee. All the people in the photographs were thin and wearing rags. I could not care if he drove me somewhere or not. I just wanted to go down the waste ground. It was peaceful and empty down there. On the TV now the people suddenly had no clothes on. They were starving or they might have been dead but it showed you their arses. There was a whole pile of naked bodies and some had big, long dicks. My dad sighed. It kept showing you dicks and arses.

'Well, well,' he said. He screwed his face up. 'Dear me.'

I was very embarrassed and I felt sad and heavy. He was shaking his head. It would not stop, it showed you more arses and even tits. He wiped his forehead with a tissue and said, 'Is this entertainment? Who do they think wants to see this on television?' I decided to grin. He leaned forward in his chair and knocked the TV off with his stick. 'It's all buttocks on that programme.' He poured milk in his tea. 'And people's private parts. On television.' Then he looked straight at me hard. His eyes were red and he made them narrow. 'Is that the kind of image you wish to see portrayed?'

'No,' I said.

He took a sip from his tea. 'Buttocks.'

I went out into the front garden and sat on my bike supported by the hedge. There were loud smashes from the skip on the road. I wanted to think on my own about things but then I heard my old man open our front door. I took the bike off the hedge but I did not look round. He stayed there getting some air. Then after a minute he limped with his stick past me to the gate and looked at the Toyota. Without turning round he said, 'What about tomorrow then?' We were breathing dust from the skip. 'I don't want to get your hopes up but . . . I think we could.' I kept quiet so he turned round. 'A drive?' he said. He let that word hang in the air.

It was my turn to speak but I did not know how to answer. I

wanted to say, 'Off you go then,' but I just mumbled, 'Oh.'

He looked like he was hurt. 'Oh?' he said. He came close to me. I back-pedalled a few times. He stood right next to me, not saying anything, only blinking. At last he whispered, 'I thought you wanted to go on a drive.' I shrugged my shoulders and there was just silence. Then he reached his hand out towards me. He touched my button on my T-shirt. There was something like blood in his eyes. 'Just you and me.'

'I do,' I told him.

He would not stop fiddling with my button. He said, 'You don't have to go.'

'I want to.'

I could hear him breathe. He mumbled, 'I don't know what to think.' I was feeling tense all over, but then he took his hand back. He limped back up to the door saying, 'Oh ! Oh!' to himself.

When the door clicked shut I cycled up to watch the men loading the skip.

The next morning I spotted Delmar and Ancel perched on the rim of the skip from our front room. I went out the front door and stopped at the gate. It was a very quiet day. Everything was pale. There were birds in the air like a flying dotted line. My old man was sitting on the footpath changing a tyre. His stick lay beside me. I hoped he was not going to take me out, which was possible because it was a bank holiday. I had to get down the waste ground in a minute or I would go mad. He was watching me, waiting for me to make a move. I took a breath and started walking towards my friends. As I passed him, I mumbled 'Hi.' I joined my friends and we slouched down the road together without talking. Before we had got to the corner he called after me.

'Tomorrow.' I stopped and looked back at him. 'You, me. A drive.' He tried to say it firmly but he was getting his breath. He was staring hard at me, then he narrowed his eyes. 'Unless you have . . . a prior engagement?' I shrugged my shoulders, and he called out simply, 'Think on.'

I walked with my friends to the top of the road. There was no air and the day was like whitewash. All the streets were empty. An ice-cream man was eating a cone in his van. We nipped in behind the hoarding. We were happy now. We decided to go looking for perverts and stone them. We trailed our shoes through the rubble. I upturned a heavy stone with my heel. Everything was quiet like after a nuclear disaster. Ancel said you could find pornography at the back of the disused shops. I have never had the opportunity to see pornography, but I want to learn. I daydreamed about it as we walked along. I could picture a pile of dead people showing off all their arses and their tits. It was very interesting.

We bumped down the slope. As we walked across the loose stones there were good things to prod at. Ancel picked up a dark half bottle. We idled along the wall, talking about sex. Delmar said you got urges. He stamped on a can. A shadow appeared beneath us and faded away. I saw a tiny bit of paper on the ground, the corner of a magazine.

'Hey, look at this,' I shouted, snatching it up.

They darted towards me, but I dodged them and belted back up the slope. I crouched in the grass and examined it. It was a bit of a picture of a person. I could not guess what part of the body it was because it was so close up. I did not know if it was pornography or not, but it looked sexual. I wanted to know. I leaned on one elbow and rubbed my dick to try to make it go hard. While I rubbed I glanced up to see where Delmar and Ancel were. But then I saw a man on the slope. All of a sudden, my elbow slipped.

I fell forward on my face. A thistle was beside my cheek.

When I looked up again the man was passing me and trotting down to the bottom of the slope. He was a white man but he had a weird blotch on his face. My heart was pounding.

Ancel hurried over to me and I sat up. His words splashed out. 'Is that a pervert?'

'Yeah,' I said. 'He tried to touch me. He's a kidnapper.'

Delmar skidded up on his knees. 'Did he do anything?'

I made out I was laughing but I felt a bit mixed up. 'I told him to fuck off and he legged it.' We watched the man disappear behind the corner of the shops. I kept talking but my voice had become very dry. 'Did you see his red blotch? It was mad, wasn't it? You should have seen his face when I threatened him. It turned as white as that sky.' Ancel dug for a marble sunk in the mud and lobbed it at the shop corner. They both looked at me again. 'He's a pervert,' I told them.

After a minute we got to our feet and walked back across the waste ground. There was not much to do. Ancel scooped up a rusty battery and swung it. A tiny bird flew into the corner of my eye. I felt a bit sad. I did not understand why the man had a blotch on his face. Someone like him might adopt me. 'What'll we do now?' said Delmar but we could not think. We just walked over the waste ground throwing stones up into the sky for a while.

The car was ready for a drive the next morning but it was a dark day. My old man and I sat out our back on deck chairs waiting for the sky to brighten up. He said he did not feel well. He was reading a magazine called *Leisure* and I lay back with my eyes closed thinking. I was starting to get an urge to go out and play. But he decided we would drive somewhere, so we stood up and went inside to get ready.

I took my Gameboy out to the car again and got in but this time he did not even notice. He flung his stick on the back seat and climbed in his door. He had taken choc-ices from out of the fridge. We sat on the seats sucking them for a minute before starting off.

'All right,' he said eventually and he turned the key. It had got even darker while we sat with our lollies. We drove past the big bill poster and I saw Ancel standing underneath it on his own. A cream ambulance was parked on the main road. I was trying to get the seat at the right notch when all of a sudden he pressed his horn. He pulled in outside a newsagent's and gulped down the rest of his choc-ice. I put the seat back and finished mine slowly.

A woman came up to his window and he wound it down and started chatting to her. Two men walked in front of the car and one touched our bonnet. My dad talked about his car to the woman. He called it a beauty and said, 'He loves it. He'll tell you.' He talked very fast. I had my lips right against my window when he pressed his thumb into my side. 'Tell her,' he said with a laugh. 'Tell her how good our car is.'

I wiped my lips and looked at the woman. She seemed dreamy. My dad's face was a bit purple. Behind the woman the two men were standing talking. My dad was going on about the car in a weird way and I was embarrassed. I bet his dick was sticking up under his jacket. I thought if I had to say something about the car maybe I could get him back now. 'It just glides over the road,' he was saying. 'He can't get over it.' He looked hard at me now and said again, a bit nervously, 'Tell her.' I was sick of him saying that. I could get him back and tell her lots of things about him. She was smiling at me.

'Are you not going to tell me?' she asked. She winked. She was OK. Just then, one of the men behind her turned his head to the side. He had a big blotch on his cheek. It was the pervert. Suddenly I freaked.

'Go ahead,' said my old man. 'Just tell her.'

'What car!' I mumbled as if it was a heap of junk. The woman glanced at my old man. She made a jittery laugh. My old man was blinking and smiling. I hoped the pervert would not see me.

'That was a good answer, son,' said the woman.

'Well, now,' said my dad. 'Well, that was . . . unexpected.'

'He's not interested in cars,' said the woman. She was right about that, I was just dying to get a peek at the pervert because I had a picture of him walking down the slope with a big blotch.

'Him? I don't know what I'll do with that bloody clown. He can hardly change his own underpants.' Now I wished I had kept quiet. I slipped down on my seat to look at the pervert without my old man knowing. I was mixed up. The woman chatted on for a bit. But soon she went away.

My dad switched off the engine. He tugged his collar open. I was waiting for the pervert to look round because I had to see his blotch, but my dad stared at me. His eyes had gone big and watery. He spoke sadly, 'What car? Just the bloody car that could take you . . . out of the slum you . . . you seem to be so suited to.' He took the keys right out of the engine. All of a sudden the pervert turned and started walking right in front of the bonnet. But I could not get a look at his face because my old man had turned to me. 'Let me tell you. We can always manage independently,' he was saying. 'You can play on that dump till your heart's content.' I was not listening. I started thinking about the waste ground. I love it down there. His voice had become a whisper. 'Expect nothing from me. No time, no knowledge, information, no . . . drives . . .' He was still rabbiting on. I wish my dad would die. He made me miss seeing the pervert's blotch. He was wiping his eyes. He would not drive.

Unspeakable Hunger

Kamila Shamsie

During all the years my aunt, Mariam, lived with us she only spoke to order meals.

I should explain, she wasn't exactly my aunt, nor related from my mother's side, though I always called her 'Khala'. Cousin, I believe, would be more accurate a term. Her grandfather and my grandfather were cousins, but while my grandfather was at Oxford, studying how to be an Englishman and do well in the world, her grandfather decided to protest the British colonial presence in the subcontinent. He did this by leaving home without warning and nearly giving his mother a heart attack.

Two weeks after his disappearance he wrote from someplace with an indistinct postal stamp to say that he was in the employ of an English army officer, as a valet. This act showed, he wrote, that he had accepted his historical role, and the only real difference between him and all his relatives who were Civil Servants or businessmen in English-run companies was that he was required to wear a grander uniform. The family would not hear from him again because he was repudiating English and – alas! – his tutors had never seen fit to teach him how to write Urdu.

This letter was passed around the family, who returned the

unanimous verdict: he's lying. I'm still not sure if this conviction arose from a knowledge of my great-uncle's character, or a mere unwillingness to accept that a scion of such an old feudal family would demean himself so far as to become a valet.

This was all before my father was born. He grew up in Pakistan thinking of his uncle as a family legend, one whom he mentally put alongside the ancestor who had committed suicide by swallowing one of the largest diamonds in the world, and his grandson, the one-armed ancestor who killed a tiger with his bare hand (the tiger-skin hung in the library of the family home in India as proof).

So it was something of a surprise, to say the least, for my father to receive a letter informing him of his uncle's death and asking him to please do his family duty and look after his niece Mariam (that is, his uncle's orphaned granddaughter) who would be arriving at his house shortly. At the bottom of the page was an official-looking signature. That is, an indecipherable scrawl.

Hollywood-style, he had just finished reading the letter out to my mother when the gate bell rang. My parents gaped at each other, assured themselves no, it must be coincidence, probably the milkman with the monthly bill. But then Masood entered the room to say a begum sahib is here . . . she is waiting in the drawing room . . . she did not give her name, but she's brought two suitcases.

'Well,' my mother said, 'if she comes up to the servants' snobbish standards sufficiently to be seated in the drawing room she clearly isn't a valet's daughter. Even my cousin Shehla only made it to the TV room, and she likes to think of herself as a princess!'

I have so often imagined that first meeting between my parents and Mariam Khala that I sometimes feel I must have been there. I was, but only in a foetal way. My parents entered the drawing room, pausing in the hallway outside only long enough to see that the suitcases were of a fine quality.

Mariam Khala stood up as they entered, quite self-assured, as though she were the gracious host, they the needy relatives. She was wearing her blue chiffon sari, three gold bracelets on her left arm, a gold chain with a diamond-studded pendant in the shape of an Arabic 'Allah' around her neck. Her black hair, parted to one side, fell half-way down her back and swayed ever so slightly, though she was standing still.

'Oh, er . . . hello,' my father said.

Mariam Khala just smiled that exquisite smile of hers that became known to cause roses to burst into bloom, and my mother rushed across the room to hug her. It is always possible to measure my mother's reaction to a person by multiplying the time, in seconds, that she speaks for without pause, by the number of words she utters in that time. The greater the result, the more she likes the person. When she met Mariam Khala she went into seven digits. So my father tells me, and he's always been good at calculations. At any rate, the warmth of my mother's reaction to Mariam Khala's smile was so overwhelming that nearly ten minutes went by before my father realized that Mariam Khala hadn't said a word.

He stopped my mother's monologue with a tap on her shoulder and said, 'I was so sorry to hear about your grandfather. What happened?'

Mariam Khala looked heavenward and raised her hands and shoulders in a gesture of resignation to a higher will.

'Well, yes, of course there's that,' my father said. 'But can you be more specific?'

Mariam Khala tapped her heart.

My mother reached over, grabbed Mariam Khala's hand. 'Can you speak?'

Mariam Khala nodded.

'Oh,' said my mother. 'Well . . . well . . . oh. I suppose I should show you your room. We only found out . . .so the bed hasn't been made up but it's a lovely room, my favourite in the house actually, I prefer it to our room but he doesn't like it because of some reason he's never seen fit to share with me. But I know you will . . .'

That's when Masood walked in. He had come to work for my parents when they got married, a year earlier, and had been hailed by all who had sampled his cooking as 'a cook to be hired but never fired'.

'Begum Sahib,' he addressed my mother in Urdu, 'what should I make for dinner tonight?'

Before my mother could answer, Mariam Khala said: '*aloo ka bhurta, achaar gosht, pulao, masoor ki daal, kachoomar.*'

And my parents knew she was part of the family, for she had ordered their favourite meal. By the time I was born five months later, Mariam Khala's silence in all matters unrelated to ordering meals had become part of the norm in our household. My father still tried to coax out of her some details of her grandfather's life, convinced that if he guessed correctly she would nod and let him know as much. So, 'he was a spy!' he would exclaim after watching the latest James Bond movie. 'A pimp!', after he had drunk too much and sung bawdy songs with his friends. 'A Shakespearean actor in Papua New Guinea.' No one ever knew where that came from. But Mariam Khala always shook her head, and to this day I don't know what my great-uncle did after he left home.

But for some reason I still cannot quite explain, no one ever asked her why she never spoke except to dictate menus. And that, too, only to Masood. She spoke only to him, ate food that only he had cooked. The week he was in hospital, when I was five, she did not speak a word, not even to the substitute cook, and she did not eat a bite.

Once I asked my parents, 'Why? Why is she this way? Why does she only speak to order meals?'

My father shrugged. 'If you ask me she's taking the whole goddamn notion of a woman's traditional role a little too literally.'

But my mother laughed at this and reminded me of Mariam Khala's encounter with Dr Tahir.

I must have been about eight when that happened. It was December, and Karachi's social élite were feverishly getting married and throwing parties before the hot weather and riots and curfew returned and impeded social activity. (Mariam Khala was, incidently, extremely popular in the social milieu, praised for being discreet, a good listener and for never interrupting anyone's flow of loquaciousness.)

My parents and Mariam Khala were at a party, the last of their social stops for the evening. Mariam Khala was draped in a lovely sari that was covered in intricate sequined designs. As she and my mother wandered to the buffet table, a liveried bearer tripped on the uneven ground and sent a dozen glasses of pomegranate juice crashing to the floor to splatter Mariam Khala's sari with red blots.

'Oh, too bad,' a male voice exclaimed, and she turned to see Dr Tahir – the man infamous for diagnosing mosquito bites as measle bumps – standing behind her. 'Well, you'll never wear that again,' he said cheerfully. 'That's the problem with these fancy sequined clothes. Can't wash them. I always say, "You want proof that men are more practical than women? Go compare their clothes."'

Mariam Khala did not sleep that night. She sat in the TV room, and unstitched every single sequin in the area around the stained section of the sari. When I woke up to get ready for school she was in the bathroom handwashing the sari. And when

I returned home that afternoon she had just finished stitching back every sequin in its original place. That night she did the unthinkable and re-wore the sari to a dinner where she knew she would see Dr Tahir.

'So you see,' my mother told me, 'she is . . . I don't know . . . determined, stubborn, she has something that can make her do these things. So maybe sometime in her past someone said something to her, someone like Dr Tahir, and to prove him wrong she decided to stop talking, and discovered she could.'

I never found out which of my parents was right, or if they were both as far from the truth as my younger cousin who said, 'Maybe she doesn't know any words that aren't related to food.' To be quite honest, I didn't really care.

It was enough for me to sleep curled beside her in the afternoons, our heads sharing the same pillow, enough to watch her fingers rise, curl, tap, fall in the hand-dance of music as she listened to Beethoven being played or Ghalib being sung, enough to know she was watching me as I did my homework, watching me for the simple reason that I was not invisible in her world. And enough to eat the meals she ordered.

Poor Masood, I suppose I should give him some credit. He was the one who cooked, after all. But my parents maintain that although he was a fine – indeed superior – cook from day one, he only became a magician the day she arrived. Never more so than in the month of Ramzan.

Officially the month of fasting, Ramzan always seemed to me synonymous with feasting. Abstaining from food and drink from sunrise to sunset had less to do with religious devotion than it did with culinary devotion. For in order to truly appreciate the Iftar meal that Mariam Khala ordered we had to build ourselves up to a pitch of hunger that enabled us to sit and eat and eat for an hour and a half without pause.

In drawing rooms across the country frazzled Begums complained that all this fasting, combined with the heatwave, made their cooks so horribly bad-tempered – and, of course, one felt guilty asking them to stand over a stove and cook under these circumstances. Masood, however, loved it. He liked nothing so much as to shoo us out of the kitchen with the warning, 'If you smell my food you will be so overcome with temptation that you'll break your fast on the spot. Leave, leave, before you make me into an instrument of Shaitan and send you to hell.' The only person he allowed in was Mariam Khala who would chop and stir and watch, as she never did during any other time of the year.

And oh! the meals that resulted! We started with the requisite date, of course, to symbolize fidelity to the first Muslims in the deserts of Arabia, but then . . . on to gluttony! Curly shaped *jalaibees*, hot and gooey, that trickled thick sweet syrup down your chin when you bit into them; diced potatoes drowned in yoghurt, sprinkled in spices; chickpeas similarly created; triangles of fried *samoosas*, the smaller ones filled with mince-meat, the larger ones filled with potatoes and green chillies; *shami* kebabs with sweet-sour *imli* sauce; spinach leaves fried in chickpea batter; *nihari* with large gobs of marrow floating in the thick gravy, and meat so tender it dissolved instantly in your mouth; *lassi* that quenched a day-long thirst as nothing else did and left us wondering why we ever drank Coke when a combination of milk, yoghurt and sugar could be this satisfying; an assortment of sweetmeats – *gulab jamoons*, *ladoos*, *b'rfi* . . .

There were always at least ten people at our house for Iftar and, at some point, someone would look up from his or her third helping and say, 'Mariam, have you finished eating? That's an insult to the food. It's divine!' And Mariam Khala would make a gesture as though plucking the words from the

air and swallowing them, to indicate, 'I am eating your praise.'
Then she would look across at Masood, who had walked in
with hot *naan* to go with the *nihari*, and smile her smile of congratulations. Masood would incline his head in a gesture that
was half salaam of deference, half acceptance of well-deserved
praise.

The only meal that ever surpassed those Ramzan meals was
the one Masood and Mariam Khala prepared for me the day I was
accepted at a college in Lahore. Half-way through the meal I
burst into tears to say, 'But who will cook for me when I'm
there?' And Masood patted my shoulder, 'Don't worry, bibi, when
you come home for the holidays I'll feed you so much they'll
have to roll you back on to the plane.'

'Promise?' I said.

'Promise,' he smiled back.

The next week he was gone.

I knew something was wrong the moment I returned from
school and the only smell to assail my nostrils as I walked up the
drive-way was that of the manure recently delivered to my neighbour's garden. My mother was standing in the kitchen as I ran in,
staring in mystification at Masood's rack of spices.

'What's happened? Where is he? Is he ill?'

'No, no, not ill. He had to leave. His father just died. Masood's
the head of the family now. He has a mother, sisters, a daughter –
did you know that? Hmm . . . his wife died in child-birth just
before he came to us – but, yes, all these women, and he's the
head of the family now. So he went back to his village.'

'For how long?'

'Jaan, he's gone. They need him there. It seems his father was
the cook at the home of the feudal landlord, and Masood will be
taking over that position. He said to tell you he's sorry he didn't
have time to say goodbye, but he had to catch the morning train.'

'But . . . how could he . . how will we . . . what about Mariam Khala?'

My mother shook her head. 'I don't know. We've already found a new cook – the one who worked for your grandmother when Mohammed was on leave – and he's starting tomorrow, but I don't know if Mariam . . . what . . . I just don't know.'

'Where is she?'

'In her room. When Masood was leaving he told her to keep eating, otherwise she'll fall ill and cause him much pain. And she just smiled and . . . hugged him. Briefly. She hugged him good-bye.'

I stared. A hug – across class and gender! And he wasn't even much older than her! Before this, had their fingers even touched as they passed a tomato from one to the other? I doubted it. A hug! I wouldn't have, and Masood had carried me piggy-back style, when I was a child.

But when I walked into Mariam Khala's room she looked as she always did, seated on her bed, reading the afternoon papers.

'Will you eat?' I burst out, as I flung myself across the bed. She ruffled my hair, shook her head, and handed me the comics page.

A week later she still hadn't touched a morsel of food, and my father was raging through the house, railing against the stubbornness of women. He was looking for a fight, of course, but my mother and I were too despondent to rise to the challenge.

In the silence that followed his latest outburst we heard the door swing open. Auntie Tano, an old family friend, walked in.

'Guess who I just met?' she said, after proffering her cheek all around to be kissed.

'Why don't you just tell us,' my father said.

'Pinkie!'

'I thought she was in London.'

'No, no. The other Pinkie. Rash's wife.'

My mother attempted interest. 'Oh, really. How is she?'

'Why do we care?' my father asked.

'You care, my dear man, because she has just spent a week on the family lands with her brother Jahangir.'

'Jahangir! How is he?'

'Why, really, why do we care?'

My mother slapped my father lightly on the wrist. 'Of course we care. Haven't seen him in what . . . three years. Ever since his wife died. He's just stopped coming to the city. I don't know why. You'd think he would get so lonely on the lands.'

'Such a tragedy,' Auntie Tano murmured. 'So young. I have a picture of them at our New Year's party. They look so happy.'

'Yes, well, it was a masquerade party,' my father observed drily.

'Honestly! What a thing to say! They were quite happy together,' Auntie Tano insisted.

'Happy? Come on! It was common knowledge he was having it off with any number of women.'

'Yes. But that was his habit, you know.'

'What?'

'Yes, yes. He acquired the habit before he got married. You can't expect a man to change his habits just because he gets married.'

A long pause followed this remark. Finally my father said, 'Why are we having this conversation?'

'Well, this is what I've been trying to tell you! Masood is Jahangir's cook!'

Next door, in Mariam Khala's room, the bed creaked.

'Of course,' my mother said. 'How stupid of me. That's why the name of Masood's village sounded so familiar.'

'Don't you see?' Auntie Tano said. 'Don't you see how you

can solve Mariam's problem? Jahangir, widower. Masood, his cook. Mariam, single and starving to death.'

No, I screamed to myself. No no no no no.

'Are you mad?' my father yelled. 'Do you think I would send my cousin off to be married to a man she's never met, in some remote village and . . . and . . . and . . . to a man of those habits! Just so that she can dine well! Over my dead body.'

'No,' my mother whispered. 'Her dead body. She's not going to eat anyone else's food, you know. Not at all.'

'Can't she just . . .' I had to say something. 'Can't she just, you know, live there or something? Or buy a house in the area?'

'Alone?' Auntie Tano raised her eyebrows.

My father waved his finger in the air to indicate a thought. 'No, of course, not that. But maybe . . . now that we know where Masood is . . . perhaps, yes, why didn't we consider this before . . . we can pay him to send a supply of food over every week. Send it by train. We could arrange that.'

Mariam Khala glided into the room, a newspaper in her hand. She lifted my mother's hand, pointed to her wedding ring, then pointed to her own unadorned finger, and nodded.

'No,' I pleaded. 'You can't.'

For the first time ever, she ignored me. She held the newspaper out to my father, pointing to something on the page.

'What's this? Train schedules? Wh . . . Mariam, you can't be serious.'

But she was. I knew it immediately by the sudden burning at the back of my eyes. I could not stay then. Could not stay for Auntie Tano's attempt to achieve self-obliteration now that one of her ridiculous schemes was being taken seriously; could not stay for my father's baffled rage; could not stay for my mother's pleas to wait a while, don't be hasty, even if you decide to marry, not him, and if him, not now, wait, weddings have to be planned, this is just not the way things are done. I could not.

I ran to my bathroom, locked the door, curled myself into a ball inside the tub and wept dry tears, my fists banging against the wall's pink tiles. And when half an hour went by and Mariam Khala did not knock on the door, I wept some more. But when I heard my father dragging suitcases down from the store-room shelves, I pushed myself out of the tub, out of the room, into her room where she was waiting for me, arms open just wide enough to fit me in. Something of the fierce tension inside me uncoiled then, for though I knew she would leave, I also knew he – Jahangir – would not be able to help but love her.

'There was a boy in my class called Jahangir,' I gulped between sobs. 'We used to call him Jangia – Underpants.' And then we both laughed, our heads thrown back, our shoulders shaking, our arms still around each other.

She and my father left a few hours later, by the evening train. She had packed all her clothes, much to the consternation of my mother, who kept saying, 'But you're only going to meet him now. That's all. The wedding won't be for a while.'

But she knew Mariam Khala well enough to know there would be no planning and preparation and attention to custom and drawing up guest lists that would include everyone whose shadow had crossed paths with Mariam Khala and her closest relatives.

There was a strange silence in the house when they left. My mother and I both retired to separate rooms to try and imagine what would await Mariam Khala at the end of that train journey. But I could not imagine the Underpants Man as anything other than a caricature, and found myself wondering over and over how she would greet Masood, and would she hug him again? And why, why, I wondered, why was it that when we tried to think of ways to save Mariam Khala there was one we never mentioned?

My father returned, two days later, alone.

'Well?' my mother and I greeted him at the door.

'Well, she's married.'

I looked at my mother, and she looked at me, and I knew she was thinking what I was thinking, only she was thinking it with greater horror, and we both wondered, how? How can we say it? And so we just said it the simplest way we knew:

'To whom?'

The Foot

Michelle Huneven

Sooner or later, everyone finds out. Five years ago, when I was twenty-three years old, I shot my boyfriend in the foot. And was arrested and punished. It would seem at times that the shooting is the most interesting thing about me. Most people have never shot anybody. By the end of every party I go to, all the people I don't know are surreptitiously observing me.

I'm not secretive about the crime, although until now I've never employed a confession as my opening line. Felonies thrive in the public domain, so most people don't have to get the story from me. My friends and even my family happily supply the details. I've gotten so I can spot it when somebody knows. They treat me deferentially. For example, if the subject of violence or, say, gun control arises, they'll attempt to steer the conversation back to gentler topics. I'm not fooled. Such honed sensitivity is really a form of unconscious urging: I can trust them, I can tell them the entire story.

When I do indulge the curious, I'm invariably surprised by their willingness to absolve me. 'You were helping him avoid the draft,' they say. Never mind that the war was over in '75. Or this: 'You must have a deeply passionate nature.' Or this: 'You must have been under a lot of pressure at school.' Oh, I realize that the impulse to ignore any evil intent on my part is a friendly impulse, but such goodwill serves only to underscore the fact that extenuating circumstances merely mitigate punishment and do not erase guilt. Once or twice, while riding the reasoning of my lawyer's arguments, it occurred to me that through some logistical kink I might actually be innocent. The rest of the time, I've felt guilty.

I'm a printmaker. Intaglio. I moved to the Midwest to study with a famous master printmaker. On my third day in town, I met Jon Doppinger while apartment hunting in the rustic decrepitude of Krantz's Kottage Kourt. There were three vacant cottages, all scarcely larger than playhouses. Doppinger and I revolved around and around each other like the figurines on a cuckoo clock. I couldn't help but notice him: he was seven-eighths leg, and tall. So tall that he cracked his head on a lintel as we both left cottage number four. In sympathy, I covered my mouth with my hand. He shook his head. 'Not my day,' he said. 'It started out punk and it's getting worse.' His eyes were shiny blue candies. I smiled and he kept on talking.

'I repair TVs,' he said. 'Today, one just popped out of my arms. Like an idiot, I tried to stop its fall with my foot, and now I've got a bruise on my shin like the aurora borealis. Next, I get this concussion. What's my name? Why is it I never forget the right things?' Doppinger rubbed his head. His hair was tufty and blond. Really, he was very good-looking in an oddly proportioned way.

He rented number eleven. I rented four. I moved in but he never did. I saw him again when he came to get his deposit back from Mr Krantz. He knocked at my door and I asked him in for coffee. When he sat at my table, he looked perfectly normal. There was no clue that his legs were curled like hanks of rope under the tabletop. His face was rubbery and expressive. He gazed at me as if my next words might complete an enormous puzzle. It was flattering, but nerve-racking. I asked questions in self-defense. For example: Why wasn't he moving in?

'My wife and I are splitting up,' he said. 'Last week she wanted the house. This week, I get it.'

'What do you want?' I asked.

'Out,' he said. He didn't look happy. He went on to explain that it was his grandmother's house in Breezy, some twenty-five miles away. He really didn't own it – yet. 'Besides,' he said, 'my wife wants to go to school, and it's easier for her if she lives in town.'

'You haven't been to college?' I asked.

He laughed. His cheeks looked like halved rubber balls had been implanted under the skin. 'Ph.D., American Studies. My thesis was on the Knights of Labor, the first union. Ever need a sedative? You can check it out of the university library.'

He came back a few days later carrying a six-pack and an old Philco, which he gave to me. 'All my friends have to have TVs I can fix,' he said. We drank beer and watched ten minutes of a soap opera. A woman was in the hospital. She had something going with the doctor. Her husband came to see her and was rude to the doctor. The doctor left and was rude to a nurse. The nurse wept and told the doctor she was carrying his child. Back in the hospital room, the husband gave his wife a bracelet. She dropped it on the floor, and when her husband bent to pick it up, she made a nasty face. Doppinger turned off the TV. 'Ugh,' he said. His face was a knot. 'Grab the beer,' he said, 'and I'll take you to a polka palace in Cedar Rapids.'

We drove thirty miles and danced one polka on a beer-slick

bar room floor. I hadn't polkaed since the eighth grade, and I fought for balance as Doppinger twirled me around. It was like trying to dance with a scissors, or with a man cleft nearly in two. The music stopped and Doppinger kissed me. 'I'm going to take you home and put you in cement shoes so you can't ever get away from me,' he said. Only we didn't go to his house. We drove north instead, and spent our first night together in an old hunting lodge a block from the Mississippi. The mattress sucked us down into a deep softness. I fit entirely within the arc of his body. It had been almost a year since I had slept with anyone, and his pulse, the hiss of his breath, and the thought of those infinite legs kept me awake, energized me as if I were lying with a radioactive statue, a Giacometti.

In the morning he dropped me off at Krantz's. Distracted, he didn't even turn off the car. 'I have pickups and deliveries to make,' he said. 'I have some jobs I should've finished last night.' I poked him around the floating rib. No response. I wondered about those cement shoes.

'I've got to get in myself,' I said. 'I have a houseplant dying of thirst.'

I didn't see him again for almost three weeks. The first week I rarely left the apartment. I bought a begonia at the Eagle super-market lest he come and find me plantless. Then school started. The print studio was a huge rectangular room that shivered under scores of fluorescent lights. My new mentor, a diminutive, silen-tious Eastern European, issued me one copper plate. 'File the edges,' he said. At home, under the blinking screen of the Philco, I filed the edges. I filed until I had blisters and until the blisters turned into whorled yellow calluses. After seven days my teacher nodded and asked for a burin. I pulled one from the bun at the nape of my neck. He wiped it on his apron and with one swift stroke scored a deep flesh-pink gash in the middle of the plate. He handed me the burin, which was ruined. 'Use this plate until there's nothing left of it,' he said. I sat on my single bed in Krantz's Kottage Kourt and contemplated the wound in the copper. It meshed with nothing I thought of. I thought of the pale sculpted cup of Doppinger's pelvis and the inestimable distance to his toes.

I opened the door one afternoon. 'Dove and partridge season opens tomorrow.' Doppinger's face was crosshatched by the screen between us. 'Interested?'

Until that moment, I'd thought of hunters as bullies and vandals.

'Interested?' he repeated.

I nodded, let him in, and packed an overnight bag.

His house was an elaborate pink Victorian encrusted with dark rose and green gingerbread. Among the neighboring white clapboards, it stuck out like a beribboned negligee on a wash line of diapers. Doppinger held the door open for me. The kitchen was a dim room with ancient, discolored wallpaper. The sink was stone, very primitive. The counter, however, was lined with electrical appliances. One could see the archaeology of women – generations, one on top of the other.

'Pardon the mess,' said Doppinger. 'She's still moving things out.' I noticed then that the floor was cluttered with half-filled boxes. We both looked into the box at our feet. There was no order to it: a couple of historical-romance novels, some home-canned tomatoes. The handwriting on the Mason jar labels was flowery and girlish and in perfect keeping with the mawkish portraits on the novels' covers.

'Come on,' said Doppinger. 'Come see the good stuff.'

The living room was dim, too. Heavy curtains, dark old flowered things. Half a dozen disemboweled TVs sat on newspapers on the carpet. Doppinger introduced them to me by their problems: Unstable Picture, Vertical Jitters, No Video Information. He kicked boxes violently from his path to show me his uncle's comic woodcarvings of gnarled old men and women. My gaze rose to a sepia photograph: a row of Doppinger's ancestors standing in front of the lacy house. They were fair and socket-cheeked, and I could trace the source of Doppinger's shocky blond hair and Slavic eyes. They scowled, a straight line of them, some with their arms linked as if to challenge any intruder into their home.

We slept upstairs in the guest bedroom, away from the haunted marriage bed. He held me by the upper arms. Waist to head, we almost matched. His muscles were a fine system of ropes and pulleys. But we had trouble. I was computing boxes, the three weeks of silence, the prospect of hunting, possibly killing things, in the morning. Doppinger stroked my back. 'Don't worry,' he said. 'It's a simple convergence problem. Comes from over-heated resistors.'

I looked down the barrel of a four-ten as over the spine of a tiny black wave. I sighted the blank face of Vertical Jitters. Doppinger came up and pushed the barrel down. 'Never never never,' he said, 'Never aim in the house.'

We hunted all morning, which meant we followed fence lines and railroad tracks in a strangely perpendicular pursuit. I had a hard time keeping up with his seven-league legs. He stalked on, alert, feral, camouflaged in old brown clothes except for the red button of his hat. His fractious setter ran about us in hysterical glee, then raced far ahead, too far. 'Dimby, dammit, Dimby,' Doppinger shouted. He waited for me. 'And *you*,' he said. 'You stop swinging your gun.' My wrist went rigid. He pointed to the dog's tail, a wispy red flag. 'If she keeps this up, I'm going to have to shoot her.'

'You're what?'

Doppinger chucked me under the chin. 'At this distance, it'll only frighten her and irritate her a little. And teach her not to run so goddamned far ahead.'

I'd had no idea that guns had such a range of expression.

A bush loosed a flurry of doves, and Doppinger shot so fast that I cried out. Two birds landed soundlessly on the ground. Tears popped from my eyes. Doppinger walked up to the birds and with a dainty twist of his toe mashed skulls and beaks into black soil. He lifted them by their feet and offered them to me, a gray bouquet. It wasn't as bad as I'd expected. They were tiny birds, virtually weightless. The next time he shot, I did not cry out. I was no longer ignorant. Compared with the doves, I had superior procedural knowledge.

As we broke down the guns at the car, Doppinger suggested I shoot one round. He handed me his double-barreled twelve gauge. I discharged both barrels into a naked blue sky. The butt skidded cruelly against my collarbone. The blast burned away all other sound. I blushed a lava flow and understood why men liked guns. Now, I too liked guns.

Doppinger kept to a tight schedule. TVs were his first priority. He genuinely loved them, not to watch, but to fix. He'd learned how by taking a night class after receiving his Ph.D., when he decided he was sick of academia. He still spoke of research, even teaching, but he also talked about going to truck-driving school. He didn't know what future he wanted. In the meantime, he had more work coming in than he could finish promptly. We could manage only two days during the week together. I wanted to spend more, no, all of my time with him. I couldn't help it, I just did.

He made me laugh even when I was furious with him for

neglecting me. I had to adjust to his humor, which was boyish and a little on the grisly side. Once, he chased me around the house with a dead mouse. The mouse's tail, stiff from rigor mortis, stuck out straight, and Doppinger wielded it like a sword. 'I'll run you through,' he shouted as I dodged him. Doppinger always laughed at his own pranks. His tomcat came home after a week-long ramble with a huge abscess on his neck. When the abscess drained, we saw windpipe. The next time we ate spaghetti, Doppinger held a fat forkful to his Adam's apple. 'Who does this remind you of?' he asked, and laughed with a quiet, funny catch in his voice, almost a sob.

If I pushed for more of his time, his boyishness turned sulky. 'Don't I have enough things to feel badly about?' he'd say. To kill the blocks of days alone, I did what I had done for years. I worked in the print studio. I hovered helplessly over the scarred copper plate until my teacher, disgusted, ordered me to put it aside. He gave me a number six pencil. Its line was hairlike. 'Draw! Rupture space!' he yelled.

I drew televisions. Televisions in formation, televisions leaking images, exploded diagrams of televisions. My teacher growled over my shoulder. He was famous for tearing up student work. He made fun of my obsession, but my work remained intact. I drew on. Televisions weren't exactly the point, but they were as close as I could come.

I didn't meet Doppinger's wife until the shooting, but the house yielded an after-image of her as if she'd just vanished. The curtains, the magnetic butterflies on the refrigerator door, the houseplants fading for want of sunlight – she couldn't take everything with her. Still, she left an awful lot behind. Her registry china in the oak buffet. Her wedding dress in plastic in the closet, preserved, then abandoned.

Doppinger never talked about it. In fact, when Patsy Cline sang 'Why why why did you say goodbye?' he turned off the radio. When there was a marriage counselor on *Good Morning America*, he turned off the TV.

'You get first shot,' said Doppinger. This time it was opening day, pheasant season. The sky was gray and mum. The fields were the color of brown paper bags. We traversed dagger-sharp corn stubble. A pheasant flew up chortling like a small airborne electric motor. I fired. The bird dipped in flight, defecated, and flew on. 'I've hurt it,' I said.

'Not enough,' said Doppinger.

Minutes later, he got a long shot. Two hundred feet or so. His bird fell. I reached it first and was shocked by its beauty. The feathers shimmered prismatically: pale blue, emerald, rust, white, scarlet. The stipplings and lines were as intricate as the detail on a Chinese vase. What could such a bird be doing in this sullen landscape? It should be strutting in Byzantium.

'It's just so gorgeous,' I said.

Doppinger smiled, nodded, and lifted the bird by its scaly yellow feet.

'What a shame to kill it.'

Doppinger considered this. 'You have to admit,' he said, 'it was one hell of a shot.'

I thought of his motor response, the speed with which he sighted, followed, and struck. 'Yes,' I said, but I remained confused until I figured out that I was feeling the way one was supposed to feel. Apparently, people hunt in order to open themselves up to complex, contradictory emotions. They hunt for the joy of the kill, but also for the shame of it. Birds of empyrean beauty were imported to this prairie, set free, and killed. It was a situation designed for both the appreciation and the wanton destruction of beauty. I wasn't entirely won over to hunting, but it began to make a little more sense.

We rested on a weedy embankment near the car and drank whiskeyed coffee. 'Don't feel badly about your bird,' Doppinger said. 'It was a damn good try. It's almost impossible to bring a bird down with a four-ten. You need a twenty gauge, more power, not too heavy. Let's keep our eyes open for one.'

We couldn't spend Thanksgiving together. He had to go to his mother's. He hadn't told his mother he was separated yet and planned to break the news to her then. He couldn't exactly bring a new girlfriend home. I understood. And complained anyway. I complained until he agreed to spend the weekend before the holiday with me. Saturday morning, when he was already late to pick me up, he called.

'I must be crazy,' he said. 'I completely forgot that every year my cousins come from Davenport. We hunt until Tuesday and then go on to Marshalltown.'

'I don't mind hunting,' I said.

'No,' he said, 'it's just the boys. A ritual. Their wives don't even come until Monday.'

I said nothing.

'Listen, I'd rather be holed up with you than hunting with them. But what can I do? They pulled in this morning. They're in the back yard sighting their guns by blowing up Hubbard squashes. You can probably hear the shots.'

I listened and then I hung up.

That afternoon, while doing my laundry at Suds City, I began to relent. I already missed Doppinger. I found myself searching for his card on the bulletin board. There it was: EXPERT TELE-VISION REPAIR. A reality check: I felt better just looking at it. Nearby a scrap of paper caught my eye:

20-Gauge Shotgun
Box of Shells
Cleaning Kit
Take if off my hands for $20

I had an idea. I tore the paper from the cork and went over to a pay phone. A woman answered. 'Yes,' she said. 'I've got the gun.' We agreed to meet at six-thirty at the feminist bookstore.

I arrived early and stood out on the sidewalk. The temperature was dropping fast. It was freshly dark and the sky had that slight phosphorescence that comes with a major temperature change. My plan was simple. I would use the gun as an excuse to drop by Doppinger's house. I would say I bought it in Cedar Rapids and that I'd stopped by on the way home to have him take a look at it. He'd be pleased, I knew. So pleased, he might invite me to stay on and hunt with them in the morning.

The Milky Way prickled out overhead. Chilled, I stepped inside. A fat woman sat reading behind the register. She glanced up at me and returned immediately to her book: *Male Power – How to Get It, How to Use It.*

Eventually, the woman with the gun arrived. Her hair was shaved in a butch cut and glistening with grease. She greeted the fat woman, then shook my hand. The gun was encased in two brown socks, a misshapen sock monkey.

'It's brand-new,' she said. 'I bought it when I lived in Hyde Park and wanted some protection. I didn't want a registered gun, and some crank in a K-Mart convinced me that this would be my best bet. I've never used it. I've since been told that as an anti-personnel weapon, it stinks. It's only a single shot, you see. You miss with the first shot and your rapist is ten times madder than before. Also, it's only a twenty gauge. Might slow down a rat, but it won't do much damage to a man awash in testosterone.' She unsheathed the shotgun and handed it to me. 'What are you going to use it for?'

'I hunt,' I said. 'Birds and squirrels.'

'Yeah, well, you'll like it then.'

'Any trick to loading it?'

'Here.' She took the gun, broke it down, pulled a cartridge from the box, and pushed it into the barrel. She snapped the gun shut and gave me a deep look. Reversing the process, she handed me the shell. I put the ribbed yellow cylinder into my pocket. Again, I held the gun. The butt was wood but it had a freshly pressed, plastic look. It was light, solid, a perfect side-saddle of a gun. I gave her a twenty dollar bill. She insisted on breaking down the gun into two pieces before piling it and the cleaning kit and the shells into my arms.

Doppinger's house was well lit, festive. Light poured from all the windows and a yellow slice zigzagged down the front steps from the open door. I parked behind his cousins' van. As soon as I got out, I heard Dixieland jazz.

I assembled the gun. The frozen grass crunched under my feet. The setter flew around the corner of the house, barked once, then recognized me. When she saw the gun, she broke into paroxysms of delight. 'Cool it,' I said, and stopped beside the skeletal hydrangea to check my smile, compose myself. For some reason it hit me that the gun might still be loaded. If so, Doppinger would kill me. My fingers fumbled with the wing-shaped lever. The gun fell open. I saw light through the end of the barrel. Reassured, I climbed the front steps.

I was hardly stealthy. In the kitchen, I called out his name. Then I saw the tomcat crouching on the table, chewing the remains of a tied roast. The tom gazed warily at me and continued gnawing. Across from him were two place settings, impossibly close and composed of crystal, china, and silver, the equipment of Doppinger's marriage.

Even with the evidence of a connubial feast before me, I strode into the living room. I was convinced I'd see Doppinger and two or three men. The music stopped. I would've called out his name again, but I heard a woman's voice coming from the bedroom. The marriage bedroom. Doppinger answered her, said, 'I can't find it,' and the music started up again.

The old piano blues were perfect cover and I surely could've left undetected, but mortification fouled my better impulses. I looked down at the gun in my hands and came close to laughing aloud at my foolishness. On the shelf across from me, Doppinger's uncle's woodcarvings contorted in unholy glee. Surrounding me, the televisions sat in grim, silent judgment. I didn't want the gun any more, not one bit. Doppinger could have it, an appropriate going-away present. Let him find it lying around the living room. I started to set it down and had an idea. I'd load it. The symbolism, however vague, gratified me.

I pushed the ribbed cartridge into the barrel, closed it up, and laid the butt on a sofa pillow, but any dramatic effect was lost in the busy flowers of the upholstery. I lifted the gun and looked about for a better place.

Jon Doppinger stood at the bedroom door. He was ten, twelve feet away. He wore a dark green robe, which was absurdly short and made his legs look extra long and pink, as if skinned. I looked right into his eyes, two dull dimes spinning to focus. His face was skullish. He raised one hand slowly, then let it drop. I waited to hear him speak. After maybe fifteen seconds, I remembered that I held a gun. I blinked in surprise. Yes, it was as if he knew what I was going to do before the idea even occurred to me. And in his certainty, I could swear there was a trace of acquiescence. I didn't know what to do next. I was on stage without my lines. If I had to shoot him, I thought, I certainly didn't want to shoot him in the face, the chest, the stomach, the groin . . . And then, like a voice-over in a movie, a sentence came to me: *She shot him in the foot because she found him in bed with his wife.* It was like some kind of joke. I fired.

Before his blood rallied, I saw the foot: it looked like a computer card with a spate of clean, squarish holes. The woman screamed. Piano music tinkled. Doppinger jerked into motion, clawed for balance along the wainscoting. Close, he swung in arcs, a furious great ape. I threw down the gun. He came on. His hand found my shoulder. I absorbed the weight of his body's swing. He went on by. Like a dog hit by a car, he was running to outstrip the pain.

The screams distracted me. They were a child's terrified, chordal screams, violent seizures of the voice box. I went to the bedroom. She had her pants on and was clutching an orange sweater to her chest and trying to burrow into the mattress. I dug my fingers into her black curls and pulled. Her mouth was a loud red hole. 'Stop it,' I said. 'You've got to stop it. It's just his foot. He's all right.' She closed her eyes, screamed. 'Goddamn it,' I said. 'I'm not going to shoot *you.*'

I must have reassured her. Abruptly, she shut up.

I ran out to the porch. Doppinger was on the lawn, convulsive, a cartoon character trying to pull himself free from a puddle of glue. The setter was barking and feinting coyly at him. I tried to get closer, but the dog turned on me and snarled. I retreated to the house, to the bedroom where Marie Doppinger was fumbling with her sweater. I took it, pulled the sleeves right side out. 'You've got to get that dog away from him,' I said. The phone by the bed began to ring. 'Forget it,' I said. I bunched up each sleeve. Obediently, she pushed her hands through. 'Up,' I said, and she raised her arms above her head. Like Doppinger, she was

wildly tall. Her breasts swayed in front of me, the nipples crin-
kled cookies. I yanked the sweater down, and once it sat snugly
at her waist, her helplessness vanished. She shoved me aside
and answered the phone.

'Yes,' she said. 'Jon's been shot.'

I knew I had to get out. The bedroom adjoined a sleeping
porch, which had a door to the backyard. I ran around the house
and got into my car from the passenger side. In moments I was
out on the highway, heading home.

I arrived back at Krantz's Kottage Kourt around eight-thirty.
Without turning on the light or the heater or removing my coat,
I curled up on the bed. It had been a mistake to leave
Doppinger's. Now, I would have to wait. And think. And specu-
late if I had done any real damage to Doppinger's foot and if I
might be arrested. I had no clear idea of what I had done. I
wasn't worried about Doppinger. I was finished with him. No
more to say. I worried for myself. When I tried to remember my
past, my former habits, the people I loved, it all seemed to belong
to another person. I bit my hand, trying through muscular con-
traction and localized pain to offset a rising terror. I got some
hope from recalling the woman who sold me the gun. According
to her, Doppinger had a load of rat shot in his foot. Maybe twelve
little BBs, which, when I thought about it, were paltry retribution
for three months of lies: it measured out to one BB a week.

But I couldn't hang on to anger. Like acid, guilt ate it away. I
felt wronged but knew it was possible that I'd done a greater
wrong. Remorse and outrage were inexhaustible dance partners
in my head. Intermittently, I resolved to turn myself in to the
police. But what if charges hadn't been filed? I couldn't just walk
in and demand a jail cell. No, I had to wait and see what my life
had become.

The knock at my door came just as the sky was turning gray. A heavy-set man, not in uniform, pronounced my name. Instantly, I understood that a great many people I'd never heard of would be materializing and assuming places in my life. The firing of the gun had created a hole, a vortex that sucked me into a new, strange realm. I unlatched the screen door and let him in. He wore a DeKalb hat. His hands and cheeks were chapped and pink from the cold. He looked around, I think, for a source of warmth. Finding none, he turned to me. 'I hate to have to do this,' he said, and read me my rights.

In the patrol car, he told me Doppinger had been in surgery all night. 'His foot was mush,' he said.

The details of the month before my indictment are numerous and unappetizing. I quit school and gave myself wholly to the endless coils of the legal system. My crime replayed itself non-stop behind my eyes. My state-appointed lawyer, a twenty-six-year-old woman fresh out of law school, had high hopes of setting some kind of feminist precedent with the case. I never understood quite what she had in mind, but I had enormous difficulty convincing her that I had not bought the gun in a bath of victimized passion to wreak revenge on my wayward lover. When I repeated my modest story and detailed the desire to impress Doppinger with my purchase, she shook her head and said, 'Won't do.'

At one point, I was desperate to talk to Doppinger, just to verify that he existed and that I had shot him. He answered the phone, said, 'I have nothing to say to you,' and hung up. I guess I got what I wanted.

In a deposition, he volunteered his reasons for pressing charges. I'd terrorized his wife. On principle, he believed that anyone who shot at another person required formal punishment.

The fact that he had taught me how to shoot only exacerbated his fury at my gross breach of gun etiquette. Also, I'd trespassed, interfered. Right in the transcripts he said, 'A man has every right in the world to sleep with his own wife in his own house without getting shot.'

In the end, I pleaded guilty to 'assault with a deadly weapon' and listed some extenuating circumstances. Doppinger was at the sentencing on crutches. The judge was a fine-boned man with a white friar's cap and salmon-colored skin. He rustled papers and whispered to the bailiff while my lawyer read her statement. When she finished, he looked up and sentenced me to one year in jail. With his next breath he suspended the sentence and put me on a year's probation. Pleased, my lawyer took me out to lunch.

Later, in the solitary darkness of number four, Krantz's Kottage Kourt, I cried all night.

Within a week my probation was transferred and I was home in my parents' house in Monrovia, California. My parents thought I was just a little late for Christmas vacation. It was a balmy night. We sat in the living room and drank egg-nog. I told them what I had done. Their opinion of me changed right before my eyes.

Nobody ever spoke directly to me about my crime, but my criminal nature was constantly alluded to in embarrassed silences, unfinished sentences, gentle pats on my hand. I had to learn to ignore other people's discomfort. I'd had my trial. I'd been assigned my punishment. It was a relief to visit my probation officer. Compared with her other customers, I was Pollyanna. We talked about modern art for half an hour and I was free to go.

Not too long after my probation ended, I had an experience.

I was attending classes at UCLA. On Wednesdays, I took Anatomical Life Drawing, which offered the option of going over to the med school and drawing from cadavers. Morgue time, we called it. I went on principle. If I could make mush of a foot, I should certainly be able to learn anatomy at its source.

It was not really a morgue, but a basement classroom set up laboratory style. Three amused medical students were our hosts. A sweet, pungent odor clung in the nose. The bodies lay refrigerated in stainless-steel drawers. Male, female, young, and old, they all had names: Sybil, Harry, Hulga, the Nun. One drawer was labeled *Soup Bones*. A student pulled it open. Inside were hands with wrists, and feet. I couldn't stop staring.

'See something?' the student asked.

'That,' I said, and pointed to a foot.

'Want me to pull it?'

'Please.'

He drew on membranous plastic gloves and carried the foot to the tray on his desk. The skin was gray. The meat encircling the pearly bones was brown, the marrow inside the bone was pur-plish-black. The toes were tucked around almost to the ball.

'The foot,' said the student, 'is the terminal part of the verte-brate leg. Acupuncturists believe the entire body can be manipulated through the foot, but we Westerners haven't mapped out that nervous system . . .' Over the top of the foot, I noticed a door-like flap cut in the skin. The student flicked this open with tweezers. 'The metatarsus is composed of five elon-gated bones . . .' He tapped the gnarly white bones, which were attached to yellowish cartilage and skeins of grayish muscle. 'The talus, or ankle, has a marvelously complex system of mus-cles which are responsible for the suppleness and dexterity of the foot. We call it the wickerwork. You see it?'

The foot, its innards revealed, revealed only its lack of life. I started to shiver. Quickly, I left the classroom, but it was too late: already, everything had shifted. Around me, I saw only the complicated braiding of matter, the endless intricacy of structure. And no life. It was a dizzying vision of filaments and pithiness. A tree was all threads. A bird was brittle skeleton and hairy feather, a dog ropy muscle, spiky hair. I tried to get hold of myself. Look, I thought, the tree grows, the bird flies, the dog saunters down the street. Movement seemed a trick of simple physics. No life in it at all.

The thought of seeing this way for the rest of my life made me panicky. I had to work it all back together again.

At home, I rummaged through old boxes until I found the naked and defiled copper plate I'd abandoned over a year before. The scar had tarnished over, but it was still there, a jagged trough in the center of the rectangular surface. I chose my finest burin, its line as delicate as a synapse.

For four months, I worked exclusively on that plate. My concentration was total, possibly escapist. Except when I was working, panic lapped darkly at the corners of my eyes. The gash posed an enormously difficult problem of composition. At first, I worked away from it, pretended it wasn't there, that I had a clean plate like I'd been used to before this one was assigned to me, before I'd gone to the Midwest, when the world was comfortable and complete and everything seemed possible. The more I worked around it, the more dominant the gash became. I didn't sleep well at night. I didn't talk to anybody. I wanted to be working all the time. In a state of agitation, I started digging into the scar itself, drawing it out to the rest of the plate. My fingernails became rimmed with ink at the trial printings and remained so for two more months. I awoke nights with pain against my skull and pulled forgotten burins from my hair.

I was still living at home and making the long commute to

Westwood. My studio was mostly my parents' kitchen table. One morning, I got up to reheat the coffee and pour myself a cup. I looked down at the plate, and right before my eyes the myriad little lines popped into place. For a moment I didn't see the scar at all. I saw the image as a whole. It was a kind of wacky, very complex image not unlike some Chinese scrollwork: a foot that was also a tree and a map and a freeway and a mountain. It held together, though. I looked away, then checked again. Again, a gentle pop, a surprising settling into place. As a foot, it would never leap off the plate and dance or strut or curl in love, but it made me laugh. I chuckled throughout the final printings. I made an edition of ten. Eight sold immediately. I gave one to my probation officer and kept one for myself.

In a seminar on pre-Columbian art, I'd learned how Woodland Indians used to crack their funerary pottery so that the spirit in the pot would be free. That's what I thought about the day I sawed the plate in two.

One more thing.

Just about a year ago, I got a Christmas card from the woman who'd been my lawyer. She wrote:

I thought you might be interested to know that I ran into Jon Doppinger at the opening of the new historical museum last week. I wish I could say that he doesn't limp. Still, he's got it down to an art. At least in a tuxedo, he managed to make that limp an enviable trait. I'm not saying this just to make you feel better. Really, he looked quite dashing and the limp didn't hurt. He cringed a little when he recognized me, but seemed eager to talk. He's remarried. His new wife looked all of twenty. He's teaching at a small college in Mt. Vernon. He asked how you were and said to send his regards and let you know that he was doing all right. He looked down at his foot and shook it and laughed. 'Tell her,' he said, 'that I think of her every time I don't polka.'

So there you have it. All the gory details as complete as I can make them. Anything more is unfounded speculation, party talk, and gossip.

On the Terraces

Peter Ho Davies

My brother lies in a Midlands hospital dying of Aids and I can't think of a single thing to say to him. I sit by his bed reading a newspaper while he sleeps, carefully turning the pages. Every few minutes I try to look up to see if he's awake. I watch the circles of condensation bloom and fade against his oxygen mask, and then go back to my paper.

My mother knits when she's here. A warm sweater for me, she says, holding up the pieces, pressing them against me. She smooths the wool over my chest or shoulders and tells me I don't look after myself. She goes on knitting even if my brother's awake and the snipping of the needles fills the silence between them when he's too tired to speak and she can't say a word without out crying.

She calls her crying, 'Waterworks'.

I take her home each night at ten or eleven and we have a cup of tea together. I put a hot water bottle in her bed and leave her in front of the TV before I drive back to the hospital. She can't go to sleep straight after seeing him, and often I come back in the morning and find her snoring softly on the sofa. She thinks one of us should always be at his bedside when my brother wakes. She wants us to make the most of his last conscious hours, and when the crisis comes she doesn't want to rely on the hospital to phone us in time. This shift system was the only way I could make sure she got any sleep.

By the time I get back the next day's newspapers are piled in bundles in front of the small newsagent's kiosk in the lobby and I buy two or three of them – *The Times*, *Telegraph*, *Guardian* perhaps. I've been doing this for a week now, but it's still strange to see tomorrow's news on the front pages so late at night. Events seem to float free, as if they could happen as easily today, or tomorrow or the next day.

On my brother's ward, the nurses know me now and we exchange whispered good mornings in the dead of night.

I've taken two weeks of annual leave to be here and my brother feels bad about that. He tells me I don't have to stay. But I don't mind it at the hospital. It's peaceful and I can't remember the last time I had the chance to read a newspaper from cover to cover. It wouldn't bother me if my brother slept right through the night but usually he wakes every couple of hours, sometimes for a minute or two, sometimes for much longer. The medication makes him drowsy and has messed up his sleep rhythms.

He wakes, blinking, from a doze, but if he's been sleeping heavily he kicks his legs, swimming back to consciousness. He might go on like this for a minute or two and I put my paper away and watch him until he wakes or falls back to sleep. His body makes only a slight ripple under the blanket when he's still. The bed looks unmade, as if someone had just slipped out for a moment, closed the covers to keep the warmth in, but left those thin rumpled folds. A sharp tug from one of his brisk nurses would make it all neat.

The problem is we've already said all the things we should say.

Last week when I came down he'd been rushed into hospital and they didn't think he'd make it. In the few hours after he regained consciousness, he made me go over the arrangements with him. I told him not to worry about our mother. He told me he loved me and I told him I loved him, too, and at that moment after not seeing each other or even talking on the phone for maybe three years I think we actually meant it. At least we both wished we did. Since then the crisis has passed and he's stronger now, though not out of danger. For a few days we just repeated things we'd already said until we began to sound insincere and since then we've had nothing to say to each other. I think we're afraid. Things are better between us now than for a long time and we're afraid we'll say something to spoil it.

Tonight, I look up and see he's awake. I've become engrossed in my paper – something about Major and Europe – and I feel a sudden flush of guilt, caught out, more interested in the world than him. But he's not watching me. He's reading the back of the paper, the headlines, the sports news. I hold the pages very still and watch his eyes move. When he's done with what he's reading he looks at me and I say, gently, 'How're you feeling?'

'Bored,' he says.

And then he asks me to tape the football match the next day and bring in our mother's TV and VCR tomorrow night.

'Will you do that for me?'

'OK,' I say, a little dubiously, not sure if I've been insulted, if he's bored by me.

'Only don't watch it,' he says. 'Don't listen to the score. I'm not watching it with you if you know how it ends.'

The first time I ever saw my brother in a hospital was when he was eight and I was five. He'd had his tonsils out and he wasn't allowed to eat anything but ice-cream. 'The doctor said so,' he told my mother. I was speechless. I thought he meant for ever. I thought he meant he got to eat nothing but ice-cream for the rest of his life. A bowl came while we sat there and we watched him eat it. Each time he took a mouthful he twisted the spoon before withdrawing it, licking it clean. It slipped slowly between his lips, like a bright steel tongue.

On the way home my mother bought me a block of neapolitan ice-cream – stripes of strawberry, vanilla and chocolate like a flag. My father had left us about a year before and all she cared about any more was that the three of us got along.

The next time, my brother must have been fourteen. He'd broken his leg. My mother sat beside him at the head of the bed and I sat on the other side by his foot with a felt tip in my hand. I looked at the huge looming cast and studied the strings and pulleys that held it up. I couldn't think of anything to write on all that whiteness.

Later, once his friends from school had come and scribbled on it and the plaster had gone grey with dirt at the edges and picked up fluff, I could have done it, but just then, when it seemed so bright and perfect, I had no idea what to write. I had carved grafitti on desks at school with my compass point. Once Jase Johnson and I had drawn an arrow above the urinals. 'Follow me,' the arrow said. 'Not much further now.' Jase had had to get on my back with me grabbing his legs to stop him sliding off to write the last bit, right in the corner where the ceiling and the wall met, a sign saying, 'You're pissing on your shoes.'

But I couldn't think what to write on my brother's cast.

'Time to go,' my mother said.

'Just a sec.'

She said she'd meet me down the hall. She wanted to talk to the doctor.

When she'd gone my brother said, 'I didn't tell.'

He meant he hadn't told anyone that I had pushed him off the low brick wall at the end of our drive when he'd broken his leg. At school, in the toilets, I'd seen his name in a line of grafitti. Just his last name. I thought it meant me for a moment and then I realized it meant him.

I didn't say anything. I stared at his cast thoughtfully and sucked my pen.

'It'll be our secret,' he said.

I stooped down and pretended to scribble something on the base of his foot.

'What's it say?' he said. 'What's it say?' But I just ran off.

I leave him at eight or nine each morning and drive home to pick up my mother. I roll my newspapers into a tight tube and when I set them down on the kitchen table they slowly unclench. We have breakfast together and then I drop her at the hospital and come home to sleep. My room hasn't changed since I left for college, the same movie posters on the wall, the same clothes in the drawers. I can't sleep in it, it feels too small, and often in the afternoon I get up, pull on my old, short robe, and look in my brother's room. His is the same, unchanged, with pictures of footballers all over the walls. He took them down when he came home a few months ago, but didn't put anything up to replace them and after he went into the hospital this time my mother put them all back. They'd been up so long that the wallpaper had faded around them and she just had to match the posters to the gaps. I walk around his room now, hands behind my back, peering at them, not wanting to touch anything. He never let me in here when we were kids. If he caught me, he'd push my face against the wall and twist my arm back until tears came to my eyes.

When he was fifteen he used to catch the train to London every fortnight to go and see a game. This would have been in the mid-seventies. He wore flared jeans and a denim jacket and a silky team scarf thin enough to keep folded in his pocket until he got near the ground. Once he showed me the Stanley knife he'd taken from our father's old tool box. He slid the blade in and out and told me if he ever had to use it he'd go for the chin or the cheek. Autographing, he called it. The hooliganism was just getting bad then, but he told our mother he knew how to look after himself. He only pulled his scarf out when he found a crowd of home fans, and he peeled it off again whenever he was on his own. I was three years younger and my mother said I could go if he took me, but he always refused and when I was old enough to go myself I went to the movies instead.

I stand at the window and look out at the street for a moment and then draw the curtains and get into his bed.

I followed him once. As far as King's Cross station. It was odd seeing him there, the only person I knew in such a large crowd. It was hard not to call out, to run up and surprise him. He crossed under the departure board and went into the gents and I waited in a newsagents looking at comics. I started to smile thinking he'd been caught short. But he'd not come out after fifteen minutes. I thought he'd given me the slip, or he was waiting in there for me. Men came and went and every time I heard steps I prayed it was him. It was as if he'd vanished. I waited another twenty minutes, panicky with impatience, too scared to go in after him. In the end, I just left.

He is awake and in pain when I come to pick my mother up the next evening. She tells me he's been refusing his medication and I can see that she's upset. He didn't think I'd wake him if he was asleep. 'Of course not for a stupid football match,' my mother says.

When I told her earlier about taping the game she didn't know what to make of it. I could tell she disapproved, but she couldn't say why. All she made me do was check that it was OK with the hospital, but when I told her that the nurse had said it was a wonderful idea, she pursed her lips with disappointment.

'It's what he wants,' I told her when I had her home and settled on the sofa. 'I didn't think I could say no.'

'Tell me,' she said, 'did you know? When the two of you were young?'

'No.' I was bent over the dark TV, one arm behind it feeling for the cables. I watched her reflection in the screen. We've had this conversation before, but tonight something about her disapproval made me add, 'I might have suspected.'

'And you never thought to tell me?'

'I didn't know for certain.'

'You should have told me anyway. I'm not saying I'd have done anything different. But I'd have wanted to know.'

'It wouldn't have changed anything.'

'I would have known him better.'

'Well,' I said. 'He hasn't always been that easy to know, has he?'

'You could talk to him,' she said. 'And not watch that rubbish.'

I unplugged the TV and the VCR and carried them out one at a time to the car. When I came in to say I was going she was still sitting on the sofa staring at the space where the TV had been. The whole room looked empty, all the chairs facing in at nothing. 'Go on,' she said.

At the hospital my brother watches me as I struggle in with the TV and the VCR. I balance them on separate plastic chairs and fiddle with the cables.

'You don't know the score, right?'

I shake my head.

'I'll know if you're lying.'

'I don't know the score,' I tell him and he says, 'All right then.'
After a minute, he says, 'How is she?'
'She'll be fine. How are you doing?'
'Just put the game on,' he says.
Sometimes I want to shake the IV stand next to his head.

I press Play and the screen fills with snow. I have one sickening moment of doubt that I've taped the wrong thing or brought the wrong tape, but then the screen fills with the bright green of the floodlit pitch.

My brother makes me turn up the volume until the commentary makes conversation impossible and the crowd noise fills the room. He has trouble hearing over the sound of his breathing. A male nurse comes to the door attracted by the sound. He smiles and leans on the door frame and calls, 'Didn't they play earlier?' My brother ignores him. I nod and pray he won't give the score away. He smiles and pulls the door shut after him.

We are silent for a few minutes and then, responding to the game, my brother says, 'Shot,' and I find myself nodding.

I've only asked my brother once about his sex life. It was a Christmas Eve about ten years ago, and we'd escaped a house full of relatives for the pub. It was heaving. We were only going to have a pint, but it took us so long to fight our way to the bar we ended up ordering doubles of whisky too. We found a place to stand by the cigarette machine, a glass in each hand. I bent my head close to his and told him I was interested. 'Not in who does what to whom or anything like that. Just how you live your life.' I had the earnest intensity of someone on the verge of drunkenness and he must have been in a similar state, or just carried away by the heightened holiday mood. He told me about 'cottages', the public toilets where he met and had sex with men, sometimes two or three a night.

'Two or three a night?' I was dubious. 'These are total strangers?'

He nodded.

'What do you say to them?' I was talking too loudly and I felt heads turn towards us.

'I don't *say* anything,' he whispered. 'I look them in the eye. I smile. There's a shared assumption. You don't need to talk about it.'

It made me feel oddly unmanned. I leaned in, my arms encircling him, holding my drinks clear. I told him I couldn't sleep with women like that, even if they were available.

'Me neither,' he said. I smiled, but he didn't mean it as a joke. 'You can't compare them. It's not that I fancy men and you fancy women. It's about wanting the same or different. The sameness is what makes it all right.'

No, I told him, I couldn't understand it, I didn't have a clue what he was talking about. He took a step back and shrugged and said it wasn't his idea to talk about it. I asked him why he couldn't just have one lover 'like normal people' and he said, 'I don't want to talk about it any more.' He took a long sip of his beer and looked away over the rim of his glass.

I've done a lot of reading since my brother's diagnosis. I know how the pneumonia is filling his lungs. Spreading until he has no room to breathe. Crowding him out. But at another level, I realize, I have no idea why my brother is dying, what he's dying for.

At half-time I turn the volume down and offer to fast-forward through the commercials and the analysis.

'Are you in a hurry?' he says. He asks me if I watch a lot of football and I say, 'Now and then.'

'Are you having a good time?'

'Sure.'

He is silent for a moment.

'I'm glad you're here,' he says at last. 'I can't stand watching a game alone, especially a taped one. It feels sort of pointless, like you're wasting your time. It's easier to pretend it's live if there's two of you.'

'I usually watch on my own,' I admit.

'It's not the same,' he says. 'You need a crowd, even if it's only two.' I look over at him, but he's staring at the screen, not me and I look back at it. 'When I used to go to games you'd be jammed in so tight you couldn't raise your arms. You all had to breathe together.'

'It sounds dangerous,' I say, but he shakes his head slowly, turning it on the pillow so that I can hear his hair rubbing against it.

'Warmest I've ever been in my life,' he says. 'They used to say it could rain cats and dogs on the terraces and your feet'd never get wet. When someone scored I used to lift my legs and be carried twenty, thirty yards on this wave of men.'

'I've never been. Not to a live game.'

'You should. Once. Before they rip 'em all out.'

He means the terraces. Since the disaster at Hillsborough when all those fans died the government has decided that the terraces should be replaced by seats.

It pleases me that my brother likes football. I used to think that he'd only pretended to be a fan, only gone along with it to fool us. After I knew he was gay, knew for sure, it was tempting to doubt everything I knew about him before.

'Tell me something,' I say. 'Why did you keep doing it?' He knows what I mean.

'Where do you want me to start?' There's an impatience in his voice. 'What do you want to know?'

I must hunch my shoulders, flinch somehow, because all he

55

says is, 'I don't know. It was freezing down there. Bloody fucking freezing.'

The second half begins. After a few minutes he says, 'Thanks for doing this.'

'No problem.'

'Really,' he says softly, and then, 'I'm going to sleep now.' The way he says it makes it sound as though he has no choice.

'Should I switch this off?'

'No. You've got to tell me how it turns out.'

I watch the rest of the game. I turn the volume right down until the players float soundlessly over the turf, and the fans shout silent clouds into the cold night air. My brother's breathing settles, gets shallow and ragged, then settles again when I'm just about to call a nurse. The game ends in a draw and I unhook the cables, turn everything off and sit with him for a while after carrying the TV and VCR out to the car. I've a new paper and I open it slowly.

I've often thought about what he told me that Christmas. I still don't understand it. I imagine him down in one of those old Victorian WC's, tiled and echoing. I think of the casualness of it, the anonymity, the giving and the holding back. The silent understanding. It seems oddly familiar. There's a surprising maleness to it.

When I was thirteen I had a dark line of down along my upper lip. What we used to call bum fluff. My mother wouldn't let me shave. I was the clumsy one and she was afraid I'd take my nose off or something. Instead, she got my brother to do it. He grinned. This was about a year after I'd broken his leg. We'd never talked about it again. He carried one of the high kitchen stools into the bathroom, put a new blade in his razor, and tied a towel tightly round my neck. 'To soak up the blood.' He rubbed a handful of shaving cream over my face like it was a custard pie, filling my ears, covering my mouth. He ran his fingertip lightly across my lips to uncover them. The blade scraped against my skin and pulled at the fine hairs, but I didn't say anything. He was very close, leaning over me, silent except for his breathing. He was concentrating hard, but he must have met my eyes once, because he said, 'Don't look so worried. I won't cut you.' When he was done, while I washed my face, he told me shaving would make my beard come in faster. The water felt like oil on my skin. 'It's so smooth.' I looked in the mirror, touching my face, and he stood behind me grinning. I smiled back, but when I looked at my face again there was a tiny globe of blood just beginning to swell at the corner of my mouth.

My mother is getting breakfast ready when I get home and she asks me how he is and I say fine.

'What did you talk about?' she says and I tell her, 'Football.' It's so ludicrous, I whisper it.

She looks at me and for a moment I think she's going to say, 'Men!' but all she says is, 'You don't even like football,' and I shrug.

The local team are at home in February. The ground is at the end of a narrow terraced street, the brick walls rising over the houses, the floodlights above them. I stoop in the darkness of the narrow turnstile and pass my money across to the ticket taker behind his grille and say, 'One.' He is so close I can smell the damp wool of his coat.

I lean on the turnstile and it gives slowly, depositing me in a dank brick tunnel, gently sloping, leading up to a broader concrete passageway. I can see the curve of the stadium for the first time in the distance. Banks of steps lead up to the left and I take them quickly into the daylight. After the darkness, the smell of the brick, the closeness of the walls, the pitch is a revelation. The dull day seems bright; the muddy pitch glows green. It makes me wonder if this isn't the point, if the Victorian architects who built this place hadn't meant all the darkness and dampness to lead up to this moment.

It's only a moment though. It's a biting day and I stand on the open terraces cowering in the wind. My brother died two months ago. I'm home for the weekend, as I have been for every weekend since. I wanted to see what he saw in something, but there are only two or three dozen men around me, gathered in little knots and huddles, stamping their feet on the bare, cracked concrete. We keep a wary, respectful distance. The stands with their plastic seats and bright red corrugated roofs look more modern, but this part of the stadium must be pre-war. Shallow slabs sloping down to the field, broken up here and there by chest-high iron stanchions. I cross my arms and lean my elbows on one of them waiting for the game to begin.

Opposite, at the far end of the stadium, they've already begun the demolition. The home terraces will be rebuilt over the summer, but the away end is already half gone. Last night I read in the local paper the contractors are working flat out, even during games. The club has erected a tall hoarding to hide the work from the pitch and YTS lads have painted it to look like a crowd scene. I can't make out any faces from so far away, but there was a photograph of it in the paper. Men with their mouths open, men with their hands in the air. The only sound coming from them is the ring of scaffolding and the thump of pneumatic drills. A local lady councillor has complained that there are four hundred and sixty-three figures in the crowd and not a single woman.

The home team are terrible, heavy legged in the mud like

cart-horses. 'Wankers,' someone on the terrace shouts. At half time boys with their hands stuffed in the pockets of dirty jeans come out and wander around the pitch stamping down divots.

The players run out again and the floodlights come on although it's only four o'clock. The home team attack the goal in front of the terrace. They win a corner and have a shot fly just over the bar. It rises over the fence and lands among us. The men around me chase after it, running stiffly with their hands in their pockets. The ball skids off the concrete, bounces up off the edge of a step. One of them gets close enough to swing at it, but he misses and it bobbles down towards me. I think about letting it roll past, but as it comes level I stoop and catch it. The men running towards me stop. I hold the ball for a long moment, feeling the slight tackiness of the damp leather. Then I throw it out in front of me and swing, catching it on the full so that it sails over the fence. It's caught by one of the gusts of wind trapped in the stadium and for a moment it hangs in the night, shining in the floodlights.

Somewhere in the crowd a thin cheer goes up and behind me someone calls, 'Shot!' I feel their eyes on me and I stand very still, not looking round while the sensation of striking the ball, the sweetness of the contact, slowly passes.

Karma

Alan Isler

A stray bacillus of the madness that had swept through America with the virulence of the Spanish Flu at the end of the sixties and through most of the seventies found unexpected lodging in the bloodstream of Harry Kollitz, even as nationally the fever had just about run its course. On the morning following Diana's graduation *magna cum laude* from Barnard College, now a little less than twenty years ago, Harry announced to his startled wife and daughter that he was henceforth a Jew for Jesus. This man, who had always fasted on Yom Kippur, who had cheerfully presided over the Seder tables, who had invariably tsk-tsked whenever he had found meat defrosting on the same refrigerator shelf as the milk and sour cream, this man had suddenly been granted a vision of the Truth. He had received the Call. He had been Washed Clean in the Blood of the Lamb. He had been 'told' to go to Detroit, there to take up His ministry.

The family was in the living room. 'Sit right there,' said his wife, getting up. 'Don't move. Take it easy for a minute.' And she hurried about the apartment, taking photographs from frames, collecting family albums, finding snapshots in boxes and drawers. She returned, her arms laden, and sat down. 'Watch this,' she said. 'I want you to watch this.' And before his eyes she took each photograph in which he appeared, wedding photographs not excepted, and tore it calmly and decisively into small pieces. 'OK, Mr Jew-for-Jesus, what d'you think of that?' Harry Kollitz regarded the heap of photograph fragments with the smirk of a man who knows of and who is going to a far, far better world. 'Wait, there's more,' said his wife. This time she returned with sheets that she hung over the living room mirrors. 'OK, smartie,' she said. 'You know what that means.'

Harry Kollitz averted his eyes from his wife and turned them, filled with appalling compassion, to his daughter, who, torn between horror and laughter, saw herself on the brink of an abyss. 'Forgive her, your mother,' he said unctuously, 'for she knows not what she does.' And off he had gone the following morning, taking with him no more than a briefcase, in which he had stuffed a change of underwear and socks, a New Testament, and a kosher salami (some old habits dying hard).

It was from this moment that Diana dated her entry into the maelstrom known as life. Within six months mother and daughter received word from Detroit that Harry Kollitz had been summoned to his Savior, shot to death, an innocent bystander, by a nervous grocer who had thought himself being robbed. Sophie Kollitz had received the news with a calm that showed how certainly Harry had transmitted the bacillus to her. She was by this time deep into Madame Blavatsky and theosophism. Diana watched nervously and with growing alarm as her mother expanded her range of dottiness. Sophie devoured books on the occult, on astrology. She began to attend seances, moved toward eastern mysticism. Plump Sophie, who had loved nothing better than boiled flanken, potatoes roasted in chicken fat, and a little horseradish on the side, became a vegetarian, grew specter thin, subsisted on bean sprouts, leechee nuts, and raisins. Diana would come home now to the smell of incense. The living room had become an ashram, on every surface a shrine, a lighted candle before each photograph of some mischievously grinning Hindu. In her conversation, Sophie had left the this-worldly far behind; her topics floated on the Astral Plane. Not that she had much to say, for she spent long hours in formal meditation. By the time five years had passed, she was painting a dot between her brows with a red marker pen. 'My real name,' she told Diana, 'is Lakmé.'

Since graduation from college, Diana had worked at the American Musical Heritage Museum on East 80th Street, beginning as a humble cataloger in the Popular Music Division but rising with exemplary speed to the custodianship of the Aaron Klopstock Collection. The work offered a welcome refuge from the madness at home, as did the courses in the humanities she enrolled in from time to time, at the New School or NYU.

One winter's evening, on a day when New York trembled beneath an unexpectedly severe snowstorm, a day not long after Sophie had become Lakmé, Diana cut her course in 'Classics and Romantics: the Eternal Struggle' and fought her way home through frantic traffic to see whether a near-blizzard had somehow penetrated the mental miasma within which Lakmé luxuriated. Lakmé, in fact, was sitting in the lotus position on a small rug in the centre of the ashram. Her eyes wide open, she was deep in meditation. Diana knew better than to speak to her now. How thin her mother was! How her sari floated in its folds! How beatific her smile! It was hard not to believe that she had found her happiness. The red dot this evening was slightly off-center, which gave her a curious cross-eyed look. Outside the windows, fat snowflakes, whipped by the wind, sped past through a grey-blue sky tinged with red. Diana sat and waited.

Suddenly, out of her trance, Lakmé spoke, her eyes unwavering, unfocused, staring. 'Diana, honey, I've got to go.' The voice had the strength of a sigh.

'Go where, mother?'

'To India, to the Kush.'

'Oh, for pity's sake!'

'I've been given notice that soon my spirit will transcend its shell.'

'Mother,' said Diana gently, despairingly, 'you need help.'

'But I have all the help I need.'

'We're all we've got. You can't do this to me.'

'I'll always be with you, honey.'

'In India?'

'Wherever.'

'But what if I have to get in touch with you, an emergency, something?'

'Call me,' breathed Lakmé, smiling gently. 'Call me. I'll come.'

She's done it again, thought Diana bitterly, she's caught me up in her dottiness. I'm arguing with a fruitcake. 'I get it. All I do is call out "Here I am, come and get me" and here you'll be, right?'

'That's it. We'll have a code, yes, a message.' Lakmé's eyes began to glow strangely. She seemed now actually to see Diana. 'You'll put it in the paper. "Here I am" at the start, "Come and get me" at the end. Never mind what's in between.'

'You'll read it?'

'So to speak.'

'In India?'

'Wherever.'

'But why do I need to put it in the paper? Why can't I just call out?'

Lakmé's gentle breath bore the merest hint of impatience. 'I don't know how to put it into words you'll understand. The

Ineffable Oneness in which you and I and All are gathered, the Oneness that is *of* this world, not *in* it, needs a physical trigger to set the vibrations in motion along a Field of Communication. Don't you see, honey? It's like touching hands at a seance.'

'But you said you'd always be with me.'

'Of course I will.'

'Well, if you can be with me while you're in India, why can't you be in India while you're with me? There's no need to go anywhere.'

'But you *do* understand! Oh, I'm so glad. It can't make a difference to you where I am, and, where you are concerned, it can't make a difference to me. We'll always be together.' Lakmé dropped her voice to a whisper. Diana had to strain to hear her. 'Now, I haven't told you this in as many words, but I'm about to enter the seventh Triad. It's true, I'm on the verge. Well, you must see that I can't make a satisfactory transition to the Zone of Quiet in New York. The electricity!'

'The Zone of Quiet? You could go to Vermont.'

Lakmé smiled in unruffled derision.

'Come on, Mom, you need to rest, we'll talk about it tomorrow.' Diana helped her mad mother to her feet. She weighed nothing any more, a feather, a bubble.

In the weeks that followed Lakmé said nothing more about India. Diana even began to hope that her mother was groping her way out of the miasma. Lakmé stopped painting the red dot on her face, she left the apartment occasionally, she asked a question or two about the Museum. But then one evening Diana returned from her Classics and Romantics class to find an empty apartment, her mother gone, a counterfoil of an airline ticket to Calcutta on the kitchen table. She disassembled the ashram.

Diana continued to live in her parents' old apartment on

Central Park West, not always alone. She had, after all, surrendered her virginity to one Axel Lautsprecher, painlessly but without passion, during her sophomore year at Barnard. The earth had not moved, and to be cruelly frank, neither had Diana. 'Only connect,' she had been taught in Philosophy 201, and for years following Lakmé's departure for the Zone of Quiet Diana had certainly tried. But the men who drifted into her life and into her apartment drifted out again – even as she drifted into and out of failed sessions in various therapists' offices – Diana after every departure a little more desperate. The words 'What's wrong with me?' echoed in her head like a mantra. The disaster area was growing, and through it she wandered sending out small, scarcely audible cries for help.

When Teddy entered her life she thought the connection had at last been made. He had a sheepish grin that made her loins melt. She could not tear her eyes from his shapeliness in brushed cotton jeans. The touch of grey at the temples of his permanently tanned and heroically craggy face sent shivers of delight through her. Oh, she had it bad all right. With him she felt herself radiant, awakened, a whole woman at last, a *femme fatale*. Teddy Greene at forty taught music theory at the High School of the Performing Arts, a temporary position, his contract annually renewed. That arrangement suited him well enough since he thought of himself as a composer on the brink of the Big Time: TV commercials, movies. He continued to wait for his break. After all, who knows?

First he tuned Diana; then he tuned the piano, a survivor from her mother's pre-Lakmé days. And then he moved in. Diana quit her course at NYU, 'Romantic *Angst* and Romantic Posturing: the Schizophrenia of a Movement.' Now she hurried home from the Museum, bags of groceries in her arms, eager to produce mouth-watering delicacies for Teddy's refined palate.

With her key in the door, she could already hear him at the piano. Tears would come to her eyes. In the kitchen, chopping onions, she would hear his arpeggios. Down would go the knife and she would hug herself with delight. Mozart himself at the piano could not have moved her more.

Diana had a friend at the Museum, Mitzi Rosensaft, a woman with a tempestuous love life, most of it imaginary. This summer, however, Mitzi had an actual lover. His name was Lionel Beilis, an intellectual with an Old Liberal bent who appeared in all the left-of-center Jewish publications. Lionel was currently completing a book on Labor Zionism in the thirties. Its final polish was being applied in a house he had rented for the summer in Sag Harbor. Mitzi joined him for the weekends and expected to spend her vacation there in August.

Diana and Mitzi were waiting for the crosstown bus. It was rush hour, and bus after crowded bus passed them without pausing. The smelly heat that New York had accumulated during the day, its buildings were now giving off in late afternoon. Diana dreamed of a cool shower but knew that once across town she would first have to shop for the makings of Teddy's dinner. A lobster salad, perhaps? Teddy was not to be fobbed off with prepared food that fell short of gourmet.

'How's about you and Teddy coming out to Sag Harbor this weekend?' said Mitzi. 'The four of us, we'd have a great time. OK?'

'I'll have to ask Teddy,' said Diana.

No sound of the piano greeted Diana when at last she let herself into the apartment. No sound greeted her at all. She dropped her bag of groceries in the kitchen and ran in panic through the large, empty rooms. The closet where he hung his clothes was empty. She pulled open empty dresser drawers. His papers, his piles of sheet music, all were gone. He had left no note. She searched madly through the wicker basket in the bathroom, throwing her bras, her panties, her blouses, into a heap on the floor, looking for some trace of him, anything, a sock. He had taken his dirty laundry.

Teddy's betrayal struck Diana like a physical blow to the intestines. She doubled over with cramps, gasping for breath, her heart thumping wildly. It was more than an hour before the pain left her. She felt drained and numb. But she managed to phone Mitzi and tell her in an unwavering voice why she and Teddy would not be going to Sag Harbor that weekend. It was Mitzi's warm sympathy that caused her to break down and cry. 'What's wrong with me?' she wailed.

There was nothing wrong with Diana, said Mitzi. It was the world that was all wrong. It was men.

'I love him so!'

'To hell with him,' said Mitzi, 'he's a crumb.'

'What am I going to do?'

It was a bummer, Mitzi conceded, but Diana was to come out to Sag Harbor anyway. They'd think of something.

Mitzi, oiled and glistening, her trim figure in the briefest of bikinis, lay stretched out beneath the scorching eye of heaven, a bright beach towel between her body and the Sagaponack sands. Black plastic discs covered her eyes, dabs of white cream her nose and chin. Her weekends had already given her a deep, impressive tan. Beside her, but on a beach chair and beneath a colorful umbrella, sat the neophyte, Diana, city-pale and fearful of a burn. She wore dark sunglasses, which masked eyes red from sleeplessness and sporadic weeping. Mitzi, exhausted from her attempts to cheer Diana up, had lapsed into temporary silence. She no longer responded when Diana, perhaps for the hundredth time, apologized for ruining the weekend. Before them the sands yearned downwards towards the ocean's eager embrace. A lone gull stalked the water's edge. Diana reached into her tote bag for another tissue.

They had left Lionel back at the house, a nicely restored relic of Sag Harbor's whaling days. He took a break from his writing on weekends, but he was not keen on the beach and preferred to spend his afternoons in various tasks around the house, returning the barbecue to its pristine condition, sweeping the old-brick patio in back, hosing down the deck, and so on. They had left him scrubbing the spotless kitchen table with an antiseptic solution. It had come to him in the night, he said, that the cracks between the planks were home to thousands, perhaps millions, of germs. 'God knows how long they've been proliferating.'

Now, Mitzi popped the black discs from her eyes and rolled on to her stomach. Overhead a small airplane flew the length of the beach trailing behind it a long, indecipherable banner. The seagull at the water's edge flapped its wings briefly, as if considering flight, but then resumed its earnest stalking. Tears trickled unchecked down Diana's cheeks.

'Cut it out, Diana,' said Mitzi, a trifle sharply.

'I'm sorry. The thing is, I feel fine. Really. I'm not even thinking about him, honest. It's just that I can't stop this damned crying. I shouldn't have come.'

'Anyway,' said Mitzi. 'Did I ever tell you how I met Lionel?'

'OK, so tell me,' sniffed Diana. 'How'd you meet him?'

'I advertised for him.'

Diana's mouth hung open. Mitzi giggled with delight.

'You heard. I advertised. You know, in the Personals at the back of *Books in Review*? "SJF, thirties, petite, beautiful, looking for sensitive older man and blah blah blah." Anyway, Lionel wrote back.'

'It's not true.'

'I was getting desperate, Diana. I was sick of the whole scene. I'd had it with the singles' bars and the synagogue socials. The best men were gay, the rest were animals. What was I supposed to do? It wasn't the sex. You know me, I'm not shy. But I wanted a real relationship for a change, I'm not even thinking marriage.'

Diana was too astonished to speak.

'The reason I'm telling you all this is maybe you should advertise too.'

'I couldn't do that.'

'Why not?'

'I just couldn't, that's all.' Diana got up and walked down the sand to the water's edge. She stood and stared at the horizon with an intensity that sought to traverse the Atlantic and Europe beyond and find the distant subcontinent and the Kush. Here I am, Mom, come and get me. The tears began again to trickle down her cheeks.

HERE I AM, young SJF, slim, appealing, nurturing, sensitive, intuitive, looking for a decent, loving, old-fashioned, intellectually stimulating, less-than-perfect, non-smoking male alter ego. Photo please. If you're out there, COME AND GET ME!

Books in Review 59132

Diana received only six responses to her advertisement and only one of these merited her attention. Enclosed with this letter was an undated cutting from a newspaper, the *Greenwich Village News*. On it, a photograph depicted two British officers from the days of the Raj. A hand-drawn arrow pointed to one of them, the shorter of the two, who was shown in profile, an indecipherable expression on his face, his elbow resting rather awkwardly on the shoulder of his taller fellow. The letter explained that the photograph might be slightly misleading: the writer did not ordinarily wear a moustache, and stage make-up may have altered, albeit slightly, his features. It went on to suggest that they meet for dinner. A date and time a week hence were proposed, and a venue, the Hungry Horse on West 65th Street. No need to reply if all suited.

This response to her advertisement threw Diana for a loop. It was not the letter itself, nor yet the photograph, which could scarcely register on eyes still dazzled by Teddy. It was what was printed beneath the photograph: 'Charles Timko (tenor) as Gérald and Norman Tarnopol (supernumerary) as British officers in Delibes' *Lakmé*, The Village Amateur Opera Society's production, all this week at the D'Avanzo, Bleecker Street. Tickets still available.' The arrow pointed unequivocally to Norman Tarnopol. Diana struggled to still an inner trembling. The opera was *Lakmé*! She gulped. Lakmé!

Diana had to tell someone. She phoned Mitzi right away.

'Don't rush into things, Diana. Hey, what's one letter? Wait. There'll be others.'

'There *were* others. This is the one that counts. Don't you *see*, Mitzi? My mother found him for me. *She* sent him.'

Mitzi knew all about Diana's mother. 'Give me a break,' she wailed. 'Not you too?'

'I'm *not* crazy! Just *listen*, OK? I used the secret code. In my ad, I mean. "Here I am, come and get me." She *said* she'd hear me. She *said* she would. Well, she *did*. She's sent me a sign.'

Mitzi sighed. 'Sure she did, sure. Only . . . what was the sign?'

'The photograph. He's in opera, sort of, an amateur. The picture shows him in costume, him and this other guy.'

'So?'

'So the opera just happens to be – wait for it, Mitzi: you sitting down? – it just happens to be . . . *Lakmé*!'

Mitzi was momentarily deprived of speech, but her intake of breath was audible.

'So maybe I'm not so crazy, huh?'

'I don't believe it!'

'So what do I do? Just turn up at the Hungry Horse? You're the expert.'

'I'm scared, Diana. Don't do anything. Not yet. Let's think about this, OK?'

'There's nothing to be afraid of, Mitzi. My mother wouldn't hurt me.'

'Lakmé! Holy cow!'

The Hungry Horse, across Broadway from Lincoln Center, was very popular with the concert, opera, and theater-going crowd, a vast cavern with many tables scattered on the ground and mezzanine levels. In the early evening and late at night these tables and the stools at the long, shiny bar near the entrance were filled with chattering, bright, mostly young people, gesticulating, laughing, leaning towards one another in an effort to be heard above the cheerful din. Waiters on roller-blades flashed recklessly between the tables, bearing aloft trays laden with food and drink. The Hungry Horse at such times was the place to be. But at eight-thirty, the time of Diana's rendezvous with Norman Tarnopol, the restaurant was almost empty, its crowds vanished across Broadway, not to return until Lincoln Center disgorged them, culture sated, two hours or so from now. The resulting atmosphere in the restaurant was sepulchral, invested with an echoing gloom only augmented by the votive candles flickering on the few occupied tables. Diana, whose nervous shyness and unseemly excitement were already being overtaken by depression, followed a mini-skirted hostess to Norman Tarnopol's table.

The man who rose to greet her looked very little like the

photograph in the cutting. She towered above him. He had a round pale face topped with thinning, dry, pepper-and-salt hair, hair not fashionably long but in need of a haircut. His eyes were red-rimmed and darted about the restaurant as if looking for spies. The hand he held out to her was plump, its nails bitten to the quick.

'Norman Tarnopol?' he said interrogatively, glancing from the long bar to the hostess.

'No,' said Diana, who wanted to run but who opted instead to put him at his ease. '*You're* Norman Tarnopol. I'm Diana, Diana Kollitz.'

Tarnopol looked puzzled. They shook hands and sat down.

'Can I order you guys something from the bar?' said the hostess.

'You want a drink?' said Tarnopol, his eyes darting from Diana to the next table. 'Maybe we'll have some wine with dinner.' He fingered the wine list.

Diana felt the onset of a headache, at the moment no more than a dull pain above the left temple. Surely, surely, there was some mistake. Please God, let it be a mistake. After lovely treacherous Teddy, Norman? If not a mistake, a joke, a bitter joke. Ah, but Diana knew that she was not for all markets. ('What's the matter with me?') Besides, had not her own mother, now securely within the seventh Triad, heard her daughter's cry for help and sent her, from the inexpressible vastnesses of the Kush, this man? It was wrong to embrace first impressions. There must be more to Norman Tarnopol than the seeming zero who sat opposite her.

Diana fixed a bright smile on her lips. 'I know you sing with an amateur opera company, but I don't know much else about you. What d'you do professionally?'

Tarnopol's red-rimmed eyes flicked from the salt cellar on

their table to the distant windows. 'I used to be an actuary. You know, death tables, and like that? But I got shafted. Ever been to the Scala Milano on West 17th?'

In fact, Diana had been there with Teddy. It was an Italian restaurant that offered indifferent food but that made up for its deficiencies with 'entertainment,' operatic musical diversions. In any case, eating out with Teddy was its own guarantee of joy. They, and others at the tables throughout the restaurant, had revelled in the rollicking oom-pah-pah of the music and the determined badness of the singing. She had nothing but happy memories of the Scala Milano.

'It's a wonderful place!'

Tarnopol, his eyes leaping about madly, sneered. 'I'm a singing waiter there. For me maybe it's not so wonderful. People come to laugh, not to listen. OK, OK, I'm not knocking it. It's a start. You never know who might be listening. Anyway, I need the work.'

The custodian of the Aaron Klopstock Collection at the Museum of American Musical Heritage and former mistress of Teddy Greene, talented musical hopeful, gulped.

'Hi, I'm Garry. I'm your waiter tonight. Let me tell you about our specials.'

Tarnopol, his eyes darting furiously around the Hungry Horse, ignored the pony-tailed waiter. 'You ever eaten here before? What's best is their hamburgers. I'm having the Hungry Horse Opera. Maybe you'd like the plain burger? With coleslaw and pickle?. But you gotta try the shoestring fries, OK? That's it, Garry.'

Garry was a trifle put out. 'You folks want wine with your meal?'

'Yes,' said Diana quickly.

Tarnopol, disconcerted, turned the pages of the wine list carefully. At length, he was satisfied. 'A glass of the house red for the lady.' He pointed to the empty tumbler before him. 'A glass of water, with ice,' he said. 'My voice,' he explained to Diana.

They sat for a while in embarrassing silence.

'That's life,' said Tarnopol.

'Yes,' said Diana.

The silence resumed.

'The truth is,' Tarnopol suddenly blurted out, 'I'm a married man.'

Diana abased her eyes, ashamed for him and for herself.

'Not married, exactly. Separated,' said Tarnopol. 'She threw me out. Can you believe that?' His red-rimmed eyes seemed on the point of tears. 'So there it is. Go know, for Chri'sake. It's not my fault, it's not what I wanted. Did Sharon care what I wanted? She was always ambitious. Thank God, there are no children. Not that that's my fault either, believe me. Nothing wrong with my equipment.' He grinned nervously at their table's guttering candle. 'No offense.'

Diana's headache became palpably worse.

Garry reappeared. 'The Opera? Great!' He put the plate in front of Tarnopol. 'So you're the plain?' He recognized a possible *double entendre* and consequent loss of tip. 'Hey, I'm talking about the burger here. Wine? Good for *you*, madam! It's a Bordeaux.'

'Bon appetit,' said Tarnopol, a degree of irony in his tone not warranted by anything he had said before.

'Oh, Norman,' said Diana, cutting with her fork unwillingly into her plain burger. 'How could you?' She pierced two shoe-string potatoes and pushed a tiny wedge of pink chopped meat on to them.

'Look, Diana,' said Tarnopol. 'You gotta understand. OK, I'm not trying for a new relationship. Let me tell you the truth. What can I say? I shouldn't have answered your ad. You're right. OK, I'm total crap, no question. But what I need is a place to stay. I'm fragile, Diana, raw.' His eyes scampered about the Hungry Horse. 'Long range? What I want is that Sharon and me, we should get together again. That's the truth. Meanwhile, I need somewhere to stay. So, what d'you say? Look, what you think a singing waiter nets? *Bubkas*, right? Makes no difference, whatever's your rent, I'll pay half.' He took a fastidious sip of water, his eyes skittering around the restaurant. 'Sharon's got someone else, I think – between us, probably not Jewish. Probably? What do I mean "probably"? No question, he's a goy. OK, so what? I'm as liberal as the next guy. But what's to become of me? Jesus, Diana, what's to become of me?' He sobbed.

'Norman, I've got this headache. It's real bad, honest. Listen, you've got a problem, I can see it, hey, it's no joke. But I've got to get home. I'm dying, Norman. Look, I've got to get out of here. Take me home, OK. If not, I'll take a cab. No problem.' Swaying, she got to her feet. 'It's OK, it's OK, never mind.'

On Central Park West, before her apartment building, she shook hands with Norman Tarnopol. Her headache now split her forehead with real pain. 'Look, I'm sorry,' she said. 'Perhaps I'll be in touch.'

Diminutive Tarnopol, his eyes strafing uptown eagerly, said, 'Sure. Hey, I understand. I had no right. Be well.'

Once in her apartment, Diana ran to her bathroom, knelt, and threw up neatly. There went the plain burger and the shoestring potatoes. The good news was that her headache diminished and soon after disappeared. She took a shower.

On her answerphone was a message from Mitzi: 'So what happened? I'm *plotzing* here. Call me.'

Diana went about her apartment collecting photographs of her mother. Sitting cross-legged in her nightgown on the floor before the piano, she tore the photographs into small pieces.

'Hah!' she said.

The phone rang. She ignored it.

She went into the kitchen and found a book of matches. On the glass coffee-table the heap of torn photograph fragments beckoned. She struck a match and watched the heap ignite. 'Good,' she thought.

In her bedroom, she examined her face in the mirror. 'Too bad,' she murmured, observing the lines across her forehead, the lines at her mouth, the lines at the corners of her eyes, 'but that's how it is.' Then she went to the linen closet and armed herself with sheets, which she draped over the several mirrors in the apartment.

In her bedroom once more, she picked up the receiver and phoned Norman Tarnopol. 'Listen,' she said. 'About your moving in. We can *talk* at least. Tomorrow? Sure, let's talk tomorrow. We'll see how it goes.'

She got into bed, turned off the light, and stared dry-eyed into the darkness.

Nitrate

Christopher Burns

Old film is perishable and mutable, able to transform itself into a liquid or a powder, or even to ignite spontaneously. The safety film archive is housed in air-conditioned vaults; nitrate films are stored in refrigerated bunkers beneath tanks which will empty and flood the racking if fire breaks out.

I have worked for the institute for twenty years, and my name is known across the world. Film historians, archivists, and restorers seek my experience and advice. My name has appeared on the end credits of more than two dozen documentary compilations and in the acknowledgments of over thirty accounts of the birth of cinema. I am a success, but I seldom talk about my work to Barbara.

She knows, of course, that I spend my working life salvaging ancient images and writing the occasional academic monograph about subjects in which she has scant interest. In the early days, when I restored footage of the 1898 Boat Race and the 1900 Lord Mayor's Show, she could see a point in what I was doing. Barbara appreciates pageantry, history, ritual; they offset her sense of fiscal prudence. Latterly, however, I have specialized in the work of pioneers who shot amateur dramas in their back gardens and developed the film in their kitchens. I have preserved short reels by Cecil Hepworth, R.W. Paul, and other film-makers whose identities will always be unclear to us.

My wife regards such films as flippant and expendable. She believes it a waste of resources to preserve them. For about two years I have not asked Barbara a serious question about her own work, and she has not asked me one about mine. The smoothness of cliché is currency enough for us – *Several clients called* or *Nothing much happened today* or some comment about driving conditions or the weather or what we ate for lunch.

Perhaps a sense of drifting apart mentally makes us also keep our physical distance. Or perhaps it was mere familiarity, and its attendant twin of boredom, that led us to a kind of separation from each other.

Barbara is still an attractive woman; I can see that plainly. On film, expertly lit and on a big screen, her good looks would be even more evident. But I have no physical interest in her. We have not shared the same bed for almost three years. It is even longer than that since we made love.

Letters arrive with Barbara's name on them. She picks them up from behind the door as I am about to leave. As she looks through them I notice a sudden change in her stance as she reads one particular envelope. Barbara gets dozens of letters at home, but I get very few. Only at the archives am I sought after.

Without asking any questions I close the door behind me. I do not know what time I will return. If I am working on a particularly tricky or interesting section of film, I often stay at my bench until the security staff tell me they must lock up.

Before we married, Barbara and I worked in cities a hundred miles apart and wrote to each other every few days. Although we phoned as often as we could, there was something especially intimate about writing. In those days I said things that must have been over-ardent and hyperbolic, things that turned out (although I did not suspect it at the time) not to have been true.

Barbara still keeps my letters somewhere. I don't know where; at the bottom of the upright metal cabinet in her office, I suspect. Certainly her other personal files are locked away there. I do not have access to her records, but I once stole a look at her keyring and made a note of the lock number. At the archives there are several cabinets from the same manufacturer. It was not difficult for me to obtain a key with an identical number to Barbara's.

And her letters to me? Why, I burned them years ago.

When I reach the archives I check the morning's mail, answer a few queries, and then visit the nitrate vaults. A particular stack of cans, recovered from the attic of a Victorian house that was demolished two years ago, has interested me since it was brought to the institute. I have already restored several reels from the stack.

To modern sensibilities these restored works are naive in the extreme. There is no sense of the narrative ambition of *The Great Train Robbery* of 1903, and no trace of the tracking camera which Nonguet and Hatot began to use in post-Méliès productions. Instead the films only last for a few minutes, and almost invariably the camera is fixed in a position five feet from the ground and twenty feet away from the subject. There are no close-ups, no pans, and no real sense of montage; these arts were all being developed elsewhere.

Perhaps even more notably, the narratives belong to a vanished age. Tales of loyal dogs, thieving gypsies, ludicrous blackamoors, and resourceful infants were the stock-in-trade of popular newspapers and music-hall sketches of the time. But the historical value and the strange poignancy of the footage – the performers long dead, the gardens long since vanished – become more potent with each passing year.

That evening Barbara asks what kind of film I'm working on.

I am taken aback, and instantly suspicious. Why such a question now, after all this time?

When I demur she asks if I'm not pleased by her interest. Her direct stare dares me to challenge her. She has recently had her hair tinted so that when she turns I can see shining gradations of blonde, as if she has been professionally backlit.

I reply that I'm not quite sure what kind of film it is, because the can is unlabelled and there's nothing on the feed. I suggest that it could be a primitive travelogue or the record of a celebration or festival. But the likelihood, I concede, is that it will be a pleasant little drama from the days when seeing images move was novelty enough for any audience.

I do not tell Barbara the full truth. I have already taken a magnifying glass to one or two frames, and found a man spying on a woman standing in a bathing costume outside a beach hut. A large towel is spread on the ground. The film is evidently a piece of titillation for gentlemen's clubs, a kind of *What The Butler Saw* which to modern tastes will seem either relatively or entirely innocuous, but still not the sort of thing that my wife will consider worth viewing, let alone salvaging.

'Why don't you know?' Barbara asks. 'I mean, why don't you just project it and see?'

I have gone through all this before. I am sure she has not forgotten. More likely she is deliberately making conversation. I do not know why.

'Because heat from a projector bulb can make nitrate film burst into flames. The stock's dangerous, a kind of cousin to nitroglycerine. That's why we have to transfer nitrate to safety before anything can be properly shown. Originally projectors had a scissoring device to isolate the strip if it suddenly ignited. If it did, the flare couldn't be stopped and that section of film was destroyed. All its images disappeared for ever. If there was only one copy, no one would ever know what had been on it.'

Barbara nods as if she is only pretending to be concerned. I can tell that she feels she has done her duty, or possibly indulged me in some kind of way.

'I'm invited out to lunch next week,' she suddenly announces.

Barbara is often invited to lunch or dinner. She is a freelance tax adviser whose clients are sometimes grateful enough to buy her meals. Six or seven years ago I occasionally accompanied her. Not any more. I had little in common with the people I was required to socialize with.

'Good,' I reply, uninterested.

I am thinking about my own work and its dangers. Sometimes there are nitrate fires at the archives. Combustion continues even when the strip is submerged. A noxious yellow smoke streams from the water surface; breathe in these fumes, and they turn to acid in your lungs. Those outside the profession never think of an archivist as leading a hazardous life.

'Why do you make a special point of telling me about a lunch invitation?' I ask after a short while.

'Because it could be important. There could be a job in it for me. It's with an old friend, Martin Tiplady. Remember him?'

Barbara is so eager for me to acknowledge that she is being open and honest that I immediately suspect there are things she is not telling me.

'Tiplady? You worked with him.'

'Six years ago, yes. I reported to him, and sometimes we went to conferences together. We used to do presentations on VAT returns for small businesses.'

'I remember him. I think.'

'I got a letter from him today – he's not with the same company any more, he's with a much bigger one. And he wondered if we might discuss matters. So I rang him and he suggested lunch.'

'I thought you were happy being a freelance.'

'Two days' work a week with Martin's company would provide a reliable and fairly high income. I'm attracted to that.'

'Yes,' I say, 'I can see why that would be attractive.'

Sometimes one becomes an expert by chance. I have examined, authenticated, and preserved several dozen little dramas by now, and seen hundreds more. I recognize the beach hut. It is the same one used in a short diversion (one could hardly call it a comedy), in which an ardent young blade's pursuit of two virtuous sisters is ruined by the girls' dog, which runs off with the man's hat, harries him to play games, and so on. Despite the beach setting the film must have been shot in a studio open to daylight. The hut is a theatrical flat, the background of dunes evidently painted, and the thin sand is scattered over an all-too-obvious floor.

Perhaps I recognize a performer, too. The girl in the new film is very similar to one of the virtuous sisters. She wears an identical horizontally-striped bathing costume, with a similar if not identical ribbon tied in a bow above her forehead. It fastens up curly hair which is, I would guess, auburn in colour. She is heavy-set, with wide hips and large thighs – not the kind of figure that would be considered glamorous today.

My detective work is not as extraordinary as it might seem. In the early days of cinema, sets, furniture and props were often used several times. For instance, historians recognize a particular feathered hat which makes an appearance in at least four films made by Film d'Art in 1908, the most famous of which is *L'Assassinat du Duc de Guise*.

So while Barbara meets her old colleague and talks about tax laws, old friends, and the chance of employment, I begin to get my new film, my little piece of voyeurism, into as good a shape as possible so that a viewable copy can be made.

Almost from the start I know that it can be saved. Always when I open a can of nitrate stock there is a distinctive and unpleasant smell, like unwashed underwear. I learned a long time ago not to be alarmed by this. But sometimes I have found the contents turned to dust, and often the entire reel has melted into an unusable mass of what restorers call honey residue. Sometimes only one or two random frames can be saved as prints. At such moments I always wish that somehow, some-where, I will be able to locate a near-identical copy. It is always a forlorn hope.

Lying in its circular metal can the new film has a strangely organic look, as if it is the remains of something that was once alive. The surface is coated with grime and several of the frames have shrunk. Parts have become brittle and some loops have stuck together. Certain sections have crumbled badly at the sides, destroying the sprocket holes and eating into the edge of the emulsion.

A few frames have become detached within the reel; perhaps the film tore at its last projection and was never spliced. I take the separated frames from the can as a pathologist may lift an organ from a cadaver. Deep scratch marks run down the sur-faces, the image appears unclear, but I can still bring the film back to life. The frames show the girl rolling down the top of her bathing suit so that her breasts are exposed.

'What happened?' I ask Barbara, and she looks at me, startled.

'What do you mean?'

'Did you get the offer of a job?'

It seems that at last she understands me. 'Oh, you mean from

Martin. No, it didn't quite work out like that. In fact, our meeting was something of a surprise.'

'Oh?'

'No, well, you see, his new boss is being unhelpful at the moment. I didn't quite understand that when I spoke on the phone.'

'So what's happening? Nothing?'

'You're quite interested in my work all of a sudden, aren't you? I'm not used to this.'

'Don't tell me if you don't want to.'

'I don't mind. There is something happening. Martin's thinking of going it alone. It was always his ambition, and he's been working towards it for years. He says he has the contacts and that a lot of his existing clients will follow him.'

'He's doing the same as you did, you mean.'

'Not quite. Martin's in a much more powerful position than I am. And he thinks that, if it does happen, we should work together again. As business partners.'

'I see.'

Now Barbara's speech becomes quick and nervous.

'I'm quite honoured, really. And a little, well, touched. I knew Martin thought I was efficient, but I didn't realize how much he really appreciated my work. We haven't discussed the details of the partnership but we'll have to do that soon. I think he expects to take the leading role. I've no objection to that because he has more experience than me. So we have to meet again, several times, and try to sort everything out.'

'You're considering leasing office space?'

For a second Barbara appears bemused, as if such a move has never occurred to her.

'Yes,' she says, 'yes, of course we will. Eventually.'

Later, when she is taking a shower, I sidle into Barbara's office and open her desk diary. Her lunch date is marked. A large M has been carefully written, almost crafted, beside the time and place. I close the diary and look round. The locked cabinet stands in the corner.

Before I leave, the fax whirrs into life. A handwritten message spools from it. There are three words, *Missing you already*, and the initial M.

I leave everything as I found it and close the door behind me.

The next day I take a spare reel of safety film and scissor from it several short, narrow strips that contain usable sprocket holes. These I fix onto the nitrate film, replacing those that are torn or missing. It is a delicate, laborious, time-consuming process. The alignment has to be exact and each new strip has to be held in place with nitrate cement, a clear liquid which reeks of acetone and has to be applied with a very fine brush.

A few days later, when all the torn and damaged sprockets have been replaced, I splice together the broken ends of film.

Then, wearing white gloves of Nigerian kidskin, and using a soft absorbent cloth, I clean the film by hand. This also takes days to complete, but the time does not pass slowly. Prior to cleaning, the images have been difficult to make out, but now I know that this is no piece of mere teasing. Instead of a disappointing and anti-climatic end, the last section of the film shows a brisk emotionless copulation which takes place on the towel in front of the hut.

When I am confident that the footage can be left to rest I carry out research in the library. I consult catalogues, lists, histories, and arrange special screenings for myself in the small theatre. Soon I am convinced that I have discovered the earliest extant film of a type that came into existence almost at the same time as cinema itself.

Within a year or so of the very first films being shot, men and women were engaging in uninventive but energetic sex solely because of the presence of a movie camera. Because of the subject matter, little of this material has been passed down. The earliest surviving example is thought to be *La Bonne Auberge*, sometimes known as *A L'Ecu d'Or*, made in 1908. Some historians believe that the Eugene Pirou's 1896 *Le Coucher de la Mariée* must have been pornographic, although only the first two minutes (which show a bride disrobing to her petticoat) survive.

My own film, I am certain, belongs with the varied batch produced in England in 1905. I can imagine the sly complicity with which they would be distributed. Along with the family films for general exhibition there would come a reel for discerning customers, to be screened in a smoky room with only men present, each one of them noisily determined to show himself a man of the world, each one secretly astonished and aroused. In both the frank depiction of sex, and in the detached efficiency of the performers, the film must have been unsettling and audacious. For me, it still is. Forget the filmed idylls of family life, forget the silly dramas, the sporting events, the military parades. This rushed and squalid little act is more important. This is what really drives the world.

Many of the old nitrate reels have been transferred to cellulose acetate stock, but I am having my new film copied on polyester triacetate. Cellulose acetate breaks down, too. Polyester triacetate, on the other hand, is tough and virtually indestructible. This is the appropriate medium for my string of images.

Why? Because I am dealing in history here.

Barbara is seeing a lot of Tiplady, and they have begun to meet in the evening. She tells me that sometimes a solicitor joins them to give advice. Usually she returns late. One night I sit up for her, but she says I need not have worried; it was just that the meeting had lasted much longer than they had expected.

'You can come with me if you want,' she declares blithely, 'but you'll be terribly bored if you do. Remember what happened last time.'

'I remember.'

'You didn't even get on with Martin. Not at all.'

'No.'

'You said he was boring.'

'Did I?'

Barbara is exasperated. 'Of course you did. I thought it was mean and spiteful of you to talk about my colleagues like that.'

But I don't even know if I remember Martin. And many of Barbara's colleagues were invariably much too confident, slightly overbearing, and absorbed only by their own interests.

I wonder if somewhere my wife has a photograph of Tiplady. There's probably one in her cabinet. If I could see it, perhaps I might remember him and put a face, and a body, to his name.

'When is this likely to happen, this partnership?' I ask.

'There are still a few details to sort out.'

Barbara is stripping lacquer from her nails. I am so familiar with the smell that I usually do not sense it. This time it seems so pungent that my eyes feel as if they are beginning to water.

'And I have to go on a course. Martin thinks it would be a good idea.'

I can hear the hands move on the dial of the clock.

'What kind of course?'

'One for professionals running a small partnership. It's supposed to be very good.'

'Don't you know all that anyway?'

'I know it for my own business. Working with another person

is very different. You have to have agreed procedures, decide responsibilities, sort out areas of decision-making, that sort of thing.'

'I see. You're both going on this course, are you?'

'It would be wise.'

'Together?'

'That would make more sense, wouldn't it?'

'Yes, I suppose it would.'

After a while I ask another question.

'Is this within easy travelling distance?'

'It's residential.'

'Where at?'

'Oh, I don't know,' Barbara says, affecting irritation, 'some coastal resort somewhere.'

I think of the first time Barbara and I made love, and I wonder if she and Tiplady will meet at that same resort. A cold wind tasting of salt buffeted the seafront and rattled the windows of our cheap hotel. We lay together, arms around each other. Barbara giggled and said she wanted to make love in the open air, among the sand and marram grass to the north of the resort, but I said it would be too cold and besides, we might be disturbed. She coaxed me, made me promise, but we never did. Three days after I returned home, I took up my job at the institute.

The reel is being copied now. It is being transferred on to stock which will last for ever. The old nitrate footage is being coated with perchloroethylene, which has the same refractive index and will eliminate the scratch marks by effectively filling them in. Inch by inch, the drenched stock is being fed into the printer; frame by frame, a stronger, immortal twin is being created. At the far side of the printer, drying boxes and fume extractors cradle the unspooled films. The nitrate reel will be returned to storage when everything is completed, but the images on polyester tri-acetate will be available for showing to anyone who is interested in the development of cinema, or legal and social history, or human behaviour.

This is what they will see.

A young woman in a bathing suit is standing in front of a beach hut. A man, dressed as if he has been strolling on a prom-enade, peers at her from the top of a fake dune. She strikes certain poses meant to be coquettish, at the end of which she pulls down the top of her bathing suit. The man approaches with the exaggerated walk of a music-hall Lothario. There is a certain amount of pretended coyness, banter and extravagant gesturing between the two. The woman rolls her costume down to her ankles and steps naked from it. She has a surprisingly small patch of pubic hair. Then she lies down on the towel while the man strips off his trousers and shoes. He seems embarrassed by his erection and contrives to hide it from the camera. They copulate quickly. The man's long shirt, which he has pulled up around his midriff, creeps down across his buttocks as he moves. Just as there is no foreplay, there is no languorous satiation afterwards. When he has finished the man stands up, picks up his trousers and shoes, and walks quickly off-camera. The woman struggles awkwardly into a sitting position as if nothing mattered at all. The film ends. The reel unspools. It has lasted less than two minutes.

The young woman is the same performer who appeared as one of the virtuous sisters; the man is different. I am certain that I have seen him before, but I cannot recall in which film. I am aware that this uncertainty, this sense of being on the edge of remembering, will not let me rest until I finally discover the answer.

*

89

Barbara is away on her course with Tiplady. She has telephoned me. It was a short conversation, because although she was determined to be friendly and to put me at ease, I was even more determined to be unreachable.

I stand in her office with the duplicate key in my hand. I have rehearsed this moment for weeks. In case Barbara detects that her things have been tampered with, and suspects a break-in, I am making sure I will not leave any fingerprints on either the cabinet or its contents. This is why I am wearing the kid gloves I use for cleaning film.

After several minutes' delay, during which time I wonder again if I am doing the right thing, I open the cabinet. The click of the lock is metallic and ugly. I hesitate for several seconds before I slide open the drawers, pushing them back in again if I find nothing of interest. The drawers rattle loudly on the runners and close with a crash.

I find what I want in the bottom drawer, and squat down beside it.

Inside there are sheaves of paper, accountancy sheets, tax publications, a trove that must date back years. Arranged in neat little bundles, tied with ribbon, and slipped edgeways down the inside of the drawer are envelopes. I life out a bundle as delicately as I lift detached frames from a film can. I do not recognize who the letters are from, but they are addressed to my wife. Wallets of photographs are inserted between them.

I lift out a second bundle. On these the stamps are very old, the letters quote my wife's maiden name, and the handwriting is my own. If I prise them slightly apart I can detect a faint smell of mould.

For a few moments I kneel on the floor with my old letters in my hand. Barbara and I loved each other in those days, before we drifted apart, before I began to devote all my energy, all my interest to the archive.

And I think of my film being printed, made permanent, fixed forever. It is all thanks to me, to my discovery, to my dedication. If I had run the nitrate copy through a projector it would have burst into flame and been destroyed. No one would ever have seen it. No one.

I return to the first bundle of letters. The stamps are more recent. The topmost envelope was franked six years ago; it was posted in a town only a few miles away from our home. I do not recognize the handwriting at all. When I lift the letters to my nostrils there is no smell of mould; they are completely dry.

I loosen the ribbon that binds them together.

An Immaculate Man

A. L. Kennedy

'Yes.' Hot little word, slightly angry, very solid, very meant. 'Yes.'
All she said.

How old was she? He couldn't tell by looking. The paper-
work gave her birth date and it wasn't exactly beyond him to
work out that she was ten. But he would have guessed twelve, or
older, because she seemed so tired and so deeply still. This meant
he must, somewhere, associate exhaustion and immobility with
age. They were certainly associated with *his* age. Next stop death,
at his age.

*Ten. Jesus God, what in Hell has happened to her yet? What can
she possibly know? And here she is landed with this.*

Clothes like her mother's: good and clean, but distressed
somehow, unhappily mismatched. The pair of them were dressing on the run; out of suitcases and despair, he would imagine.
The mother wore the wrong shoes for this weather and she knew
it and didn't care. Sometimes separation would take people that
way, making them want to act biblically, to seem on the brink of
rending garments and putting ashes in their hair. He'd seen it
before.

The daughter was staring again, focusing herself at one meaningless point on the top of his desk and giving him her forehead instead of her face. She was trying some type of self-hypnosis to keep his best efforts away from her mind when he'd already made it quite clear that he was on her side completely and only had to ask unpleasant questions to determine what she genuinely wished. The comprehensive and accurate fulfilment of all her desires was almost undoubtedly well within his gift. She could and would get what she wanted to get. This was something which rarely, if ever, happened throughout the course of anybody's life and he was offering it to her now, as her perfect right. He was her *friend*.

'I'm your friend, you do know that, don't you?'

She leaned further forward, her elbows resting on her knees and he somehow doubted she could hear him, although a mild shudder showed in her back when he spoke. Was she permanently round-shouldered, or simply wincing herself temporarily away from things? She wouldn't be so pale in the summer, he was sure, and she would know how to smile. Of course she would.

The mother shifted her weight, looking, as was customary, close to tears. She never did cry, though. Considerate. Still, no need to test her endurance beyond its strength. He'd already got the answers he required.

'Fine. Well, thank you. You've been really very clear. If you want to stay with your mother and not g –' The child's attention leaped at him, made him swallow half his word. '– go to your father. Sorry. *Not* go to your father.' He felt the air unclench. 'Then we'll try to ensure that happens. Fine. I'll fix it. That's what I do: I get things fixed.' He raised his head to the mother, cooled his voice, gave it the proper, professional pace. 'If you don't mind . . . Excuse me for one moment.'

The girl didn't stir as he passed her, although his jacket must have tapped her arm, at least. Prudence suggested he should pause by the mother, bend vaguely at his waist and accept her brief, ferocious smile which fought to suggest that her daughter loved her and that she was, therefore, still essentially loveable.

He nodded and pursed his lips to imply his agreement and support, or at least an understanding reached, or simply to let her know that he was deserting her now with good reason. His absence would allow them to talk and let their feelings calm. They could then be appropriately loving with each other and settle down before he came back to join them in the ghastly little interview room with its overheating and underlighting and dying rubber plant. Jesus, it was appalling – the pastel motel carpet and the stolidly tasteful furniture intended to imply reliability and a courteous use of client's fees, unblemished by unreasonable charging and other extravagance. He really did have to go now – the human mind could only bear so much terracotta ragging.

His offer of tea was refused. 'Something for the girl, then. Milk? Lemonade? Actually, we have none.'

'No, really, Mr Howie. We're all right.'

Rather than pat the mother's shoulder, which he felt she wouldn't like, Howie straightened and nodded again, confidingly.

'Perhaps if I might telephone tomorrow, we could discuss the aliment. And I do feel Mr Simpson's comments over custody won't come to much: pursuing it could only represent a pointless expense.' Her eyes wailed at him suddenly. 'Back in one moment, Mrs Simpson. Excuse me. Fine.'

Out in the passageway, Howie felt cleaner immediately. He detested the fug and the panic, the terrible malleability of words – all of the paraphernalia that straggled around clients and the law. His working life had started to have a particular, dragging smell, like the after-prison-visit tang he'd never been able to clean from his suits in his bad, old criminal days.

He paused, pushed back his shoulders till his backbone let out a series of grinding snaps. How best to pass the time . . . He could either make a phone call, or take a leak. The leak won.

He washed his hands and face before he started, trying to get the misery out from under his fingernails and cool his skin. Salter came in.

Howie knew it was him without looking. Salter had a way of half-whistling and half-exhaling between his teeth while he walked about. Some people found this annoying, of course, but Howie took it as a kind of reassurance. The sound was almost melodious, mildly contented and instantly recognizable. Salter's sound was a part of what made him; like the quiet shoes, usually suede, and the little gap in his lower teeth that he worried between with his tongue while he was thinking. If you thought of him at any time while he wasn't there, these were the things that might very easily spring to mind. But above all, the whistling.

Howie stood, breathing inaudibly, moved his thumb a touch along his prick and then moved it back again, feeling foolish and observed. Salter. A good man, Salter. He looked as if he might be confided in with safety. If one ever had anything suitable to confide. The base of Howie's neck felt odd, it tickled a bit.

Before a pressure dunted hard in at his chest and he looked down, half expecting to find blood, or something awful and ridiculous like that. A tightness rippled implacably round his ribs.

Fuck. Oh, shit. Oh, fuck.

A man's arms were fixing him, hands buckled together above his breast bone. And he could see where his own hands were locked clumsily in place, one of them holding his prick while he still pissed, because he couldn't help it, because once you've started pissing and passed the point, you really can't stop and you just have to keep on pissing until you're all emptied out. This was unfair.

It's a joke. It must be. Please.

He shook his head without meaning to and felt a high, inappropriate noise burst in his throat.

This is a fight. But this is Salter. This is Salter's hands. I can't fight Salter, he'll win.

A definite exhalation nudged past him and then Salter's chin dropped, solid on Howie's shoulder. Howie shut his eyes and felt his thinking rock and swim. Salter's body steamed in close, one of its legs bending warmly to fit the soft curl behind Howie's knee. Another squeezed in to the side, thigh to thigh. Howie's breath fought back against the swell of another man's lungs while his scalp greased over with an unwanted sweat.

When you're drowning, it must be like this.

He couldn't shift his hand. Even though he'd stopped now, was all done, he couldn't move. He couldn't put himself away.

'Howie.'

The voice loped in like a blow while Howie felt the shape of his own name working soft, fierce changes in another man's mouth, set tight at his cheek. And under his shirt and his jacket and under his blood and his skin something stalled. He felt himself drop and waver in a grasp of precarious flight.

Please. You mustn't do this. You don't mean what I want you to mean.

But he leaned back in any case and let himself rest on a body he couldn't trust. He twitched his neck to turn, to speak, but Salter bore up against him like good water, like a promise within reach.

'Sssh.'

The rush of that tobogganed down Howie's ear to fracture

him completely, bits and pieces of thinking spun off, crumpled, were entirely misplaced, with all the time Salter's arms there and now deciding to tense harder, to constrict.

Howie coughed up a spasm of nonsense, shrill as his brain. 'I can't . . . I can't . . . when you're holding . . .' Nerves lit up his spine, 'Is this . . . did I do . . .?' caught the thin, round pressure from one of Salter's hips, 'please,' the rising line of his prick. 'Please.'

'Sssh.'

And then nothing more. Howie stumbled back, slipped into a queasy turn, suddenly and coldly freed. Salter was already reaching for the door and leaving and not speaking and not making an effort to signal, to communicate in even the smallest sense: no turn of the head, no self-consciousness in the shoulders, no especial grace or tenderness in the curl and turn of his hand; no goodbye, no clue.

Howie still cradled himself, now facing the doorway and knowing a thick lift of want was taking his weight from his hand. He was yowling with solidity, pressing his thought up and forward into one or two beads of clarified despair. Before lack and embarrassment and, almost undoubtedly, fear slammed at him and started to wither his hopes.

If I'd done something back.

To either side, reflections snagged his attention with mirrored angles on a man who blinked, who had bewildered hair, who was shrivelling back in his own hand and swallowing hard.

If I'd done something back.

The interview room was silent and probably calmer although he was in no state to tell. He noticed, as he walked, what must be a line of piss, staining in a stripe across his shoe.

'Is there anything?' His voice sounded no different, his clothing was not in disarray, but how long had he been away for?

Anxiety crept a sweat across his palms. 'Was I . . .? I didn't keep you waiting, did I?'

Two pairs of identically grey-blue eyes blinked at him neutrally. The mother shook her head.

'Well, there were no . . . messages. So. Since you've had a while to think, are there any other points you'd like to make?' He tried to meet the daughter's eyes and didn't manage. Really, he should get behind the desk and hide his shoe. But he'd have to show them out soon – better stay where he was. Once the leather dried it would be fine, most likely. 'Questions? No? Good.'

He tried an unwieldy smile and allowed his arms to initiate vaguely ushering movements. Mother and daughter took his hint rather more keenly than was complimentary. Anxious to leave the room. Anxious to leave him. Not surprising, really – he must look remarkably like a man whose hands were now slithering with confusion, whose shirt was sopped and plastered across his arms and under the shoulders of his jacket and down against the small of his back, and who wanted to fuck, just to fuck, just to fuck.

No, to come. No, to fuck – the one you can't do on your own.

'Take care, then. Both. And I'll call tomorrow. Would tomorrow be good? We have the new number. You'll be . . .' He didn't have to offer them affection, they didn't want affection, they wanted appropriately professional behaviour and sound advice. But if they didn't go now he would scream. Then he would run and beat his head through the window and scream very much louder for a long time. 'Bye, then. Bye.'

Howie turned from them in the corridor and began the walk to his office, stupidly afraid of what it might hold. Afraid, to be more precise, of finding his office utterly undisturbed: without a note, a change of his usual good order, somebody in there and waiting for him.

The girl and her mother – should have called them a cab. It'll still be sleeting. You should have thought. You should have taken care.

Almost at his office door, he caught again the feel of a brush at his cheek and recalled that Salter didn't always shave quite thoroughly. There would often be those few hairs overhung by the broadest part of lower lip. The effect was not untidy but it drew the eye.

You'll have to go out yourself soon, get home for the evening. A cab might be the best idea, this weather. No need to decide now, though. It could pass, these things sometimes do.

His office was just as he'd left it, not touched.

I almost wore a pullover, this morning. I wish I had. It would have been soft for him. It would have kept his smell. Jesus.

He could have been joking. He must have been joking. Except that I know he was serious.

I hate my room, it is too small for me and makes me feel as if I will have a skin complaint soon, or asthma, or some other physical reaction to constant discomfort.

I don't look gay. I don't act gay. I don't ever say that I am gay.

There are gay people with the firm, people who are openly orien-tated in that direction. Barnaby is gay and, I think, Curtis. They are not mocked or humiliated, they are only themselves and accepted and relatively efficient – no more or less appreciated than any of the rest of us. I could be gay here in safety, like them, I do know that. I don't hate the idea, the actions, the thought. Being gay as a concept, that's probably something I love. I do, very probably, love that I am gay. I only hate me.

But Salter, I was sure he wasn't, hadn't – I thought he had another type of life. I thought I remembered hearing – something I now can't recall. I don't listen enough. Keep oneself to oneself, then there's no need to lie, confess, confide, that stuff people do when they don't mind finding, being found out. I don't want to be out.

I didn't want to be out. I didn't want to be found. I didn't want to find no one was looking.

I should not, do not, should not wish to find out about Salter. I do not wish to be told this is impossible.

But this couldn't be more impossible than it is now.

And this couldn't be more wonderful. Really.

At the far end of the building, a Hoover muttered and worried to life. Howie should go. All he'd done since he left Mrs Simpson was fumble blankly through his files and almost trash a phone call. He'd pleaded flu to excuse himself and then settled back to staring at his hands. His fingers were tapered, not stumpy, which he seemed to remember was a sign of sensitivity.

Ha, ha, ha, ha.

He should get his coat. There was no point waiting.

He really should go home.

Where it was just exactly warm and light enough and he'd done all the paper and paint work himself so each room was absolutely the way he wanted and ideal for being comfortable in when alone. Alone being the standard state: what the firm's new computers would probably call his default.

Bath. Relax. And then the good dressing gown, the long one and no slippers because they were a sign of age and shuffling and the wholly pathetic type of domesticity.

Howie came to rest in his living room, hot and washed, but still coated with recollections that watched and pried. His movements were hobbled and muffled with self-consciousness, as if the attention his mind was giving another body was being consistently equalled by that other body's mind, as if his substance was being pondered, fingered, in thoughts beyond his reach. He found himself folding his arms, shifting, shielding his face from the glare of nothing and no one.

When he went to bed early, it was only for some kind of privacy, only for that.

What does he mean?

Howie's ankles had started to sweat.

From a look – you can't tell from a look. But a look like that, it couldn't be an accident.

His whole feet were wet now, even the soles, which was ludicrous – as if he'd stepped in a basin when all he'd done was answer a smile with a smile. A pleasant insanity was flaring and hopping up from rib to rib, lifting him, lifting him entire.

Dear God. I'll be sick. I'll touch him. I'll be sick.

They were tucked in together in the tea room, slipping and straining to dodge the heat of the urn, the unstable clutter in the sink, the thrum of space closing and yawning between unavoidable, small contacts. Salter had good hands, no one could deny it: those tapering fingers allegedly so indicative of a sensitive man, the beginnings of dark hair turning close round the curve of the wrist, nipping in under the shirt cuff.

A man's hands. The things to hold, the size to hold, to move under. These hands, like my hands, like more of a better me. A me I could love.

'Not much room in here, eh, Howie?'

Cheeky smile, naughty smile, bad, bad, bad boy's smile. God let me not be imagining this.

'No. No, it's –' Facing each other and overly close. Howie thought they were overly close. 'I suppose it's –' Although, of course, not close enough. The need to reach forward was slapping and twisting in Howie like a flag. 'Difficult.'

'Mm. Difficult.'

Salter lifted his mug and drank, slowly, perhaps tenderly,

perhaps only being cautious of the heat. He swallowed and a liquid motion stroked down the length of his throat. The thumb of his free hand rose to dab at his lips, to press, to pause.

Please.

Howie began to understand the turning of the world, the slewing of continents and oceans, the problem of ever, at any time, keeping one's feet.

Please.

Then he let himself have his way and pushed his hand out through the thick, unpredictable air until he could stroke the side of Salter's face. Leaning forward, he tried to hold steady against the broad mayhem of information roaring in from that one moving touch: the warm of flesh, above and below the shaving line; the upward twitch of a blink; a small resistance of bristle and then an ear's gape, its soft lobe and cool rim; the fabulous close nap of Salter's hair set trim at the start of his skull and the final, searing, glorious skin, whole and smooth and taught on Salter's neck.

Oh, Jesus.

Salter shut his eyes, rocked his head back and to the side, pressed Howie's palm.

He'll stop me. He'll move away. He'll stop me. I won't. He will.

'Stop.' Salter's voice was low in his throat, gentle and, somehow, grinning. 'Oh, do stop.' This, an approving whisper, while Salter slipped a hot glance over Howie. A break of winter sunlight licked through the room, showing lazy constellations of dust rolling between them and the bright grains of steam leaping up from their mugs like flame. 'But I mean it now. Please. Stop.'

Howie brought his hand away. Hope bobbed absurdly in his chest when Salter stepped nearer, then picked up the milk. 'Need a little drop more of this stuff, I think. You?'

'Mm?' Common sense dodging round his kidneys, out of sight out of mind. 'I?'

'Do you need any more?' And a kiss so fast and light against Howie's neck that it might not have happened, but it did, it undisputably did. Salter gave him the milk and walked away.

Howie blundered back to his office, slopping his mug and smiling – he hoped – in only a minor way.

I'm too hard. I can't be like this and not do something about it. If I sit, if I sit down and breathe and think of work, it'll maybe go.

Like fuck.

I HAVE AN ERECTION I DIDN'T MAKE. I am not responsible. This belongs to Brian Salter. I want to give this to Brian Salter. I want him to have this. Me.

One of the secretaries passed him with a nod, looking studiously overworked.

Afternoon, Mrs Carstairs, blessings upon both you and the state mental hospital bearing your name. I have, in case you wondered, a massive fucking hard-on, caused by my immediate superior, dark horse and senior partner of this parish, Mr Brian Salter. YES.

Howie became a collector. In a handful of attentive days he snatched hold of glances in the hallway, a hand brushed in the midst of other company while the lift dipped three dizzy floors. He also kept an inventory of pauses where explanations might have been shown, or even one more kiss, perhaps a little longer, fuller, more likely to offer a taste. It took very little to dash him, but so very, very little to make him shine.

Christmas bore down on the city and even on the firm, which allowed its interview rooms and its offices and the secretaries' open-plan nest to sport a familiar ration of weary foil and tinsel. No mistletoe.

By half-past four the city sky would smudge out to a coffee-coloured blank and the knowledge of night closing round them all would fill Howie up with risky possibilities. He'd taken to working late, even after the cleaners had gone, busying himself in his office, alone, available, ulterior motivation harrying quietly. Everyone knew he was here, that this was now his habit. He made sure that everyone knew.

And each evening, he would sit with his door a quarter inch ajar and listen to the building as it came to rest. The silence never broke, although his heart would buck in him, now and then, at some distant disturbance. He would beat missives towards conclusion and tease couples' lives apart, then make himself a fresh coffee, drink it as his mind lowered into heat.

I know how to do it. I never have, but I've heard the talk. In the cubicle, it would be easy, I'm sure. A bit of conversation, then we'd walk past the stalls and lock ourselves into one cubicle together. Hope no one else turns up outside. But if they do, we wait until they've gone. It's not a problem, that's the whole point about doing it this way. We would be safe – effectively safe – at any time. I'll have to get a bag.

The bag is important. I need a good one, the type they put good clothes in, one of the kind made of something like almost thin card, instead of plastic. Paper would be no good. We'd need something rigid. Definitely. Stiff.

We close the door and I fold out the bag and step in it. No. I'd be taking him, so that wouldn't work. I ask him to step in the bag and then I put the lid down on the bog and sit. Sit in front of him, head at the height of his waist. Anyone looks, there's one pair of feet where they should be, a little spot of shopping in evidence and the right number of feet. But I'm inside, feet in the bag and lifting my eyes to his face and he wouldn't have to do anything, not if he didn't want to, I'd do it all. Take down his fly. Calm, definite moves – too light is annoying and too rough is too rough. As if it was me. Touch him as if he was me, strip down the cloth and lift him out, probably also let him out, really, with the pressure of blood already there and doing its bit to make him spring. To watch him spring, just to watch him.

But then I'd want his prick on my forehead, the silk roll of that, heavy and tight and a fat weight in it. Not for too long, though – kissing his balls, it would be while I did that, I'd press him and rest him so the tip of him touched my hair. Maybe more than the tip, I'm not receding. I've got more hair than when I was twenty, actually. The same, anyway.

He could stroke my hair. Put his hands down on my neck. Steer me. If he wanted.

I don't know how he'd smell. A bit pissy maybe – cloth, or talc, or soap, or nothing but him straining. Private skin and sweat – private and only for us.

I do still remember that. Breathing round the rush of a prick, licking down everything it wants and rolling, nodding for it, bowing to it. I don't see how a woman could do that. I don't see they could properly know how.

I think I love him.

'And?'

'Mrs.'

Howie's mind clawed over itself to get off and away, scrabbling, tripping over his clutter of hopes.

'Mr and Mrs.' Mrs Carstairs spoke slightly more slowly that time, repeating herself, as if he'd become stupid. Which of course he had. Recently, he'd become more stupid than he could believe.

He nodded and found it strangely hard to stop. 'Mr and Mrs Salter. Fine. Any little Salters?'

What are you doing? You don't want that answer. You don't want to know. Leave it, for fuck's sake.

'Any?'

'You know. Family. What a thought, eh. With those genes . . .' He mugged badly, something cold and liquid rising faster than his breath. 'Just a joke.'

Ha, ha, ha, ha.

'I don't know why I've never sent cards before. Then I would have known all this. I just don't really . . . like Christmas.'

'Well, I'm never sure if I do, I suppose. The idea's always better than the reality isn't it?'

'Always. Yes.'

'Actually, I think he has a little boy, Mr Salter.'

Hold firm on her face, keep looking in her eyes, smile. This is not important, this is not any of your business. But you had to fucking ask, didn't you? Fucker.

'Oh? Nice.' *Swallow. Get a grip. Swallow.* 'And is that everyone?'

'There's the usual big card for the cleaners. Unless you want to do something for them yourself.'

'No.'

'Then, no, I didn't think so.'

'Don't want to overdo it. You can have too much Christmas spirit.' *Breathe.*

'Yes.' She was giving him a kind look and he could only assume this was because he seemed such a sad, old bastard – all of a sudden wanting to join in, pass out office Christmas cards, have his bit of festive fun.

'Yeah. No need to overdo it. No need at all. Thanks for the help, Mrs Carstairs.'

'No trouble.'

Which she said nicely, with a dab of affection that he couldn't acknowledge, being already in motion and heading for the gents. Guaranteed privacy.

Ha, ha, ha, ha.

Bolt the door and lose it. Sob. The effort vacuum pumping at your lungs – no noise happening, just a heaving rock – until the air bangs in like a new type of pain.

Ha, ha, ha, ha.

He tried to believe this would break from him and be brief, get all the nonsense out of the way. There was the toilet roll to clean his face with when he'd stopped. It wouldn't be so bad, only a necessary release.

Except he didn't stop. Howie yanked breath in between his teeth, wincing at the hiss, and cried and folded his arms around his head and cried and held himself tight around the ribs and cried. He sat on the toilet with the lid down, in the way that he would for Salter, if Salter had been there, and he cried.

He might come in. Not now. In a bit. I'll get myself back together. Then he might be there when I come out and I might not have to say anything, because things would be clear in my face. He could take me in his arms and I could take him in mine. Take him. What I need. Fuck.

Shut the fuck up.

No one's ever done that.

Shut the fuck up.

Howie stayed off work for a while with flu. It did feel like flu. Without warning he would be sick, although he had no appetite and had nothing much to speak of that he could bring up. Nasty business. His sleep was also irregular and, perhaps as a result, his attention span diminished and he was prone to bouts of excessive weariness.

Then he woke up at five one morning with an absence lying heavy on him from the back of his throat to his balls and he knew another day of stammering round his flat would make him want to die in ways that he might take to heart. He should go back to work, learn how not to be foolish where he'd been such a fool before, carry on with whatever was left of his dignity.

```
I hope that you are feeling better now.
All the best. Brian.
```

The note was lying in wait for him on his desk. He'd managed the corridor and the secretaries and the enquiries after his health and then two sentences' worth of ink dropped him cold where he stood. He wanted to go home and to resign and to go into Brian Salter's office and thank him so much for caring, or beat in his fucking, prick-teasing head. But the phone rang and took him into what he knew: the law and how it worked in people. He was safe.

Hours congealed around him, made one day, two: he learned that he need not meet Salter's eyes and that even a wafer of air could insulate him from the bite, the lunge of Salter's skin. He didn't always want to retch when he moved away without completing a contact or making a sign. But when Salter came into his room, soft shoes hushing at the carpet, hands slow and graceful when they closed the door and made them the only two there, he didn't in any way know what to do.

'But I do know – you should come.'

Resolution was shuddering loose from each of Howie's joints. Salter seemed nervous, *Brian* seemed nervous, a raw edge in his face. 'Come.'

'I don't think. I can't. I've never gone.'

'I know.' Salter licked his lips, flicked a glance at Howie. 'You've been missed. This year . . .' He drove his hands into his pockets. 'It's Christmas. People go to parties.'

'I don't.'

'But you could. If I asked. Otherwise I'll be there on my own.'

'I shouldn't.'

'But you will.'

'If I . . . What would I . . . You're not being . . . fair.'

'Thanks.' Salter sent him a boiling grin, began to turn for the door and then stepped back. Howie understood he would do nothing but sit still now and let expectation lash him open while Salter walked up to his desk and then round it to find him.

He parted his lips for the kiss before he could tell what it was, easing in the muscle and eloquence of Brian's tongue, sucking until he was sure he was testing its root, then slacking and lolling and giving and being drawn forward himself into a perfect comfort. They sounded so loud, so unmistakably like kissing, so much like a proper couple, tailspinning off towards a fuck.

He was aware of being very happy.

'One day,' Salter spoke into Howie's hair, 'I'll make you so full.' Then he gentled himself away and the start of that idea arched and exploded in Howie like a Very Light. He gleamed with it all week, shivered whenever he let it out to play.

Stupid fuck. What are you doing? Have you thought what you're fucking doing? Are you insane?

No, I am just desperate. That's enough.

By the time he got there, the pub was more than full: God knew how many office parties hazing and blundering into each other. Howie stood quite near to the entrance for a while, checking faces and wondering how he felt.

I should go home and change, I'm all wrong.

Tarting up for him, silly fucker. Trying too hard. No one will see you anyway, it's so bloody dark.

Music broiled around him like a physical force and a volley of cheering spattered up. He tried to enjoy the pound of amplified percussion in his chest and knew he should leave. There was nothing he could have here, nothing he would be allowed.

But he stepped down and started to wade forward through the

barrage of bodies, because going home after coming so far would make him seem more feeble than he cared to be.

That's him. Shit. That's. That was the side of his face, it was, but I can't tell which way he's gone. The thought of Salter bellowed through Howie, scooped the muscle out from his legs.

Fuck. This is ridiculous. Pathetic. He was shaking down into a sweat, hands thumping with senseless blood. *I'll fall. And I don't want to. People will think I've been drinking.*

A bed, mine. If I could take him to my bed. Once. He could do anything. There's nothing I couldn't take or wouldn't want.

A hand caught his elbow. 'You made it. I am glad.' Salter. In a lovely sweater, jeans. Howie felt himself blur irretrievably.

Oh, God, Jesus, thank you. Let me make sense.

Salter tilted his head to one side and let half a smile slip for the two of them to share. 'I wasn't sure if you would.'

'Nor was I.'

'But you're not thinking of leaving.'

'No.' *Liar.*

'Listen, I'm in the middle of something inappropriately business-like with Billy Parsons –'

'That's OK.'

'But I'll be back.'

'That's fine. I'll be here.'

'Good. Make sure you are.' Then, leaning in as he passed snug at Howie's shoulder, Salter breathed out a shot to the brain, to the cock, 'I will see more of you later. Don't go.'

Howie watched Salter retreating and then fitting himself into a ring of conversations, his hands making lazy curves whenever he spoke.

He's not wonderful, only good; but my kind of good. Sweet. I'd take care of him, I would.

Let me take your wife and child and make them go away. Let me

*wreck your life, because I don't have one. Let me love you as much
as I'd like.*

Fuck, if he's asking for it, then he must want it, mustn't he?

Please.

I can't do this.

Please.

For ten or fifteen minutes, people Howie worked with came
up and threw words at him. He listened with such small attention, he felt sure they would be offended and move away, but
they smiled and milled around him, as if they were entirely satisfied. He had to go.

'No, you don't,' Mrs Carstairs, patting his shoulder, 'you can't
leave now. I've come to fetch you.'

'What?'

'To fetch you. I'm being a good secretary. Even if I am off-duty.'
She offered him a hoarse, off-duty laugh. Perhaps a bit of a goer,
Mrs Carstairs.

'Fetch me?'

'No questions. Come one.'

So he let her tug him between knots of talk, glistening faces,
day time acquaintances relishing their annual slur into lechery.
Naturally, Salter had sent her and was waiting, neatly ready to
give her the Christmas peck on the cheek, his eyes finding
Howie while he kissed.

'Just a thank you would have been fine.' Was she blushing?
Howie thought she might be.

'Don't worry. We'll all be back to normal after the break.' Salter
the genial boss, tolerant of humour, but ultimately serious.

She'll go and we'll be alone.

Mrs Carstairs giggled. 'Don't remind me. Well . . .' Howie
knew she'd rather not kiss him and shook her hand before she
had to try.

But I'll leave soon, because I have to.

'Merry Christmas, Mrs Carstairs. Mary.'

Please.

'Merry Christmas, Mr Howie. You'll be fine now.'

His body stammered while he tried to understand her. 'I'll be . . .?'

'You wanted to go early. Brian – Mr Salter – is leaving early, too. You can share a cab. That's why I . . .' She let her explanation drift away. 'You know. You'll work it out.' Howie realized she was quite drunk. 'Night, night. Merry Christmas.'

Salter scooped him in with an arm round his shoulder.

I can't.

'The wonderful thing about Christmas . . .' Their hips met. Good fit. 'It lets men be mates.'

'Please.' *Please.*

'Sssh. We'll go out and hail a taxi. Get you home.'

'I –'

Please.

'That's what you wanted, isn't it? To go home.'

Tell him now, tell him. Make it not hurt, make it stop. You have to stop.

'Isn't that what you want?'

No. No. No.

'Isn't it?'

'Yes.' Hot little word.

Thanksgiving

David Treuer

It hasn't snowed yet. The buildings on Third Avenue rise dull and gray into the morning air. The city is huddled in on itself, and on the margins, in the Indian neighborhoods of South Minneapolis, no one is out.

It is one of those days when you look outside, at five, nine, noon, whatever, and there is the feeling of pre-dawn lead in the way the clouds stoop level and low over the people and buildings. No snow, but the ache of cold creeps from the cement. The cigarette butts and wrappers lie dead by the curbs. Simon leans into his coat.

Franklin is deserted as he takes the corner and crosses over 35W. The traffic butts up against itself in a slow pour into town. No one honks or passes on the right, each just follows the car ahead as if it were a first car, with no cars in front of it. An initial car leading the others out of the suburbs and into the city.

On the bridge the wind pushes his chin down into his jacket. The zipper rubs his chin. He'd grow a beard if he could, but like all the Indian men in his family, he has the smooth skin of a boy, nothing to use as a disguise against the wind or the law.

At the Charities a voice from the stoop pulls him from his coat.

'What up, Chief?'

'Hey.'

'Where you headed?'

'Hell if I know. They closed?'

He stands stiff with his hands in his pockets, jerking his chin toward the door of the Catholic Charities.

'Been and gone. Been and gone. You missed breakfast. Least they could do is leave the door open.'

He shakes his head.

'Yeah. I suppose. You got money?'

'Naw. I'm flat, man.'

'Yeah,' says Simon, his eyes taking in Franklin, the cars parked as if they are waiting for orders.

'Let's head Uptown, see what's cookin' over there.'

'Yeah.'

T-Man hops up from the steps and pulls his coat tighter with his hands still in his pockets.

'Let's get the fuck off Franklin, anyway.'

With that they cross over, trailing their breath behind them.

T-Man pulls out a cigarette, clears his throat and spits expertly on a dead squirrel frozen flat in the gutter. He lights his cigarette and hands one to Simon and they set off down Clinton. Since Simon met him, next in line at the St Patrick's food kitchen, T-Man has always been this way. He has always enjoyed a casual disregard for his surroundings. Though they have both been in prison, Simon has emerged more careful, recently released and tenuously paroled, always easing into the streets and lives around him, while T-Man is determined to be off-hand, as if nothing can affect him.

*

The trees grow up over the street, a cage of thin fingers holding the low slung clouds from the old houses, beaten and showing ant-eaten wood through chipped paint.

They cut over in front of the Institute of The Arts where leaves that haven't been squashed or washed down the gutters into the river flip and jerk over the wide, shallow steps.

'You ever try to go in those doors?' T-Man asks Simon.

Simon shakes his head and flicks the resinous cigarette butt against the steps where the cherry splits from the filter and hisses as it hits a pocket of rain water in the stone. The butt tumbles harmlessly down the steps like a spent shell.

'Well, they're locked. They never open 'em. You gotta go around back. Why the fuck they put the Art Museum in the ghetto beats the shit outta me.'

'I been in the back,' says Simon, shoving his hands back in his pockets.

They look up at the huge wooden double doors, like castle doors, squinting against the wind that stings their eyes and against the stone building that looks too solid to ever fall down or be razed.

Uptown is empty. The bars are closed down Hennepin. The thrift stores and prostitutes aren't showing their rags down the length of Lake Street. Simon and T-Man see a bum tottering from side to side on the cement sidewalk, bordered by the street on one side and the battered store fronts on the other. He moves as though fixed on an invisible rail over a precipice.

T-Man snorts. 'Shoot me if I start walking like that.'

'Don't have a gun, T-Man.'

'Well choke me or somethin'.'

They stare after the bum until he stops. He senses he is being watched. The bum pulls himself straight and moves his head from side to side, squinting through the post-dawn gloom. Seeing that T-Man and Simon aren't cops, he pulls his ratty hat lower on his head and flicks them off with one hand while scratching at an itch on the front of his thigh with his other.

T-Man laughs and starts coughing.

'Fuck you too!' he shouts cheerfully, breaking into another cough. He wads the phlegm together with his tongue and spits the ball out, skipping it off the sidewalk into the gutter.

The old man turns and walks off down Hennepin, past the Uptown Bar and Grill.

T-Man shakes his head. They hear voices down Lagoon, an argument, maybe a crowd gathering.

'You hear that?' asks T-Man.

'Yeah, yeah.' Simon turns his reddening ear upwind. 'Yeah I hear it.'

They start walking down Lagoon to the lake, turning their heads right and left at each intersection. A couple of cars stroll glumly past, trailing bluish exhaust.

The voices grow louder. It sounds like an auction mixed with the barking of long-kennelled dogs.

'Jesus, we're missing some action,' says T-Man.

He walks ahead of Simon, craning his neck in every direction. Simon stops.

'Hey, T-Man. Those aren't people.'

'No?'

'Naw. They're geese. Listen.'

Sure enough, through the murmur and low city noises they hear the rubbery bark of geese mixed with the throaty chatter of ducks.

'Why didn't they fly south for the winter?'

'Why didn't we?'

'Yeah, yeah, good point. Let's go down there.'

So they walk again, quickening their pace, and cross Lake Drive, dead of traffic. Along the iced bank they see hundreds of geese. Some sit up on shore stabbing at the dead grass. Others pump along in the freezing water while still more set their wings and tilt in with a splash. The mallards skitter over the water to get out of the way.

Simon and T-Man walk up to the shore. The geese part and close in behind them. A couple jog by on the path eyeing the geese and Simon and T-Man as they try not to step in the scattered goose shit.

'They're bigger than they look,' says T-Man, squinting at a big gander beating his wings against his breast and shaking them back into place again.

'Hey goose,' he says. He takes a half-step toward the gander.

The goose pushes his chest out and rushes toward T-Man.

'Whoa! Whoa! Mean fuckers, too!'

The gander backs away and starts combing the ground with his nose for some invisible food.

'Yeah,' says Simon, 'and messy.'

The shore is slicked solid with goose dung.

'You know how to cook one of these things?' asks T-Man.

'Sure,' says Simon, 'rip off their feathers, throw 'em in an oven and turn it on.'

'Let's kill one,' says T-Man.

'How?'

'Strangle him. Can't be that hard. Looks like they only weigh about twenty-five. You're all of two hundred.'

Simon looks over the gathered geese and shivers into his collar. His feet hurt in his mis-sized shoes and snot drains slowly from his nose on to his upper lip. He shrugs his shoulders.

'Come on, Simon. All this food . . . Just sittin' here. Just reach out and grab his neck and twist his fuckin' head off.'

Simon looks around at the feathered chaos around them; the geese strutting and fighting, shooting their beaks like bullets at the mallards, picking at food dropped by park-goers. One goose has a hot dog bun clenched in his beak and tries to hiss at the other geese who are closing in. The bun is too big and he drops it to the ground where the rest of the geese peck it to pieces.

Simon steps toward a pair off to his right. The female snakes her neck out, draws it back, and shoots it out along the ground again, glaring at Simon with one eye. The gander stands tall, opening his beak and hissing at him, his wings drumming half bent against his chest.

'Holy shit!' T-man jumps back. 'They sound like cats!'

Simon steps away from the geese. He shakes his head.

'They're too mean. Way too mean.'

'Come on Simon. It's just a bird for christ's sake.'

Simon stamps his foot to loosen the goose shit lodged in the cracked sole of his boot. With his hands in his pockets he begins to stroll lightly in a small circle.

The geese part and sway a few feet in every direction he turns, like a sea of gray feathers rolling and rolling. To the left a medium-sized goose shuffles through the collected shit and snaps his beak. He looks away and it bends its neck double and bites at the feathers in its wingpit.

Simon knows that for a moment it can't see him with its wing raised over its head. Simon pauses and jumps with his hands out in front of him.

He falls short but the ground is so slicked with goose shit he slides into the goose. His hands close on the scaly feet and it jumps back in surprise.

Simon scrambles to his knees holding on to the goose's feet with both hands.

It hisses and opens its wings, whipping its neck around in

every direction like an unmanned fire hose. The other geese retreat nervously, calling their calls and stamping their cold webbed feet, forming a ring around Simon and the goose he holds by the feet.

It hisses again. It flaps its wings, trying to fly away from Simon. The goose pumps the air and Simon feels the gusts in waves against his face, sees the great clenching of the goose's breast underneath the mantle of feathers and skin.

His grip is tight and the legs feel so thin, no thicker than broom handles. They are cold and the skin is aubergine, scaly like the skin of a dragon. Simon feels the tendons pulling and pulling as the goose tries to take off.

T-Man is shouting.

'Kill him! Kill him!'

The other geese squawk and move back. Some turn and pop up, settling down in the wintery water where they paddle nervously back and forth like sentries or nervous witnesses.

'Kill him. Grab his fuckin' neck and kill him!'

T-Man is shouting but Simon can barely hear him. All he can hear is the woosh of the struggling wings, the snap of his wrists as the goose jerks right and left, the sharp edge of his own breathing as he tries not to fall back in the carpet of goose shit.

It quits struggling. The wings drop down and Simon staggers to his feet.

'Is it dead?' asks T-Man, looking out from behind one of the battered ornamental trees the city planted next to the lake.

'I don't know,' says Simon.

He turns the limp goose in his hands. His knuckles are skinned and raw.

It beats its wings once and rides up above Simon's head. The sun is weak over the lake and the spread wings block it out. Simon sees the sky go dark and the world emerges as a thin light through the flexed guard feathers trailing along the edge of the goose's wing, filtered through some terrible, rearing angel.

Simon steps back and the goose dives at his head with a hiss like the breaking of water on rock. Simon tries to raise his hands to fend it off without letting go, but the wings sweep in from the sides. He raises his elbows but can't keep them high enough. The goose knocks him in the ear with its wing. His head spins and his ear feels hot. He takes another step back and the goose hits him on the other side of his head.

'Aw shit!'

He hears T-Man laughing and yelling but the words are lost on the far side of the goose's wings around his head like a violent blanket.

Simon pivots around but the wings keep beating him from the sides. The goose's neck whips this way and that. Simon tries to tuck his chin in and bring his ears below the grade of his hunched shoulders. The goose's head looms, its neck uncoiling like a cobra and he feels a sharp sting on his cheek.

He throws his head back and sees the wing coming at him level, a feathered tide sweeping across his vision. Simon tries to dodge but is too slow.

The ridge of the wing catches him on the bridge of his nose. The pain sears up and across his forehead and tears cloud up his eyes.

'Damn it! Fuckin' die!' he shouts as he turns and whips his arms out. With his eyes closed he steps back and swings the goose away from his body and slams it on the ground. Simon lifts his arms and swings the goose in an arc over his head and on to the ground again. He raises it up once more but his feet slip and they both go down.

Simon lands on the goose and it lets out a honk as his full weight crushes it into the grass. He rolls over and grabs it by the

neck, then struggles back to his feet and swings it around and
around, like a happy parent holding a child by the hands and
twirling it with its body turning and turning in the fall air. Simon
feels his grip slipping and sees blood on his hands. He lets his
arms drop and the goose's head falls from its ragged neck. The
body lands in the goose shit, rolls and stops. Simon tosses the
head next to the goose's body. Its wings are broken, feathers
stuck out at improbable angles from its body, no longer part of
the geometry of flight. Feathers float down lazily from where
they hang suspended above the battlefield, like constellatory
witnesses whose job is over.

'I think he broke my nose,' says Simon.

Blood drips down his chin and he tries to suck in air. It feels
like splinters are being driven up his nostrils. He hacks and spits
out a clot of blood. His cheeks are raw and a bruise has already
formed where the goose bit him.

T-Man starts to move out from behind the tree.

'What's going on here?'

Simon and T-Man turn. Two policemen walk briskly down the
path.

'Aw, shit,' says T-Man.

He turns, and runs back up to Lake Drive.

Simon stands planted next to the goose.

The police walk stiffly along the asphalt path, pause as if
trying to decide if they wanted to get their shoes clotted with
goose dung, and walk up to Simon blowing twin plumes of
breath into the air. They look down at the goose. One looks
back up at Simon.

'You kill that goose?'

Simon's ears ring. He wipes the blood off his chin with his
coated shoulder.

'I hope so.'

His voice feels small against the throaty honks of the surviving and circling geese.

'He sure did a number on you, didn't he?'

'Yeah I suppose so.'

The policemen rock in their shoes in unison as if listening to the same inaudible song.

'You know it's illegal don't you?' The cop's voice comes out in almost a drawl.

'Really?'

'We're bringing you in.'

'For this?' says Simon, looking down at the dead goose.

'Yeah, for this.'

Simon looks at the cops and then back at the goose. It hasn't moved.

'But it was self-defense.'

'Sure.'

'It was.'

'Uh, huh. Come on, let's go.'

They turn and start walking to the car idling in the parking lot.

'Don't suppose I get to keep the goose?' asks Simon.

'Nope,' says one cop, 'don't suppose you do. It ain't dinner anymore. It's evidence.'

'I was just protecting myself,' says Simon.

The cop looks back over his shoulder at Simon.

'Don't look like you did much of a job of it.'

The other cop laughs out a puff of steam.

They reach the Caprice and open the back door and motion for Simon to enter and he does, ducking his head and sinking into the warm interior. One cop walks around to the trunk and opens it, taking out a yellow garbage bag marked 'Evidence'. He starts down to the lake and over to the dead goose. He lifts it by the feet and drops it in the bag. He scrutinizes the ground for a minute before he finds the head.

He walks back to the car with the bag thrown over his shoulder and puts it in the trunk. Stepping to the passenger side, he knocks his shoes on the sill and climbs in. They pull away from the lake.

Simon looks back and sees more geese landing and swimming back and forth, talking. A society of strangers. More geese swivel in on the nose of a northern wind.

The car turns out on to Lake Drive and Simon sees only the long darting necks of the geese as they close over the circle cleared for Simon's fight.

He closes his eyes. It's been a while since I been here, he thinks. It feels the same. Past the idle cop talk and radio static, past the hum of the tires and the gentle clawing of the heater he hears the parting of air between the feathers of the geese as they rise and fly to some other distant place.

At the Hennepin County Jail they book him and give him a washcloth and soap to clean the blood off his face.

They lead him feeling numb down the familiar halls, past still doors into the holding cell.

There are only four others in the cell. Two men play cards. One is reading on a bunk covered in a stiff wool blanket. The fourth is curled up against the wall with his back to the others, sleeping. The door slides shut behind him. He stands and looks around the room and touches his nose with his raw index finger. He feels the bones shift but he does not wince.

The card players look up and Simon nods. The reader flips a page with one hand and scratches his chest with the other without glancing at Simon, who walks over to an empty bunk and stretches lean along the rough wool.

There are rust and piss stains on the bottom of the sagging mattress above him. He crosses his booted legs and gently puts his arm over his eyes, trying not to touch his nose. He hears the slick of another magazine page and a low sniffle. After a few minutes the sound of cards sliding and snapping starts. They have been looking at him.

The jailer comes with food. The card players throw down their cards lazily and unfold themselves from the chairs.

Simon sits up slowly and makes sure that he isn't too dizzy from his broken nose and hunger to walk steadily to where the food waits on plastic trays. The reader tips the magazine down and surveys Simon and the card players and begins reading again. Simon takes a tray with a glop of stew and another lump of what looks like creamed corn. He brings it back to the bed and begins to eat. After two spoonfuls he pauses and looks up from his food at the sleeping man. He looks across to the card players.

They are watching him.

Simon swallows and gestures with his chin at the sleeping man.

'He dead, or what?'

'Naw,' says one of the card players around a mouthful of stew. 'He just wished he was.'

'Why?' asks Simon, picking at the creamed corn with the dull metal spoon.

'Got drunk, beat up his wife.'

The other card player shrugs.

'Won't be long before she bail him out either.'

Simon looks back at the sleeping man.

'You think?'

'Any woman stay mad at you for hittin' her a few times?'

'Ain't ever hit a woman.'

The card player with his back to Simon half-turns and pushes his chair sideways. He spoons a lump of potato into his mouth and chews. He taps the side of his nose with the greasy spoon.

'Cops do that?' he asks, looking at Simon sideways in the green light.

Simon shakes his head as he swallows the corn, wincing at the pain shooting through his nose and at the snot-like texture of the creamed corn.

The potato-chewing card player keeps looking at him.

'Whatcha here for then?'

'I killed a goose.'

'No shit?'

'No shit.'

The other card player shakes his head.

'Who busted you up then?'

'The goose.'

'No shit,' he says again.

They hear the jailer cough and the squeak of his metal chair against the cement down the hall.

'They're lockin' you up for gettin' beat up by a goose?'

'I guess so.'

'That don't sound right.'

The reader sets down his magazine and sits up on the bed.

'Them geese is mean fuckers.'

Everyone turns to look at him except for the man sleeping off his binge in the corner bunk.

'They are,' he repeats. 'I remember back in the fall my dad would take us from the city. You know most people took vacations in the summer. Well. He'd work straight through. Even in August when it got real hot and all the other kids'd be on the lakes, some water-skiing. We'd be stuck in the city. Dad'd come home and it was too hot even to get out the barbecue. Too hot to get drunk, he'd say. So we'd sit there in the basement and he'd drink iced tea and me and my brother'd watch TV and wait for the fan to swing our way. Even our T-shirts stuck to us. It was that hot.

'So we went on vacation in the fall. By that time it was cold. Not snow yet, but it'd sleet some mornings. You'd think we'd get to sleep in, piled under our blankets we brought up from the city. Funny, waking up under the same blankets in a totally different place. He'd wake us up at 4:30 in the morning, way before dawn.

'We'd eat hard-boiled eggs – our mother wasn't there, just the Guys, Dad said – and get dressed in the dark and take the boat out. It was still dark and I had to sit up in the bow, with a big flashlight so we wouldn't ground out the boat in shallow water and burn up the prop in the weeds. Dad sat in the back with his hands on the outboard tiller, smoking a cigarette, and my brother sat right in the middle shivering, and complaining. Though he didn't complain too loud cause Dad would get that look on his face.

'Dad had put out milk jugs on the lake, anchored to the bottom with tractor bolts so we'd know where to go. I mean, it was impossible to see the shore, even with the flashlight. You could see it, but it all looked the same: just trees and more trees.

'When I saw the milk-jug buoys I'd whisper to Dad and he'd nod, his cigarette dipping in the dark, just a little red dot where his face was.

'He'd nod and angle the boat in where there was cut in the weeds. My brother complained that it was cold, but me and my dad didn't say anything. It was cold. What could we say?

'Once it got real shallow, so I could see the bottom with the flashlight, just green weeds and the stunned minnows, I'd whisper at him again. He got mad if we talked loud. Even though the motor was louder than we were.

'And he'd kill the motor. Pretty soon we'd stop moving. We

weren't to shore yet. The weeds pulled us to a stop and Dad got out in his waders and pulled the boat closer to shore, into the cattails and we'd hand him the decoy bag and the backpack and the guns and he'd set them in the blind there in the cattails.

'Me and my brother'd climb out and put on the waders. Dad'd smoke a cigarette while we untangled lines and weights. Then he'd direct us as we threw them out, tell us how to organize the spread depending on the wind and how late it was in the season. Then we'd arrange the blind, putting our shells in reach and throw the camo deke bags over the thermos and the backpack while Dad moved the boat further down shore so it wouldn't spook the birds. After he walked back along the shore and we settled in, we'd wait for dawn and for the first flights of birds.

'One time, it was late in the season, all the locals were gone and the northern flight hadn't come in yet, we'd set up for four days and hadn't seen a damn thing. A few singles flyin' somewhere else, but that was it. Not even a coot or a mud hen, not even a grebe. The weather turned and even though it was a north wind with a little sleet, there weren't any ducks landing. We'd seen some bills come in but they'd rafted up out in the middle of the lake and didn't pay any attention to our dekes or calls.

'Anyway, it was on the fifth day and still nothing. Dad always said that just being outside was enough. But, the way he was real grumpy and smoked one cigarette after another, you could tell. Don't let anyone tell you hunting isn't a lot of work. It was getting dark. We'd been sitting there all day. We're pretty froze up and all the coffee was gone, and we heard her come in. A single. She didn't call or anything. All we heard was her wings, when it's real quiet and you're listening and used to sittin' still you can hear a lot. A goose's wings are about three feet from tip to tip and we heard her dip down about twenty yards out from our spread. It was just gettin' dark and we saw her struttin' back and forth.

Dad didn't want to use the call so close cause it might startle her. So we waited and waited but she didn't pull any closer.

'So my dad says Take it. Take the shot. Now we were loaded up with four shot and one two to kill anything we winged when it hit the water. We weren't planning on seeing any geese. So . . . Bam! I opened up with a four and she jumped up and Bam! I hit her again – I could see my spread go right around her – and she settled back down. She tried to fly again but I could tell I broke one of her wings because she sat down again and just paddled out further away from us. By now she was a good sixty yards out and even with two shot we wouldn't of been able to bring her in. So Dad starts down to the boat and me and my brother shuck our waders and we can see her still paddling away through the dark. Dad finally gets the boat in the water and we jump in and motor out toward her. Only, with the motor on we can get up on her cause she starts diving so we kill it and my dad posts the oars and he and my brother are rowing. We saw her, still paddling out, her neck pumping, she was about forty yards out so I shoot again, with two shot, cause she's on the water and she dives. I think I got her and I say so to my dad. But she just surfaces fifteen yards further away and he keeps on rowing. I load up and when we get to where she was we see her pop up thirty yards to our left.

'You wouldn't think a twenty-pound goose could dive but let me tell you. So I swing left and shoot and she goes under again. We rowed up . . . and there she was to our right this time. I shot again and she went down again. This time she didn't dive so we rowed in and got real close, maybe fifteen yards and I raised up and – Click. I was out of shells. Totally out. Dad and my brother had left their guns in the blind and all the boxes too.

'But Dad said I'd hit her pretty hard three times and that even a goose would tire out and die so we kept on closing in on her. It was almost pitch black and every time we drew near she'd dive again. Our arms were numb from sprinting behind the oars and stopping and sprinting again. Dad's breath was coming out raspy and my brother's hands kept slipping from the oar and it fell in the water and jerked the boat around and Dad would yell at him and cough. We kept getting closer though and we moved up to about four feet away and then she'd dive but without the shells four feet could've been forty yards. I threw one of the extra paddles at her before she could dive and it hit her square on the neck but she just dove anyway and it was as dark as it'd get and we couldn't see her any more. So we stopped and we were all breathing hard. We heard her paddling and saw in the little light some ripples. But we had to pack it in and get the decoys and we never found her.'

The man scans the room: the food steaming dankly in the flickering fluorescent light, the card players, Simon, the still sleeping drunk. He nods to himself, lays back down, and puts the magazine over his face. He starts snoring in a few minutes.

After a while they all take to their bunks and with the light still flickering, they close their eyes and go to sleep. All can hear, faintly, hard-soled shoes, the rasp of metal, and the jingle of keys, like bells, in the cemented distance.

The next morning at his arraignment Simon shifts uneasily in his crumpled and bloody clothes. In the clean courtroom he can smell the goose shit on his shoes and pants, the cigarette smoke clinging to his jacket.

The judge sits leaning forward, his arms stuck out from the black robes like sticks. He cocks his head when the bailiff reads Simon's case from the docket. When the bailiff finishes the judge remains leaning forward looking at his clasped hands. Simon sways back and forth in his torn and bloody clothing.

'You're being charged with poaching and disrupting the peace. You understand that?'

He pushes his glasses from the crease in his nose.

'Yes sir,' says Simon.

'You killed a goose by Lake Calhoun.'

Simon doesn't say anything.

'You killed a goose.'

Simon squints through the court light and picks a leaf from his jacket cuff and puts it in his pocket.

'Well. Don't you have anything to say?'

'You're doin' all the talkin',' says Simon.

'Don't get smart. It's eight-thirty in the morning.'

'Yes sir.'

'Well.'

'Yeah, I killed a goose.'

'So you're pleading guilty.'

'I suppose.'

The lights seem to pulse. Simon hears the other people waiting to be called sniffling and fidgeting in the benches behind him. The judge sighs and looks down at some papers in front of him. He takes off his glasses, pauses, and puts them on again. He looks at Simon.

'You been in jail before.'

'Yes.'

'In fact, you've been in prison.'

'You're sending me to prison over a goose?'

'You broke parole.'

Simon is silent. He tries to speak, but looks at the judge, sitting high up in the cruel light and he averts his eyes and stares down at his bloody boots.

'Oh,' he whispers.

The judge taps his hand with a pen. He looks at the paper in front of him again and back at Simon.

'Wasn't ten years enough for you?'

'Yes sir,' says Simon, his voice cracking. 'Yeah it was enough.'

The judge sighs.

'Sixty days,' says the judge to no one in particular.

Simon hears the ruffle of papers and a new name being called off the docket by the bailiff.

A police officer comes up to Simon's side and touches him gently on the elbow. Simon pivots as if he and the officer are part of some graceful dance and the officer leads him out of the court-room.

Eileen Dunn

Erica Wagner

I am pared to bone and whiteness now. There is nothing left but the hard of me, the rattling core that clatters in the wind, stones on the beach, washed clean by the sea, turned over and over like thought until there is only the pure centre, clean and smooth and adamant. When the rough wind comes again they will sit close in the dim light, drinking, watching the red sky, the black sea through greasy windows, looking for a change in the weather. They will think of me. I am storm and sunlight.

I was hanging out the wash. The big white sheets of my bed flapped and snapped and curled wet tentacles around my arms, holding me to myself. My fingers had puckered, two-day-old fruit, and my shoulders had gone thick and stupid from reaching. Winter just allowing himself to be courted by Spring, the garden bright and cold, the ground buzzing under my feet with the knowledge of something about to happen.

He passed on the path to the harbour.

One was sun and the other shade, or so it seemed to be. The first, the sun, the one I married: broad and fair and fine, pale as seashell beneath the collar of his shirt, the skin of his hip soft as the breast of a gull. The other, the shade: and you would not know one without the other. When he passed on the path to the harbour my husband was mending nets; on the wind, if I had listened, I might have heard his voice. But I did not listen, for over the wall I saw a wing of dark hair, petrel-black, and my heart lifted like the petrel's wing and my mouth was full of sudden breath. He was a stranger to me. He had a sack across his shoulder and his shirt, I could tell, had once been a much darker blue.

Do you want work? I called. I could count the steps between us.

He turned in his tracks and put his dark eyes on me. There was nothing in them except what he saw: I was a woman in a garden, a woman with sheets on a line, with her hair pulled back tight and her hands red from washing.

My husband has a boat, I said. He stepped close to the wall between us, and put his hands on the grey flints that rose as high as his waist. His thumbs hooked together; his fingers, with their black-mooned nails, curling towards his palms. His wrists were white beneath the whorled dark hairs, beneath the frayed cuffs of his shirt. The edges of men: all pale and unexpected, like a creature crawled out from the dark.

Fishing boat?

For something to say, he said it. His words sidelong, his eyes sliding off mine like weed from a rock.

The *Eileen Dunn*. You cannot miss her.

Are you Eileen?

I am, I said. And then I felt the flush in my skin, like a sunrise. She is a fine boat.

You might have thought he would say something then, about a fine boat and a fine woman, but he only smiled. In my hands I still held a sheet, cold and wet in the weak sunshine.

Thanks, he said. I'll find her.

He turned his back and went. Down the path to the harbour, the stones grumbling beneath the soles of his boots, his shoulders broad as sailcloth billowed by the wind, his suncreased neck, the shine on his cap of hair. I watched until he turned a bend and vanished, but I could see him still.

My husband and I were married in my mother's house. It was a summer's day, but all the same the rain came down in hard bolts, like the spray from a wave against the sea wall. It churned up the ground into a thick red mud that slid into my shoes and clung to the hem of my new-sewn dress so that when my husband lifted me to carry me through his doorway it might have been just to keep his swept steps clean.

But I have never minded the rain. To me the sound of rain on a roof seems a kind of heartbeat, human, sorrowful, the high blue of the sky brought down closer, the world a smaller, more containable place. At night, too, the rain blots out the hard cold stars that only show how small we are, how made of nothing. The North star shows the way: from before we are born until after we die, for ever. What hope is there against such eternity? But then my husband would say: it is the North star brings me home to you.

That night we could see no stars, not North nor any other, and yet I felt less lost than I had ever done. He boiled up water until steam filled the room, our very own indoor cloud, and washed my muddy feet and lifted my wet dress from my body while I stood on his stone floor and shivered though the room was warmed by the fire. He looked at me as if I were a woman he had never met before, a selkie risen from the sea, and though at first I was frightened, when I stepped into his arms and felt his rough hands I was not. I moved like a seal beneath him until his eyes opened wide and the candlelight caught their moist surface, my own pole star to follow.

He smelled of the sea, of smoke; his skin when I licked it was salty and bitter. The white of his body shone against his dark arms and face, the sweat that streaked him like the sea full of fire on a summer night. He lay on his back and I ran my hands through his hair, down his flesh. I imagined myself the selkie his eyes had made me, wild and strange, skin and fur, his salty shell-taste like the ocean in which I was born.

In the days that followed, the sun rolled across the sky, the stars turned through the heavens, the same as ever they had, and I found that being a wife was not so different from being a daughter. I knew how to do what I needed to do, to cook and clean, to make and mend, to watch and wait – as my mother had done all these things before me, until the day she waited and waited and my father did not come home. That last gale my father sailed through tore a slate off our roof: it cracked on the ground in the night and made my mother a widow, its break the break between this world and the next.

Five years passed. Twenty seasons, sixty months, the invisible numbers that make up a life. When my husband was gone I filled the house with the sound of my own voice, enlisting the aid of the windows and walls as I went about my business, as if I might vanish in silence. I had not expected silence: I had expected company, but none came. Each time my husband left for the sea he left in expectation: each time he returned he hid his disappointment in a kiss.

At first I did not mind. I liked my own company, I liked my husband's, when he was home, the unbroken quiet between us in the fire's glow. But there came a day that I walked down to the village and saw two women, neighbours of ours or nearly so, for they lived on the other side of the bay. They were two sisters who had married two brothers; one was dark and one was fair and the dark one held a strawy-haired bundle, the fair one a child with a tuft of inky down floating off its scalp. They talked as sisters will, all at once, together, catching words before they have time to fall. They did not see me until I was close upon them: and when they saw me they had no more speech but hurried to the other side of the road, clutching their little bundles to their milky breasts. When I turned to stare at their shawled backs I heard nothing, but saw their heads bent together, as if they walked under a cloud.

Evil is like fever, a disease that passes from eye to eye and it is in you before you know it. It was that night, three nights before my dark friend hooked his thumbs over my garden wall, that I felt something shift inside me. I accepted the dark in their glance. I did not know it would happen. I did not mean this to be.

It was my husband told me his name. He had taken my advice and gone down to the harbour, found the *Eileen Dunn* and this time made a compliment about a pretty boat and a pretty wife. He seems a good man, my husband told me, he seems like he will work hard. He comes from down the coast, but doesn't say what made him leave. I shrugged and wiped the table with a cloth, the wet-streak catching the light and shining like a lie. I dried it with my apron. He leaned back, closed his eyes. I could look without being seen. That evening his familiar face seemed new to me, another man's, as if my new eyes had made it so. My heart jumped and rumbled.

I kept the name I learned in my mouth, tucked away, did not say it out loud although I felt the shape of it, whole and round, set atop my tongue like fruit.

Then the first storm came. The men thought they would be

sailing soon, but the winds dropped from the northeast and slapped their notions down. Some said they would go anyway: said they needed the fish and the money. Some, and my husband among them, said money's no good to those in the grave.

I should have been glad to hear him say it; and I did not want him to go. But somehow his voice sounded different in my ear, buzzed like a fly I wished I could bat away.

Before I knew it I stood before the place where he lived. He had taken a room, upstairs, with a door of its own down on to the street. I knocked, and stood. I knocked again. He opened the door and his dark eyes stared, closed and opened so that I wondered if he might shut me out in the rain. But he did not. He stepped back, and I walked in.

When I was young I learned to dance. I was a fine dancer, or so my mother said, light on my feet and with a straight back and eyes that did not care to see the ground. I learned the steps so well that the knowledge of them came away from my head, went into my body. The dance led us on, took us without our will until we were a dozen people made one animal that wove and lashed like a dragon.

So it was just then. My feet moved without my will, my hands reaching out, my face hot despite the cold and there was only this movement, this dragon, two steps forward, one step back. I saw small things: the oily lamp, its blackened glass; the window sooted and shadowed; the eyes of the low fire's coals. His blue shirt hung stiff to dry. His skin dark and secret and new. He was not like my husband. He was rougher, coarser, no fine white silk beneath his cloth – and seemed stronger in his quick action, his clasping hands. But I think he was not. For I chose to go to him, and once I arrived he was weak at the face of me, his strength sweated out as we lay out by the fire, the bones of my shoulders and hips bruised by the floor. A splinter of wood dug into my heel as he shouted out, not my name, just a cry like rage or pain. He kissed me and I felt the draw to him, the dark pull in my blood to this stranger, still strange. Small things: the lamp, the window, the coals, his shirt. Nothing different and nothing the same.

He watched me as I dressed. He took my hand when I stood at the door, squeezed my cold fingers hard enough to hurt. I ran home through the rain, mud on my skirt, on my feet, warm and suety between my toes. When I unlaced my shoes, squatting on our neat steps, I found the splinter had dug right in above the bone of my heel and would not come out until I had dug a needle under my skin. Two spots of blood dropped on the clean flags; I threw the splinter and the needle into the fire.

The weather would not lift. The sky pushed down against the backs of the hills, the spun spray rose from the surface of the sea and knitted itself with the rain. There was nothing left between water and air, no distance. I pulled the wet into my lungs day after day until I was sure I was drowning. Wood grew slimy; bread grew mould. My husband grew restless, kept to the edges of the house, walking by the walls that confined him as if by brushing his shoulder against them he might make them disappear. Soon everything was mended; his busy hands were empty, fingers reaching like blindworms for something to occupy them.

Sometimes they found me, his hands. They reached out to me at midnight, at dawn; they crept across me cautiously as if they knew my skin was not the skin they remembered. He is the same, but a stranger; or I am the same, but a stranger; or there is just a stranger between us, a shadow in the drifting dark.

I did not see him again, my lover. I had what I had wanted: and now the thing I want has no name but a voice in the wind, a howl in the wind that will not abate as if it voiced my silence, and my eyes were grey as the sky, my brow lowered like the clouds, my gaze dark, dissatisfied, a wind whipping inside me, blown through my heart until it was emptied of blood and feeling and held only air.

Three weeks passed this way. Howling wind, prowling husband. He knew nothing of me; he hardly thought of me now, only the weather, little knowing that the weather came from in me, that this was my weather, my storm. To him I was the same woman, the same wife, who went each morning to the barrel that stored our fish, salted, dried, reached down to pull out supper, reached lower and lower each day until I had to stand on my toes and put my head right inside the stinking staves and one day felt my nails scrape on the barrel's base.

We must go out, he said to me one night. We have no choice.

In the lamplight I saw fine lines at the corners of his eyes, in the turn of his mouth. He was older, and I had not noticed.

I did not answer. There was nothing for me to say. He took my hand, and we sat skin to skin. The firelight showed the shape of his skull; his eyes were deep in their sockets. Still I was pulled to him, like the tide, but like the tide too I rushed away towards another shore. That night, his palm in mine, I tried to remember how my lover's palm was different, how it felt on my flesh – and I could not. That night, it seemed, my husband returned to me, or I returned to him, and for a few hours it was possible to believe that nothing had changed, perhaps because I knew that the greatest change was to come. I told him I was carrying his child. His eyes opened wide, the light shone on them at last. I knew what I told him wasn't the truth. I knew it didn't matter. Thunder cracked and the ocean roared and I knew that nothing mattered but that.

*

There was only a tawny stripe of light at the bottom edge of the sky when I walked with my husband down the path to the harbour. It was a crack in the still-lowering cap of grey cloud that pressed down on our heads; and it was too red for my taste. But I said nothing. I walked in step with my husband, heel and toe, and he told me what he would build for me on his return. A cradle made from wood he would season himself. A tall rocking-horse with jet eyes and a tail of real hair. A bone rattle, a teething ring: in the bag slung over his shoulder were his delicate scrimshaw tools, cleaned of old ivory dust and wrapped in soft cloths. While he was carving, he would be with me, he said.

The sickness first struck me then. I knelt by the side of the path in the long wet grass, soaking my skirt, and he held my hair back from my forehead as I vomited up my meagre breakfast. He stroked my head, soothed me: he almost seemed pleased. It was proof, of some kind. But proof of one thing to him: of quite another to me. I imagined I could feel the child kick me for my lies.

She kicked again when I stood on the quay. I stood by the painted side of the *Eileen Dunn*, moss-green, slick paint, some-times seeming the colour of the sea but not today: the ocean was like a chopped scree of basalt, flinging foam hard as little flints on to my cold skin. As soon as we reached her my husband was stolen away by the ship, my ship, he often said, so I suppose I should not have been jealous but I always was, even then, even this last day. In his heavy boots he strode his deck, slipping through baskets I had woven, nets he had mended, coils of glass floats like dark frozen bubbles from the water's depths, his head dark gold ducking beneath the boom, shouting to his men who answered him without speaking, who would not meet my eye, as if their going out in this dirty weather were the fault of her who had named the boat. All the men but one.

By now the crack of dawn had opened wide and the seagulls wheeled and screamed. The wind rose and the rain fell and my clothes clung close to my body but I stood stone-still and would not leave. I was waiting to hear one of them say it: for one of the men to say to my husband, we will not go – but none of them did. He was the master, they were the men, and besides, their wives were hungry too, though not fools enough to stand like me, my hair growing knotted and wet as the rigging of the *Eileen Dunn*.

They would lose the tide if he did not come. The sun made a high, sallow streak in the tarnished sky; its light struck the water and sunk straight in, there was no glow to anything. My husband had disappeared below.

I never saw his face, only his back as he ran by, knocked me, almost made me fall. My lover leapt on to the *Eileen Dunn*, his long legs wide over the water, landed hard on her deck on his knees, his face down by her planking, his breath coming hard as if he had run for miles or had felt some evil spirit at his back. I see him there still, crouching, bent at all his joints and slick with rain, the sinews of his arms taut through the wet blue cloth of his shirt, a thread of water running off the black of his hair. I see him there still, as the rough walls of his room closed around me again, the air thickened with our bodies' heat, and I hardly knew that my hands closed around my belly, my child. It was then that he looked ashore, his stone-black eyes on mine.

In the next instant, my husband, hearing the clatter, was up on deck. What happened then is hard to say. A woman sits by her fire with needles in her hand and skeins of wool on her lap: when does the garment she is knitting become more than an accretion of stitches? Which stitch, which row? There must be one – and yet it could never be accounted for. And so it was then as we stood and knit up between us – my husband on deck, myself on the shore, my lover, just rising from his knees – a garment of glances that told a story as a pattern in wool will, soundless, say the name of the drowned wearer. The wind was the only one of us that spoke, shrieking in the rigging and wire, a sudden gust battering against my breast and stealing the breath from my lungs as if its cry were mine.

I turned and ran. I did not watch her sail, but there was a fine thread between us, between me and the ship named after me, spooling out from my heart. As the days wore on it drew and drew, pulled by an invisible spinner, and the thread was the life of me.

My fever had begun to rise when I heard the knock on my door. I lay in my bed, just awake after a nightmare sweat in which I seemed to float above myself, swollen and enormous as a thundercloud, tethered to my tiny shape below by rain-fine silver pins. It was not unpleasant, drifting this way, though the height and distance made me dizzy; sometimes when I looked down, down, I thought the tiny shape was my baby, unnaturally still in my dream as I feared she had become in my belly.

I rose to answer, the breath of the wind pushing impatiently against the latch, a scatter of rain on my cold bare feet. Lying still in the nest of my bed I had felt almost content, had hardly been aware of my illness except in my swelling dreams, but standing the fever shook me, pushed cold and hot into my marrow and made the dull grey sky too bright for my eyes so I had to squint to see who had come to call.

It was my husband's cousin. A fisherman, too, once: until the too-quick blade of a gutting knife had taken the fingers of his right hand. Gold-headed, like my husband, but with a hard-set face. He carried his blunted palm shoved in a pocket; under his arm he cradled a splinter of wood.

Broken board. Clay-cracked green paint. The edge of a letter, downstroke or upstroke I could not tell, bow or stern I could not tell, could only know what he had come to tell, no more words or letters needed. With his good hand he reached under his arm and pushed the shard at me like blame. I reached out to take it, and as he shoved it into my uncertain grasp a sliver of wood, the length and sharpness of a mending-pin, pushed under my nail and made a bright line of blood beneath the shell of my finger. I cried out, I think. Perhaps he caught me as I fell. I don't remember any more.

It was he, my sickle-faced cousin, who said they should take me out to the storm. He was shouted down, I know – how I know I cannot tell, but know I do – for he, a cripple, would not be at risk. He would stand on the shore and watch another boat sail to the depths. But he was insistent, and his wry mouth could make fine words. At last they listened, the men; and the women too, even those sisters who had swerved past me in the town persuaded that the lifting of the storm could be bought with such a price. It was the sisters' men, the brothers, who allowed they would be my boatmen, my guides. The *Shepherd* was their ship; and I suppose that was about right.

So they wrapped us, me and the child curled silent inside me, in fine linen, and placed smooth stones in my set hands and bundled stones by the soles of my feet and the crown of my head. After linen, a sail: heavy canvas from our loft, green-edged with mould from the unceasing rain, a sheet from the *Eileen Dunn* sewn round. All that was left of her for all that was left of me.

The *Shepherd* set sail on another yellow-black dawn. They took me up shoulder high, brought me below, and when she struggled out of the harbour's grasp the wild swell of the open sea pulled at my cold bone, my settling blood, my sinking veins.

I could believe I was their compass: for how otherwise could they know where to take me, where the *Eileen Dunn* had sundered and sunk? How else could they have seen what I did? The wracked sky and moiled sea, wrought with the tempest, turned against them, and the nets drifting, tangled, useless, my lover's black head bent into the maddened water, already taking it into his lungs as he worked to bring the nets back aboard the boat. My husband, clutching the other man's legs, his coat, his back, suddenly and desperately as if he were himself the lover – but no embrace of theirs was stronger than that of the wave that took them, almost tenderly, lifted them on its seething shoulder high above the ship before drawing them down to its belly's calm. It was done in a moment. And only another moment before the next wave came and heeled the *Eileen Dunn* to starboard until her mast dipped into the laden waves, not to rise again.

She filled with the salt-fat water. She swelled with it, as if she had been greedy for it always. She split silently, no noise louder than the waul of the wind as she came in two, her refuge in the still depths. Spinning down to soft sand, to silence.

How could they know this? They could not: but I did. I knew it as the needle knows North, and I felt them carry me to the deck, strong-shouldered as the waves, as the sea that had swallowed my love opened for me, too. I was weighted. I sank, spinning like the broken *Eileen Dunn*.

And as I spun I could feel the warmth on my back, on my cold bones through water and sail and linen and stone as the sun broke through the black. The *Shepherd* settled in a trough of the waves, the abating rain lacing her rigging with diamonds. The men with their bare heads in the soft breeze were silent. In awe of me.

I am pared to bone and whiteness now. There is nothing left but the hard of me, the rattling core that clatters in the wind, stones on the beach, washed clean by the sea, turned over and over like thought until there is only the pure centre, clean and smooth and adamant. When the rough wind comes again they will sit close in the dim light, drinking, watching the red sky, the black sea through greasy windows, looking for a change in the weather. They will think of me. I am storm and sunlight.

> Gura mise tha fo eislean
> Moch sa mhaduinn is mi g'eirigh
>
> *O hi shiubhlainn leat*
> *Hi ri bho, ho rinn o ho*
> *Ailein Duinn, o hi shiubhlainn leat*
>
> Ma's en cluasag dhuit a ghaineamh
> Ma's en leabaidh dhut an fheamainn
>
> Ma's en t-iasg do choinlean geala
> Ma's en Righ do luchd-faire

The woman was to be buried on the far side of the sound; but a tempest came upon the boat so that the coffin was put overboard. It went against the tide and wind, and sank where her sweetheart had been drowned. Then calm came upon the sea, and the men, who had been in great danger of losing their lives, were saved.

Iris

Tobias Hill

No questions. Shut up and listen. That's the way I do it.

Is that thing working? Because I'm not doing this twice. The little wheels aren't going round. That's better. Alright?

Iris. I had her on Christmas Eve. On the TV thing. Pouffe. It was Brenda's pouffe but my TV. It was my flat. She bought the pouffe round to sit on because the sofa was manky, can you believe her? I sat on it, though. Ravenscar Estate. Not a nice name, is it? Raven. Scar. It scared me, when I was little. You can get your media mates to put up a plaque for us. Me and Iris.

I was poor, that's all. If you understand that then you understand why I did it. Now it's different. I get paid just to talk, can you believe it? You won't get a bed fart out of me for less than fifty quid. I met Ronnie Biggs here the other day, Ronnie gets paid to be in photos with tourists. Tenner a go down on Copacabana. Ten pounds goes a long way here. Phuket, that's where I'm going next. That's a nice name. Phuket.

Have you got the money? Ta. And my glass is empty. Mary. Without blood. Lovely.

Iris. Like Irish but without the aitch. The Permanents were the first ones I told, Brenda and Del. Eh? – No, not like the

Supremes. Christ, what are you like? *Permanents*. As in not temps. Secretaries, alright? Oh good.

There were always more temps than us. Four, five years slimmer than us, always getting younger. It kept us together, something we had in common. I liked Brenda. Del made me laugh but she was too hard. The Permanents! I would've been the singer.

Iris like Irish. It was in a baby-book in the library. Tiny little book, like it might grow up bigger. I opened it on page thirty-six and it said *Iris (girl)*. *The goddess of rainbows. A shy and accommodating child*. I did all my homework in the library. Personal Health, between Romance and Horror.

Brenda squeaked, 'A baby!' like it was six right Lottery numbers. 'Oh Helen, a baby! Oh, my God!'

Del said, 'Maternity leave. You lucky old thing.' Not old as her, the lipsticky moose.

Brenda said, 'I thought you were putting on a bit. Didn't I, Del? Only I wouldn't have said.' She tried to feel my belly but I wasn't having it. 'Oh Helen. Oh bless!'

'Oh come on. It's a baby, not the bloody second coming.'

That was Del. A bit too hard for me. Bit too sharp.

We worked in Customer Enquiries. Telephones and computers, chattering like teeth. The smell of fifty women in a small room, that's what I remember most. Sweet sweat. Trees outside black as wet concrete and motionless, like concrete. And the rain. When it rains here you can smell shit and mangoes. I like that. It smells better than fifty women in a small room. I've got all the room I need now.

I told them at lunch. We didn't eat lunch, the Permanents, we smoked it. No lunch, no breakfast. Keeping up with the temps. Del lit up and I waved the smoke away; I was ready for that. She said, 'So. Who's the lucky father?'

I said, 'Sean. He was a friend of my dad. He's Irish. Red hair.'

Del said, 'You're getting a bit old for older men, ain't you? What does he do?' Brenda just sat watching, cow-eyed, leaning forward at me. Excited, like it was her going on nine months' maternity, not me. Three months' half pay, six months' full. Seed money, that's how I think of it now.

I said, 'Farms.'

Del said, 'What, pigs? Maggots? Health?'

'Plants. I don't know, do I? Weetabix trees. I'm having the baby there, though. In Ireland. On my maternity leave.'

Brenda said, 'Maternity leave. Ireland.' All breathy and dying for it, like she was doing a TV chocolate ad. Foreign travel, as seen on TV. 'What are you going to call it?'

'Iris.'

Brenda said, 'Iris.' Weighing it up. 'What if it's a boy though?'

'It ain't. I know.'

Del said, 'Blimey, that's quick. Still. Iris.'

'What?'

Nothing. Bit of a granny name.' She said it again. Rubbing it in. 'Iris.'

I said, 'That's right, Del. Iris. Easy, isn't it? Like Irish but without the aitch. Can you give us a fag?'

I bolloxed it up, you see? And it didn't matter. The first two people I told, and I made three mistakes. The cigarette and the sex, and the granny name. All the books I read, and I still made mistakes. I'm a terrible liar. Do you believe me?

They could have told it was all bullshit, but they didn't. Why would they? I was their dream; big and fat and sweetly pregnant. They all wanted it, that's what I'm saying. It was an easy lie, a good lie. Smooth as a baby's bottom.

What's your name? Adolf. That's a bit of a grandad name, too. Do you want to be my toyboy, Adolf? No. You just want the story. The wheels have stopped on your little widget there. Turn it over, that's right. Good boy.

I'll tell you about Christmas. My immaculate Christmas conception.

So there was the TV in the background and the pouffe with me on it and Brenda sitting on the manky sofa. There was Del pouring drinks in the kitchen, and the smell of old Brussels sprouts and instant stuffing, it's like a seasonal mushroom cloud over Ravenscar. Only the Permanents don't eat Christmas dinner, we drink it. Vodka, because spirits have got less calories. I was rat-arsed, nasty phrase. I felt dirty like that, drunk and unwashed. I fell asleep for a bit. When I woke up I was on the sofa with Brenda, Del was on the pouffe, and the local news was on the box. There was a special report about maternity leave. Proud mums and company men. Seasonal joy. I was so pissed, I couldn't get my eyes off the screen. A judge came on and said that maternity leave is a woman's natural right. He had a bright smile. Baby teeth.

What? No. No families. That's something else we had in common, after my dad died. Later we went crawling round Camden. We didn't have any money left so we ended up at midnight mass. For the free wine. I didn't like doing that. I don't have to do that any more. I can make you buy my drinks, Adolf, just by telling you a story.

I didn't think about the wine. All I was thinking about was the TV special. Maternity leave. A bit of money and a bit of time. We went up for the bread and wine together. Everyone shut up and there were little bells, Christmas bells. When the cup got to Del she drank it all. Chugged it back. I could hear it over the bells. Jingle chug, jingle chug.

We left with everybody else. No one said anything. Right by the door there was a plastic baby Jesus in a manger full of hay, a little scrap of new life. My new life, that was. I didn't have a name to put on it yet, but I was thinking of Iris then. Planning it. My iris valve. My great escape.

It was the first break I ever had. Iris was the time and money to sort myself out. When I was little I thought I was rich. We had a council flat and my dad had his saxophone. He said it was worth loads and I believed him. It stank like a pub toilet and the metal was green but I believed him. He worked in the Bowens Cricklewood sausage factory and we got trimmings, no one else had that either. He tried to look after me, my dad. He pawned the saxophone to put me through secretarial college. Afterwards I couldn't find the ticket. He said it was in his trousers but it wasn't. He only had one pair. He died nine years ago. There's only me now, but I look after myself.

I didn't want a baby; all I wanted was my maternity leave. Why should I miss out because I don't want a baby? Maternity leave was my natural right. What are you going to do, lock me up?

Haven't you ever phoned in sick? You wake up to the alarm and you think, I don't want to be in this life any more. Then you lie into the telephone. Hello, yeah it's me, I was just ringing to – Something going round, I know – Oh thanks, really, thanks. Tomorrow. Bye. And you don't feel that guilty for ruining the country, do you? No, you feel nasty and ratty and glad of it. I know your type. You're the selfish kind. Like me.

It was an easy lie. Not because I was good at it, but because I was fat inside. Oily in my bones. Have you ever been on a crash diet, Adolf? I mean, really, *crash*? No. You don't have a clue. That was the last thing we had in common, the Permanents. We kept up with the temps. Fifteen years of nicotine lunches and no breakfast. I was bony then – sharp at the edges. But inside I was like this; rolls of fat, oil on my lips. I just had to bring it all out.

Food is what I remember about Iris. I started three days after Christmas. I went into one of the Arab grocers on the Edgware Road – away from home, just to be safe. I bought pastries and three pork pies, big ones. There were chips of fat in the pastry and the pork was the colour of tea. When I got home I locked the door and ate in the kitchen standing up. I couldn't finish, but the next morning I kept going. I could feel my belly, stretching when I breathed. By the time I got into work I was hungry again.

My new year's resolution was to gain one pound every day. I kept it up right through until the beginning of February, when I told Brenda and Del my news. I ate everything, everywhere. I saturated myself with fats. On the tube, in the bath, in front of the box. Never at work; not to start with. Baltis and Red Stripe, kidney pudding and Peking duck. Licking off the greasy spoons.

There were great damp sweat-patches under my arms. I ballooned – the only problem was building it up in my belly. Lots of fried rice. Like those Japanese wrestlers. Right little love-handles I was getting. Iris the love-handle. I kept packs of pork scratchings in my purse, for between meals. I stopped using make-up. I only smoked in the bath with the ventilator on. I exercised till I glowed.

I started working when I was seventeen. Ted Broughton was head of department and I got the job off of him. When I told him about the pregnancy he started crying.

'I'm so glad for you, Helen, so glad.' Then he went quiet, staring at me. 'Bloody hell. You're going to be a mother. I used to think I was like Charlie when you first came here. You know, him and his Angels. And now you're going to be a mother.'

He whispered that last bit. He was staring at my belly and I thought he was going to try and touch it. Then he started again. While he talked he picked the hairs of out his nostrils, looked at them, and put them in his jacket pocket.

'Well, I know you'll be coming back to us, Helen. I know that. You'll go mad on a farm. Watching the grass grow. No need to get married these days just because you're preggers, eh?'

He got a paper out of his Twinlock files. 'This is the company form. Then you'll need a DF6 from your doctor – or have you filled that in already? Not to worry. Write this up now. Then take the afternoon off, eh?' He held it up and the sun filled the yellow copy-paper with gold.

The hospital form was harder. The DF6. You need a blood test for that, and I wasn't having none of that. I used to dream about that form, like mothers dream of babies. In my dream the DF6 paper was warm and lovely and it smelled of milk. I'd wake up in bed with all the food around me, waiting. Litres of yoghurt in their pale plastic pots. Tin trays of takeaways shining in the dark.

Every other day for a week I went to the walk-in clinic in Kentish Town. I sat in the waiting room and read the agony mags. Watched the routines. There was only one receptionist and mostly she was out of sight, drinking tea or doing paper-work. Young doctors belting about with eyes like coal sacks. When I stood at the counter I could see all the forms, blue and pink and white, hanging out of filing cabinets like tongues. Begging to get ripped off.

The third time I went, I got the DF6. I just opened the office door and went through the drawers till I found it. Pink, it was. Baby pink. Third drawer. It only took a tick.

I was leaving in March. It wasn't long to wait. We were in the Black Cap. It was hail outside. White like grease chips in pastry.

Brenda said, 'Are you getting broody yet? Because you've always been a bit, you know. Frigid. About babies. But you probably feel different now. You look like a new woman.'

Del said, 'She looks like a cave woman. Her man must be neanderthal too, seeing as how he doesn't phone the office.'

She knew, Del did. She was always too sharp for me. If she knew, she could have grassed me up. If she knew, I owe her. I wish I didn't.

Faxes helped. I used to send them myself from the local newsagents. Changed the heading to McGILLIS SALMONRY, NEWCASTLE, COUNTY DUBLIN, EIRE, and changed it back when I finished. Letters, too. Up all night, writing myself love letters.

It was tricky, not having a man. Iris was hard work. Eating wasn't such a laugh by then. Stuffing my face every night, then drinking myself straight to sleep – that way all the fat goes into your legs and belly. I had to study, too. The way women walk in the first months, not striding yet. Just a bit slow, like they're on ice. What they cut down on, what they eat more of. A man could've helped. Buying tickets, setting up the accounts – Credit Suisse, posh or what, only it was easier because it had branches in Dublin and over here.

But I did it all myself. I don't owe no one nothing.

They had a party, when I left. That sounds wrong: they weren't glad I was leaving. That surprised me. It was a celebration party, ugly pink tinsel hung all over the desks and office lights. I just walked out of the lift and they were all there, blowing those butterfly-tongue horns. Clapping, some of them. Like champagne, the sound of it and the way it lifted me inside. I felt so proud. And then –

No. I had plenty to be proud about. Not because of the money. It's not that much, really, is it? Just enough to set me up. But it changed me, Iris did. Once you've given birth to a bank balance you can do anything.

I smiled for them until it hurt. You ever done that, Adolf? Smiled till it hurts? After a while it's like you've twisted all the muscles in your face. Del bought me a dryer, 'For all the babysuits'. She couldn't afford it. She shouldn't have done that. Ted got me this bracelet with beryl and amethysts. Birthstones for the baby, he said; two kinds in case it was a bit late. There was a cake too. GOOD LUCK HELEN AND IRIS in pink. I couldn't eat it. I was full.

She got hold of me the other day, Brenda. I reckon Del helped her. Phonecall. On and on, *how could you Helen? Who am I supposed to trust after what you did? It feels like Iris died. I'm glad she weren't real. People selfish as you always die out.*

Did I say you could ask questions? That's right. You just sit there and pay for the drinks, that's what you do. You don't need to know what I felt.

I know what you're after, though. You want trauma, don't you? FRAUD MUM HAUNTED BY PHANTOM PREGNANCY, is that what you'll write? That's what they all write. Still, it's not much of a place for ruined lives, this, is it? I'm jet set, son. I'm liquid.

Tell you what though. I'll give you a new ending. A little exclusive, because I like your arse. Ready? I'm pregnant. Really. Cross my heart. You're supposed to say congratulations.

Go on. Guess what I'm going to call her.

Avoiding Mrs Taraniuk

Alice Kavounas

'So. I told her I was going out. I said my son and his new wife *they insist*, tonight we eat out.'

The five-foot tall, candy-floss blonde kept stealing furtive glances past them down the dim corridor towards the elevator to make sure the coast remained clear. Her apartment door, open only half-way, had already begun to close as she grabbed at his coat sleeve to slide him and Andrea inside.

'*Hurry!*' she was whispering. '*Hurry Bobbela* – in case Elsie comes to say goodbye! We're supposed to be at the restaurant. God forbid she should find us here together . . .'

Visitors safely inside, she quickly double-locked her door, leaned back against it, and at last allowed herself a long, bottomless sigh of painful welcome.

His mother deployed these gut-wrenching sighs on so many occasions: always when commiserating with relatives over the neglect inflicted by a wayward son or daughter . . . or, like now, to exonerate herself from guilt. To turn her white lies into tragic necessities. Was anyone *ever* fooled? Of course he'd been taken in plenty of times, but years ago, when he was a kid and didn't know any better. Damn her sighs. She was probably recycling the same turgid one that she'd exhaled earlier that day (maybe only ten minutes ago!) aimed at Mrs Taraniuk herself, trying as usual to anchor those skimpy little lies with the sad weight of truth: *So. Elsie. It's out of my control. My son and that new wife of his (SIGH) they insist . . .*

'Listen. Bobbela – you hear something?' His mother froze. There they stood, still clustered in the cramped foyer; he and Andrea still holding their things. They hadn't even said hello, how are you. A sigh escaped him. Elsie Taraniuk lived three floors below. The elevator grunting into motion would give early warning of her arrival.

'I hear *nothing*. OK, Mom? Now relax.'

He took Andrea's jacket, shrugged off his own coat, loosened his tie. 'How about telling Mrs Taraniuk the truth for a change? That we don't see you very often and could she *not* stop by just this once. I know she lives alone, but can't she stay put for an evening. Is that such a big fucking deal?'

'You have to use curse words, in front of your poor mother?' Another one of her sighs, but airy and fake. Robert knew she was flattered, not angry. They both knew it. Arguing, like sighing, was a Jewish form of conversation. He found that hard to explain to his wife. Her family was Greek. They sighed but didn't argue.

Robert bent down to kiss his mother's creased, Miami-tanned cheek. 'You know I can't stand the woman. Besides, we've come to see *you*.'

Andrea, meanwhile, had drifted off into the living room. She was standing by the window, gazing down at the dull Brooklyn street. She motioned to him.

'Look, Robert. Down there. Like you used to be.'

He left his mother's side to follow Andrea's eyes. Two young boys on shiny new bikes. 'Yeah, I guess so.'

But he wasn't in the mood to reminisce, not with his mother

staring after him, that quizzical, hurt look on her face as if he were her suitor and he'd suddenly abandoned her for another girl. Then, inexplicably, her expression brightened, like someone turning on artificial light to fill a dark corner.

'So you two! You're not going to come and sit? We're going to stand up all night, like at a fancy cocktail party?' His mother, thrilled by her analogy, chuckled coquettishly and pretended, even, to sip at a drink.

Oh God, thought Robert. His mother's preening, her feigned cheerfulness, how he detested it. And those brave little stabs at dressing-up, Brooklyn style. Pink toreador pants with floaty, fake silk blouses. She never used to dress like that when he was a kid. He'd seen pictures of her in sober, tailored suits, and her hair was dark, soft. Come to think of it, all those old photographs were in black and white. Maybe he'd deceived himself, even about that. Now his mother was linking arms with his wife, dragging Andrea from the living room toward the L-shaped eating area where the table was.

'Come and sit, sit, Julia!' his mother insisted merrily.

'Mother . . . *Andrea*. Your daughter-in-law's name happens to be Andrea. She produces commercials. Julia was an actress – *got it*?'

'Forgive me! *Andrea*. Of course. These names . . . you're not hurt I hope – Bobbela, Robert – I'm sorry –'

'It's OK, Bob. Don't worry about it. I'm getting used to it.' Andrea shook her head.

'She didn't even like Julia.' He turned to his mother with a flash of his old anger. 'I don't know why you can't manage to keep it straight. I'm your only child, and Andrea is my wife. Is it so much to ask?'

Robert inhaled deeply, then stopped mid-breath, turning his sigh into a loud cough, a clearing of his throat. He was determined not to let his mother get to him. He pulled out the flimsy dinette chair opposite Andrea and sat down at the food-filled table.

Only two places were laid.

'What about you, Mom? We've driven all the way over here to have dinner with you. Andrea had to break out of a meeting.'

'I ate already. You think I can eat so late? Now you two eat. You and, and – Andrea.'

'I don't get it – what do you mean so late? We work. We have demanding jobs. We always get here around seven-thirty.'

'And your mother's always eaten,' said Andrea, smiling patiently. 'Bob. Relax. Would you like some bread?'

Andrea passed him the chartreuse plastic basket filled with a fresh loaf of *challah*. He took a slice, broke it in two and began to scrape a thin glistening of margarine on it. Andrea began doing the same, putting off, he knew, the moment when she'd have to manage the first swallow of his mother's cooking.

'One slice? Only one slice each?'

His mother hovered over the dinette table, nudging and rearranging the unappetizing array of mismatched, seriously overcooked food.

She pointed accusingly at the sweet, butter-coloured egg-bread. 'So who's going to eat the rest of this loaf?'

Maybe she's right, he thought, chewing silently, trying to calm the knot of tension in his stomach. This bread was the only truly edible thing on offer. Maybe I *could* eat the whole goddamn loaf.

But of course, he had all the rest of the meal to get through, and Andrea's portion besides.

That was their deal. Whenever they came to his mother's for dinner, he had to help her eat the long-dead, boiled chicken, the sodden rust-coloured broccoli, the acrid cabbage. And worst of all, the final course: soup, served last *à la Russe*, as murky and indigestible as his mother's tangled Polish-Jewish-Ukrainian background. Andrea described it as 'those suspicious balls of meat floating in a seasick broth.' It was only funny when you weren't spooning into it.

If only they could all go out; tell Mrs Taraniuk the truth. But the restaurants in this part of Brooklyn served food that tasted even worse than what emerged from his mother's kitchen. Andrea had found that impossible to believe. One visit to the local Kosher haunt had quashed all further suggestions and sent them, however reluctantly, back here to Mom's.

'So how's work, Mom?' He was grimly attacking the flaccid chicken now, under the close observation of his mother who continued to hover at her son's elbow. She worked as a cashier at a nearby movie theatre and all anyone could see of her was her head, with that fake Hollywood hair-do.

'Work? It's a job,' she answered, throwing up her hands. 'Mr Baum tells me to speed up, but how can I speed up? With four pictures playing, the people don't know what they're saying – "two for three, four for two" – such a business to punch the right tickets. I tell Mr Baum I'm doing my best. "You don't like it, fire me!"' His mother bustled around to Andrea's place. 'You're not eating tonight, Julia?'

'For Christ's sake, Mom, it's *Andrea*! If you can hold down a fucking job, you can remember my wife's name!'

'OK, OK! You give me another heart attack if you scream like that! It's enough I had to tell poor Elsie that she couldn't visit tonight. Already it's upset me. I can feel my heart.' His mother grabbed his hand, the one holding the fork: 'Feel, feel.'

Bits of moist cabbage came loose from the jiggling fork, dropping on to his new, Ralph Lauren, burgundy corduroy slacks. '*Goddamn it*, Mom. Now look what you've done! These stain like crazy. I don't want to feel your heart.'

'They'll dry-clean, honey. Don't worry.' Andrea had cut up her chicken and camouflaged it with a large, limp branch of broccoli. She was waiting for his mother to go into the kitchen so she could switch her full plate with his own, emptier one.

'Elsie, if she's standing in the hall, she'll hear you screaming. She'll know we're here."

'Well, it's your own fault for lying in the first place. You should've told Mrs Taraniuk the truth.'

'Oh, Mr Truth, here. All along he tells me he loves his wife, then suddenly he gets a divorce. A shock like that? Of course it gives me a heart attack.' His mother's hand remained on her breast, as if to prevent another one. 'Did you know that, Andrea? I never had a heart attack before he got divorced from that woman.'

'You mean his first wife. Julia. The one you mix me up with.' Robert looked hard at Andrea to see if she was mocking his mother. But no, she seemed to be stating a fact. An unpleasant fact, much like the statement that this plate of cabbage smelled like sweaty gym socks. Unpleasant but unbiased. Andrea didn't go in for clever, underhanded jibes. She didn't manipulate. Not like Julia. There was no similarity between his two wives. Only his mother would confuse them.

'My Robert, he only likes gentiles. First that woman Julia, now you.'

'You like gentiles too, Mom.' Robert smiled slowly.

'What?' His mother looked wary, sensing a trick.

'Elsie,' Robert persisted softly. 'Isn't Elsie Taraniuk your best friend?'

'So?' His mother was frowning.

'Well, she's Catholic . . .' Robert allowed himself a laugh.

'Oh *sure*. Always the joker. I'm talking about marriage. Divorce.' His mother paused briefly to peer at him more closely. The daggers were out. 'Even when your father died, I didn't get a heart attack.'

'Congratulations, Mother. *Mazeltof.*'

'Don't you dare make fun of your father.'

'Fun? Who's talking about fun?' he muttered.

But she ignored him and turned her attention to Andrea. 'My Abner was the best husband a woman could ever ask for. The best. No woman in this world could have a better husband than his father was to me. I was a lucky woman. That's the truth.'

'Well,' said Robert, 'not much point in even trying, I guess.' Poor sweet, dead Abner. Had he really been that good a husband, or just so weak she'd pushed him around until suddenly, one night, he simply keeled over? *Don't think about that now.*

Robert put down his knife and fork neatly on the plate. God how he hated eating off this plastic. It wasn't as if his mother couldn't afford decent china. Oh no. Just that in this section of Brooklyn, *plastic* was like a totem. And how! He lifted his gaze to the living room beyond. Every damn piece of furniture was in a coffin of clear thick plastic. No zips – the covers were meant to stay on for guests – for ever! Even the fucking lampshades crackled in their plastic hats. It was like living in a showroom, or a funeral home. What was it protection *against*? His mother lived entirely alone. No kids, no cats, no dogs. No one even visited, except him and Andrea once every couple of weeks, and the ever-persistent Elsie Taraniuk.

'How come we never had plastic covers when I was a kid?' he ventured, thinking he'd veer off the abyss of those treacherous topics: his divorce; his father's death; his abandonment of his mother; his neglect of their relatives in general; his love of non-Jewish women. It went on and on.

'Who could afford it? In those days it was a struggle to put food on the table. Now, thank God, there's a little extra for nice things.' She turned to address Andrea: 'I'm not a fancy woman, but . . . a few special outfits . . . once a week the hairdresser, *chachkas* for the house, every winter a little trip to Miami . . .'

Andrea nodded, her hand pressed up against her temple. Robert knew the sign. One of her migraines was starting. By the time they managed to get out of here, drive the forty minutes back to Manhattan, park their car at the Hudson Pier and cab it uptown to their Westside apartment, the pain would be blinding.

'Mom, Andrea would probably love some tea.'

'She hasn't touched a thing, and already she wants tea?'

'I had such a big lunch – I had to, it was business, so I'm afraid I'm not as hungry as usual.'

'Big business, eh? Me . . . I have my little sandwich, I walk around the block, I don't know from big lunches.' His mother turned decisively toward the kitchen, dismissing the world of restaurants, Manhattan, and Robert's wives, now numbering two. There was soon a deafening clatter of pots and pans indicating general disapproval and, possibly, that tea was underway.

'Bob! Here!' Andrea thrust her full plate towards him and grabbed his empty one like a drowning swimmer catching a life raft. And this soup . . . *please*.'

He ate soundlessly, rapidly and without pleasure while Andrea watched, relief momentarily easing her tensed features.

All Robert's memories of being a fat child flooded back with each mouthful of his mother's food, every gulp of salty, yet tasteless soup.

It had taken years of living away from home to wean him off this lie; the lie that his mother was a wonderful cook, that this food was nutritious. Above all, that it was a good idea to eat until you burst. Until the other kids laughed at you for being fat. Until all you ever thought about was how to get out of your body by any possible means.

Later had come the drinking, the drugs. And, when he was finally thin, and, women insisted, really good-looking – the fucking.

It all helped to blur, if not exactly wipe out, the memory of what he'd been as a child in this dreary part of Brooklyn, imprisoned in this hermetically sealed, cling-film apartment.

Trapped at this small square table, first with both his parents, then alone, with his hysterical, grieving, endlessly sighing, permanently widowed mother.

He'd barely turned eleven when his father died.

Heart attack.

Eleven years old . . . that's when the eating had really gone berserk.

'So! You managed to finish,' his mother said to Andrea accusingly, as she re-entered the fray. '*Mazeltof*.'

She whipped away Andrea's plate with one hand and planted a cup of tea there in its place. The label dangled into the saucer by its wet string.

'Give it to me when you're finished.'

'You mean this,' commented Andrea, dunking the tea-bag in and out of the stained, pink plastic cup. She was slowly getting used to his mother's ways. Her thrift knew no bounds. No one except her re-used tea bags. No one.

'Too strong it's no good for you,' she warned, and began clearing the table. She darted around them like a career-waitress in a diner, noisily scraping cabbage into broccoli, skeletal chicken remains into the dregs of meatball soup.

Robert wondered if she'd get out the deafening Hoover next and begin vacuuming around their feet. Maybe the spectre of Mrs Taraniuk patrolling the corridor would spare them that commotion. 'You see? It's like no one was ever here,' his mother had observed one evening, as he and Andrea were forced to lift their feet – then shift the table a few inches – not that they'd finished eating of course, to accommodate his mother's zealous urge to clean.

'You never sit down – let me clear these plates,' Robert offered, crazed by her desire for perpetual motion.

'Shhhh. Children! It's the elevator!'

His mother stood absolutely still, her hands motionless on the stacked, dirty plates. Andrea, meanwhile, had allowed the teabag to sag back into her cup, sensing a hitch in the proceedings. She looked across at her husband and smiled weakly.

'This is ridiculous,' he hissed, trying to wrench his mother's grip from the plates.

'Sit *down*!' his mother hissed back, a flush of anger visible beneath her tanned complexion.

Suddenly there was the sound of a key against metal, of a bolt dropping, a door opening then slamming shut. His mother let out a huge sigh. 'That was only Bea Feldman, next door. Still, I hope she didn't hear us. She might say something to Elsie.'

'This is worse than living in the ghetto,' Robert said dryly. 'Now let me do this. You sit and I'll bring you some tea. You can keep Andrea company.'

'He talks about the ghetto,' his mother said, willing now to conspire with his wife against him. 'He doesn't like Elsie but she's a good woman. She's from Lvov, like me. A Catholic, but so what? She suffered too . . .'

'Twenty-five years in America,' came Robert's voice from the kitchen, 'and she can hardly speak English. I suppose you speak Polish together. Or Russian. What the hell country is Lvov in these days, anyway?'

'Ech, what does he know? This young American son of mine.'

Andrea was massaging her right temple, nodding as Robert's

mother complained. It looked like a gesture of sympathy if you didn't know about her worsening migraine.

He'd returned to the table with a matching pink plastic cup. It was brimful of plain boiling water, just the way his mother liked it. He put it in front of her. She didn't thank him. Instead, she smiled at his wife. 'Andrea, sweetie, your tea-bag?'

His mother took the dripping dark square and dropped it into her cup. The saucer took the overflow. He stood and watched the water turn amber. No one said anything for a full minute. Robert knew how Andrea would hate him for what he was about to do – he did it every time they visited – but he couldn't help it. Any longer with that woman and he'd throw something.

'I'm just going into the bedroom to watch the news,' he announced, leaving them both sitting there in a parody of polite tea drinking. The tacky cups. Everything. 'I don't want to miss the weather report,' he added, before Andrea could object.

His mother tried to fix him with a serious look. 'You keep the sound low, Bobbela, in case – you know –'

But he was past caring and laughed out loud saying, 'What, Elsie?' slamming the door to his mother's bedroom hard behind him. How that glitzy chandelier hanging in the centre of her room shuddered and swayed – as if the entire apartment were a ship, and the seas that night were rough, and getting rougher.

Robert sprawled out on his mother's massive bed, momentarily safe and distanced from the two women. He picked up the remote. Channel 2. Even before the picture resolved itself, the important-sounding signature music filled the purple bedroom. He slumped uncomfortably against the fake Louis Something white-and-gilt headboard. For a few minutes, the rapid-fire delivery of the newscaster soothed him. It didn't last.

'Now please! Turn that *down*, Bobbela.'

His mother had opened the door and was standing there bravely in her electric-pink toreadors, that floaty blouse. Her stiffened bleached hair comprised at least the top eight inches of her meagre height. At that moment, she appeared to him like a wizened page out of the French King's court begging for some kind of dispensation, or arriving with a terrible message from his queen. He passed his hand over his eyes. Suddenly he was extremely tired.

'OK, OK. Just shut the door and leave me *alone*. I'll turn it down, I promise. And tell Andrea that after the weather we're leaving.'

She sighed one of her all-encompassing tragic sighs, turned and left. He clutched a large, lace-covered pillow to his chest and eased the sound way down so she'd have no excuse to barge in again.

Those damn sighs of hers. He wondered if she'd ever sighed as deeply with pleasure, here in this bed, in the arms of his father.

Robert had pondered on that a lot lately. He knew that she'd never tell him the truth, so he'd never asked. She was incapable of it. Just as she'd waited until he was twenty to tell him that he was adopted; that she wasn't his real mother. Nor was poor gentle dead Abner his real father.

In certain ways he was glad that he'd never known the truth while his father was still alive. And Robert was relieved, too, to realize that this crazy mother of his wasn't a blood relation: her genes hadn't been passed on to him. He couldn't pass them on. But to be given that huge hand-grenade of knowledge at twenty had taken the ground from under him. It had destroyed his sense of reality – no matter how glad he was about those particular genetic aspects.

Finally, to know the truth. What could he do with it?

His mother had even told him his real name. It was eerie, being two people suddenly, both alive. Or was his past just a shadow? Who knows what had happened to his natural mother. There was, apparently, no record of the father.

Robert didn't know what to think. Sure, he bitched and moaned about his adoptive mother, but he owed his life to her and to Abner too – that perfect husband of hers. They'd done their work, their best and their worst. Two frightened immigrants whose own families were scattered like so much small change every time a new treaty was signed.

First Lvov was part of Poland, then, after 1939, it was absorbed into the Ukraine. And in the Nazi massacre of the Lvov Jews, the children were killed along with their parents. He knew he should feel damn lucky to be alive, free, and in America. His problems were as nothing, really, compared to the Jews who were caught up in that struggle. Even his mother – how serious were her problems compared to the terror, the endless suffering endured by those who never got out, whose children died in their arms?

But he could never stay feeling grateful for long. He was constantly anxious, unsure of his identity.

He knew that the answers to his problems were locked in places he had no access to: parents he'd never meet; new parents who'd taken him in but who, when the truth emerged, felt like complete strangers. His own life was a puzzle to him even so many years later. It was as if the clues were hidden somehow behind these newly painted purple walls, and that he'd never decipher any of it. Maybe the most important clues had already been destroyed.

The bedroom door opened again. His mother, of course, the wizened page.

She was motioning wildly, as if the walls of the castle had just been breached. 'The elevator! Elsie! She's coming – *turn it off.*'

Robert groaned and killed the news. He threw the pillow he'd been hugging straight at the screen. If only he could douse everything. His mother, this room, the world.

Andrea tiptoed in. Now they were *all* in the bedroom. Christ, he thought. This was a normal woman when I met her. She's only been married to me a year, now she's as crazy as I am.

'How long do we have to stay in here, Bob?'

His mother had carefully shut the door behind his wife, then handed Andrea her unfinished cup of tea. Andrea looked at it, placed it on top of the TV and came over to him. She sat on the edge of the bed and took his hand, stroked it gently. He thought what a terrific nurse she would make. You'd want to get well, just so you could fuck her. He tried to smile. 'How's your head, precious?' Robert hoped he wasn't going to mess up this marriage too. Andrea's job as a producer put her under a lot of pressure. She didn't need this. His mother, meanwhile, had her ear glued to the inside of the bedroom door. 'Try to hang on, Andrea,' he pleaded.

'I'll make it, but can't we leave? We're on location tomorrow – I have a six am start.'

His mother was nodding vigorously. He didn't know what that meant. Was Elsie out there . . . was she leaving . . . or was it another benighted neighbour going out for a disgusting meal? Robert slid down further, his neck scraping against the carved headboard. Andrea continued to hold his hand, patting it slowly, as you would a terminal patient or a small child.

His mother was tiptoeing towards them. Now she bent over the double bed from the far side. Her hair-do moved with her. When her lips were one inch from his ear she whispered deafeningly, '*She knows we're here* . . .' She shook her son's shoulder for emphasis – '*Elsie knows we're all here!*'

Please God, thought Robert, let there be an earthquake. A meteorite. Even a PLO bomb. Anything to get us out of here. Don't worry about the human sacrifice, the loss of innocent lives. Don't spare anyone, dear God. *Just let your people go.* Let us get home!

But it was Andrea who spoke:

'Why don't you let Mrs Taraniuk in? Tell her we changed our minds. People do change their minds.'

Amazing, thought Robert. Fucking amazing. He's married a brilliant woman. No wonder she was being paid a mint. 'There, Mother. You see? A simple, honest solution. Just go and open the door. Say "Why hello Elsie, do come in, my children are just leaving!" because goddamn it we ARE!'

And Robert sprang from the bed, nearly knocking Andrea on to the floor, picked up the large pillow and flung it at the headboard, narrowly missing his mother.

'We're worse off than the whole fucking Ann Frank family! They were stuck in one room hiding behind a bookcase –' He gestured wildly around the florid surroundings. 'We don't even have any *books* in this room to keep us sane!'

Robert threw open the bedroom door, then strode across the dinette area and lunged at the door to the outside hall. Andrea was right behind him, leaving his mother to cower in the bedroom, her mind racing for excuses, devising Byzantine white lies.

'Mrs Taraniuk!' Robert called out.

It was like trying to surprise a burglar. Opening the door seemed to create blank space, a breeze. For some moments he couldn't register whether there was someone there or not.

Then he saw the unmistakably large form of his mother's friend, shuffling in slow retreat down the long dim corridor towards the elevator. A Polish mama-bear in scuffed fluffy mules.

'We're home, Mrs Taraniuk,' he barked. 'Mother's been expecting you!'

The immense figure turned. Elsie's doughy, featureless face was a picture of misery. Even Andrea, standing alongside him, took pity. 'We're just having tea – why don't you join us?'

'We didn't go out after all. Changed our minds. My fault, really – just can't get enough of my mother's cooking,' continued Robert, blabbing on as if searching for kind words that would magnetize this Polish/Russian dumpling; entice her into his mother's crumb-free, plastic-covered home.

Such a long way from Lvov, he thought, watching Mrs Taraniuk's thick, slippered feet shlump, shlump towards them. He sensed his mother's presence now, even felt her quickened breath pulsing against his back. Maybe she'd have another heart attack. Who knows? *I'd be wholly responsible.* Me and Andrea. I can see the doctor's certificate now. Cause of Death: Trying to Avoid Mrs Taraniuk.

Robert turned to face his mother. 'Hey, Mom . . . whatta piece of luck! Just as we're leaving, you'll have some company!' He flashed her a completely manufactured grin.

'You shoore?' managed Elsie at last, lumbering forward towards the threshold, her journey nearly over. 'I ken leef . . .'

'Mom – Elsie wants to leave! Imagine. Your best friend. Now *that's* a friend. Always thinking of the other person. Andrea, don't move! You have a migraine – I'm taking you home. Let me get your jacket.'

Robert returned with Andrea's jacket, holding it for her as she slipped into it gratefully. They stood to one side as Mrs Taraniuk finally crossed the threshold. His mother steadied her by the elbow as if Mrs Taraniuk was fording a fast-flowing river. 'My Bobbela is right. You're a good friend, Elsie. Here in America it's not so easy to find good friends.'

Damn if his mother wasn't nearly in tears. What a little actress. No wonder his father had fallen for her. His mother had certainly missed her calling. She was wasting her time standing behind that ticket booth – she belonged right out front on the goddamn Silver Screen, starring in one of those tear-jerker B movies. The kind that kept everyone glued to their seats in the old days, a box of buttered popcorn in one hand and balled up Kleenexes in the other. Mrs Melodrama.

Meanwhile, Mrs Taraniuk was moving forward into the apartment, slowly closing the distance between herself and the dinette area, sighing massively in response to the emotional situation but saying nothing. Each sigh moved her entire upper body, imparting a sense of tragedy that outdid even his mother. Robert hadn't witnessed anything like it.

Elsie Taraniuk's heaving breasts seemed to express the entire sad history of Lvov, shunted pitilessly between Poland and Russia, overrun by Germans and now, a source of deepening nostalgia to Elsie, to his mother, to anyone who would listen.

'Bob, we have to go now, OK?' Andrea was tugging at his arm. If it weren't for Andrea he was sure he'd gradually be pulled under by the sheer weight of unexpressed pain. He would drown.

'You look tin. He looks tin, like rake,' said Elsie suddenly, as a way of goodbye. She was cantilevering her body on to one of the toy-like aluminium dinette chairs.

'They eat nothing, Elsie,' his mother sighed. 'I cook but they eat nothing, not even bread. Look at her –'

'*Her* is Andrea, Mother. And we're fine. OK? In fact, for the first time in my life I'm goddamn fit and healthy.'

Robert took his wife's hand and turned to go.

'So. When will I see you?' His mother stood at the door, her back to Mrs Taraniuk. He imagined the rest of their evening.

There they would sit, Elsie and his mother – she in the role of the blonde waitress, jumping up to bring plate after plate of food, all his and Andrea's left-overs, to try and cheer up the gloomy, insatiable Elsie Taraniuk. So what! Let them eat. God only knows what they'd suffered in that damn town, Lvov. Who was he to judge?

'So. You're not going to answer your mother?' She repeated, 'When will I see you?'

Andrea had disengaged her hand from his and gone to get the elevator. She'd had enough. His mother shrugged her shoulders at Andrea's departure. 'I did something to upset her? Next time, maybe you come on your own . . .?'

Robert's breath was coming fast now, too fast. It matched his mother's. He felt completely wired. His eyes burned. He jammed his fists in his pockets, slowly clenching his car keys with his right hand until they dug deep into the palm. It was possible, just possible, that in this mood, he could kill.

But when he spoke, his voice was low, measured, completely betraying his wild emotion.

'Andrea and I will visit when you have a free evening, Mother. When Elsie isn't coming over.'

And then, because he saw that his toneless voice had frightened her, he squeezed a small, tight smile out of himself, adding, 'OK?'

His mother's stiff, candy-floss head bobbed up and down in mindless agreement, but he knew she didn't understand. How could she? How could anyone.

Some Loose Change

David Rabe

Red was depressed, but not the way assholes or sissies get depressed. He felt he had no fucking stake in anything any more. No fucking stake in the system. No fucking steak in the refrigerator. Haw, haw, haw. Him and his raggedy-assed buddies, the bunch of them has-been, used-to-be high rollers, who had just ransacked their own goddamn vehicles out in the goddamn parking lot, tearing apart the upholstery to scrounge up nickels and dimes and stray fucking quarters. So they could get one more round of beer.

'I got forty cents.'

'All I got's twelve.'

'Twelve! Keep looking.'

It was sickening. It was pathetic. Red had checked in about one in the afternoon at The Backhoe Bar and Grill. Bobby and Jake and Macky were already planted at their favorite table, the one under the *Sports Illustrated* calendar showing this long-legged bitch on her belly at the beach, sand caking the gold of her ass, the bikini bottom creeping up the crack. Now they were flopping back down under her serene, superior glow to count their change and mutter about the amazing, unbelievable fact that it was already night outside.

'What the hell time is it?'

'You been here the longest, Macky. When did you get here?'

The bar was a long rectangle of weird light like the spill of an arcade game. It looked pretty much the same in the morning as it did after dark. But there was no denying the Dallas skyline they'd just seen firing up the sleek black starless sky. Nothing they could do about it.

'What we need is a little venture capital,' said Jake.

'Right.'

'So we could make a venture,' said Bobby.

'In?'

'Right. In what? Hypothetically, if you had some capital to play with where would you put it?'

Stomach acid turned Red in his chair. He burped, shrugged and scanned the room, looking for something. A couple of nervous kids were huddled up in the corner. Not far from them a snoring drunk was crumpled over the bar. This gym rat dripping tattoos in a sweat shirt with the sleeves ripped off was brooding at the juke box, like it had just asked him a very difficult question that he was determined to answer.

'What'samatter, Red?' said Bobby, 'do we bore you? Sorry if we bore you. Look at him.'

Red turned and squinted at Bobby. It wasn't that Bobby bored him, but he didn't feel like trying to explain.

'Red.'

He had nothing to say, and nothing he wanted to do either, except turn away. All along the walls neon signs advertised different brands of beer, each exuding their own mechanical pulse of artificial color. On the table in front of him were a couple of ashtrays. The one that was overflowing had butts with lipstick

on the filters so there must have been a woman around sometime. But he couldn't remember. Probably the waitress at some
point, bored and annoyed and stubbing out a smoke. Because
now there was just Jake and Bobby and Macky and this new
guy, who had crouched down beside Jake and started talking to
him about the golf cart concession at the club where Jake
worked as a fucking caddy. In the years of the boom, Jake was a
real estate speculator. Red met him in the Lear Jet Red leased and
piloted in those days. Charter flights had been Red's way of dipping into the money-stream gushing through Texas at the time.
It had been hurricane force. Jake and some of his partners were
on a junket to Vegas when Red stepped out of the cabin, and
there was Jake, settled back in his chair, this blonde attached to
his dick like a fly to a horse's ear, and she was sucking just as
single-mindedly. After giving Red a shit-eating smile, Jake
reached and wedged his hands into the tops of this sequined
halter the blonde was wearing till he got some nipple. His eyes
kind of sparked like he'd just made a shrewd maneuver in a
stock deal, then he sank from sight, his lids closing. He looked
like he was vacationing on the beach. His partner and three
clients were aboard, along with four other bitches, all of them
nasty little show dogs dressed to make the most of their enter-
tainment/market value. After those flights, the waste cans
overflowed with empty booze bottles. Red would find soggy rub-
bers clinging to the nozzles, or nestled with the empty coke vials
and broken poppers. He found a G-string more than once, a lacy
bra hooked over the back of a chair, somebody's floral bikini
panties in the crack of the cushions. Once he hit the jackpot with
this actual living breathing little bitty brunette passed out in the
john. He couldn't remember if she was part of one of Jake's flights
or not, but whoever left her, she took the option of smiling her
big smile up at Red. He ushered her into the flight deck to show

her the instrument panel. As per her request, he fired up the engine. She sort of made this cheerleader kind of noise and swung her legs over his, so his lap was like her horsey and if he'd found any underpants that time, they damn well could have been hers because she didn't have any on to take off.

The drinks arrived. Red watched the waitress setting down tap beer in mugs for everyone except Macky. Somehow he'd managed a shot of bourbon.

'Well,' said Bobby, 'the best wheels won't get you out the driveway without some fuel.' He tipped the beer to his lips and made a sad sound as he drank.

'What we need is a little venture capital,' said Jake.

'You said that.'

'Did I? When?'

'Somebody did.'

'If people paid their debts, I could take us all anywhere we wanted.' Red probed the foam with his tongue, and added some salt. It was true. More than one dipshit had left him hanging. Some just ducked him, ducked his bills and then the collection agency he sent after them. People seemed to think their charter Jet tab was the last thing they had to pay. Maybe they declared bankruptcy and then he couldn't even chase them any more. It wore him the fuck out. So he declared bankruptcy. That was a brilliant fucking law.

Jumping up, Macky tipped his head back, taking the bourbon in like oxygen after he'd just surfaced from some overly-long underwater stay. 'I'm goin' home,' he said.

That scared everybody. If he left, it could start a trend. 'No, no, no.' Then they'd all be going home and then they'd be home, and the next thing that happened would be the alarm clock screeching at them, or some asshole on talk radio, welcoming them to the new fucking day, and the morning would drag them off to their stupid jobs. Jobs that had no status; no opportunity to advance. Jobs like treading water. They wore you out and got you nowhere, until you started to think maybe you wanted to drown.

'I'd like to go to one of them pudenda bars,' said Bobby. 'That's what I'd like. Whata you think of that, Macky?'

'Yeh,' said Jake. 'C'mon, Macky.'

They were talking about The Velvet Spotlight or The Animal Club, or the new Stringfellows, where these gorgeous, golden, extraterrestrial cunts danced topless and for twenty bucks would come over and squirm around between your legs. For a slightly higher dollar incentive, they'd take you into a back room, and give you a 'Friction Dance' which was in reality an old-fashioned dry hump.

'We don't have the money,' said Macky.

'Would you wanna do that, Macky? If we had the money,' said Jake. 'Maybe we can figure out a way to get into one.'

'How?'

The question, though it was his own, seemed to confuse Macky so that he stood there looking more and more tired until he slumped back into his chair.

Red thought, What the hell! He'd said it once, he might as well say it again: 'If people paid their debts, there is no place I could not take us if we wanted.'

'Somebody owe you money, Red?' said Bobby.

'A lot of people .'

'Yeh? Like who?' Jake wanted to know.

'I don't remember their names. It's all out in the computer.'

'Wait a minute? This is legitimate. It's on the computer.'

'I swear I just said that. Didn't I just say that?'

'Like who?' said Jake. 'Who owes you?'

'It's on the computer, Jake. I don't have it fucking memorized. That's why I have the computer.'

'Gimme a name.'

'Part of the reason I went under was people waltzed me and held back what they owed me. They waltzed me, I took the hit. You know.'

'Gimme a name. One name.'

Red was glaring at Jake. He tossed back half the mug and leaned on to the table. 'Are these questions somehow your way of expressing doubt about the fact that I was screwed just the way I'm saying?'

'No, no.'

'People didn't pay me. I met my obligations and flew these seeming trustworthy, very affluent people where ever the hell they wanted on time and safely, and then they didn't meet their end. They left me hanging. You're probably one of them.'

'I payed you.'

'I wonder.'

'I payed you. I always payed you.'

'Did you? I think I'd like to see.' Red guzzled the last of the beer and headed for the door.

'Where you going, Red?'

'I'll be right back.'

'But where are you going?'

In the parking lot, he popped open the trunk of his 'Beater', a red, rusty 63 Ford. He shoved aside the briefcase with his daily calendar, one reefer, divorce papers, pictures of his three kids. He lifted the Smith and Wesson .38, wrapped in oil cloth and placed it carefully off to the side so it snuggled in with a set of Anthony Robbins audio tapes he'd ordered off the 800 number one night when he was drunk and alone at home. The lap top in its vinyl carrying case was waiting under a cardboard box full of old files and random junk.

Back at the table, he set up, jamming the plug into a wall

socket a few inches below the *Sports Illustrated* bitch's crotch. The bunch of them were watching him closely. They'd collected behind him, as he booted the machine. The glow of the screen went cloudy, then filled with icons blipping up, the green halo tainting his fingers. He hit some keys and the data started popping up. He could feel Jake and Bobby and Macky shifting behind him, peering over his shoulder. The screen was full of names, dates, figures. Just seeing the names pissed him off. It was like a burning building as everything started to slip from reach, and disappear in this smokey blinding choking indignation. The muscles in the back of his neck were squirming like rats trying to get out of the fire. 'Look at these fuckers,' he said.

'I ain't there, am I?' said Jake.

'Not so far.'

'I payed everything.'

'This guy owes you fifteen thousand dollars, Red,' said Bobby. He was smudging the screen with his finger, as he pointed at a name. 'Is that right? Look at that.'

'Wait a minute, wait a minute!' Jake said, leaning in.

Red, who was scrolling through the names, each one causing him a nasty little twinge, stopped.

'That's Thomas P. Harlow. Is that Thomas P. Harlow?' Jake was using this tone of exaggerated shock.

'That's what it says, doesn't it. That's what I'm reading.'

'I had some dealings with the bastard. He was the brains behind that development over at Twin Creek. What an asshole.'

Red was having a little trouble remembering Harlow. 'He's probably working the window at a Burger King now. Real Estate got butchered.'

'No, no. He was getting out of Real Estate. I remember that. Just before everything went south. Actually, I heard about him lately.'

Red didn't like this kind of news. One of the key ways he'd kept himself sane was to imagine everybody who had fucked him getting screwed and dumped down the shitter on the same flush that washed him into the mess he now lived in. Some sort of hidden force for equilibrium focused around Red and what happened to him. He didn't really want to know that Harlow had escaped, but he asked anyway. 'What's he in now?'

'I don't remember, but they were complaining about him.'

'Who?'

'I don't remember.' Jake leaned in to the computer screen like it was whispering and you had to be close to hear it. 'Is this all legitimate, Red?'

'Of course it is.'

'How did this happen?' Bobby wanted to know. He sounded dismayed and disappointed in Red like it was Bobby's fucking money. 'How did you ever let this happen, Red? How?'

'You know how it goes.'

'Yeh, sure. But still. This guy owes you big money. Fifteen thousand's a lot of money, Red.'

'Is that right, Bobby? Really. I didn't know that.'

'You know what he did with it, of course,' said Jake. 'He no doubt used it to slam dunk his own fucking life. So he's some kind of low-level Fortune Five Hundred kind of guy, which is what I hear. You know, he's in the land of abundance, his portfolio is diversified while what is left of you is sitting here with us.'

'What's your point?'

'We're roadkill!'

'This person who you can't remember, who knew about Harlow, who knew what he did, who knew how he's doing –'

'Yeh,' said Jake.

'What'd they say about him?'

'They said he was fat-assed and arrogant, but nevertheless in truth a slime ball, who had somehow survived the boom, and come out richer than he went in.'

'You oughta collect, Red. Something, anyway,' said Macky. 'We could go with you.'

'I mean, he owes you, Red,' Bobby added. 'It ain't right.'

Red knew it wasn't right. He accessed everything he had on Thomas P. Harlow and just seeing the high end address sickened him. Then along came some vague memory of Harlow. It was fuzzy like a channel you can't afford to subscribe to – this hub of fat and annoyance and smug contempt flickering on and off. Red's brain was burning again and he was back inside the smouldering walls, the flames eating away at his cherished belief that everybody who deserved to go down when the bottom fell out had taken the fall. 'Look at that,' said Red, gazing at the computer. 'The fucker lived in Hurst.' Hurst was one of the more affluent of the Dallas Suburbs. 'You think he's still there?'

'There or better,' said Jake. 'That's my information.'

They took Red's car and Red drove with Macky slouched beside him. Bobby and Jake were in the back. Everybody had a can of beer. They'd had to borrow the price of a six pack from the waitress. She had a thing for Macky and he'd boned her a couple of times which explained her interest and her resentment, because before and after he'd boned her, he treated her the same. Like a waitress. She agreed to help them out only after they promised to pay her back double. She even scribbled the deal down on a slip of paper, and then asked her boss to witness it, because she was 'really, really' serious about it. They were serious, too, they told her, because they knew what it was to get screwed by people who didn't pay their debts.

Now they were rattling through the night on their way to Hurst. Macky suddenly groaned and guzzled whatever remained of his beer in one big breath. A six pack gave them one beer each and two to fight over. Macky flipped the can out the window and looked at Red. Macky had been a foreman on an oil rig during the boom. He'd worked his way up after coming back from Vietnam. At the moment he pumped gas and was on several waiting lists to become a security guard. 'I want another brew, OK, Red.' Macky reached out with both hands, his forearms like cables with human skin stretched around them.

In the back seat, Bobby started laughing, as Red fumbled one of the two remaining beers up from the bag and handed it over to Macky. 'What?' Red said, peering into the rear view mirror in hopes of catching a face and a clue. 'What?' But Bobby couldn't stop laughing. 'What'd you say to him, Jake? Did you say something?'

'I don't know.'

'I was an investment banker,' Bobby giggled. Bobby'd been a Vice President at an S&L in Balch Springs just outside Dallas. When the S&Ls started flying apart, he jumped for cover, hunkering down, looking for a hole. He ended up fined and filing bankruptcy. He just escaped jail time, though he felt those cold concrete walls moving in so close he heard the doors slam in his sleep for months. 'Don't you see the irony, Red?' said Bobby. 'Now look at me.'

'We all see the irony, Bobby,' said Jake. 'We just don't think it's funny.'

'Irony is always funny.'

'Not this time.'

Red sure as hell didn't think it was funny the way all their lives had slammed to earth. Red's Lear Jet might as well have crashed and burned once Jake and Bobby and all the others like them were stripped down to their posh shorts. The leasing payments on his plane went from being a kind of afterthought, to this big guy pounding on the door. Strangers started showing up in a steady stream to take away his possessions. Everything was gone in a matter of days. He made a living now installing and repairing car stereo systems. Bobby worked part time in one of those copy places that make endless, pointless xerox copies for other people. Jake was a golf caddy.

It took a while to find the street, once they arrived in Hurst, then they went a couple of blocks in the wrong direction. When at last they pulled up in front of Harlow's fake Tudor style house, the bay window was full of light. The car port had three cars in it, two Beamers and a racy maroon Mercedes.

'Whata you think, Red?' said Jake.

Red was staring at Harlow's house. He climbed from the car. They were all sucking on a beer as they followed him on to the lawn. The Mercedes was pretty much irresistible to Red, pulling him straight up to it. He stood peering in at the interior. The pang he felt had some nasty dimensions. Here was actual, tangible proof of the lies he'd told himself over these last years. The Mercedes was like an organ ripped out of Red's own body.

Jake and Bobby were maybe twenty feet away admiring the Beamers. They sort of crooned and cooed with the memory of what they used to have. It hurt, Red thought. It fucking hurt. A scraping sound whirled him. A clotted shadow that made him feel hemmed in and fearful turned out to be Macky easing up.

'Listen,' Macky whispered. 'I been looking in the windows. What's in there is this fat, short guy in a linen suit. He's wandering around barefoot from room to room. A bottle of vodka in his hand. It looks like Absolut. He's got the bottle by the nozzle and he's walking around with the bottle swaying by the nozzle in his hand.'

'No shit,' said Red. 'The miserable prick, the slick two-faced sleazy prick! I shouldn't have let this happen.' It was clear to him that Harlow's life was an intentional public flaunting of the way he'd tricked and screwed Red. Harlow was mocking him and taunting him, and he was half-way across the lawn when Macky jumped in front of him, shaking his head in this worried way. 'Wait a minute, Red.'

'He can pay me what he owes me.'

'You know what I'm thinkin'.'

'Not until you tell me.'

'He's a Texan, ain't he? I'd say the odds are we go barging in on him, we are going to be lookin' at some kind of firepower. We better make a plan.'

'Look at the house and shit – *three* goddamn cars! We don't need a plan. Fucking bullshit. I have firepower of my own.' Red was already on a detour back to the street, his car, the trunk, the .38 in the oil cloth. By the time he returned, he couldn't see Macky. Then he heard a low murmur and spotted Macky with Jake and Bobby huddled together in the car port. He must have raced off to tell them what was going on. They were probably going to try and stop him, but nobody was going to stop him. He mounted the front stairs. Something about standing there like that, ringing a doorbell and holding a pistol, made him light-headed, these goose bumps streaming through him. He waited, then rang it again. Macky and Bobby and Jake were headed towards him. The latch clicked and the door pulled open, and Red felt like he did when he'd made his one and only bungi jump. Holy shit, motherfuck. It was a world of free fall.

Something about opening his front door and facing the upwardly tilted muzzle of a pistol made the fat guy standing there in his linen suit wrinkle his nose and then snigger. Or his mouth sniggered, while his eyes focused, blurred and then refocused. On the edge of the door, his fingers fidgeted, the way he would if he was annoyed and in some way bored. The noise he made was a sort of squeak, and then he actually said, 'Ha ha.'

'Remember me,' Red asked. He put his foot against the frame. 'What's going on here?'

'I asked, "Do you remember me?"'

'What do you want?'

'I'm here to balance the books.'

'Is this a hold up?'

'Don't you call it that. I want my money. This is debt-collecting.'

The fat guy registered the approach of the other three men behind Red. 'What money?' he said and took a slug of vodka.

Red wanted a drink, too. He grabbed the bottle. 'The money you owe me.' He took a gulp of vodka and handed the bottle back.

'Who are you?'

'You know me.'

'I think you've come to the wrong house. I think you've made a terrible mistake.'

'You owe him fifteen thousand dollars!' said Jake sticking his head in.

'You know what, Red?' Macky said, stepping past them and into the house, his eyes darting about. 'Standing in the doorway like this could get you in the shit real quick. You're backlit. You're standing in fucking silhouette. Whata you look like? Let's get inside or get into the car and find some shadows somewhere.'

Red didn't know what was warning and instructing him, but some ill-defined aspect of the situation would favor Harlow, if they entered his house. Harlow would gain some kind of authority, owning everything the way he did, every stick of furniture, even the land, knowing the floor plan, being familiar with the decorations. But if they fled into the night – if they took him off into the night he was theirs.

'Let's go.'

'What's going on here?' Harlow wanted to know. 'I don't owe you any fifteen thousand dollars.'

'Fuck you.' He grabbed Harlow by the arm.

'This is crazy. Wait. I don't have my shoes, for crissake. Look at my feet. Are you fucking blind? I gotta have some shoes on. Just gimme a goddamn minute!' The outburst disoriented Red. He didn't know how far he should let this abusive trend in Harlow develop. Impulsively, he pressed the tip of the .38's barrel against Harlow's ear. It must have felt cold as an ice cube the way Harlow's mouth stopped and locked up in this crooked shape.

'Let's go.'

'What are we doing?'

'I'll see if I can find his shoes,' Macky yelled.

They herded Harlow across the lawn. They were shoving him into the car when Macky joined them with a bottle of scotch in one hand and a Jack Daniels in the other. 'I couldn't find the shoes.'

'They were right in front of the couch,' Harlow told him.

'I looked there.'

'They were just laying there.'

'I didn't see them.'

'Maybe they were under the coffee table.'

The doors were slamming. Red yelled for Macky to drive. Red wanted to sit in the passenger seat and be able to concentrate on Harlow, who was wedged in the back between Bobby and Jake.

'Where to?' Jake wanted to know as the engine rumbled and the Beater struggled off from the curb.

'Go north on the Jacksboro.'

Bobby and Jake were drinking scotch, while Red and Macky worked on the Jack Daniels. Harlow still had his vodka, but he didn't seem all that interested in drinking at the moment, though he took a half-hearted sip every now and then. The houses got fewer and fewer, the flat desolate strips increasing, the signs of city life diminishing. Red was trying to figure out exactly what he wanted to do. He wanted his money, that was for sure. And maybe some payback. He just had to figure out exactly how to go about getting what he wanted.

By the time they got on to the Jacksboro, Macky was flipping radio stations, giving each one about a two seconds before he raced on, Jake and Bobby were arguing about the interest rates – whether or not they were going to continue in their downward trend, or if the current dip was simply the last depression before the start of an unavoidable rise. Neither one of them had a solid position. Seated between them, Harlow was frowning like he might be struggling to come up with a way to ease their concerns. The scotch bottle moved back and forth across his body, as they exchanged it and talked and drank.

'How the hell did you avoid going under, Harlow?' Jake suddenly yelled. 'You were in Real Estate, for godssake. The great bitch of business chewed the rest of us up and shit us out, but you stayed close to her fucking heart. If you were in Real Estate, the rule of thumb was your dick was in the shredder.'

'I wasn't in Real Estate any more.'

'So the rumor's right. We heard a rumor.'

'What rumor?'

'That you got out before the crash.'

'It's not a rumor, it's what happened. I liquidated and reinvested. I was in computers.'

'You went into computers.'

'Software.'

'Did you ever have any dealing with an S&L in Balsh Springs?' said Bobby.

'Balch Springs? I don't think so.'

'It's just outside Dallas.'

'I know Balch Springs. But I don't think I did business with any S&L there. Why?'

'I was a Vice President there. It was like getting hit with lightning when the bottom fell out. The oil stopped, and the money stopped. I mean, how the hell did you know to get out? I didn't have a clue. Then all of a sudden it was like the boom had never been flesh and blood, but it was all along this kind of virtual reality projection that fucking mesmerized us all until the central tube in whatever system was generating it just blew. That's how I felt, anyway. Does this make any sense to you?'

'Sort of.'

'Did you see the bust coming?' said Jake. 'Is that what happened? You saw it coming?'

'No, no, I don't think I had the –'

'Sure, sure, you sensed it. So you got out.'

'I don't think so. I was just bored. I don't remember why.'

'You had an instinct.'

'I don't think so.'

'When is it going to end, though?' Bobby asked. 'What do you think?' He sounded whiney and pathetic, like he did when he was pleading with some gorgeous woman to fuck him and she wouldn't. 'When is this recession going to bottom out?' he said. 'It's gotta recover, don't you think?'

'I'll tell you this,' Jake said, 'they have to get inflation under control, and they won't the way they're going about it. Not if Greenspan keeps parading around scaring everybody about inflation like he's been doing in front of congress. Now it's going to skyrocket. You mark my words. It has to.'

'Where are we going?' Harlow asked.

Red whirled in the seat, and knelt there facing Harlow. 'Enough of this crap! Do you remember me now? I flew a plane. I had a Lear jet.'

'I don't remember you.'

'Do you remember a Lear Jet? Do you remember Vegas? Broads?'

Blades of illumination fanned over Harlow's face as the car shot under periodic street lights. It struck Red that Harlow was sorting the questions and debating what to say, trying to remember, and then trying to sort out what he should admit remembering. 'I'm getting a divorce,' he said. 'I'm in the middle of a divorce proceeding. It's a fucking hemorrhage in my finances – it's gushing out. I'm losing everything.'

'I think he remembers you,' said Macky and then he took a swig.

'You were very shrewd, Harlow,' Red said. 'You made me real comfortable, paying me the first couple of times right on schedule. So when you didn't pay, I hesitated.'

'It was somebody else, who did this to you. That's what I'm trying to tell you.'

'No, no. He trusted you and you betrayed him, you prick,' Macky yelled.

'You broke his heart,' said Bobby.

Harlow shook his head in this exaggerated, amazed way and then he scanned them, his expression making him look like he'd just heard that something terrible had just happened to somebody really stupid who was somehow very dear to him. Red was watching closely, looking for the edge he needed to find a way into Harlow's head, a flaw to pry open, so he could work the guy over from that vantage, from the inside. Fuck him up good. He took a sip of Jack Daniels and contemplated the unexpected way things were developing. He had to give Harlow credit because the guy had come up with a completely original bluff. Who would have ever guessed that Harlow would be ballsy enough to risk everything on a tactic as ridiculous as pretending to be someone else.

'You know what we were wondering, Harlow?' said Macky. 'We were wondering how far you thought you could swim with a stop sign tied to your leg.'

'What?'

'What?' said Red.

'I know I couldn't swim very far,' said Macky.

'I couldn't, either,' said Jake, 'and I'm a good swimmer. Could you Red?'

'Swim with a stop sign tied to my leg? Is that what you're asking?'

'I don't think you could. I think you'd sink.'

'Of course I'd sink. Anybody would.'

'Wait a minute, wait a minute,' said Harlow. 'This is nuts. You guys are nuts.'

'No, no. It's you!' said Bobby. 'It's pricks like you, failing to pay your debts, so the whole economic system gets thrown out of whack. We're all interdependent, you know that. Cheaters hurt everybody.'

'I didn't cheat.'

'The hell you didn't.'

'Everybody cheats,' said Harlow. 'Everybody cheats. It's expected. It's business.'

'You cheat until you get caught,' said Red. 'And so that explains what's happening to you. You been caught.'

Macky veered off the concrete into a wooded section of scrub live oak and mesquite, startling everybody. The car bounced and jostled them as he slammed to a halt and popped the door open.

'What the hell are you doing?'

Macky plunged out the door.

'Where's he goin'?' said Harlow.

Macky sprinted through the dark to the intersection where he started wrestling with the stop sign on the corner. Red looked around at everybody inside the car and they were all staring at Macky, heaving against the pole, straining through minutes of shadowy struggle. He tried various angles, pausing and gathering himself to lunge again and again.

'I'm going to help him,' said Jake, jumping from the car.

'Me too,' said Bobby.

Macky had his back against the pole, his heels dug in when they arrived. The three of them reeled about, groaning and gasping. Several times they consulted and then they began their fight all over again, positioning themselves, counting to three and attacking, until abruptly they all crashed to the ground. The dirt made a loud cracking sound and the sign clattered against large stones and scattered gravel, the concrete base popping up like this gigantic uprooted onion. For a second, they lay there gasping, then they ran towards the car, lugging the sign.

'I can't give you fifteen thousand dollars. For crissake, I don't even remember you.'

'Well, then you're going to fucking drown,' Red told him.

'What?' The way Harlow said this and then met Red's eyes somehow highlighted the odd fact that they were alone just then, and that they were only a few feet apart. Red sensed a change in Harlow, a shift in the way he was looking at things. Wanting to press Harlow, to make him crumble right here and now, Red lifted the .38 into view.

'What's this about?' said Harlow.

'I told you.'

'No. Really! Who sent you? Did my wife send you? Because it won't work if she did. It won't fucking work.'

Macky and Bobby and Jake were loading the stop sign into the trunk, so the car bounced and shuddered with their effort. Red could hear them arguing about the best way to do it. Then the lid slammed. With Macky once more at the wheel, they tore off, plunging down a lightless back road. 'We'll need a boat,' Macky said.

'There's lots of them.'

'Listen,' said Harlow, 'this is gone far enough. I have to pee.'

'You miserable sonofabitch!' Red screamed at him. 'You stiffed me! You owe me!'

'I don't remember you.'

'Is that my fault?! I mean, I'm sorry I can't give you a god-damn presentation with flip charts and memos, but I can't. I do in fact have the bill, the date, the itinerary, the passenger list in the back on my computer. I have a series of letters we exchanged on this matter. I even have a Polaroid picture of you getting sucked off by one bimbo while you finger fuck this other one. I have the photo.'

'It's not me. That's what I'm trying to tell you.'

'It's useless,' Macky said. 'I don't think he's got the money.'

'I gotta pee. I'll goddamnit piss in my pants.'

'Don't you dare piss in my car,' Red yelled.

They were bucking and jolting down a dark side road, enter-ing a little marina. The water appeared, a glittering inky slab. Boats bobbed in the shallows, or lay turned over on the shore.

'The computer doesn't lie,' Red said, wishing he could reach back and wipe the shadows off Harlow's face. He wanted to con-firm beyond all doubt that Harlow was Harlow. But everyone was getting out of the car, Jake and Bobby pulling at Harlow, gravity hauling at them all. Macky ran into the night. Red reeled side-ways for several steps, fighting back the knowledge of how drunk he was with another aggressive slug of vodka. He was staggering towards the wooded fringe, vaguely intending to find something to row the boat with. If they found a boat. He ven-tured to the boundary between the clearing and the forest, peering into the tangled murk. He had to pee, and his piss muttered and shook the leaves, their shadows feathery. It seemed the underbrush was too thick to enter and look for logs to row with. He felt like he might never get back out. He retreated, zipping up, angling towards the flat black gleam of water. When he came upon a little storage shed, he found some planks piled up along the wall. A couple of them would serve as oars.

The commotion near the shoreline was Macky in the water up to his ankles, lugging an aluminum twelve footer through the shallows. Either the owner forgot to lock it up properly or Macky had ripped it loose. Jake and Bobby had tied Harlow's hands behind him with his belt. Macky tossed them a piece of rope loose in the floor of the boat, and they started lashing the stop sign to Harlow's pudgy leg.

'I got oars,' said Red as he sat down in the dirt drinking and watching the white linen of Harlow's trousers balloon above the bulge of the knot. Macky sloshed out of the water and bent over to pick up the sign. Jake and Bobby hefted Harlow on to his feet.

'Look,' he said, 'I'll write you a check.'

'A check? Jesus Christ, you are not talking to children here,' said Bobby. You know that, I hope, Harlow. You know you are not talking to children here.'

'What else can I do?'

Red walked up, leaning in close to Harlow. 'I took a check from you now, by the time I went to cash it, you would have cancelled it.'

'No, no. I wouldn't.'

They were on the move, struggling to get into the boat, arguing who should do what, who should sit where. 'Stiffed again,' Red went on, though no one was really interested. 'That's what I'd have to say, wouldn't I? What an asshole I'd be. You beat me once. I can't let you do it again. I couldn't look myself in the eye in the mirror, I let that happen.'

Macky was the last one aboard, landing with an aggression that prompted groans from the hull and turbulence in the water. Bobby and Jake were all set to use the planks to pole away from shore, but they waited for Macky to settle before starting in. The riveted aluminum of the hull gave up a creaking sound that slid through the sighing of the waves they passed over. 'Listen,' Macky said, in a voice that made Red look at him. It was like Macky was using somebody else's voice. He'd adopted a sort of formal quality that made him sound like he was pretending to be a minister or teacher. 'For all you who've never killed anyone before, it's not what you think. It's just not. It's different.'

In the past, Red had never known whether to believe Macky's lunatic claims about Vietnam or not, but looking at him in the sheen rising off these dark polluted waters, he felt himself becoming a believer. This strange set of eyeballs appeared to have been implanted in Macky's head. He swayed a little, staying in harmony with the rocking of the boat, the movement shifting him in and out of the moonlight.

'Macky,' said Red. 'Whata you mean?'

'Just listen. Wait. Watch.' He was back on his 'Nam frequency' which the rest of them could never quite pick up. It wouldn't be the first time they'd seen this kind of spasm take him over, turning him into a refugee from COPS on TV, motor-mouthing about 'bringing smoke' and 'vils' and 'zapping' and 'fragging'. More often than not, this shit hit him after a case of beer or a dozen whacks of reefer, so tonight was prime. Now he was looking off into deep shadows along the shore. Then he raised his glance to the smoky clouds revising themselves around the moon. Nostalgia seemed a pair of pliers closing deep inside him.

'Who pissed? I smell piss,' said Jake. 'Look at this, he pissed himself.'

'This has gone far enough,' said Harlow, closing his legs over the shameful dark stain.

'You stink,' said Jake.

'Whata baby. You big baby,' said Macky. 'Let's get on with this. I'm getting eaten alive.' He was swatting at mosquitoes. 'There's too goddamn many mosquitoes to just cruise around out here.'

'Fucking bullshit,' said Harlow. 'I told you I had to go.'

'We're not really going to do this are we?' said Bobby.

'God-fucking-damnit, Bobby!' Red yelled. 'You got the intelligence of a landfill! Can you shut the hell up? Goddamnit!' They had to get the money or do it, didn't they? What the hell was Bobby thinking? The only way to avoid killing Harlow was for Harlow to believe there was no doubt they were going to kill him. 'Whether we do it or not is up to Harlow, Bobby.' Red took the vodka bottle from Macky.

'You guys must really think you are hot shit,' said Harlow.

'The fuck we're not.' Macky grabbed Harlow by the shirt front. His awkward violence started the boat rocking.

'Wait a minute,' said Bobby.

Who would know? Red was thinking. Who would care? Nobody. Nobody cared about any-fucking-thing these days. Everybody knew everything and nobody cared about anything. Macky pushed Harlow away and bent sideways secretively, huddling over something like a guy protecting a match from the wind. With pinched fingers he was jamming something tiny into his mouth. Then he looked at Red, his big eyes fixed on some distant intrigue, which he was inviting Red to join. He reached inside Red and touched something Red didn't even know was in there.

'It's a free one,' Macky said. 'It's a free one.'

Red nodded, then looked at Harlow. What the hell was Macky talking about? What was a 'free one?' Did he mean they could kill the guy and get away with it and just go on? Harlow had a weird gleam in his eye. He was pretending to be some kind of tough guy who knew every inch of the difference between what could and couldn't happen. He didn't, though. Nobody did. It was real thin anyway. It might not even be there.

'Red,' said Macky, 'you know the way Saranwrap keeps one thing separate from another. But you can go through it. You can go right through it. Just poke your finger. It's nothing.'

'Yeh.'

'It's like the water. It looks like it could hold you up, but it won't.'

Harlow started to cry. At first he sounded like somebody was strangling him, and then this big cough came out of him, and he said, 'Oh, oh, oh. Oh, God.' It was like he was barking and spitting snot. 'Please,' he moaned.

'Save it for the fish,' said Macky.

'Wait! Wait!'

'It's too dark,' said Macky. 'It's too dark.'

'Whata you mean? What does he mean it's too dark? Please!'

'You hear that, Harlow?' Red said. 'I thought you were a real savvy deal-doer!' He was enraged at Harlow for pushing things this far and leaving Red with no choice that he could see. Did the stupid miserable prick want to die? If he did, fuck him.

'Gimme a minute.' Harlow was barely able to get the words out through all the groans and gasping. 'Just a minute. One minute to think. I want to come up with a counter offer. OK? OK?'

'Whata you think this is, a press conference?' said Macky.

'What?'

'Give it up,' said Jake. 'Or you're going over!'

'What are you talking about?' Bobby yelled, like he was being threatened himself.

'The fish will ask you all the questions,' said Macky.

'What? What fish?'

'At the press conference. "What are you doing down here?" they will ask. "What are you doing with a stop sign tied to your leg?"'

Harlow turned to Red, and it was like they were both remembering each other fondly. Maybe it was that moment in the car when they were alone before. Or some good time they'd shared during the boom that they'd both forgotten. Red shook his head, as if to push aside Harlow's appeal. This was business. He had to keep his business head on. In every deal, a moment like this arrived, where the worst outcome appeared unavoidable. Red had to harden himself. This was how he lost out the first time. He forced himself to meet Harlow's beseeching eyes by reminding himself of the first rule of negotiations: if you didn't think you could handle the worst consequence a deal might bring, then you would lose out for sure. It was Harlow's position that he could afford to gamble on Red turning out to be more afraid of killing him than Harlow was afraid of dying. At the same time, Red's position was just as sound, if not better. The odds were good that Harlow should be more afraid of dying than Red was of killing him.

'I'm not Harlow,' he said.

'Fuck you,' Red told him, making sure to hide the fact that he was seriously asking himself if this guy in the boat could just be some misplaced fat guy who lived in Hurst in a big house. He wished he'd checked the Polaroids. Letting him drown, whoever he was, wouldn't get the money back, anyway. The thought of this pudgy figure descending into the black water annoyed him and left him resentful, as if the money was sinking with him. 'We're like the goddamn wet backs,' Red said. 'That's the problem, Harlow. That's what you gotta understand. The goddamn niggers and greasers. You know how they're always complaining they've been disenfranchised. Well, that's what's happened to us. We've been disenfranchised just like them so we have no part to play in the normal course of things. That's the problem. We been tossed out. You can't appeal to us. You don't have the means any more. It's like a foreign language. We're talking Hip Hop rap crap.'

'You mean I should talk to you like you're a spade?'

'All we understand is money.'

Macky was grunting to lift the stop sign and hold it out over the side of the boat. Harlow gaped, watching every move Macky made like it was this amazing, really interesting athletic event.

'Jesus God Almighty, I've got eight thousand in a safe at home.'

'You owe me fifteen thousand.'

'The degree of difficulty on this thing is going up,' said Macky.

'You can't kill me. I'll drown.'

'What time is it?' said Macky.

'Why?'

'All right, all right!' Harlow said. He was gasping for air with each word, his voice getting littler. 'I've got it. I've got it in cash at home.'

'Don't bullshit me!'

'Red, please!'

'If you're lying, I'll bring you back here, you hear me? You swear it. You got the whole fifteen thousand!'

'I remember you,' he said. 'I suddenly remember. You're Red.'

'That's right,' Red said.

'I just remembered,' said Harlow.

'All right,' Red told him. 'Deal.'

'Yes, yes, yes.' Harlow was looking at Macky who still stood holding the sign out over the water. His big hands and forearms were straining, his biceps swollen like they were filling up with this irritating liquid making him grimace.

'We're headed for the pudenda bar,' said Bobby.

'Bring it back, Macky,' Red told him. 'Bring it back. We got what we wanted.'

'And could you do me a favor?' said Harlow. 'Do you think you could do me a little favor and throw in those Polaroids you mentioned, Red? I mean, the ones with me and those bimbos. Just throw them in to sweeten the deal. If my wife got her hands on them, I mean, good Lord, armed with those fuckers, the divorce settlement she could get would bust my ass for sure.'

Macky dropped the stop sign. Bobby lunged to grab hold of Harlow, but it was too late. As Macky's empty hands flew skyward in a magician's flourish of presentation, water plumed over them in high cold spray, the boat bucking, the black sky heaving and shaking. Macky was laughing, while everybody else screamed and Harlow didn't move. The water came down like rain. The sign was gone, but Harlow sat there, this weird look in his eyes, like he was taking a painful shit. The rope ran from his leg to the frayed end, dangling through the oarlocks to brush the black water.

'Musta broke,' said Macky.

'Damn.'

'He's going to give us the money, Macky,' said Bobby. 'What the hell are you doing?'

'Some things are more important than money,' said Macky.

When they arrived at The Animal Club, Red had fifteen thousand dollars in his pockets. There'd been two safes in Harlow's house, one in the master bedroom, the other in the floor under the couch and the shag rug in the living room, and between the two of them, there was a hell of a lot more than fifteen thousand. When Harlow counted it out, he still had plenty to put back. Red thought about adding in some interest charges, but decided against it. He just went out to his car and dug up the Polaroids from the trunk where they were stashed in an envelope in the bottom of the cardboard box. He met Harlow in the kitchen, and they sat down at the table to make the exchange over a couple of beers.

Now Red, Macky, Bobby and Jake were striding the aisle of the 'pudenda' bar, rocking and rolling to the heavy beat of the music. Red had paid the cover, tipped the door man and the bouncer, and he felt huge and bossy. They all did. The money was rolled up in two lumps, one in each of his trouser's front pockets. He was swaggering side to side, his head high, his chin stuck out, he was riding a mood fueled on left-over nerves, waning adrenaline, and lots of alcohol. Bobby was mimicking the look in Harlow's eyes when the sign hit the water, and they all burst out laughing.

On a small stage to the right, a blonde was slipping out of a satin gown the color of fresh blood. The lights scorched her with jelled streams of cloudy color and the stereo system was so high tech that the music assaulted them, this huge coiling embrace of sexy sound and sentiments.

They felt like a gang Red had just guided through a dangerous escapade and now they had come to this place for their reward. They strode past several other small stages, each topped by a quality woman sprayed in light and driven to dance by the music. Ahead was the main stage. They settled at a table directly in front of it. Colored lights circled the floor and girls sailed across the polished surface, light rising off it in thick waves.

The approaching waitress had on a kind of Bo Peep outfit and she smiled and wrinkled her nose when she asked them what they wanted to drink. They all ordered doubles and started throwing back the single malt scotch and Maker's Mark and crying out their appreciation for the women performing on the stage. There was Maggie and Pirate and Misty and Amanda. Macky bought a table dance for Red, and this sparkling, perky brunette with sassy eyes slipped from her gown and wavered around between his knees. After that everybody started buying dances for everybody, so one after another, women appeared to look into Bobby's eyes, or Macky's or Jake's, or Red's, as they bumped around between one guy or another's thighs, nothing on but a G-string and these shiny pasties glued on to their nipples.

Red thought Amanda was the best. Macky liked Pirate and Jake was crazy about Misty while Bobby said he liked them all, but if he had to choose – and it was a big 'if' – he would pick Amanda. They weren't arguing, but it sounded like they were, because even when they agreed, they yelled, their voices clanging against one another with escalating drunken excitement.

'Her tits are real,' Macky yelled. 'I know they are.'

'Bullshit,' said Jake. 'Hers are Styrofoam just like they all are.'

'Styrofoam?'

'They're not real. I think maybe Misty's are real. Hers might be real, but –'

'What're you talkin' about – styrofoam?'

'What are you talking about? What they put in 'em in these plastic bags and sew them in. The plastic surgeon.'

'That's not Styrofoam.'

Red was taking the last of his Maker's Mark in a jubilant throw-back, the tilt of his head sending his gaze into a chance encounter with this blonde with a long nose and a sweet ass. She had just finished table dancing for two corporate stiffs in suits, and she was slipping back into her dress.

'It's not Styrofoam, for God's sake, I know that,' said Jake.

'What is it? Celluloid? Celluloid!' His intonation left no doubt that he believed himself to be right at last.

'That's film, you dickhead,' said Macky.

'What the hell is it? They're not real, that's all I know.'

The girl with the two corporate stiffs had just picked up a glass of water. The stiffs were done with her, so they were turning to look back to the stage. Glancing at Macky, Red said, 'What?' to something. He'd heard his name. But his interest in the girl pulled him back. She was standing there as still as a rock, her lips parted and the glass a few inches from her mouth, this sad expression taking over her face, like she was beginning to recall some really terrible memory. He was thinking maybe he'd buy a dance off her, maybe get a friction dance. Her expression hadn't changed, the memory dawning on her, coming back. But Red knew it wasn't a memory, not really, even though that was the way she looked. He had no idea what exactly made him know she had an ice cube stuck in her throat in that place where you can't get it out without help, but he was sure.

'Silicone,' said Macky.

'No, no, no, that's computers.'

'You're jerking me around,' said Macky.

There was fear in the blonde's eyes now, her mouth open. She can't breathe, he thought. She can't breathe or speak. He got up and walked towards her, knowing exactly what to do to help somebody in trouble like this. He'd picked it up somewhere in his endless TV watching. He put his arms around her. The music was in the midst of a lush, romantic move, this ballad with Whitney Houston singing. Red locked his hands just beneath her tits and pulled her to him. Because of the way she was standing, his need to get behind her had him facing Macky and Jake and Bobby, and one by one they noticed what he was doing, as he slammed his fist into her solar plexus with a force and effort that drew him forward so his mouth was pressed up to her ear. She was struggling, moving against the length of him, and she didn't feel real somehow, but unearthly and sweet like her body was spun of cotton candy, only electric and full of perfume. His arms around her were squeezing, her ass pressed into him and she was in this state of perfect helplessness. She felt weak and sad, sagging against him. She's going to die, he thought. I can't stop her. He could feel misery filling her up, and he pumped her again. Begging to be able to save her. She drifted into him. She was giving up. With the music dreaming on about love, Red felt like they were dancing, and her ass sort of shifted and his dick felt it. He searched for the spot and tried hard. He slammed her again and then out of nowhere an ice cube arced from her open mouth into the air and the breath came back into her. He felt it at the same time that he saw the ice cube flying, this white light bursting out of it. Her teeth closed and opened like she was starving and biting hard into what she had to have, and over and over she filled with precious breath. He felt sentimental towards her, kind of maudlin and tender. There they were, the two of them, like these characters in a sad song embracing. And then he thought of Harlow, and the lake, and the black water. She was crying now, tears just sprouting in her eyes the way they do sometimes in a little child's. She seemed to be getting ready to turn and look at Red. He was eager for that. He could hardly wait for her to hug him and thank him. He let her go and she stepped away. Her eyes started darting, searching the room for something or someone. She took another breath and ducked her head and ran away.

The guys were all yelling at Red. A few people at the surrounding tables had noticed that something unusual was going on, but most had remained oblivious. Macky and Jake and Bobby herded Red back to the table, wanting to know what the hell he had been doing. He was picking up his drink and sitting back down, getting ready to explain when a bouncer came up to tell him the girl was all right now. It was weird the way the guy was acting, because there was definitely something threatening in the way he looked at Red, the way he talked. His whole thing was belligerent and mean. 'Just sit back down,' the guy said, like Red had misbehaved somehow, like he'd broken a rule.

A few minutes later, the girl returned, but she never gave Red a look. Not even a peek. She seemed embarrassed about what had happened, like she was trying to put it behind her. Just forget about it. She got right back to business, working two new corporate stiffs on the other side of the room. Red ordered a triple Maker's Mark straight up and when it arrived the waitress told him it was on the house. Then the bouncer swaggered back up to tell Red the management wanted to give him a free table dance, and up came a different girl to swirl around between Red's legs and wave her titties in his face.

Beetroots

Matthew Sweeney

Rockets watched him through the spyglass, getting off the bus and heading up the hill road. He was unsteady on his feet and carrying a paper bag. It didn't look like it held much, though. Rockets shook his head, put the spyglass down and looked at the clock. Five-past six again! He filled the kettle and replaced it on the hot-plate of the range, then went with the tea pot to the back door to throw the cold tea over the pebbles.

He stood there, leaning on the jamb. Presently Bancelor's head bobbed above a hedge, and then the whole man came into view. He looked at the road as he walked. It was thinner he was getting – if a big wind were to come along it would blow him to Mayo. The coat was torn, and the lining was hanging out. It was a long time since the shoes had seen polish.

At the turn in to the lane he stopped, left the bag on the ground and pissed against the stone wall.

– Oh, oh, here comes Wag at the Wall, shouted Rockets. And what might that be in the bag?

– Beetroots, said Bancelor, with a slur in his voice, as he buttoned up and continued towards the house.

– *Beetroots*? In God's name, what good are they?

– They're supposed to be lovely, so Joe Neddy says. And good for you, too. Joe eats them every day.

– He does, does he? And I suppose it was the same Joe that was selling them to you? Aren't you the eejit! I've told you many times to give up the drink.

– Joe never sold them to me, he *gave* them to me. And I'm going to boil them now. And you can eat them or not, as you like. And it would do *you* good to make the odd trip into town, instead of sitting here, waiting to make sarcastic remarks when people get home.

– Mind you don't cut yourself, that's all I say.

Then Rockets started whistling a jig, and went outside for a walk.

It was a dry evening, and no rain was lurking in the sky. If this weather kept up, as it had done for weeks, it would be great for the turf. Theirs would be good and dry by now. They'd do well to bring it in soon, at the end of next week maybe. You couldn't trust the weather and it was better to be sure.

He could see the sea from here, and the island long and flat in the distance. Fifty-three years ago he'd lived there, and he hadn't been back since. He could barely remember it, being five when they'd left, and Bancelor would remember nothing, as he'd been a baby. He hadn't missed anything, but at the same time what difference would it make if they lived there now?

He turned to go back to the house. You could probably see that from the island – up on its hill, painted bright green (keeping the rust off the corrugated iron), with the chimneys and gables white. You would nearly see it from the moon.

The smell of beetroot met him at the door. Bancelor had the table set and the salt and pepper in the middle. You would think they were having a feast. He sat down heavily, even though there wasn't much meat on him either. He watched Bancelor's stooped back as he jabbed the beetroots with a fork to see if they were done.

– If you're going to go into town like this, you'd think you'd do something about how you look. That ould coat's fit for the bonfire. And you'd be better off getting a haircut than buying beetroot. The smell of it would scunner a donkey.

– Aye, that's right, said Bancelor. Moan, moan. Would you listen to him, he said to the beetroots as he teemed them, and the red water disappeared down the plughole. He put the steaming pot on the table, sat down opposite Rockets, spiked a beetroot with his fork and started peeling it like he would a potato.

– Joe Neddy says the people of Russia eat little else. If it's good enough for the Bolsheviks it's good enough for me.

Rockets grunted and took a beetroot himself, a small one. It reminded him somewhat of a turnip. As he cut into it, his knife and plate were stained red. Even his finger had a red blotch. He hoped it would come off. But the taste wasn't too bad when you put plenty of salt and pepper on it – not that he was going to say this to Bancelor.

He pronged another one, a big one this time, as it was only when he'd started eating that he'd realized how hungry he was. And Bancelor was devouring the beetroots like a pig would turnips. It was funny that they'd never had them before while someone like Joe Neddy ate his fill of them. He imagined they'd go well with beef.

The thought of Joe Neddy brought back to him Bancelor's trip to town. Every week he went in there and every week he came back half stocious. Sitting around in pubs with cronies like Joe Neddy instead of bringing back useful things for the house. There were any amount of things that would be useful. Not beetroots, he thought, even though he had eaten four.

– I think *I'll* go in to town next week, for a change. You can stay here and mind the fort.

– Well, it's about time, said Bancelor. You've been rotting away here too long. What's happened to rouse you?

– Beetroots, said Rockets. That's what's happened. Beetroots and beer.

– I didn't see you refusing the beetroots. You should have said this earlier and I could have had your share.

He collected the plates and left the beetroot skins out for the hens.

That night about two in the morning Rockets woke with a very sick stomach and immediately ran out to the toilet. When he got there he heard the sound of vomiting. Debating whether to wait or head for the back door, he heard a mournful cry.

– Ah God, another blood vessel!

Sick as he was, he went in to investigate. The bowl was red but it wasn't blood.

– It's your frigging beetroot, he said, as he moved Bancelor over and contributed his own vomit to the bowl.

Bancelor never heard the end of it all the next day. He had a pain in the centre of his stomach and was still a bit queasy. So was Rockets but he had no one ranting at him.

– Joe Neddy didn't tell you about the vomiting, did he? What do the Russians do with their red vomit? Do they dry it and export it? As long as they don't export it to Ireland I don't care.

On and on he went, so that Bancelor spent most of the day walking on the hill. He was puzzled by why the beetroots should make them sick. He had half a mind to go in to Joe Neddy in the pub but that would bring more abuse on his head. Joe could eat all the beetroots he liked – it was a free country – but Bancelor wished Joe had kept them to himself.

For the next day or so even the hens' eggs were contaminated

208

with red. Still, Tuesday morning came without any murders in the green house, and Rockets set off bright and early for the town with all their savings (unknown to Bancelor) in his inside pocket, and his best suit on. As he stood at the bus stop he calculated that it had to be two years since he'd last made the trip. Bancelor was right, it was about time he went into town. Sitting at home made a being odd, and people would be talking. He would be as sociable as possible today, but he mustn't forget his trip had a purpose. And it wasn't the acquiring of beetroots, either.

The town was bigger but the mart was the same. Rockets walked the length of it, stopping to pass the time of day with anyone he knew. He listened to one man tell how two of his bullocks were struck by lightning within three months of each other. Another demanded that Rockets admire his horse. The auctioneer was shouting and banging with his hammer. Once he held a goose up by the neck, and at the point of sale, the goose shat on his head.

Rockets went into a café for a pot of tea and an Ulster fry. He took his time with it and ordered more fried bread and another pot of tea. He read the paper, eavesdropped on the two old women at the next table and exchanged a few words about the weather with a man who sat at his. Then he sauntered into The Golden Horseshoe and sat on a barstool and ordered a glass of Guinness.

It was already quite busy. Joe Neddy was there, and Rockets nodded at him. He wanted to ask him about vomit and beetroots but wouldn't lower himself. Joe would probably laugh in his face, saying he'd never vomited from beetroot, and the people of Russia never did. Rockets enjoyed sitting alone in bars and he'd forgotten how much he did so, especially in early lunchtime, before anyone got too drunk. He'd always been a good listener but every year he spent on the hillside with only Bancelor to listen to made him even better. He had another glass of Guinness, sipped it slowly, then slipped back outside.

By now the market was in full swing. He went straight to where he'd seen three donkeys earlier. All three were still there. He eyed them up and down, conscious of their owners eyeing him up and down. He went towards the smaller of the three and had a closer look. The beast appeared healthy enough. The owner came up to Rockets.

– That donkey's so light in his foot that if you sprinkled turf mould on a lake he could walk on it.

– It would seem so, said Rockets, but tell me, could he carry anything? Could he carry creels of turf?

– He could carry a cart-load if you could balance it on his back.

They struck a deal for a tenner with two new creels thrown in. Then they went to The Golden Horseshoe to make the deal lasting. The man was called Tom Fagen and he was from the edge of the Gaeltacht. When he'd get excited he'd break into Irish, a language Rockets had never been good at. When Rockets told him that he wanted the donkey because his turf was in a really boggy place, Tom Fagen said he knew exactly what Rockets meant. Hadn't he the same kind of useless stretch of bog. Walk on it and you'd sink to your knees. That donkey was perfect for a business like that.

– If he's that perfect, said Rockets, and you have the same trouble, why are you selling him?

– Oh, I have another one at home that could walk on air.

Rockets stared at him, and had a mind to demand his money back, but after a few gulps of Guinness he'd forgotten about it.

It was only on the fifth pint, when Tom Fagen was singing, that Rockets remembered to ask him what donkeys liked to eat.

– Oh, I know about grass, he said, but what do you give them every now and then to keep them sweet?

Fagen stared at him like he was soft in the head.

– What do donkeys eat? With *their* big teeth? They'd take a moon-bite out of your hand, if you gave it to them. They love carrots, spuds, turnips, beetroots – anything crunchy like that. They eat nearly anything. They're almost as bad as goats.

– Beetroots, did you say?

– Beetroots is one of their favourites.

He went back into his song, and Rockets looked around the bar to see if Joe Neddy was still there.

It was dark, and it was a long five miles home. The bus passed him at the outskirts of the town, but the driver would never let a donkey on, even a scrawny one like this. Every now and again when he felt tired he'd hop on the donkey's back, but he wouldn't stay on long. The donkey had enough to carry, with the two creels of beetroots. He had a few bottles of stout in there too, to keep Bancelor happy. After all, they had something to celebrate. With this donkey, their turf would be in by the weekend. And he still had a fair amount of their savings back with him. And he had enough beetroots to keep the donkey sweet for months. And he'd had the best day in years.

The moon was up and the sky was swarming with stars as he wearily but happily led the donkey up the hill road. The house was a ghostly green in the moonlight. The donkey brayed when he saw it but carried on. Rockets led the donkey into the house, right into the bedroom where Bancelor was in bed but still awake.

– Get up, get up, Rockets shouted. Can't you see this donkey I bought to help us with the turf? He's so light in his foot that if you sprinkled turf mould on a lake he'd walk on it. And can't you see what's in the creels? It's beetroots, hundreds of them, enough to keep the donkey sweet for months. And you won't need to cook them, Bancelor. The donkey'll crunch them like you would an apple. And he won't vomit, either, like Joe Neddy doesn't, and the Russians don't. Would you get up, out of that, and have a drink with me, for haven't I had the great day.

Blue Sky Like Water

Livi Michael

Yvette brought the milk in. She stayed a while on the step in spite of the stony blast of air, because the sky was the same colour as the milk, a pool of light in one corner, and because the curtains of the house opposite were already drawn back, as they seemed to be most of the time these days, night and day, no light on. Soon the cold from the bottles bit through her fingers, a bird had dented the top of one but not pierced through, probably dented its beak as well, and she went back inside where the kids were calling,

Shut the door mam.

It's cold.

Later, orange light on a blue moor, she chugged slowly behind a tractor, the road too busy and winding to overtake. She'd had a real afternoon of it, roadworks all over the town centre, and the cash-card machine still not giving her any money, though the bank had said they'd got it sorted. Then the woman in front of her at the check-out had to put half her stuff back, and now it looked as though she'd have to follow the tractor all the way home.

The road had been gritted but there were still ridges of greying snow at the sides. It was too late to call home first, Yvette had to go straight to pick the kids up and listen to them fight all the way back, Jamie called Adam a baby, Adam kicked him and Jamie cried. Cut it out you two, Yvette kept saying, and she let them out and Adam skidded on the wet snow and fell against the car and cried.

Unpack the bags while Adam and Jamie fight over children's programmes on one or three, Phil not home for tea again, waffles and sausages on the grill, Adam wants spaghetti hoops, Jamie beans, neither of them like the sausages, Adam kicks Jamie's chair throughout the meal, Mum tell him, tell him Mum, and afterwards snow falls again, a few light flakes at first, then thicker, faster, until it's like looking at the world through a mass of lace curtains. Yvette could hardly see the house opposite, but she was sure there was still no light from it.

Mum can we play outside?

Not while it's snowing.

Ple-e-ease.

Usher them into the front room, get out the train set and garage, put the video on, wonder what time Phil will be home, new management job, mustn't complain, wonder what everyone else is doing, peer into the impenetrable white and wonder what she is doing, Mrs Stowe, all by herself all day long in this weather. There was no excuse for it really, Yvette told herself, she should have called over long since to see if she was all right, if she needed anything from the shops.

Mum, can I call for Christopher?

When the snow stops.

I want to go now.

Later, after the endless chivvying that got the kids into bed, half an hour early, even though Jamie can tell the time now, Yvette began to think about food herself. Last night's cheese and onion pie was in the oven for Phil, she didn't fancy it herself, just a bowl of cereal. Her meals were getting more and more erratic, less thought out, who had time to think? But she was getting, not exactly fat, but dumpy. An Yvette should never be dumpy. Such a glamorous name, older people said, kids just took the piss. But she was definitely getting dumpy, she would be just like a barrel soon, small bust and hips, no waist. And mumsy. No matter how many instructions she gave the new hairdresser on the Brew she always came out looking mumsy.

Dumpy and mumsy. Thirty-five next birthday and no job.

She doesn't want a job.

On telly there is one of those wildlife programmes, or is it a vet? Anyway, someone is doing unsavoury things to a dead deer, probing its distended belly, probably the poor thing was pregnant. Then the man in the plastic gloves presses right down into the belly and from a wound or incision a cloud of flies appears.

Yvette doesn't feel like cereal any more.

Yvette brought the milk in. She didn't linger on the step this time because of the wind whipping the fallen snow upwards around her nightie. Shut the door quick, stand the milk in a pan of water to thaw, cold milk for Adam's cocoa pops, hot for Jamie's frosted wheats, bread on the grill for herself. There was the sound of furious fighting from upstairs, and through the kitchen window she could see birds blown in all directions by the wind, struggling to fly one way, being blown another.

Yvette knows how they feel.

Upstairs to separate Jamie and Adam, make them pack for school, wellies, lunch boxes, PE kit, books, stand over them while they eat breakfast, Adam doesn't like cocoa pops any more, Jamie wants toast, get them dressed and into the car.

*

It would be terrible, Yvette thought, if Mrs Stowe died over there and no one noticed. She scoured the bottom of the grill pan which was thick with grease from yesterday's sausages, trying to remember who did call at Mrs Stowe's. A home help Thursdays and a small van like an ambulance came every Tuesday to take her to some day-care centre. There was no family that Yvette could see. Four years ago, when Yvette and Phil first moved in, she used to stand outside her front door in all weathers, nodding at everyone who went past, but her legs must have got worse in the past year or two because now, even in the summer, she stays indoors.

But today the water board were arriving and had to dig up the entire back to get to the common supply pipe, Yvette had to be in to give them access. And Phil would be home early for once and they would all eat together, look in the fridge, nothing much of anything in but milk, far too much milk, the milkman never seemed to read the notes she left. Well, she could do a cauliflower cheese if she had a cauliflower. Or cheese. Hard to believe she had only shopped yesterday, maybe Penny next door would have the keys while she slipped into the shop.

When Yvette did go to the shop it seemed that all the old people were out, edging their way towards the one shop Blackshaw possessed, a Post Office that sold groceries, hardware and newspapers, handbags and gardening equipment, and clothes, and everyone was talking to one another, the snow made everyone talk.

Terrible isn't it.

I wish I'd got skis.

Careful Mrs Newsome, no hurdling for you in this weather.

Then Eddie Price the postman asked Yvette if she knew she had a dead cat on her head, cheeky monkey, and pretended to stop her going into the shop, and the effect of all this chat was to make Yvette think even harder about Mrs Stowe and how she got on all day with no one to talk to.

She wasn't the only neighbour, she told herself, cutting into the large and rather speckled cauliflower. There was no reason why she, out of all the neighbours, should take it on herself to call round.

Yvette couldn't see her winter-flowering pansies surviving through this lot, the third heavy snowfall that week. She had arranged them rather tastefully, she thought, surrounding the ornamental cabbage, in the two tubs she had instead of a garden. Now the snow had formed a perfect smooth cap over each tub, and there was ice on the path beneath the snow. Yvette had bought salt to pour on it in the hope of avoiding an accident.

Even from outside Yvette could hear the boys arguing indoors.

Anyway you couldn't have killed one, Jamie was saying, because there aren't any.

There are!

If she did go and knock on Mrs Stowe's door, she told herself, she might only disturb her. Suppose she was asleep, or in the bath? You never knew when it was a good time to call.

There weren't any people when there were dinosaurs.

There were.

There weren't.

Yes there were.

Anyway there weren't any dinosaurs, that's just cartoons.

Bicker, bicker, bicker, it went on all day every day, and every day went on just like the last. Yvette shook the last salt out of the carton and sighed, feeling unaccountably down.

Yvette rang Mrs Stowe's doorbell, which was connected to an

intercom, she noticed, after all that worry about making her come to the door.

Who is it? came a surprisingly strong, gravelly voice, and Yvette, feeling foolish now, said,

My name's Yvette Walker, Mrs Stowe, I live just across the way, and the buzzer buzzed and Yvette pushed the door, then, when it didn't move, put her shoulder to it until the stiffness gave way.

Inside was almost complete darkness; darkness and the old-woman smell of closed doors and windows, soiled clothing. Yvette couldn't even tell where Mrs Stowe was until the voice said,

Over here, by the back window.

Though it was dark outside, the window was a square of blue light against the deeper darkness of the room. Yvette fumbled her way towards the light, which was the deep, uninterrupted blue of a winter night, lightened by fallen snow. When a car travelled slowly along the main road a beam of light illuminated one section of the room then another, the flowered sofa, some kind of dresser, Mrs Stowe's walking frame and her legs, which were stuck out in front of her like two sticks.

Phil had talked Yvette into this; well not talked exactly, he had laughed, shaking his head, when she told him she had been thinking about calling on Mrs Stowe. She was always thinking about doing things, he'd said, and not doing them. And she had snapped right back at him, Well, I'll go now then, you put the kids to bed.

Shall I put the light on, she said, thinking that perhaps Mrs Stowe couldn't get to the switch.

I like the dark.

There didn't seem to be anything to say to this, so Yvette started to explain again that she lived across the road.

I know who you are, Mrs Stowe said, and she picked up her

stick to indicate the seat opposite and it clanged against her walking frame.

Sorry, she said. Sit down.

Yvette perched on the seat.

You've got them two little boys.

That's right, and Yvette thought of them briefly, wondering if they were playing up for their father, though when she'd left them in the bath they'd been happy enough, blowing long bubbles through their hands and using up all her soap.

very nice of you to call.

O no, I mean, it's silly isn't it, I've been meaning to for months. I just came, really, to give you my phone number and say if there's anything I can do, you know . . .

Mrs Stowe looked at her enquiringly, and Yvette couldn't help but notice what a large, craggy face she had.

How old are they?

What? O, six and a half and nearly five . . .

What are they called?

Jamie and Adam.

Is Adam the oldest?

. . . No.

Firstborn. Adam means that you know.

Yes.

It had been pointed out before.

Phil chose it. I chose Jamie's name and then Phil chose Adam.

They're nice names anyroad.

Encouraged, Yvette said,

Do you have any children, and a strange look passed over Mrs Stowe's face, but she turned away to the window and said, No, not me.

Not as such anyroad, she said, and Yvette didn't feel she could ask any further.

Outside orange light from the street lamps fell on the children's playground, which was empty now of course, swings and slide neatly capped with snow.

I watch them playing of course, said Mrs Stowe, and Yvette thought of saying that must be nice, only of course she didn't know that it was, they might be screaming and swearing, kicking balls at the window for all she knew, so she just said O.

Yvette's a nice name as well, she said, turning back from the window with a craggy smile. Unusual like. Were you named after someone?

Yvette had to think for a moment.

Y-vette

teacher's pet

she's so wet,

was what she thought, but she said, It was someone my grand-mother used to write to. So I was told anyway. Kind of a pen-friend.

Bloody silly reason for naming someone.

Someone French?

I think so.

No one French in the family then.

No.

As she said this, Yvette felt she should know more really, to tell Mrs Stowe, but she had never wanted to know the full story, she had always been so cross about her name. She wondered what Mrs Stowe's first name was, and thought of asking, but changed her mind, and remembering why she had come said,

Shall I write my number down then.

Mrs Stowe pushed a notepad towards her and there was a pencil attached to it by a piece of string. Yvette wrote her number down in a business-like way and Mrs Stowe said again,

It's very kind of you.

Well, Yvette said. It's silly, isn't it, calling someone else when I'm just across the road.

How do you manage? she wanted to say.

How do you get anything done?

How on earth do you pass the time?

She was near enough to Mrs Stowe to hear the hoarse rattle of her breath and, just as if she heard her thinking, the old woman smiled again faintly.

We none of us think we'll come to this, she said.

Yvette blushed.

No, she said, but Mrs Stowe wasn't listening. Leaning forwards into the window she said,

Stars are out,

and in what Yvette had thought was the even blue of the sky she could now see a faint, winking star.

Do you know, Mrs Stowe said suddenly, if Spiritualist Church is still there?

Surprised, Yvette said, I think so. Yes, she knew it was, more of a big house than a church, on the main road between Blackshaw and Harrop. Blackshaw and Harrop National Spiritualist Church, it said on a plaque outside. Established 1917.

There used to be a medium there, Mrs Stowe went on, called Edie May. There's a name for you. I was never much for it, all this communicating with the other side, but Maggie, my sister, always wanted to go, especially after our mother died. It'd be a comfort, she used to say to me, and so we went regular, never missed. We never got any messages though. And them as did I weren't impressed by. Anyone here know a Jack, and Doris says keep your feet warm, that kind of thing. Funny reason to cross the Great Divide if you ask me, just to tell someone to keep their feet warm.

Yvette giggled sympathetically.

She were a big woman, Edie May, with a big chin and a shilling on her head as we say in Lancashire – thought she were someone. Anyway, I got a bit sick of it all, and one night I think it showed. Because she came up to me and said, You're surrounded by spirits, young lady, but you won't let them in.

Seeds falling on stony ground, she said. Well I didn't take any notice, in fact that were the last time I went. I was a bit disgusted like. But now, well, I know Edie May must be dead long since. But sometimes I think I'd like to go again.

Couldn't anyone take you, Yvette said after a pause, but Mrs Stowe shook her head.

It's the stairs, she said. And the seating. I can't sit on benches. This is the only seat in the house I can sit on.

Yvette leaned forwards a little, almost wanting to touch the legs which seemed so cold and dead.

Do they hurt, she said quietly.

No no, Mrs Stowe said laughing. Can't feel them at all. She looked at Yvette looking at her legs.

They used to work you know, she said. I used to be fit and active.

Yvette stopped looking.

I walked miles over these hills, she said. Delivering. Groceries and stuff. Post. She paused a moment while Yvette thought of asking her about this former career, then she said,

There's no safety you know.

No, said Yvette. She knew that. You couldn't be a mother and not know that. Not when Jamie could come home from school one day perfectly well and an hour later have a temperature of a hundred and five and his neck thrown back all stiff, they had to rush him into hospital. Or when Adam could swallow the top off a bottle and nearly choke to death. Yvette often said that was when her hair started to go grey, she said it jokingly but privately she considered it to be true.

Mrs Stowe leaned towards the window again.

That's Maggie's boy, Frank.

Outside an elderly man and woman crossed the little park, the light from the lamp shading them orange and brown.

That's your nephew then, Yvette said, surprised, as the old couple disappeared into the passageway between the terraces on the other side of the park.

Maggie's boy, Mrs Stowe said, in such a disparaging tone that Yvette didn't bother to ask if he ever called by.

He were first to say he'd seen things, Mrs Stowe went on. He couldn't have been more than eight when he said he'd seen his dad's Uncle Eddie the night he died. And now he'd tell you it were all nonsense. He doesn't want to know. But I know different.

Yvette laughed again, then thought maybe that wasn't the right thing to do.

The dead are around us all the time, Mrs Stowe said. Sometimes you don't even realize you're looking right at them.

Yvette thought it might be time to go.

Little Tom now, Mrs Stowe said, I see him on playground with the other children, broad daylight and everything. I used to wonder why the others weren't playing with him, then I realized they didn't know he was there.

A beam of light passed over Mrs Stowe's face and Yvette thought it lit up her eyes very strangely.

He knows I can see him, she went on. He always looks for me now and waves. I don't think he ever had a playground when he was alive so he likes to play on them now. Makes sense really, Mrs Stowe said.

Yvette didn't know what to say to any of this. Alzheimer's, she thought. Senile dementia, though the old woman seemed calm enough.

The one in the house gave me a bit of a turn though, she went on. The first time I saw the girl she was standing by the sink leaning over, just as if she was washing up. But when I looked again there was blood pouring from her mouth.

Yvette's hand flew to her own mouth.

She wasn't trying to frighten me, Mrs Stowe said earnestly. She was trying to let me know, like, how she died. TB. Just like my mother. I never saw her haemorrhaging again. She just comes and goes around the house, quite at home. I think she used to live here, myself. And I think she's called Miriam, but I don't know. I don't mind her being here. It's company for me you see.

Yvette felt she had heard enough.

I'd best be getting back, she said, that is, if I can't do anything? but Mrs Stowe was looking out of the window.

Sometimes I wonder why I don't see anyone I know, she said. My mother, like, or even Edie May. I'd like to see her again, just once, just to let her know she was right.

Yvette stood up.

I'll have to be going, she said, and she moved towards the door. But if there's anything you need at all . . .

Mrs Stowe looked at her.

It's very nice of you, she said. Don't let me keep you.

No, said Yvette, I'd better go. The kids are with their father, and she managed a smile of collusion at the uselessness of men, but Mrs Stowe didn't smile back, she just looked at Yvette, and Yvette said quickly that she'd be in touch, and Mrs Stowe only had to ring, then she opened the door and it clicked to behind her, and she was outside, breathing in the cold, clean air.

Cars were double parked, either side of the road, though people had been asked often enough not to, and most were on double yellow lines; it was dangerous because the road was narrow enough already and the weight of traffic too heavy for it, it made Yvette angry that people did it even where children had to cross, so angry she was shaking and had some trouble getting the key in her door.

The door opened onto a quiet house and Yvette was thankful for that. Either the kids were asleep already or Phil was reading to them, Yvette had been in that dark house longer than she'd thought. And even though the light was on overhead and the little lamp she felt as though she'd brought the darkness in with her. Poor, crazy old woman, she thought, pulling off her coat. That was what happened when you were cooped up all day in a dark smelly house, and it flashed across Yvette's mind as she tapped the snow off her boots that all the things she had to do every day, shifting dirty washing, filling in forms, shopping, cutting out coupons for the shopping, cleaning the kids' shoes, all the hundreds of little jobs that filled her time and annoyed her, propped her up somehow, kept her normal. Who knew what she might be like without them? Still, she felt not so much sympathetic as repelled, as though her ears had been rinsed in dirt.

Even so, as she sank down finally on the settee, she allowed herself a small smile. All those stories, she thought to herself, in one little conversation. People were full of stories, they welled up the moment you started listening to them, and once you started listening there was no end to it, it was like water welling up from holes in the ground, or, Yvette suddenly thought, like all those flies coming out of that dead deer.

Or like the flakes of snow, she thought the next morning at breakfast, falling endlessly, everywhere. She put cereal bowls on the table in a listless way, thinking about Jamie's temperature and whether or not to send him to school, then she wandered back to the window, gazing out again into the snow, wondering if it would finish soon, feeling drawn by it, hypnotized. When she looked upwards into it the snow was very different, angled peculiarly, hurtling forwards, until Yvette drew back in a kind of confusion, reminded of what Mrs Stowe had said about safety. The snow was like all the stories, she thought, coming endlessly out of nowhere, because there wasn't any safety.

Yvette brought the milk in, glancing out of habit over to Mrs Stowe's dark windows, shivering briefly and checking the sky for more snow, sniffing at it for a moment like a dog.

Jamie was well enough now and would go back to school today, but Adam had woken up at four in the morning and climbed into bed between Phil and Yvette, wanting to talk.

Mum, why are lights yellow?

Mum, wood is made of metal, isn't it?

Phil had grunted and turned his back. Yvette said Mmm, mmm, and eventually fell asleep again, waking up to a lightening sky, and as she turned round Adam said, just as if he'd been waiting all the time for her to wake up,

Mum, the blue sky is like water, isn't it?

And part of Yvette's mind admired him for saying that, it was so pretty, and part of it, aching with sleep, was critical, because really water wasn't like that at all, and anyway, what kind of water, tap water, rain water? Now though, still standing at the door, holding her dressing gown around her, she could see that the sky was like the flat, still water of a lake, clear and cold as glass, so that as you looked up into it, you might almost expect to see, reflected there, whole and perfect, an image of the round, turning earth.

Girl

Hanif Kureishi

They got on at Victoria Station and sat together, kissing lightly. As the train pulled away, she took out her Nietzsche tome and began to read. Turning to the man at her side she became amused by his face, which she studied continually. Removing her gloves she picked shaving cream from his ears, sleep from his eyes and crumbs from his mouth, while laughing to herself. The combination of his vanity, mixed with unconscious naiveté, usually charmed her.

Nicole hadn't wanted to visit her mother after all this time, but Majid, her older lover – it sounded trite calling him her 'boyfriend' – had persuaded her to. He was curious of everything about her; it was part of love. He said it would be good for her to 're-connect'; she was stronger now. However, during the past year, when Nicole had refused to speak to her, and ensured her mother didn't have her address, she had suppressed many tormenting thoughts from the past, ghosts she dreaded returning as a result of this trip.

Couldn't Majid sense how uneasy she was? Probably he could. She had never had anyone listen to her so attentively or take her so seriously, as if he wanted to occupy every part of her. He had the strongest will of anyone she'd known, apart from her father. He was used to having things his own way, and he often disregarded what she wanted. He was afraid she would run away.

He had never met her mother. She might be incoherent, or in one of her furies, or worse. As it was, her mother had cancelled the proposed visit three times, once in a drunken voice that was on the point of becoming spiteful. Nicole didn't want Majid to think that she – half her mother's age – would resemble her at fifty. He had recently told Nicole that he considered her to be, in some sense, 'dark'. Nicole was worried that her mother would find Majid also dark, but in the other sense.

Almost as soon as it left the station, their commuter train crossed the sparkling winter river. It would pass through the suburbs and then the countryside, arriving after two hours at a seaside town. Fortunately, theirs wasn't a long journey, and next week, they were going to Rome; in January he was taking her to India. He wanted her to see Calcutta. He wouldn't travel alone any more. His pleasure was only in her.

Holding hands they looked out at Victorian schools and small garages located under railway arches. There were frozen football pitches, allotments and the backs of industrial estates where cork tiles and bathroom fittings were manufactured, as well as carpet warehouses and metalwork shops. When the landscape grew more open, railway tracks stretched in every direction, a fan of possibility. Majid said that passing through the outskirts of London reminded him what an old country Britain was, and how manifestly dilapidated.

She dropped her hand in his lap and stroked him as he took everything in, commenting on what he saw. He looked handsome in his silk shirt, scarf and raincoat. She dressed for him too, and couldn't go into a shop without wondering what would please him. A few days before, she'd had her dark hair cut into a bob that skimmed the fur collar of the overcoat she was wearing with knee-length motorcycle boots. At her side was the shoulder bag in which she carried her vitamin pills, journal and lip-salve, and the mirror which had convinced her that her eye-lids were developing new folds and lines as they shrivelled up. That morning she'd plucked her first grey hair from her head and placed it inside a book. Yet she still had spots, one on her cheek and one on her upper lip. Before they left, Majid had made her conceal them with make-up, which she never wore.

'In case we run into anyone I know,' he said.

He was well-connected, but she was sure he wouldn't know anyone in Croydon. Yet she had obeyed.

She forced herself back to the book. Not long after they met, eighteen months ago, he remarked, 'You've been to university but things must have changed since my day.' It was true she didn't know certain words: 'confound', 'pejorative', 'empirical'. In the house they now shared, he had thousands of books and was familiar with all the writers, composers and painters. As he pointed out, she hadn't even heard of 'Gauguin'. Sometimes, when he was talking to his friends she had no idea what they were discussing, and became convinced that if her ignorance didn't trouble him it was because he valued only her youth.

Certainly he considered conversation a pleasure. There had recently occurred an instructive incident when they dropped in for tea on the mother of her best friend. This woman, a sociology lecturer, had known Nicole from the age of thirteen, and probably continued to think of her as poignantly deprived. Nicole thought of her as cool, experienced and, above all, knowledgeable. Five years ago, when one of her mother's boyfriends had stabbed Nicole's brother, this woman had taken Nicole in for a few weeks. Nicole had sat numbly in her flat, surrounded by walls of books and pictures. All of it, apart from the occasional piece of soothing music, seemed vain and irrelevant.

Visiting with Majid she had, by midnight, only succeeded in detaching his hand from the woman's. Nicole had then to get him to leave, or at least relinquish the bottle of whisky. Meanwhile the woman was confessing her most grievous passions and telling Majid that she'd seen him address a demonstration in the seventies. A man like him, she cried, required a substantial woman! It was only when she went to fetch her poetry, which she intended to read to him, that Nicole could get the grip on his hair she needed to extract him.

By providing her with the conversations she'd longed for, he had walked in and seduced her best friend's mother! Nicole had felt extraneous. Not that he had noticed. Pushing him out of there, she was reminded of the time, around the age of fourteen, she'd had to get her mother out of a neighbour's house, dragging her across the road, her legs gone, and the whole street watching.

He laughed whenever she recalled the occasion, but it troubled her. It wasn't the learning that mattered. Majid had spent much of his youth reading, and lately had wondered what adventures he had been keeping himself from. He claimed that books could get in the way of what was important between people. But she couldn't sit, or read or write or do nothing without seeking company, having never been taught the benefits of solitude. The compromise they reached was this: when she read he would lie beside her, watching her eyes, sighing as her fingers turned a page.

No; his complaint was that she couldn't convert feelings into words and expected him to understand her by clairvoyance.

Experience had taught her to keep her mouth shut. She'd spent her childhood among rough people it amused Majid to hear about, as if they were cartoon characters. But they had been menacing. Hearing some distinction in your voice, they would suspect you of ambition and therefore of the desire to leave them behind. For this you would be envied, derided, hated; London was considered 'fake' and the people duplicitous. Considering this, she'd realized that every day for most of her life she had been physically and emotionally afraid. Even now she couldn't soften, unless she was in bed with Majid, fearing that if she wasn't vigilant, she would be sent back home on the train.

She turned a few pages of the book, took his arm and snuggled into him. They were together, and loved one another. But there were unaccustomed fears. As Majid reminded her when they argued, he had relinquished his home, wife and children for her. That morning, when he had gone to see the children and to talk about their schooling, she'd become distraught waiting for him, convinced he was sleeping with his wife and would return to her. It was deranging, wanting someone so much. How could you ever get enough of them? Maybe it was easier not to want at all. When one of the kids was unwell, he had stayed the night at his former house. He wanted to be a good father, he explained, adding in a brusque tone that she'd had no experience of that.

She had gone out in her white dress and not come home. She had enjoyed going to clubs and parties, staying out all night and sleeping anywhere. She had scores of acquaintances who it was awkward introducing to Majid, as he had little to say to them. 'Young people aren't interesting in themselves any more,' he said sententiously.

He maintained that it was she who was drawing away from them. It was true that these friends – whom she had seen as free spirits, and who now lay in their squats virtually inert with drugs – lacked imagination, resolution and ardour, and that she found it difficult to tell them of her life, fearing they would resent her. But Majid, once the editor of radical newspapers, could be snobbish. On this occasion he accused her of treating him like a parent or flat-mate, and of not understanding she was the first woman he couldn't sleep without. Yet hadn't she waited two years while he was sleeping with someone else? If she recalled the time he went on holiday with his family, informing her the day before, even as he asked her to marry him, she could beat her head against the wall. His young children were beautiful, but in the park people assumed they were hers. They looked like the mother, and connected him with her for ever. Nicole had said she didn't want them coming to the house. She had wanted to punish him, and destroy everything.

Should she leave him? Falling in love was simple; one had only to yield. Digesting another person however, and sustaining a love, was bloody work, and not a soft job. Feeling and fear rushed through her constantly. If only her mother were sensible and accessible. As for the woman she usually discussed such subjects with – the mother of her best friend – Nicole was too embarrassed to return. Oh, to fall in love was to contemplate the gates of hell! But what else was there?

She noticed that the train was slowing down.

'Is this it?' he said.

'Fraid so.'

'Can't we go on to the seaside?'

She replaced her book and put her gloves on.

'Majid, another day.'

'Yes, yes, there's time for everything.'

He took her arm.

They left the station and joined a suburban area of underpasses, glass office blocks, hurrying crowds, stationary derelicts and stoned young people in flimsy clothing. 'Bad America' Majid called it. He'd been everywhere.

They queued twenty minutes for a bus. She wouldn't let him

hail a taxi. For some reason she thought it would be condescending. And she didn't want to get there too soon.

They sat in the front, at the top of the wide double-decker, as it took them away from the centre. They swept through winding lanes and passed fields. He was surprised the slow, heavy bus ascended the hills at all. This was not the city and not the country; it was not anything but grassy areas, arcades of necessary shops, churches and suburban houses. She pointed out the school she'd attended, shops she'd worked in for a pittance, parks in which she waited for various boyfriends.

It was a fearful place for him too. His father had been an Indian politician and when his parents separated he had been brought up by his mother eight miles away. They liked to talk about the fact that he was at university when Nicole was born; that when she was just walking he was living with his first wife; that he might have patted Nicole's head as he passed her on the street. They shared the fantasy that for years he had been waiting for her to grow up.

It was cold when they got down. The wind cut across the open spaces. Already it seemed to be getting dark. They walked further than he'd imagined they would have to, and across muddy patches. He complained that she should have told him to wear different shoes.

He suggested they take something for her mother. He could be very polite. He even said 'excuse me' in bed if he made an abrupt movement. They went into a brightly lit supermarket and asked for flowers; there were none. He asked for Lapsang Souchong tea bags but before the assistant could reply, Nicole pulled him out.

The area was sombre but not grim, though a swastika had been painted on a fence. Her mother's house was set on a grassy bank, in a sixties estate, with a view of a park. As they approached

Nicole's feet seemed to drag. Finally she halted and opened her coat.

'Put your arms around me.' He felt her shivering. She said, 'I can't go in unless you say you love me.'

'I love you,' he said, holding her. 'Marry me.'

She was kissing his forehead, eyes, mouth. 'No one has ever cared for me like you.'

He repeated, 'Marry me. Say you will, say it.'

'Oh I don't know,' she replied.

She crossed the garden and tapped on the window. Immediately her mother came to the door. The hall was narrow. The mother kissed her daughter, and then Majid, on the cheek.

'I'm pleased to see you,' she said, shyly. She didn't appear to have been drinking. She looked Majid over and said, 'Do you want a tour?' She seemed to expect it.

'That would be lovely,' he said.

Downstairs the rooms were square, painted white but otherwise bare. The ceilings were low, the carpet thick and green. A brown three-piece suite – each item seemed to resemble a boat – was set in front of the television.

Nicole was eager to take Majid upstairs. She led him through the rooms which had been the setting for the stories she'd told. He tried to imagine the scenes. But the bedrooms that had once been inhabited by lodgers – van drivers, removal men, postmen, labourers – were empty. The wallpaper was gouged and discoloured, the curtains hadn't been washed for a decade, nor the windows cleaned; rotten mattresses were parked against the walls. In the hall the floorboards were bare, with nails sticking out of them. What to her reverberated with remembered life was squalor to him.

As her mother poured juice for them, her hands shook, and it splashed on the table.

'It's very quiet,' he said, to the mother. 'What do you do with yourself all day?'

She looked perplexed but thought for a few moments.

'I don't really know,' she said. 'What does anyone do? I used to cook for the men but running around after them got me down.'

Nicole got up and went out of the room. There was a silence. Her mother was watching him. He noticed that there appeared to be purplish bruises under her skin.

She said, 'Do you care about her?'

He liked the question.

'Very much,' he said. 'Do you?'

She looked down. She said, 'Will you look after her?'

'Yes. I promise.'

She nodded. 'That's all I wanted to know. I'll make your dinner.'

While she cooked, Nicole and Majid waited in the lounge. He said that, like him, she seemed only to sit on the edge of the furniture. She sat back self-consciously. He started to pace about, full of things to say.

Her mother was intelligent and dignified, he said, which must have been where Nicole inherited her grace. But the place, though it wasn't sordid, was desolate.

'Sordid? Desolate? Not so loud! What are you talking about?'

'You said your mother was selfish. That she always put herself, and her men friends in particular, before her children.'

'I did say . . .'

'Well, I had been expecting a woman who cosseted herself. But I've never been in a colder house.' He indicated the room. 'No mementos, no family photographs, not one picture. Everything personal has been erased. There is nothing she has made, or chosen to reflect . . .'

'You only do what interests you,' Nicole said. 'You work, sit on

234

boards, eat, travel and talk. "Only do what gives you pleasure", you say to me constantly.'

'I'm a sixties kid,' he said. 'It was a romantic age.'

'Majid, the majority can't live such luxurious lives. They never did. Your sixties is a great big myth.'

'It isn't the lack of opulence which disturbs me, but the poverty of imagination. It makes me think of what culture means . . .'

'It means showing off and snobbery . . .'

'Not that aspect of it. Or the decorative. But as indispensable human expression, as a way of saying "Here there is pleasure, desire, life! This is what people have made!"'

He had said before that literature, indeed, all culture, was a celebration of life, if not a declaration of love for things.

'Being here,' he continued, 'it isn't people's greed and selfishness that surprises me. But how little people ask of life. What meagre demands they make, and the trouble they go to, to curb their hunger for experience.'

'It might surprise you,' she said, 'because you know successful egotistical people who do what they love. But most people don't do much of anything most of the time. They only want to get by another day.'

'Is that so?' He thought about this and said that every day he awoke ebulliently and full of schemes. There was a lot he wanted, of the world and of other people. He added, 'And of you.'

But he understood sterility because despite all the 'culture' he and his second wife had shared, his six years with her had been arid. And now he had this love, and he knew it was love because of the bleakness that preceded it, which had enabled him to see what was possible.

She kissed him. 'Precious, precious,' she said.

She pointed to the bolted door she had mentioned to him. She wanted to go downstairs. But her mother was calling them.

They sat down in the kitchen where two places had been laid. Nicole and her mother saw him looking at the food.

'Seems a bit funny giving Indian food to an Indian,' the mother said. 'I didn't know what you eat.'

'That's all right,' he said.

She added, 'I thought you'd be more Indian, like.'

He waggled his head. 'I'll try to be.' There was a silence. He said to her, 'It was my birthday yesterday.'

'Really?' said the mother.

She and her daughter looked at one another and laughed.

While he and Nicole ate, the mother, who was very thin, sat and smoked. Sometimes she seemed to be watching them and other times fell into a kind of reverie. She was even-tempered and seemed prepared to sit there all day. He found himself seeking the fury in her, but she looked more resigned than anything, reminding him of himself in certain moods: without hope or desire, all curiosity suppressed in the gloom and agitated muddle of her mind.

After a time she said to Nicole, 'What are you doing with yourself? How's work?'

'Work? I've given up the job. Didn't I tell you?'

'At the television programme?'

'Yes.'

'What for? It was a lovely job!'

Nicole said, 'It wore me out for nothing. I'm getting the strength to do what I want, not what I think I ought to do.'

'What's that supposed to mean?' her mother said. 'You stay in bed all day?'

'We only do that sometimes,' Majid murmured.

Her mother said, 'I can't believe you gave up such a job! I can't even get work in a shop. They said I wasn't experienced enough. I said, what experience do you need to sell bread rolls?'

In a low voice Nicole talked of what she'd been promising herself – to draw, dance, study philosophy, get healthy. She would follow what interested her. Then she caught his eye, having been reminded of one of the strange theories that puzzled and alarmed her. He maintained that it wasn't teaching she craved, but a teacher, someone to help and guide her; perhaps a kind of husband. She found herself smiling at how he brought everything back to them.

'Must be lovely,' her mother said. 'Just doing what you want.'

'I'll be all right,' Nicole said.

'Yes,' he said.

After lunch, in the lounge, Nicole pulled the brass bolt and he accompanied her down a dark flight of stairs. This was the basement where she and her brother and sister used to sleep, Nicole wearing a knitted hat and scarf, as her mother would heat only the front room. The damp room opened on to a small garden where the children had to urinate if the bolt was across. Beyond there were fields.

Late at night they would listen to the yells and crashes upstairs. If one of her mother's boyfriends – whichever man it was who had taken her father's place – had neglected to bolt the door, Nicole would put on her overcoat and wellington boots and creep upstairs. The boots were required because of overturned ashtrays and broken glass. She would ensure her mother hadn't been cut or beaten, and try to persuade everyone to go to bed. One morning there had been indentations in the wall, along with the remains of hair and blood, where her mother's head had been banged against it. A few times the police came.

Majid watched as Nicole went through files containing old school books, magazines, photographs. She opened several sacks and hunted through them for some clothes she wanted to take back to London. This would take some time. He decided to go upstairs and wait for her. As he went, he passed the mother.

He walked about, wondering where in the house, when Nicole was ten, her father had hanged himself. He hadn't been able to ask. He thought of what it would be like to be living an ordinary life, and the next day your husband is self-murdered, leaving you with three children.

On returning he paused at the top of the stairs. They were talking; no – arguing. The mother's voice, soft and contained earlier, had gained a furious edge. The house seemed transparent. He could hear them, just as her mother must have heard him.

'If he's asked you,' she was saying, 'and if he means it, you should say yes. And if you're jealous of his bloody kids, have some with him. That'll keep him to you. He's well-off and brainy, he can have anyone. D'you know what he sees in you, apart from sex?'

'He says he loves me.'

'You're not having me on? Does he support you?'

'Yes.'

'Really?'

'Yes.'

Quietly Majid sat down on the top step. Nicole was struggling to maintain the dignity and sense she'd determined on that morning.

The mother said, 'If you stop working you might end up with nothing. Like I did. Better make sure he don't run off with someone younger and prettier.'

'Why should he do that?' Nicole said sullenly.

'He's done it already.'

'When?'

'Idiot, with you.'

'Yes, yes, he has.'

'Men are terrible beasts.'

'Yes, yes.'

Her mother said, 'If it's getting you down, you can always stay here . . . for a while.' She hesitated. 'It won't be like before. I won't bother you.'

'I might do that. Can I?'

'You'll always be my baby.'

Nicole must have been pulling boxes around; her breathing became heavier.

'Nicole don't make a mess in my house. It'll be me who'll have to clear everything up. What are you looking for?'

'I had a picture of father.'

'I didn't know you had one.'

'Yes.' Shortly after, Nicole said, 'Here it is.'

He imagined them standing together, examining it.

'Before he did it,' said the mother, 'he said he'd show us, teach us a lesson. And he did.'

She sounded as if she were proud of her husband.

Upstairs Nicole packed her clothes in a bag, then went back to find something in a cupboard; after this, there were other things she wanted.

'I must do this,' she said, hurrying around.

He realized that she might want to stay, that she might make him go back alone. He put on his coat. In the hall he waited restlessly.

The mother said to him, 'You're in a hurry.'

'Yes.'

'Is there something you have to get home for?'

He nodded. 'Lots of things.'

'You don't like it here, I can tell.'

He said nothing.

To his relief he saw Nicole emerge and put her scarf on. They kissed her mother and walked quickly back where they'd come. The bus arrived, and then they waited for the train, stamping their feet. As it pulled away, she took out her book. He looked at her; there were some things he wanted to ask, but she had put herself beyond his reach.

Near their house they stopped off to buy newspapers and magazines. Then they bought bread, pasta, hummus, yoghurt, wine, water, juice, Florentines. They unpacked it on the kitchen table, on which were piled books and CDs, invitations and birthday cards, with his children's toys scattered underneath. It was only then they realized she'd left the bag of clothes somewhere, probably on the train. Tears came to her eyes before she realized the clothes didn't matter; she didn't even want them, and he said she could buy more.

He sat at the table with the papers and asked her what music she was in the mood for, or if she didn't care. She shook her head and went to shower. Then she walked about naked, before spreading a towel on the floor and sitting on it to massage cream into her legs, sighing and humming as she did so. He started to prepare their supper, all the while watching her, which was one of his preferred occupations. Soon they would eat. After, they would take tea and wine to bed; lying there for hours, they would go over everything, knowing they would wake up with one another.

Summer of the Rats

Emily Perkins

Two winters ago the weather was especially mild. Many city rats survived, rather than dying off in large numbers as they usually do in the colder months. Their survival, aided by the piles of street rubbish left out by fast food stores, meant that the rat population of London increased by 40 per cent.
(Taxi driver, taking me to my boyfriend's flat at 3 am, 15 May)

We all stood there: me, my flatmate, my flatmate's girlfriend. We listened. That scrabbling sound was not the clicking of the immersion heater, or rubbish rustling past in the street outside. It was the noise of claws on plaster, claws in the wall, claws intent on getting out. The get-out claws, ha ha, said my flatmate as we stood, listening, waiting, trapped. Why do you live in a slum, said my flatmate's girlfriend, but nobody answered her. There was a final effort from within the wall, an almighty push, and a chunk of plaster hit the floor and shattered. Through the hole left by the plaster poked a ratty nose, ratty eyes, a long pale ratty body. It turned around and showed us its tail, ringed and thick. I thought I was possibly going to be sick.

When the rat problem came to light it was not something I could immediately deal with. It had to stand in line and queue for attention like all my other problems. Some days I didn't actually deal with any of them, I just spent my time arranging and rearranging them in differing orders of priority. Which was more important? My career, which was going nowhere; my relationship, which was going too many places all at once; my domestic situation, specifically the attitude problems of my flatmate's girlfriend, who was ten years younger than me and didn't know the meaning of respect. And then there were the by-problems of these larger issues: money, sex and self-esteem. So when Ratty made his first appearance through a hole in the wall of our flat, I looked up at his brazen little face and just said, Wait. Then over my pyjamas I put on a cardigan, a raincoat, an overcoat, a hat and a pair of boots, and I went out into the road to hail a taxi. What else could I do?

I am a photographer. My agent says I'm quite good, but not well known enough. She said I needed some free publicity. An article on me in a style magazine would have been perfect. The trouble was, I suspected, that I was not swanky enough for *Vogue*, and not street-cred enough for *The Face*. (I don't know if it's cool to say 'street-cred' any more – perhaps I am even more square than I'd thought.) Some monthly called *Zaza* professed interest in me, and for a weekend I was hopeful of imminent fame, but it turned out the proof-reader was looking for somebody to photograph her wedding. I don't do weddings. I don't even go to them. It's a source of disagreement between my boyfriend and me.

Our relationship had developed so quickly that, nine months in, we were behaving like a couple who'd been together for years. We'd almost completely stopped having sex. I only bothered to shave my legs if we were going out to a party. We both put on a

little weight, from sitting in front of the television eating unnec-
essary quantities of toast. My boyfriend was a lunch-hour chef at
an ironically trendy greasy spoon, and I liked to make him whip
up a full breakfast (bacon sausage bubble fried egg and tom-
ah'a) as practice before he went in to work. The weight problem
worsened. For the first time I was seriously wondering about
having a child. My sister said children are what people have
when their lives have hit a wall and they require a distraction. I
thought this was pretty harsh. She was going out with a man
who already had two children and I think what my sister
objected to was the specific distraction they created in his life,
the amount of time and affection he distractedly spent on them
and not on her. They're only young, I said to her (they were
twelve and fourteen), they're children for heaven's sake. You're
supposed to be the grown-up here. You're supposed to deal with
it. No, she said, it's not fair. Whoever told you that life was fair,
I said, like our mother would, and that made her laugh. What
about you, she said, you're supposed to be mature about your
flatmate's girlfriend. Shut up, I said, I am being mature.

There are certain things, I thought, that women should not be
allowed to do until they reach the age of thirty. For example, read
the novels of Jane Austen. A woman in her teens and twenties is
too undeveloped, too susceptible to the charms of a Mr Darcy,
too likely to believe in the lasting, smouldering passion of a
Captain Wentworth, too prone to disappointment and collapse
once she realizes – horror! – that love in the real world is Just
Not Like That. A woman a little older, however, will have been
around the block a bit and will recognize the yawning gap
between fiction and reality. Another thing that ought to be
banned is marriage, unless it is to a man of over thirty-five. The
mind-boggling divorce statistics these days are doubtless to do
with the fact that most men are indulging in a protracted

adolescence. On the whole these Lads should not be committed to until women are of an age to be able to keep them in line. I also believe that women under thirty should be barred from going out with my flatmate, ever. Or at least for as long as he's my flatmate. It's too much to expect a girl with minimal experience of the world to negotiate my mood swings, and besides, it's nauseating to watch her fawn and giggle over him at the same time as she turns her nose up at our living conditions. My flatmate's girlfriend is a model. This does not help.

Rats can squeeze through any gap, no matter how small or strangely shaped.
(My flatmate, 16 May)

I was at my neighbour's the next day, informing him of our rat sighting. He was not surprised. He has lived in the area much longer than us and his encounters with rats are many. Once, he told me, he was going for a night-time stroll when out of the corner of his eye he saw something dart out from a rubbish sack and felt it run across his sandalled foot. Why didn't you tell me this earlier, I asked, when we first moved in. He replied that he didn't really see the point. We had our hearts set on the area, which is both fashionable and relatively cheap, and it's true that any warnings about rodents would only have increased the intoxicating local atmosphere of urban decay. He asked me if I knew that there was currently a rat plague in Hanoi, where all the cats are being killed and served up cooked in restaurants. Then he made a crass joke about going to Vietnam for pussy, so I remembered some contact sheets I urgently had to pick up from the printers and said goodbye.

Over the phone to my agent, I casually mentioned the rat situation. She told me that the only things they cannot chew through are steel wool and cement. I was amazed at how much there was to learn about these small animals. My flatmate said yes, he'd bring home steel wool and cement, and he was cooking that night because his girlfriend was coming over with her friend. The girlfriend's friend was also a model. I didn't think there'd be much cooking required. After I'd cemented up the rat-hole I sat and watched them not eat, marvelling at the human capacity to survive on cigarettes and rice crackers. I've never had an eating disorder myself, which is why I remain behind the camera rather than in front of it. The girlfriend told her friend in great detail about our rat problem and they both squealed a lot. The friend, apparently, lived in her agency's ritzy apartment on the other side of the city, six floors up where vermin couldn't reach. For some reason I hated the idea of her going back and telling all those other skinny girls about the filthy nest she'd visited that night and how when she was my age there was no way she was still going to be stuck in grotty old London, by then she'd have made enough money off her looks to retire to a gorgeous big house in the country. Not that she said this to me, but she was one of those girls, you could tell, who liked dogs and Big Walks and who still looked beautiful with no make-up on. I consoled myself with the thought that the countryside is teeming with rats and mice. When I went upstairs to bed they were still at it. I was tempted to make a scrabbly noise on the floor, to encourage them to go home, but remembered just in time that I was the mature one in this situation.

We can't send someone round until next week because we have a lot of bookings at the moment.
(Local council vermin control department, 18 May)

The Spring wore on, full of wind and dust. Every now and then

I heard something in the walls, but I tried to ignore it. A couple of photography jobs came my way, which was good for the bank balance but bad for the ego. They were standard catalogue work, the sort of thing I'd done when first starting out, and I had assumed that after this many years I'd be permanently on to bigger and better things. As it was, I'd had one so-called glamourous job to date, but they hadn't run the photographs and ended up paying my costs and nothing more. I couldn't understand what they didn't like about the pictures, but they told me the models didn't have enough Attitude. In catalogues the models weren't required to have Attitude, unless it was to smile in an anodyne way. And to tell the truth some of the catalogues I'd been working for were from appliance manufacturers, or children's toy makers. I never needed to bother about what sort of emotion a washer-drier was putting across, only that its gleaming white surface didn't accidentally reflect me, the lights, and my camera.

The first really warm afternoon, me, my flatmate, his girlfriend and his girlfriend's friend sat drinking wine in the neighbour's back garden. Our neighbour was the only person in the street to have a back garden, and it was really the scrappy yard of the derelict house behind his. Still, he had some plants in large pots and a few deck-chairs: it gave the illusion of a tranquil country lawn. Kind of. Anyway, we were sitting there and I was playing with a new digital camera I had borrowed, wondering if I should buy one for myself. It had a tiny monitor on which you could see the image as it would look when photographed. You could take pictures on it and then decide whether or not to develop them etcetera. It was pretty neat but it was also pretty expensive, and these days things seemed to get out of date so easily it was hard to keep up.

The models latched on to the camera and squeaked and

goo-gooed over it. They quickly discovered that you could turn the lens right around to photograph yourself, and they studied themselves intently in the monitor, with much pouting and sucking in of non-existent cheeks. I could tell that my neighbour was interested in the flatmate's girlfriend's friend, but she wasn't responding to his special-attention treatment in any way. This surprised me, because my neighbour is a good-looking guy, and kind too. Girls usually go for him, and then he gets embroiled in all sorts of complicated scenarios, and sometimes he has to hide out at our place until everything blows over.

Whatever the reason, she wasn't paying much attention to anybody but herself. But we all sat there having a nice time, feeling the sun on our shoulders, sipping wine with ever-slowing movements of glass to mouth. Aren't we lucky, said my neighbour, to all be freelance? (He's a journalist.) Aren't we lucky not to be part of that mob of office-workers that stream in to the city every day, caged in their little offices, churning through their paperwork, oh it'd drive you mad. He gave the model's legs an appraising look. Thank God we have other talents, he announced. I didn't know. The freelance world was pretty precarious, I thought, and sometimes I longed for the stability of a daily grind. At that moment, there was a rustling from the unmown, straggly grass border along the side of the concrete fence. I looked, and could have sworn I saw a low brown figure streak through the grass and out a hole in the corner. Had the rat been listening? I realized that was the thought of a crazy person. We all stared at each other. I could see that the model friend was deciding between giggly hysteria or louche insouciance. She chose the latter, and rolled her eyes in an uncaring way. Rats, she said, huh. The rat population of London has increased by forty per cent these past few years. I shut my eyes, and didn't tell her that I'd told her that, last time she was round.

Rats do not have bladders or sphincters. They leave a small trail of rat urine with them wherever they go. This is why you must cover up all foodstuffs if you suspect rats in the kitchen.
(Taxi driver, 3.10am, 15 May)

My boyfriend and I really seemed to be in trouble. At the time I thought it was because his career was becoming more and more demanding and mine was in a state of – well, let's say I'd hit a plateau. Now I suspect that it's because he looked at me one day and saw somebody just over a stone heavier than the girl he'd started going out with nearly a year before. You'd imagine that women with a bit of flesh on them have more fun (and are therefore better) in the sack, but apparently not. Apparently, I read in a magazine, skinny women are the best in bed because they have greater body confidence than their chubbier sisters. And I have to say that my personal experience tallied with this probably unresearched, fabricated magazine article. My new weight hadn't filled me out in a sexy, voluptuous way. It had settled in uneven pools around my stomach and bottom, and made small thighs out of my upper arms. I lacked chin definition. This, combined with my career stasis, made me feel fairly unappealing, and our already ordinary sex life dwindled into nothing beyond the occasional shoulder rub. It seemed I was on the brink of losing both my glittering potential career, and my boyfriend.

It was in this gloomy state that I sat in my neighbour's flat, eating biscuits and drinking tea. The scratching noise in his walls was louder than in ours, like a faraway sawing sound. He was waiting for a phone call from an editor to tell him whether or not they wanted him to do a travel piece on the Seychelle Islands that month. If the answer was yes, it would mean having to go on an expenses-paid trip to the Seychelles, and having to snorkel in crystal clear waters and look at coral from a glass-bottomed boat and eat a lot of Creole food. Would he have to leave London, where nothing was air-conditioned and there were rats in the plaster, to go on this junket? If the paper offered it to him, he wouldn't want to offend them by saying no. It was a tense moment. While we were waiting, my neighbour's friend the artist dropped by. She is a reasonably well-known artist and mostly stages 'events' and 'interventions'. I didn't like discussing work with her because she always said Of course, in *commercial* photography . . . and things like that. It was hard to take that she had a) more artistic integrity than me, and b) was incredibly well paid for her work. Anyway, there she was, and there we were, three freelancers sitting around eating constant afternoon tea.

The artist lit a cigarette. She said, *What* is that *noise.*

Vermin, said my neighbour, looking pleased with himself. They live in the walls.

The artist put her head on an angle and listened. The skrtch-ing stopped and started again, as if for dramatic effect. *Brilliant,* she said. I could do an *amazing* sound piece in here.

My neighbour looked alarmed. You mean people would come into my house?

Yuck, I said.

Or – the artist started to smile. Or, do the rats venture out into the street ever?

Yeah a lot, said my neighbour and me at the same time.

OK, said the artist, visualize this. People are walking down the street, normal as anything –

They're not normal round here, my neighbour interjected.

Normal as anything, and then suddenly – around a corner – there are *piles* of rats, simply piles of them, swarming all over each other, gnawing at this piece of bloody meat. A heart, maybe. She exhaled smoke and nodded at us. Pure confrontation, yeah? That could really work.

Speaking of work, I said, I'd better get home. There are some ah, people I need to call.

But the artist had got me thinking. Maybe, if she went ahead with this piece, I could take some pictures of it to submit to magazines. That'd be edgy, that'd have attitude. Rat Art. She was right. It could work.

A mysterious telephone call came for my flatmate. The voice on the other end sounded just like the girlfriend's friend, model number two, but she wouldn't say who it was and didn't want to leave a message. The neighbour came over with a bottle of whisky. He didn't get the Seychelles junket and wanted to drown his sorrows. We were half-way through the bottle when my boyfriend came home after a cooking competition for one of the foody stylie mags. He was in a good mood because his dish, retro sausages and fried slice with a twist, had been awarded second prize. He was in a bad mood because I had completely forgotten about the competition, and especially forgotten it was that night. Well I see you were too busy to call and wish me luck, he said, and stormed upstairs to bed. The neighbour looked at me, his eyebrows raised. I shrugged and pushed my glass forward for topping up. Later, in the middle of the night, I woke up strangely dehydrated but too heavy with sleep to go and get a glass of water.

Rats' favourite food is chocolate.
(My neighbour, 22 June)

My sister and I went to the movies, even though it was a hot sunny afternoon. In the middle of it she leaned over to me and whispered, I think I might be pregnant. Will you come with me while I do a test? Sure, I whispered back, and sat through the rest of the movie unable to concentrate on any of it. If she was going to have a baby, that would be a whole new life. What would she have? What would it look like? Then again, what if she didn't want it? I hoped that her boyfriend, with his two children already, would let her get on with whatever decision she made. In the darkness we squeezed each other's hands.

But, the next day, she called to say that the test had been inconclusive and then she'd got the curse that morning. It seemed that this was the summer of things maybe happening, and then not. Do you think, she asked me, that either of us will ever have kids? Or do you think our family line will run out here, with us? That possibility had not occurred to me. Well, I said, I'm in no position to reproduce. I have no prospects and potentially no boyfriend. And there are rodents living in my house. Yeah, she said. I guess it's down to me. Yeah, I said, thinking of all she had been through in her life. You're a survivor.

More phone calls for my flatmate. I became convinced that it was the second model. That high creaky voice had to belong to her. It was astounding to me how my flatmate managed it – he was not what you'd call a looker. But he had underworld drug connections and I think the young girls were impressed by this. There had to be some explanation. I wondered if the proper girlfriend knew her friend was calling up. Somehow I doubted it.

When a group of rats come across a new, potentially poisonous, food item, the oldest rat eats it first, acting as a taster, so that if it is fatal the loss to the group is minimized.
(My boyfriend, 30 June)

It's terrible, said my neighbour, the artist has had to go to hospital with liver trouble.

Blood poisoning? said my flatmate, going yellow. As he paced up and down the kitchen the undone laces on his trainers made a noise like rat's claws on the floor.

They don't know, said the neighbour. She'll be laid up for several weeks. Maybe months. She's on an IV drip. He shuddered. I hate needles.

Yeah, said my flatmate, rubbing his arm. Me too.

So. The artist was out of the picture, ha ha. The next morning I got up extra early and went to the nearby meat market. It was so early that the sun hadn't risen, even though it was summer. It was so early that, stumbling on to my push-bike in the milky blue light, I wondered why I'd bothered to go to bed. Hauling myself out of it was worth the effort though, to cycle through the empty East End streets towards the market. London seemed soft, blurry at the edges, like a painting. There were a few people around, and minicab companies with their signs still lit, but it was as though we were the only citizens breaking a curfew, and we had to go about our business swiftly and in silence.

I'd only ever been to the meat market during the daytime, to walk through it as a short-cut. Even then, when it was deserted, the iron smell of flesh emanated from the walls and floors, curling into your mouth and under your soft palate, up through your sinuses like a bleeding nose. It was the sort of place you knew was about carcasses, and bones, and a man in white rubber boots sluicing blood off a stainless steel bench with one sweep of his arm. On several occasions, just walking past the place not even going in, I had vowed to myself I'd become vegetarian. But precisely because its atmosphere of dead animals, of marbled muscle and fat, of loosely hanging hooves, was so strong, when I saw the vacuum-packed boned chicken breasts in the supermarket later, bloodless and smooth, it was impossible to equate them with the meat market and so my resolutions were forgotten every time.

Now that I was there, the size and smell of the bodies was far more powerful than I had imagined. Long red and white carcasses, the legs stuck out at helpless angles, dangled from butcher's hooks. There was the whine of electric saws, the creaking and scraping of metal on metal, and men talking in a loud deep burble. It was surprising to see this place that sold death, so empty and haunted during the day, now completely alive. I wished I'd brought my camera. I found a stall that specialised in offal and bought a heart, a liver and a pair of kidneys. They were cold and squishy, reddy black in their plastic bag.

That night the flatmate's girlfriend's friend visited without the girlfriend. She and my flatmate were sitting in the kitchen when the neighbour came over to borrow a cup of rat poison. We'd been going through it like anything, trying to keep them at bay, but he said he'd seen some suspicious-looking droppings on his kitchen shelves. He smelt of disinfectant and was wearing pink rubber gloves. When he saw model number two sitting there at our table he tried to pull the gloves off in a surreptitious way. He sat down and attempted to engage model two in conversation. He even lied, telling her he was still waiting to hear about the Seychelles trip and that it was probably going to happen. She remained unimpressed. She was sitting quite close up to my flatmate, with a manner about her that made me sure they'd been intimate together. Their eyes locked while he was lighting her cigarette, for example. And if I leaned back in my chair I could just see their knees touching underneath the table. To my surprise I began to feel sorry for girlfriend model number one. My flatmate was a very sneaky type indeed.

I told the neighbour that we were all out of rat poison. My aim was to lure them into the street later that night, not to kill them. Why didn't we go out for some dinner, I suggested, so he could get out of his kitchen. There was a cheap Vietnamese restaurant that had just opened up the road. He promised not to order pussy. We left my flatmate and his girlfriend's friend to it, whatever it was. When I got home they were nowhere to be seen. The telephone rang and I felt a charge of guilt, thinking it might be my boyfriend. I don't know why I felt guilty, I just did. But it was the flatmate's girlfriend. Her voice sounded funny and blocked. She asked me if I'd seen my flatmate and I said he was here earlier but he appeared to have gone out. Then she asked me if he was with model number two. I didn't know what to say. Should I snitch on him or not? If I lied and said No, and then her visit turned out to be perfectly innocent, I would be creating intrigue where none really was. But if I said Yes, was that telling tales and would it land him in a heap of trouble? In the end I decided on honesty. Yes, I said, she'd been around here this evening. The girlfriend said Thank you in a quiet voice and hung up. Well, I said to the room, What could I have done?

I laid the blood-smelling organs over a drain on the corner of our street and waited. It had been a long day. I yawned. The digital camera was weightless in my hand and the night was warm, heat still exuding from the concrete buildings that lined the footpath. Sitting on the grocer's stoop, all I needed was a bottle of bourbon. The scene reminded me of a fashion story I'd been looking at that day in *i-D*: models lying about in doorways like homeless people, half-empty vodka bottles scattered on the dirty asphalt around them. You could read the label on the bottles and I wondered if the vodka company had paid for product placement. The clothes were raggy but made out of expensive materials by exclusive British designers. Where there was a leg or an arm exposed, a bruise had been painted on it. Well, I hoped it was make-up. Bruising easily is a sign of a vitamin C deficiency. The story had the title Living Rough, Looking Smooth. This was the sort of area my agent was eager for me to get into. The money on those glamour jobs is apparently terrific.

I waited for maybe two and a half hours, ignoring local nutters and youths in vibrating cars. Finally something happened. The heart started to twitch and jerk downwards into the drain. I had an old piece of pipe ready, and held the heart down with it, the whole thing at arm's length. The first rat squeezed out of the drain to check out what was going on. I grabbed my camera. Another rat emerged on to the street. Through the camera's monitor the image was in night-time infra-red, like a clip from a post-apocalyptic movie. A third rat clambered over the others to the heart, and then another. I chucked the liver and kidneys over to them as well. The offal shuddered and bled under their ratty jaws.

I was hoping that this would be my big break. My boyfriend had suggested two weeks apart, to 'think things over'. If I could sell these pictures to a good magazine, maybe I'd make enough money to take us both on holiday somewhere, and try again. I developed the best shots and wrote a proposal for a photo-essay entitled London at Night. I sent the package off to my agent and waited. My flatmate confirmed that he had indeed exchanged model one for model two, and from the way he was acting I suspected that this would be the beginning of a whole new line in models. It seemed I just had to come to terms with youthful stick-figures around my flat. The neighbour had managed to pick up model one, so there was a great deal of scuttling into houses unseen and whispering behind closed doors. The rat noise had increased. I didn't like the idea of living amongst rodents, but neither did I want to move. With luck, I thought, it'll be a cold winter.

*

Rats follow patterns and daily travel set paths that they are not easily deterred from.
(Library book on rats, 9 July)

Wonderful news. This was my agent over the phone. *C . . .* Magazine want you to shoot a fashion feature for them.

Really? I was surprised. This was the magazine that had turned down my previous effort because of the lack of Attitude. Have you heard anything about the London at Night proposal? I asked.

This is it darling, they want you to do London at Night as a fashion shoot.

I didn't understand. I said, But I gave them photos of rats.

Precisely. The models are lying in the gutter – a recreated gutter in a studio, you can see the studio floor, very Brechtian – and rats are gnawing at the clothes. Perfect.

My eyes felt dry, unblinking. Rats. Are gnawing at the clothes. And the models are lying there.

You are going to be so excited when you hear what they've offered.

Just a minute. I didn't want to hear what they'd offered. They don't want to run London at Night?

The agent sighed. They want to run it as a fashion story. Isn't it brilliant?

Brilliant? I couldn't think. I couldn't think of anything worse.

It's the break we've been waiting for. Her voice changed. Darling I have to tell you, if you're not excited about this, then . . .

The rest went unsaid. If I wasn't excited about this, then she wasn't excited about me.

I'll call you back.

That night, along with the usual sirens and shop alarms, some bloody pipe player kept me awake. I think it was coming from the Muslim community building round the corner. To tell the truth it was quite a pleasant sound, reedy and melodic, and seemed strangely incongruous in our dirty little neighbourhood. I lay staring at the wall, listening to it and sweating slightly in the heat. I was thinking about how I'd stolen the artist's idea.

Chin

Gish Jen

I was not his friend, although I was not one of the main kids who hounded him up on to the shed roof either. Sure I'd lob a rock or two, but this was our stage of life, someplace between the arm and the fist. Not to chuck nothing would have been against nature, and I never did him one he couldn't duck easy, especially being as fast as he was, basically the fastest kid in the ninth grade. He was a good climber too, you had to give him that, the only kid who could scale that shed wall, period. Because that wall didn't have no hand holds or foot holds. In fact, the naked eye would have pronounced that wall plain old concrete, you had to wonder if the kid had some kind of special vision, that he could look at that wall and see a way up. Maybe where we saw wall he saw cracks, or maybe there was something he knew in his body about walls, or maybe they didn't have walls in China, besides the Great Wall that is, so that he knew a wall was only a wall because we thought it was a wall. That might be getting philosophical. But you know, I've seen guys do that in basketball, find the basket in ways you can't account for. You can rewind the tape and watch the replay until your eyeballs pop but finally you've got to say obstacles are not always obstacles for these guys, things melt away for them.

Gus said it was on account of there was monkey feet inside his sneakers that the kid could get up there. That was the day the kid started stockpiling the rocks we threw and raining them back down on us. A fall day, full of the fine crack and smell of people burning leaves illegally. It was just like the monkeys in the zoo when they get mad at the zookeepers, that's what I said. I saw that on TV once. But Gus blew a smoke ring and considered it like art and said even though you couldn't see the kid's monkey feet, they were like hands and could grip on to thing. He said you've never seen such long toes, or such weird toe-nails either, and that the toe-nails were these little bitty slits, like his eyes. And that, he said, was why he was going to drown me in a douche bag if I threw any more rocks without paying attention, he said I was fucking arming the ape.

We didn't live in the same building, that kid and me. His name was Chin or something, like Chin-up we used to say, and his family lived in the garden apartment next door to ours. This was in scenic Yonkers, New York, home of Central Avenue. We were both stuck on the ground floor where everyone could look right into your kitchen, it was like having people look up your dress my ma said, and they were smack across the alley from us. So you see if I'd really wanted to nail him with a rock I could've done it any time their windows were open if I didn't want to break any glass, and I could have done it any time at all if I didn't care about noise and commotion and getting a JD card like the Beyer kid got for climbing the water tower. Of course, they didn't open their windows much, the Chins. My ma said it was because they were Chinese people – you know, like Chinese food, from China, she said, and then she cuffed me for playing dumb and getting her to explain what a Chinese was when they were getting to be a fact of life. Not like in California or Queens, but they were definitely proliferating, along with a lot of other people who could tell you where they came from, if they spoke English. They weren't like us who came from Yonkers and didn't have no special foods, unless you wanted to count fries. Gus never could see why we couldn't count fries. My own hunch, though, guess why, was that they just might be French. Not that I said so. I was more interested in why everybody suddenly had to have a special food. And why was everybody asking what your family was? First time somebody asked me that I had no idea what they were talking about, but after a while I said, Vanilla. I said that because I didn't want to say we were nothing, my family was nothing.

My ma said that the Chins kept their windows shut because they liked their apartment hot, seeing as how it was what they were used to. People keep to what they're used to, she liked to say, though she also liked to say, Wait and see, you know your taste changes. Especially to my big sister she was always saying that, it was because my sis was getting married for real this time, to this hairdresser who had suddenly started offering her free bang trims any time. Out of the blue, this was. He was a thinker, this Ray, he had it all figured out, how from doing the bang trim he could get to talking about her beautiful blue eyes. And darned tootin' if he wasn't right, that a lot of people, including yours truly, had never particularly noticed those eyes, what with the hair hanging in them. A real truth-teller, was that Ray, and observant as a narc. It was all that practice with women all day long, my ma said. He knows how to make a woman feel like a queen, not like your pa who knows how to make her feel like shit. She was as excited as my sis, that's the truth, now that this Ray and her Debi were hitting the aisle sure enough. Ray was doing my ma's hair free too, every other day just about, trying to fine tune her do for the wedding, and in between she was trying to pitch a couple of last You knows across to Debi while she could. Kind of a cram course.

But my pa said the Chins did that with their windows because somebody put a cherry bomb in their kitchen for fun one day, and it upset them. Maybe they didn't know it was just a cherry bomb. Who knows what they thought it was, but they beat up Chin over it, that much we did know because we could see everything and hear everything they did over there, especially if we turned the TV down, which we sometimes did for a fight. If only more was in English we could've understood everything too. Instead all we got was that Chin got beat up over the cherry bomb as if they thought it was owing to him that somebody put the bomb in the window. Go figure.

Chin got beat up a lot, this wasn't the first time. He got beat up on account of he played hooky from school sometimes, and he got beat up on account of he mouthed off to his pa, and he got beat up on account of he once got a C in math, which was why right near the bomb site there was a blackboard in the kitchen. Nights he wasn't getting beaten up he was parked in front of the blackboard doing equations with his pa, who people said was not satisfied with Chin plain getting the correct answer in algebra, he had to be able to get it two or three ways. Also he got beat up because he liked to find little presents for himself and his sis and his ma. He did this in stores without paying for them, and that pissed the hell out of his pa. On principle, people said, but maybe he just felt left out. I always thought if Chin was so smart he would've known enough to get something for his pa too.

But really Chin got beat up, my pa said, because Mr Chin had this weird cheek. He had some kind of infection in some kind of hole, and as a result the cheek shook and for a long time he tried to avoid going to the doctor seeing as how in China he used to be a doctor himself. Here he was a cab driver – the worst driver in the city, we're talking someone who would sooner puke on the Pope than cut across two lanes of traffic. He had a little plastic sleeve on the passenger side visor where he displayed his driver's license, that's how much it meant to him that he'd actually gotten one. But in China he had been a doctor, and as a result he refused to go to a doctor here until his whole cheek was about gone. Thought he should be able to cure himself, that's what my pa said, and now even with the missus out working down at the dry-cleaners, they were getting cleaned out themselves, what with the bills. They're going to need that boy for their old age, that's what my pa said. Cabbies don't have no pension plan like firemen and policemen and everybody else. They can't afford for him to go wrong, he's going to have to step up to the plate and hit that ball into the bleachers for them. That's why he gets beat, so he'll grow up to be a doctor who can practise in America. They want that kid to have his MD hanging up instead of his driver's license.

That was our general theory of why Chin got the treatment. But this time was maybe different. This time my pa wondered if maybe Chin's pa thought he was in some kind of a gang. He asked me if Chin was or wasn't, and I said no way was he in anything, nobody hung with Chin, why would anybody hang with the guy everyone wanted to break? Unless you wanted them to try and break you too. That's when my pa nodded in that captain of the force way you always see on TV, and I was glad I told him. It made me feel like I'd forked over valuable information to the guy who ought to know. I felt like I could relax after I'd told him, even though maybe it was Mr Chin who really should've known. Who knows but maybe my pa should've told Mr Chin. Though what was he going to do, call him up and say this is our theory next door? The truth is, I understood my pa. Like maybe I should've told Gus that Chin didn't actually have monkey feet, because I've seen his feet top and bottom and they were just regular. But let's face it, people don't want to be told much. And what difference did it make anyway that I didn't think his toes were even that long, or that I could see them completely plain because his pa used to make him kneel when he wanted to beat him? What difference does it make what anybody's seen? Sometimes I think I should've kept my eyes on the TV where they belonged instead of watching stuff I couldn't turn off. Chin's pa used to use a belt mostly, but sometimes he used a metal garden stake, and with every single whack I used to think how glad I was that it was Chin and not me that had those big welts rising up out of his back skin. They looked like some great special effect, these oozy red caterpillars crawling over some older pinkish ones. Chin never moved or said anything, and that just infuriated his pa more, you could see it so clear you almost felt sorry for him. Here he had this garden stake and there was nothing he could do. He had his cheek all wrapped up, and he had to stop the beating every now and then to readjust his bandage.

My pa used a ruler on me once, just like the one they used at school – Big Bertha we called it, a solid eighteen inches, and if you flinched you got hit another three times on the hands. Naturally Chin never did, as a result of the advanced training he got at home. People said he didn't feel nothing, he was like a horse you had to kick with spurs, your plain heel just tickled. But I myself was not used to torture instruments. We didn't believe in that sort of thing in my house, even that time my pa did get out the ruler it broke and he had to go back to using his hand. That was bad enough. My pa was a fireman, meaning he was a lot stronger than Chin's pa was ever going to be, which maybe had nothing to do with anything. But my theory was it was on account of that he knew he wasn't that strong that Mr Chin used the garden stake on Chin, and once on the girl too.

She wasn't as old as my sister, and she wasn't that pretty, and she wasn't that smart, and you were just glad when you looked at her that you weren't her gym teacher. She wore these glasses that looked like they were designed to fall off, and she moseyed down the school halls the way her pa did the highway – keeping all the way to the right and hesitating dangerously at the intersections. But she had a beautiful voice and was always doing the solo at school assembly. Some boring thing, the songs at school were all worse than ever since Mr Shea the math teacher had to take over music. He was so musical people had to show him how to work those black stands, he didn't know you could adjust them. He thought they came in sizes. To be fair, he asked three times if he couldn't do study hall instead. But she managed to wring something out of the songs he picked somehow, everything she sang sounded like her. It was funny, she never talked, this girl, and everybody called her quiet, but when she sang she filled up the whole auditorium and you completely forgot she wore these glasses people said were bulletproof.

It wasn't the usual thing that she got hit. But one day she threatened to move out of the house, actually stomped out into the snow saying that she could not stand to watch what was going on any more. Then her pa hauled her back and beat her too. At least he left her clothes on and didn't make her kneel. She got to stand and only fell on the floor curled up by choice. But here was the sad thing: it turned out you could hear her singing voice when she cried, she still sounded like herself. She didn't look like herself with her glasses off, though, and nobody else did either. Chin the unflinching turned so red in the face he looked as though blood beads were going to come busting straight out of his pores, and he started pounding the walls so

hard he put craters in them. His ma told him to stop, but he kept
going until finally she packed a quick suitcase and put his sister's
glasses back on for her. She had to tape the suitcase with duct
tape to get it to stay shut. Then the Chin girls both put on their
coats and headed for the front door. The snowflakes by then
were so giant you'd think there was a close-out sale on underwear going on in heaven. Still the girls marched out into the
neighborhood and up our little hill without any boots. Right
down the middle of the street, they went; I guess there being two
of them bucked up the sister. Chin's ma started out with the
suitcase, but by the time they reached the sidewalk the sister had
wrestled it away from her. Another unexpected physical feat. It
was cold out, and so dark that what with all the snow, the light
from the streetlights appeared to be falling down too, and kind of
drifting around. My pa wondered out loud if he should give the
Chin girls a lift someplace. After all, the Chins had no car, and it
was a long walk over to the bus stop. But what would he say?
Excuse me, I just happened to be out driving?

He was trying to work this out with my ma, but she had to tell
him first how Ray would know what to say without having to
consult nobody and how glad she was that her Debi wasn't mar-
rying nobody like pa. Ray, Ray, Ray! my pa said finally. Why
don't you go fuck him yourself instead of using your daughter?
Then he sat right in the kitchen window where anybody who
bothered to look could see him, and watched as the Chin girls
stopped and had themselves a little conference for a while. They
were up to their ankles in snow, and neither in one streetlight
cone or the next, but smack in between. They jawed for a long
time. Then they moved a little further up the incline and stopped
and jawed again, sheltering their glasses from the snow with
their hands. They almost looked like life guards out there, trying
to keep the sun out of their eyes, except that they didn't seem to

know that they were supposed to be looking for something. Probably their glasses were all fogged up. Still my pa watched them and watched them while I had a look at the boys still in the apartment and saw the most astounding thing of all – Chin and his pa back at the blackboard, working problems out. Mr Chin had a cup of tea made and you couldn't see his face on account of his bandage, but he was gesturing with the eraser and Chin was nodding. How do you figure? I half wanted to say something to my pa, to point out this useless fact. But my pa was too busy sitting in the window with the lights on, waiting for the Chin girls to shout Fire! or something, I guess. He wanted them to behold him there, all lit up, their rescuer. Unfortunately, though, it was snowing out, not burning, and their heads were bent and their eyes were on the ground as they dragged their broken suitcase straight back across our view.

Virtual

Ali Smith

The girl in the bed opposite was very beautiful. She had dark
hair and dark eyes and the paleness and seriousness of face of
one of those painted Pre-Raphaelite heroines, and it was only
when the nurse came in and the girl peeled back the blankets
she'd coiled round and over her, and slowly pushed herself up off
the bed, that she was shocking. The nurse helped her balance on
the metal scaffold and inch her way across from the bed to the
bathroom at the end of the ward. Her arms were like the arms of
a starving child. Her legs, swollen by the huge knuckles of their
knees and ankles, were like the legs of one of those white bodies
from the last war dead on the ground and bulldozed into a pit;
they moved beneath the zimmer like something practical and
ghastly was making them move.

What's wrong with her? I asked my aunt in a whisper.

I thought to myself that it must be something terrible. She
looked thin enough to be dead or dying.

She's a poor thing, my aunt said. She's an awful nice girl. She's
awful clever. She does the crosswords for us, she knows all the
words. She was at the university but she had to stop.

Then she leaned forward and whispered to me. There's nothing actually wrong with her so to speak. She just won't eat.

My aunt was in hospital for what she called something unmentionable down there. Something unmentionable down there had worn out, she told me when we met on the street a few days ago, and she had to come in and have it seen to. She's not really my aunt; she is my mother's old friend, one of those friends that get called an aunt; and now she is much older than my mother was when she died, her face much the same, a little more lined and bagged, smiling, ten years on and still thriving. I often wonder how it is that she can still be alive if my mother is dead, how it can be that my mother is dead if her friend is still so alive. It doesn't seem possible that one person can just be gone like that and another can still be here, shopping in the same shops or walking along the same pavements or drinking tea out of some of the very same cups even, but it is, it's the most possible, most everyday thing in the world.

It was good of you to come in and see me, she said, her hand on my arm, her too familiar face close to mine. And the flowers are lovely. She gave me a dry kiss on the cheek. The old skin folded along the hollows of her throat and stretched at her collarbone. She smelt of her house and she smelt of something else, the ward maybe, and she waved me goodbye as I left. I waved back.

I passed the thin girl on my way out; she was hunched in blankets, a blanket over her legs, a blanket piled over her stomach. She smiled a polite goodbye at me too. Goodbye. I smiled back.

But that night, as I ate supper, I stuck the fork in the food and rolled it on to the prongs, I held it in front of my mouth, then I put it inside my mouth and closed my lips and pulled the fork out, felt the food on my tongue, chewed and swallowed the food.

I thought about the thin girl. I wondered what her name was. I wondered if there was anything she wanted, anything she would like.

I went back to the hospital the next day.

What a surprise! my aunt said. But you'd no need to come again. I told you yesterday. I'm just about better.

She was sitting up in a chair, wearing her clothes.

Oh, you know, I said. I was passing, I thought you could do with a visitor. And I was wondering if there was anything I could bring you, anything I could do for you, shopping, anything?

But you know I'll be out tomorrow, my aunt said. She shook her newspaper and folded it down, smoothed it out on the bed, shook her head for the benefit of the new lady in the bed next to her. First I don't see her for years, eh Edith, she said, then I can't get rid of her. Doesn't she have a job to go to? She turned to me. What am I going to do with you? What would your mother say to that, eh? her bad daughter being so good at last?

She told me again the details of her operation, all the time really telling them to Edith who was listening and nodding and adding her own commentary. I sneaked a look across. She was still there, she was asleep. She looked like a broken child.

Actually, my aunt was saying, there is something. If you've the time, only if you've the time, mind. You couldn't nip into the house and feed the fish for me. I'm worried one more day might be just one day too many. I'm not wanting them to start eating each other. Here's the key. You only need the one key. Leave it in the geranium on the left-hand side of the mat on your way out.

Her fish were the small kind, the white ones, I don't know the name of the type. They eat flakes of food out of a plastic canister. The flakes have been made out of vegetable matter and bits of different species of fish. You're only supposed to give them a pinch of it, they're supposed to need very little. They swarmed together to the surface to be fed and I poured it out on to their heads, I poured far too much by mistake so that they were swimming in a riot of food spread across the surface of the water, red and yellow and gold. The fish lashed and fought in the food. The smallest ones, too small to fight, waited lower down in the tank for the crumbs of flake to sink to their level.

I had remembered the way to her house. I could have found it with my eyes shut, and her house was the same as I remembered. The living room was the same though the TV looked new beside the rest of the furniture; the old one must have given out. I sat on the couch and watched the fish eat. Her house was small, like ours was when I was a child, the same kind of house. My aunt must have bought hers because she'd changed the front door and changed the windows. Apart from these things it was the same, the same as it had been when we came round here and my mother swung me down in front of the television, she and my aunt in the kitchen doing some serious talking in low voices under the smell and the slow veil of cigarette smoke, the hushed tone of agreement between them, the occasional conspiratorial hushed whoop of a laugh. Can a laugh be hushed and a whoop at the same time? Theirs was, their laughter, it was both; raucous and subdued, wild and withheld; it somehow wouldn't have been quite proper otherwise.

Anyway I don't know why I keep calling her my aunt. Habit I suppose. Because she was just a friend, a friend of the family, my mother had several such friends. I fed the fish for her and I sat on her couch and I wondered what she could have meant, saying I was my mother's bad daughter. My mother's bad daughter. I couldn't think which of the things about me it was, which of the things I might have done, and she might have heard about from someone else in that same hushed secret women's tone, that constituted bad. Maybe I was about to be bad again, because I couldn't remember which geranium I was supposed to hide the key in. I was sure to get it wrong. I almost wanted to get it wrong on purpose. Maybe that was the kind of thing she meant by bad. Like how I wanted to give the fish even more food than they'd already had, though I knew it wouldn't be good for them. They still looked hungry. They were still acting hungry because they knew the light was on and I hadn't gone yet, I was still somewhere in the room.

I was hungry too, even though I'd eaten all day. All afternoon and all that evening I had been eating things. It's not that I ate more than I usually did, and it's not that I eat any more than the average person. It's just that today, for once, I had simply noticed the casual stream and variety of the things I put in my mouth. I had eaten an apple and a nectarine and some bread and coleslaw for lunch. I had chewed my fingers and the ends of several pens. I had eaten a chocolate bar and what was left of a packet of crisps and the whole of a packet of Polos. I ate a dinner of aubergine, mozzarella, tomato, garlic and pasta all mixed together, and after it I ate some lettuce and another apple. I pulled the string off a herbal tea bag, prised the little hinge out of the label and chewed the label and the string into little pieces. Then I drove round to feed the fish and on the way I was thinking about what I could buy to eat at the all-night garage on the way back if I stopped for petrol. They do hot snacks there, hot chicken in greaseproof paper, and barbecued ribs and sausages, as well as a range of sweets and more substantial things in tins like ravioli, beans and Ambrosia creamed rice.

I fed the fish more fish food. I thought of the thin girl. I thought how maybe I could drive a car full of delicious things from the garage to the hospital and spread them prettily out on the bed to tempt her, so that she would want to eat, so that she wouldn't be able not to eat. But probably there wasn't the kind of thing available at the garage that she'd want to eat. I couldn't think of anything delicious enough, or anything delicate enough for her. I thought harder. Tiny dainty scented seafood. Thin slivers of choicest chicken. Things which I had no idea how to get. But if I could get them, say I could get them, I could spread them out and let her choose. I wondered if she was fasting, like the men in Northern Ireland or the suffragettes, or like saints used to do; I wondered if it was pictures of thin women in magazines that had made her decide she didn't want to eat any more. I wondered what had happened to her. I wondered what would happen if someone picked her up and put their arms around her and hugged her close. She looked thin enough to snap into pieces.

All the way home in the car I thought about what it would be like to have someone snap into pieces in your arms. I couldn't get it out of my head; it made me wince, it made my stomach wince to think about it, but I thought about it again and again. The small crack of the bones inside the skin at the slightest pressure, like the snap of dry twigs, or the crack of the shell of a snail under your foot on the pavement before you realize what it is you've done.

Look who's here, my aunt said the next day. Look who's back. I was hoping you'd come. You can give me a lift home.

Her bags were on the bed and the bed was made. I leaned down so she could speak by my ear, but she didn't say anything. She was hiding her hand so only I could see it and jerking her thumb at the old woman next to her, Edith, who looked sweaty and yellow and uncomfortable and was staring into space. My aunt looked at me, shook her head with a slight shake that only I was meant to notice.

Right then, my aunt said cheerily. I'll get myself together.

She moved me out of the way and put her arm in her locker drawer, feeling around to see if she'd missed anything.

A family had gathered round the thin girl opposite. A man sat on the edge of the bed, looked lost and dazed. A small grey woman held one of the girl's hands, telling her things. The girl nodded back, her face white. A small boy, her brother, hung his legs off the chair kicking the metal legs of the zimmer with a dull clanging, and a teenage girl, an inflated version of the pale girl in the bed, poured water from the drinking jug into the plants on the locker table.

I followed my aunt, who had disappeared ahead of me already, out of the ward. Goodbye, the girl said as I passed.

All the people round her bed turned to look at me, all at once. Her father made room for her to see me, and she shifted up the bed, pained and graceful, and took a moment to find her breath. There was a tube attached to one side of her nose, and to a machine behind the bed.

The girl held her hand up until she was able to speak. Please say goodbye to your mother for me, she said. I didn't get the chance.

Yes, I said.

She couldn't wait to get out of here, the girl said. Me neither. She looks a lot better though, doesn't she?

Yes, I said, she does, doesn't she?

You'll be pleased, the girl said. She smiled. Her lips drew back round very white teeth. The smile made her look tired. She held up something red in her hand, like a plastic key-ring. Look what they've brought me today, she said.

I smiled and nodded. It looked like a key-ring. I didn't know what it was.

It's a virtual pet, she said.

They're Japanese. She can't have a cat in a hospital and she was missing the cat, her mother said, smiling at me.

Her mother looked tired too. I smiled back.

Look, the girl said. Look what things you can do with it.

The small boy moved his legs like he was told so that I could come in closer. I put down the case and the bags. The girl showed me how the pet needed baths and games, it needed to be disciplined and taught, and fed and watered, it needed you to push buttons to make sure of all of this, and that it was happy with the amount of heat and light you gave it.

It has this life cycle and you have to get it right, the girl said. Or it dies. It gets a halo above its head and a tombstone. Then she laughed. I hate it, she laughed. It isn't even alive and it's making me feel guilty. Here.

She put the plastic thing in my hand. I turned it over. On a small screen a creature with eyes and no mouth was moving up and down and back and fore very fast in the small space.

The Japanese are fighting over getting these, the father said.

They're really popular, the sister said from behind the bed.

Japanese gangsters are taking over selling them, they're so popular. They're a real fad, the father said.

See, the girl said. It's really irritating.

A noise was coming out of the plastic. The creature was flashing black and white. The girl took it back and peered hard at it. That means it needs a bath, she said. She pressed a series of buttons making a series of beeps. Then she showed me the happy-faced clean creature. It made a melodious beeping sound to show that it was happy.

See? the girl said. It never shuts up.

Everybody laughed. The small boy snorted on the chair. Well if you want it to shut up you could just take the battery out, he said.

Everybody laughed again.

What? the boy said. Well what? What's so funny? All you need is one of those small screwdrivers. You could just take it out. If it was annoying you so much.

As I went down the corridor my face was sore from all the smiling. I found my aunt and drove her home. I came in with her and made sure her cupboard and her fridge had enough in them to see her through the next few days. Then I drove home. At home I went from room to room in my big house, with all the books and things and furniture and pictures. I looked out of the window at the view over the bridge and the houses. I looked out of the back room at the view over the other back gardens. There was a cat asleep on top of one of the sheds. I thought about getting a cat. Then I thought about maybe getting some fish and a tank.

Up so close to the thin beautiful girl I had seen that the skin round her eyes, the skin that made her eyelids, was loosened and roomy. Her hand up close had been like the foot of a bird and you could see lines in it, and lines along her fingers, like the traceries in a leaf.

I couldn't think what to do.

I couldn't imagine what to do next, or how to be able to do it right.

Nature Near

Leslie Dick

When he got a temporary teaching job at UCLA, she didn't want
to go. But it was only nine months, September to June, and he
was completely broke, so she made a deal with him.

'You go first, and find us a place to live. It has to be close
enough to UCLA so I don't have to drive you to work. I won't
make you learn to drive if you don't want to, I'll do the driving,
but I won't drive you to work. And I need a room of my own, for
my work.'

He went ahead, and found a place for them to live on
Strathmore Drive in Westwood, near the campus. He found a
Neutra apartment. The Strathmore apartments of Richard Neutra
were very beautiful, and arguably theirs was the best one – it was
the least changed, containing even the original 'ant-proof cooler'
Neutra designed.

The 'ant-proof cooler' was a small larder-like cupboard in the
kitchen, with a circular metal shelving unit, a series of round
trays which revolved like a lazy Susan. These shelves were supported by three legs, and at the bottom, between the floor and
the lowest shelf, the tubular legs were surrounded with a lip, like

a little cup or frill. This served as a moat; by filling it with oil, ants were unable to pass beyond it, to attack the food kept on the shelves above. Richard Neutra's son, Dion, proudly showed it to them, explaining that all the others (there were eight apartments, of which four, on the right-hand side, were still owned by the family) had been torn out.

The front apartments in Strathmore Drive were separate, one-storey houses, and theirs was at street level, and therefore the most noisy and exposed. On the other hand, it was the only one that had two floor levels, a drop of about two and a half feet, which allowed a very subtle articulation of the interior space. For example, the bedrooms were lower than the living area, and therefore had higher ceilings. Huge ready-made metal windows extended in an unbroken line across the front, yet the bedrooms were less exposed because their floors were lower. It was a clas-sic of Los Angeles domestic architecture, built in 1937, exemplary in its minimalism. There was even an interior plan of their apartment in the big Neutra book, and proliferating myths of various famous people who'd lived there. The Eameses made their first bentwood chairs in the bathroom of one, Orson Welles's girlfriend lived in another, Fritz Lang's girlfriend too, and Luise Rainer, friend of Clifford Odets, had lived in theirs.

So she was pleased, he'd made a good choice. They bought a cheap bed, and a ten foot 1960s Scandiwegian sofa; they bought a small red Quasar TV, with its remote in the form of an identi-cal miniature red TV. They made two tables out of doors on trestles, and acquired four metal folding chairs. Otherwise the place was empty, full of light, showing off its complex volumes and clear lines. They moved in on October 1st, and the spider bit her just before Christmas, in early December.

It had been extremely hot in late November. Unseasonably hot – one blazing day after another, exacerbating the already existing drought. It was hell crossing the parking lot to the supermarket, it was hell sitting at her desk. She hated the heat, reluctant to invest in an electric fan, and everyone was relieved when these weeks of intense heat were suddenly succeeded by an equally intense downpour. For three days, it poured with rain, sheets of water thrown down from the dark sky. Then they had dinner with an acquaintance, who suggested the 1981 Mazda GLC she'd bought was on its last legs.

'The struts are gone,' he said, 'like my old Honda. Does it wobble on the freeway if you're going over fifty? Then the struts are gone – there's nothing you can do when the struts are gone.'

A couple of days later, Sunday morning, she woke up early, about 6 am, with an itchy bottom. The surface of her right buttock felt itchy, and she couldn't come up with a hypothesis to explain why. She'd been reading in the *LA Times* about the illnesses associated with various sporting activities – like tennis elbow, there were many others, including something called 'bikini bottom', a rash particular to swimmers. As she had been swimming regularly in the UCLA Olympic pool, she surmised this could be the cause, and they lay in bed together, very romantic, making up a blues song to contain her anxieties. The refrain went like this:

I got those
struts are gone
wobblin' over fifty
bikini bottom blues

It was funny, but the itching got worse, and by late morning it had moved beyond what could be described as itching: it was beyond itching, beyond discomfort, to unspeakable pain. Rain streamed down the big windows, it was dark in the middle of the day; they turned on the lights. Nevertheless, she had to do something, so she took an umbrella and drove down to Wilshire and San Vicente, to the seven days a week pharmacy there.

Then she was lucky – there were two moments when she was lucky, and this was one of them. She was lucky because the pharmacist told her to go to the hospital. She explained.

'I thought it was a rash at first, but now I think it must be some kind of a bite. And I've got no health insurance, and I don't have a doctor, and I wonder what oral antihistamines you can give me without a prescription.'

The pharmacist asked some questions; he said, 'Is the area hot?'

She reached behind and slid her hand under the elastic waistband of the loose cotton skirt she was wearing; she wasn't wearing underpants because of the pain. She rested the palm of her hand flat against her buttock, and yes, it was hot, it was burning up.

'Go to the hospital,' the pharmacist told her. 'This could be very serious, go to the county hospital if you haven't got any money, but go.'

So she did, she went home and told her boyfriend, and then she went to UCLA Emergency, and paid her eighty dollars, and waited. Then she had bad luck – because she saw two doctors, then, this was on Sunday, by now late afternoon, and neither of them knew what it was. The 'area' was beginning to curdle, so to speak, to suppurate, her smooth bottom skin unrecognizable. They didn't know what it was, and they gave her a prescription for antibiotics (she wanted antihistamines), and told her to go home. They said it would get better.

She went home, and it got worse. She couldn't eat, or think, she couldn't function at all. The pain was terrible, an ache and an itch so extreme it was agonizing. By Monday night she was beginning to be very frightened, and first thing on Tuesday morning she went back.

Then she was lucky, again. A young male doctor looked at her bottom and said, 'You've been bitten by the brown recluse spider.'

'I have?'

'Excuse me for a minute,' he said, and left her perched on her left buttock, sitting awry as she was forced to now, wondering what this meant. After a couple of minutes the doctor returned, and he said, 'The doctors you saw on Sunday, they told you what to expect, right?'

'No, no – they didn't. I mean, they didn't know what it was.'

The young doctor became tentative, as if reluctant to break it to her, to tell her what was going to happen. He looked down, as if unwilling to look her in the eye.

'So I . . .'

'You have to tell me,' she said, decisively. It was terrifying, his reluctance. He took a deep breath, and looked up.

'Have you looked in the mirror? I mean, do you know what it looks like?' he asked.

'Yes,' she said; she'd stood in front of the full length mirror on the bedroom door, and craned her neck over her shoulder. The bite (she kept calling it a bite, but the doctor referred to it as 'the wound') was huge, about seven or eight inches long, and five or six inches wide, a glaring oval oblong on her right buttock. At the centre, there was an irregular patch where the skin had turned dark purplish black, about three inches by two inches. This was cracked and leaking, as if disintegrating slowly. Surrounding this area was an expanse of brownish yellow, with purple tinges, about six inches by four inches, and this was enclosed within a bright swollen ridge of red itching flesh, engorged and painful, like a giant insect bite. The redness spread outwards, fading. The doctor explained, carefully.

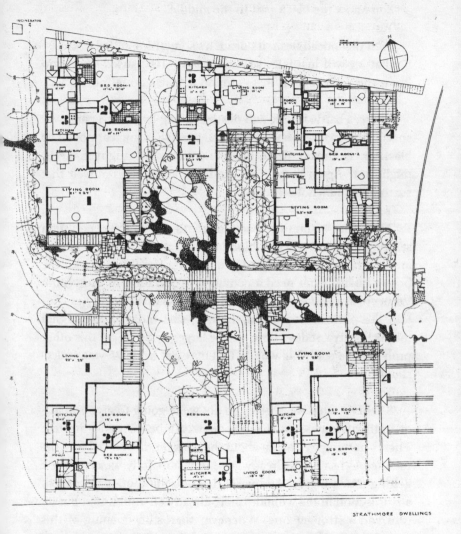

Photo courtesy Dion Neutra, Architect and Neutra Papers – UCLA special collections

'You know the black part in the middle.'

'Yes.'

'Well that's dead flesh, it's dead, it's something called necrosis. So that bit will just fall away eventually.' He paused. 'And you know the yellowish bit that's around it, like a doughnut?'

'Yes.'

'There, a battle for life and death is going on; which parts will succumb to necrosis and which will survive is unclear now. The black bit is already dead, but the yellowy bit might make it, might not.' Again he paused. 'And you know the red welt that surrounds the whole wound?'

'Yes.'

'That's the histamine reaction, that's your immune system sending millions of white blood cells to make a wall, a barrier around this invasion, to try to contain it. The thing is with the brown recluse, you need a certain concentration of the venom for necrosis to take place. So while it makes sense to try to contain the poison, within this barrier, this moat, actually that means the area of dead flesh will be larger, and you get this other problem of a really big wound that may not heal. Do you understand?'

'Yes.'

'So this is what we're going to do: we're going to give you lots of antihistamines, so the poison won't be so concentrated. There's nothing we can do about the dark bit, the black bit in the middle. As I said, it's already gone. But hopefully we can stop it getting much bigger. And we'll give you antibiotics to prevent any infection in the wound; you're already on antibiotics, but I'll give you a stronger one. Whenever there's an opening of this size, there's a real risk of secondary infection. But the problem is, by letting the poison circulate through your body, you get a systemic reaction, you get sick. We have to let it spread, to try to stop the necrosis, but it will affect your liver, and other organs, it will make you feel pretty awful.'

He looked up, and saw her face. He said, 'You know how I know so much about this?'

She was silent.

'It happened to me,' he said, tonelessly. She looked away.

'God, how awful,' she said.

'So you can expect to be sick for maybe three weeks, two or three weeks, and what I did, I just took about five showers a day. Keep the wound very, very clean, and lie down and expose it to the air, and get a lot of rest.'

'Like a burn,' she said.

'Yes, exactly,' he said. 'And come see me next week. And call if it gets much worse. You can expect it to begin to get better in the next day or two, the next two or three days.'

She was too tired to say anything; she thanked him, and got the prescriptions filled at the hospital pharmacy, and paid her money, and drove home, with difficulty, trying to sit in the car with all her weight on her left hip.

She walked up the steps to the door of the apartment; it was still raining. The doctor had told her it was unusual to see a brown recluse, because you didn't feel the effects of the bite until a few hours later. She put it together: the irregular spider web in the corner beside the toilet in the other bathroom – his bathroom. She'd got up in the night to pee, it was the nearer of the two bathrooms. She hadn't turned on the light. She figured the spider had come into the house because of the rain; the frosted glass window in the bathroom was always slightly open. She walked into the apartment and went immediately to get the broom; she went directly to the bathroom and shoved the broom violently down on the spider web, over and over again.

Then she talked, she said, 'We have to make a list, now, we

have to go to the supermarket. They told me I'm going to be ill for two weeks, maybe three weeks, so we need to get some food in, we need to get some food.' Her anxiety was overwhelming.

In retrospect, when she remembered this series of events, this was the bit that seemed hardest of all, that they didn't know anyone in LA well enough to be able to ask for help. Or that she was such a control freak, so omnipotent, that it never crossed her mind to ask for help. In the rain, she got behind the wheel once again, shaky, beginning to feel the shock seeping through, and they drove down to the supermarket and bought food.

Then she went to bed, she swept the floor of the bedroom, she showered, and she went to bed. It happened much as the doctor had described; she took the drugs and felt much worse, she felt very ill. The next ten days passed in a dreamy state: it was like having terrible flu, when you can't read, when you can barely manage to stare into space. Her joints ached, she stumbled on the steps in the hall. She had a fever that came and went without warning. She took four or five showers every day, letting the warm water pour down her back, over the wound. The dead flesh fell away, flaking, breaking up, and new skin began to grow back, slowly. Time passed.

The strangest symptom was the rash on her legs, all over her thighs and calves, scattered, intermittently during this time there appeared little patches of scabrous red marks, which he named 'scary Hawaiis', because they looked like that, a group of irregular islands, and they were scary. First they would be red, and itchy; then they became a little rough, scaly, scabrous; and then they faded, to be replaced by dramatic deep dark bruises, blossoming up from deep under the surface of her skin. These huge dark flowers gradually faded, to be replaced by more of the scary Hawaiis, until her legs were covered with dark purple and yellow blooms, making a muted pattern on her skin.

She couldn't sit down; for a couple of months she had to sit sideways on one hip while it healed. She subsequently developed serious back problems, but never made the connection until the National Health physiotherapist in London, six months later, commented that she'd suffered some 'wastage' on her right buttock, she pointed out it was smaller than the left.

'We'll have to build it up!' she said, in her Scottish accent.

'Oh no, can't we just make the other one smaller?'

'I'm surprised you haven't noticed,' the physiotherapist said, laughing. 'Hasn't your boyfriend noticed?'

When she got home, she ran upstairs to the room where he worked. 'You're a useless boyfriend, according to my physiotherapist. You never noticed my right buttock is smaller than my left, apparently I've suffered some *wastage*.'

He was serious. 'Of course I've noticed, that's where the spider bit you.'

For the first time she put it together: sitting crooked for all that time, and this disc that was out of place, this broken disc, this disc that (according to the physiotherapist) would never get better.

She remembered the complicated pattern of rectangles Neutra made in the bedroom windows, the eucalyptus leaves moving outside. Silver light, long afternoons lying flat, half-conscious. She remembered the time she took a sip of white wine and almost fell over. Her liver was shot, for a few weeks, too busy processing the poison that was dispersed throughout her body. Later she'd met someone at a drinks party, a doctor who specialized in the brown recluse. He told her the venom actually attacks the immune system, and the most up-to-date treatment is to inject cortisone at the site of the wound.

Her boyfriend found a wonderful book called *Poisonous Dwellers of the Desert*, with a lurid hot red cover and a huge picture of a spider, which made things clearer still. One reason the doctors want to limit the size of the wound, the hole in your body, is because in many cases a skin graft is required, and one of the effects of the spider's poison is the skin graft doesn't take. It won't stick, it won't take.

The book said that generally, if you were for example bit on the finger, you would lose the finger, sometimes more. And if you're under two or over seventy, you die.

Possibly she'd been lucky in another way, lucky to be bit on the buttock, where there's plenty of flesh, no joint just under the surface, not like a hand or foot. Poisonous dwellers of the desert: she thought of Los Angeles as a desert, a thin veneer of greenery spread over it. Turn off the sprinklers and it's a desert, she would exclaim with disgust. People loved the desert, they spoke of going to the desert, like going to the mountains, or the country. They spoke of going to the desert with reverence, as if it were something spiritual. She thought of the desert as a place that might kill you. A glance at *Poisonous Dwellers of the Desert* would convince anyone of that. But the desert dweller had been in her bathroom, it was in her house.

Neutra believed in undoing the architectural dichotomy between inside and outside. He thought the home and the garden should interpenetrate, he thought nature should be near, nature should enter the domestic space.

Nature entered with a vengeance, rupturing the surface of her body, leaving a gaping wound, an opening to the outside. The damage to her body was catastrophic: her lower back was gone, her liver and spleen would never be the same. She understood the dark logic of Los Angeles architecture, its misleading, deceptive promise of sunshine and health. Earthquakes and the desert: Neutra's houses are flexible, they give when there's a quake. In Strathmore Drive, it sounded like tigers leaping across the flat roof, and then the shaking started. It was the night Dion came to dinner; he held her hand as the table shook, the whole house vibrating, and he said, 'There's nothing to fear, my father's houses are very flexible; they *give*.'

She understood Los Angeles: under the surface it was malevolent desert and terrifying earthquakes, it was lethal. She understood it in a way she wouldn't have, without the gift of the Neutra house, the dark secret of the brown recluse.

Lucky's Bantam

Romesh Gunesekera

The sun sank into the sea. The fast-blackening sky over Colombo vibrated to the protest of startled crows while we spluttered, from gate to gate, in a three-wheeler examining house numbers. '15A, 15A,' I yelled to the driver above the clatter of his putt-putt motor. The light from his headlamp dimmed as his engine strained to haul us out of the potholes and bomb craters. Crossing a small, choked canal we finally came to Lucky's suburban fortress. '*Adey*, Sir, *this be it!*' The driver revved his motor high and bobbed up and down: 15A was sculpted in stone. Deep-throated guard dogs barked inside.

I was let into a huge dark room by an old man.

'Hallo-hallo, here already!' Lucky's unmistakable voice bounced across. 'Jonas, lights!' he bellowed. The old man shuffled behind me and the whole place was immediately illuminated. I had first met Lucky at a Blue Orchid convention a couple of years earlier. We had got drunk together. We had a good time. He had insisted then that I come and stay at his place the next time I visited Colombo.

Lucky's round boyish face beamed. 'How did you come? You should have phoned. We could have come for you, no.'

I said I took a trishaw.

'My God man, those three-wheelers are killers. Turtles! Turn over all the time. You should have called.' Lucky looked smooth and cheerful. He was dressed in a baby-blue polo shirt with a small crest on the breast pocket and a pair of pale Crimplene trousers. His neat open leather sandals were polished. He shone like a Bombay film star. Lucky had made good money in the last ten years out of cleanliness. He ran a soap factory and had recently diversified into biodegradable detergents. 'Lot of dirty hands these days,' he had joked that first time we had met. 'Fingers in everything.' Now he grasped me with two neat clean hands, 'Anyway, good to see you, *men*.'

'Nice place,' I said glancing around the spacious room.

'Hellava job we had building it.' There was a cackle from the garden beyond the open doors at the far end. Lucky motioned with his head. 'Those are my birds! I must show you.' He pushed me forward. 'But first, your room. You must want to clean up and all.' He looked for my luggage. 'Come, your room is upstairs on the left.'

We climbed to an unexpected white open terrace. A covered walkway connected the west and east wings. Lucky pointed to the left, 'That way. Next is my library-cum-study. Videos and all. You'll like that.' He held me back. 'You'll see the whole garden from the terrace. What do you think? Good idea, no?' We walked on. 'Here *machang*, the guest room.'

The room was carefully designed to balance the needs of privacy and of community: a neat bed, easy chairs, a writing table, a bookshelf with Zane Gray, Agatha Christie and the Jataka Tales. Lucky opened an old Dutch almirah. 'There should be a . . . Ah yes, here's the new soap!' He held up a green bar triumphantly. After a quick inspection of the rest of the room he went to the door. 'So, come down after your wash, when you are ready.' He smiled affectionately, 'It's good to see you, *men*. After so long.'

I unpacked my bag and after a wash and change went out on to the terrace: Lucky's Mogul courtyard. A slightly bruised moon hung overhead, spilling light on to the pristine white marble floor.

'So, everything all right?' Lucky asked when I came back down. He was ticking a piece of blue paper. A long list of names.

'Excellent,' I said. Lucky's face lit up. 'I'll give you the full tour tomorrow. Or Mali, she will. But I must show you the birds in the morning. You'll really like them.' He looked up at the ceiling dreamily. 'First I wanted peacocks. I had one, you know. Tail was a bit of a poor show, but a really fine *royal* blue neck. But people said it was unlucky. *Something terrible will happen*. You know how they talk.' I nodded: the violet feather eyes were protectors for some, but for others they were irredeemably evil. 'Anyway, I had to get rid of the thing. So I got bantams instead. And you should see what I got. The cock is really magnificent.' He laughed juicily. 'First-class fellow. You'll see tomorrow. I'll show you . . .' He was going to say something else but stopped. Mali, his wife, appeared from behind the stairs.

'Sorry to take so long darling, but Emily, our cook you know, has gone and there's so much to do . . .' She sighed and sat down next to me on the buffalo-hide settee. 'Anyway, has he been looking after you?'

Lucky jumped up. 'I say, must get some drinks, *men*.'

Mali picked up Lucky's blue paper and turned it around in her hands. 'You invited *all* these people for tomorrow night?'

'We need a big party, no? We have to show how we can pull these people in, no?' Lucky said. 'Don't worry, Emily will be here in the morning. First thing. There's the whole day to cook.' He turned to me. 'Tonight I ordered a Chinese for dinner. From that Dragon's Nest. A take-out. Tomorrow we can have the full jamboree.'

'Great,' I said slowly drowning in cold beer. Outside the dogs started barking again. 'It's the moonlight,' Lucky explained, 'these Dobers love to bark at shadows.'

'Or Kotta!' Mali added.

'Yes. Or Kotta, my cousin next door. Bugger gets drunk every night.' Lucky rolled his eyes. 'You can see him on the balcony, pissing at the moon. Shouting. He's crazy.'

When I woke up the next morning I walked straight out on to the terrace. The garden below was large and landscaped with cannas, lantanas, bougainvillaea and even a lime grove. At the bottom of the garden I could make out the bird cages: silver mesh shimmering in the morning sun.

Lucky emerged from the room beneath the terrace. 'Ah, Morning! You're up early. Couldn't sleep or what? Come on down, come I'll show you the cock,' he chuckled.

I went down. The lawn was steaming. 'So, what do you think?' Lucky nudged me. I said the garden was a haven. Full of colour, light and life but without the crude frenzy of most Colombo gardens. The grass was neat; the beds scrupulously weeded. Lucky rubbed his neck slowly. 'Have you seen the fruit trees?' He pointed out a *jambu* and an orange tree. 'And over there, that's an avocado! Perfect, no? My little garden of Eden,' he winked.

We wheeled slowly around and slipped into the second half of the garden beyond a low ruined wall. The three stately cages were set together in a clearing. A few white bantam hens were sitting in the sun in one. The other two looked empty. 'The cock sleeps in the middle,' Lucky said. 'The other cage was for the bloody peacock.'

Lucky went to the centre cage and pushed the door. It swung open, unlatched. 'He's out on his morning stroll,' Lucky said. 'He likes to crow outside. Free. Jonas must have let him out.' He shut the door. 'Come, I know where he will be. He usually goes near the papaw trees. There's a log there he likes to perch on, to crow. Come.'

I followed him past the neat vegetable patch along a paved path. We stooped under a jam tree and reached another clearing. I could see the boundary wall and a neighbour's tall house beyond it.

'That's the log,' Lucky whispered.

I could see nothing on it. I looked at Lucky. He shrugged. Then I saw a dark oval shape under a bush. We approached slowly. It did not stir. Lucky crooned, half moaned . . .

I watched not knowing what to do while Lucky crouched by the creature and turned it over. He stroked the feathers and looked up at me. His eyes flooded. Slowly his face hardened. As his fingers searched the body his mouth twisted as if in pain. 'Bastard,' he spat out. 'Bloody bastard.'

'What?'

'I'll get the bugger. You know what he has done?' Lucky raised his voice.

'Who?'

'Bloody Kotta!' He stood up with the bird cradled in his arms. He jerked his head at the house next door. 'Kotta, next door. That fucking bastard. Who the hell does he think he is? Bloody terrorist.' Lucky stared angrily at the house and then yelled, '*Bloody terrorist!*'

I held his arm, but Lucky shouted even louder. '*STUPID BLOODY TERRORIST!*' He shook his fist and yelled again. Then he took a deep breath and turned to me. 'He was shot. Look, this is blood.' He raised two muddy fingers. 'There's a hole here in the chest.' He parted the feathers to show me a scrawny cage of bones wrapped in yellow oily skin. I could see the puncture. 'That's a pellet gun wound, isn't it? Shot with a pellet gun, isn't it?'

I felt accused. 'Yes, it looks like it,' I said.

'You're damn right! And do you know who has a pellet gun around here? Who? Guess who?'

I nodded at the house opposite. 'Your cousin?'

'Cousin? Cousin?' Lucky shook his head. 'A fucking lunatic. A menace. They ought to lock him up. Bloody terrorist. He can't just sit around shooting birds. My bantam.' He stared at the dead bird. 'I'm sorry about this,' he said suddenly. 'Let's go back. I'm going to nail the fucker.' We hurried back to the palace.

Mali was on the terrace, her figure swollen from the heat of the night. 'Why all this shouting? What has happened?'

'It's the cock. Kotta has shot the cock.' Lucky lifted the bird up to show her.

'Shot it?'

'Dead. Shot dead in the heart.'

'No!'

'Yes. I'm going to get the bastard locked up.'

'How could he?'

'He's a drunk. This time he's gone too far. Come on.' Lucky turned to me. 'You go in. I must find the pellet. I'm going to prove he's the killer.' Lucky shouted for Jonas. The old man appeared from behind me. Lucky fired questions at him. He was terrified. Yes, he said, he had let the bird out as usual. It liked to run about. Yes, he heard it crow. No, he didn't stay to watch. He came back to make tea. No, he doesn't remember if it crowed again. Lucky looked at me. 'You know, I noticed something was strange but I couldn't put my finger on it. How stupid of me! There was no *crowing*. It was so quiet this morning. Usually he doesn't stop.' He stared at the dead bird in his arms. 'The body is still warm. I wonder how long he's been dead. That fucking lunatic . . .' I must have looked unconvinced. 'It was him. I'm sure. I'll prove it. Look, there is only one hole. So the pellet is still in the body. From the pellet you can tell the gun, you know.' His forehead gleamed with sweat. He shouted for a knife and started plucking the feathers.

Mali joined us. 'The poor thing,' she said rubbing her heavy eyes. Lucky worked fast. He ran some water from the garden tap into an old enamel basin and bathed the body. He spoke in quick bursts. 'You remember how he shouted the other day? He hated the crowing.'

Mali nodded. 'He keeps drinking until about four in the morning sometimes. Then the rooster wakes him and he goes mad.'

Lucky waved his hand like a busy poulterer. 'You see, he is different. Something is wrong with him. Fundamentally he is not sound.' Lucky's voice had turned entirely reasonable, explaining this simple but critical point. Kotta had always been trouble for the family. His mother had been killed by his father and Kotta had been brought up by Lucky's parents but the stigma of the crime meant that he was never fully adopted. He felt permanently displaced. He developed a drink problem; he lost every job he was given and lived on borrowed money, arrack and small acts of terrorism. He spent his time hurling abuse over the garden wall, gate-crashing parties and making a spectacle of himself, and now this – killing. 'I think he is sick,' Lucky said, slitting the flesh below the breastbone. He intended to demand some serious family action; he wanted to get Kotta certified insane. He cut deeper. The blood flowed in the water. Lucky's fingers poked, pulled, pushed.

Above us the sun had magnified and I could smell the earth

burning. The gully turned red. Mali brushed back her hair. 'Where is that Emily?' she said and went indoors. I followed her feeling groggy. The screen door banged behind us unsettling a piece of dry yellow plaster.

About ten minutes later Lucky marched in with a squat lead pellet pinched between his right thumb and forefinger. 'Here it is!' he said jubilantly. 'I've got it!'

But Mali didn't even look up. She paced the kitchen floor as if trapped in a cage. 'Emily isn't here,' she hissed. 'What will we do?' She shook the blue guest list in the air. 'All these people coming tonight, who is going to cook?'

'She'll come, she'll come.'

'No, she won't. Jonas says she's frightened of that lunatic cousin of yours . . .'

'Kotta?'

'Yes, Kotta. He's been at her. Pestering her, you know, with his wretched . . .'

Lucky's round shining face tightened like a fist. 'I'll kill him. I'm going to kill him.'

Then I heard a crowing outside; a clear, loud call. It came from beyond the garden. From high up: it was Kotta on his balcony. There was nothing I could do to stop Lucky as he raced back into the garden bellowing.

The Death of
Miss Agatha Feakes

Louis de Bernières

Miss Agatha Feakes summons her menagerie of animals; 'Chuffy chuffy chuffy chuffy,' she calls. It is her last day on this earth, but she does not know it yet, and the morning starts in its usual fashion. No one knows why she calls 'Chuffy chuffy chuffy chuffy' rather than the actual names of her dogs and cats, but the village has grown accustomed to it, and only the little children, whose minds have not got used to anything, wonder about it any more. Her voice is like the call of the cuckoo, mellow and tuneful, with a touch both of mournfulness and optimism. Like the cuckoo, her call carries for miles across the fields and coppices, and there is indeed a real cuckoo that roosts in the hurst, who cranes his neck in curiosity and surprise whenever Miss Agatha Feakes calls her animals at seven o'clock in the morning.

Unlike the cuckoo, which is shy, as if ashamed of its own ways and would prefer to pass itself off as a woodpigeon, Miss Feakes is outgoing and conspicuous, even though she lives without human company. She had a lodger for a while, who conducted a lurid affair with the ever-obliging postman, but now she contents herself with the companionship of rabbits, chickens, goats, cats, Labradors, West Highland terriers, and a jackdaw that she rescued when it was a fledgeling. She does not need an alarm clock any more because the jackdaw thinks that it can sing and joins in with the morning chorus. She wears a brown peaked cap because the bird sometimes sits upon her head and was never house-trained.

Miss Feakes feeds them all. The small dogs yap, bouncing up and down like quaint Victorian toys, and the slavering Labradors put their front paws up on the wooden table whose surface about the edges has been scoured by claws for forty years. The cats adorn the centre of the table, and the shelves where plates used to be, otherwise entwining themselves about her legs, which are wound permanently, not only with cats, but also with flesh-coloured elasticated bandage, reminding the village's old soldiers of the inexplicable puttees that they used to have to wear in the old days.

One of these old soldiers is the postman, who originally arrived as the batman to the general who used to own the house next door. He is thin, and very fit from cycling in all weathers. Even in winter his face and the skin of his neck is golden brown, like old waxed pine, and he wears brightly polished army boots that he has maintained ever since the 1950s. He tells the children that his bicycle clips are for catching the change that falls through the holes in his pockets. He whistles when he arrives at the gate, and the dogs come to collect the biscuits with which he has befriended them, and which, for the purposes of his correspondence with the Inland Revenue, he considers to be a legitimate business expense. He leaves Miss Feakes's house until last, because she expects to give him a cup of tea.

He hates it, but he is soft-hearted. 'Do you think the weather'll hold up?' he asks her, as he surveys the grimy newspapers that serve the place of carpets. Miss Feakes would not dream of taking a tabloid paper because the sheets are not big enough, and so she takes the *Daily Telegraph*, of whose editorial outlook she approves. In the evenings she reads about the cricket, and falls asleep over the crossword.

'The forecast's always wrong,' she says, as usual, 'I know all about the weather from watching my animals.'

'Animals can foretell earthquakes,' says the postman, 'so I hear tell.'

He looks at his cup of tea. There is a decade of tannin stains about the rim and an oily film floating on the top. It tastes of cats. Some of them are not very domesticated, and the whole house reeks of warm tom's urine, of wet dogs, of decaying newspaper, of dust. The house exhales a stupefying halitosis that makes the tea and the digestive biscuits taste solely of itself. It is so nauseating that no one can stay in there for longer than twenty minutes, and accordingly the postman rises to leave, his cup of tea unfinished. Today he will buy Miss Feakes a present. It will be a potted hyacinth, whose powerful scent of aunts and grandmothers might improve the atmosphere of the house, and he will find Miss Feakes's deserted body in the kitchen when he comes to give it to her in the morning. After the burial he will go to the graveyard on his own and plant the hyacinth in her grave, so that even death might not defeat his good intentions. Near by the yew tree that was originally planted to secure longbows for the King's army, beneath a mother-of-pearl sky that is reeling and drunken with rooks, he will take off his cap and gaze down upon the new-turned earth, and then, like a true Briton, he will restrain his tears as he paces out his grief along the rutty track that leads to the hill. He will see the deep green of the dogs' mercury, and, above the busy noise of Mr Hamden's tractor, he will be spooked by the cuckoo that sounds like Miss Agatha Feakes calling her dogs.

But Miss Feakes is not yet dead, and she conducts her day exactly as if she will live for ever. She sits in her armchair, and, one by one, she defleas her cats. They sit expectantly, according to the daily ritual, and they jump, purring, into her lap. She combs the fleas from their necks, stroking against the lie of the fur, and then she does their flanks and haunches. She fluffs up the fur of the long-haired ones, and gives them whimsical hairstyles that she then pats flat again, so as not to compromise their dignity for too long. When she does their bellies, they go wild-eyed and silly, and sometimes they embrace her wrists with their front paws, biting at her fingers from sheer pleasure. Miss Feakes extracts the fleas from between the tines of the comb, and drops them into a cereal bowl that is full of scalding water. They struggle a little and die. She likes to poke at them with a forefinger, so that they sink to the bottom and drown more quickly. Miss Feakes keeps all the fur from her combings, and puts it in carrier bags, because one day she is intending to have it spun, and then she can knit herself the softest and most personal cardigan in the history of the world. Sometimes she thinks that it might make more sense simply to use it for stuffing cushions, but really it wouldn't be the same.

When she has finished with the cats, Miss Feakes decides to go shopping. She has the same car that she has had since before the war. It is a grey 1926 Swift four seat open tourer, with black mudguards and running boards, and a high steering wheel. The car is lovingly maintained for free by the two brothers at the garage who belong to a religion that prohibits drink, but at present the hood is falling apart, and she has contrived to lose the wooden dashboard, exposing all the wiring; therefore she takes it out only when her animals have not forecast rain. With long pins she secures a hat that, like her car, was flamboyant in her youth, and heaves at the starter handle. She has been feeling a little weak and woozy recently, and between each effort she pauses for breath and leans on the car, one hand on the top of the radiator for support. After so much time with the one car she has the knack of starting it, though, and it knocks into life and settles down into a steady tick. The car has a crash gearbox, but Miss Feakes is a maestro of the art of the double declutch, and the gears grate only when she surprises it into first. At the end of her drive she honks the rubber bulb of the horn several times, so that people will know that she is coming, and she will not have to lose precious momentum by using the brakes or changing down.

In the village there are forty-two reckless drivers. Forty-one of them are nuns from the convent on the hill, who have altogether too much faith in the protective power of the Blessed Virgin, and the other is Miss Agatha Feakes, who today is going to Scat's Farm Shop in Godalming in order to buy worming tablets, feed for her goats and chickens, a blade for her bow-saw, and a new pair of wellington boots. Miss Feakes cannot easily reach her feet any more, but she has toe-nails like chisels, which destroy the toes of one pair of wellington boots every six months. She reminds herself daily to ask the doctor to cut them for her, but when it comes to the crunch she prefers to forswear the indignity. It is bad enough that he unwraps and re-wraps her bandages, inspecting her varicose veins that are always in danger of ulceration. Twenty years ago he suggested an operation, but she said, 'And who is going to look after my animals? I have responsibilities you know,' and so he never suggested it again. Miss Feakes takes her creatures very seriously; she has agreed with the vet that he will inherit her house in return for free treatment during her lifetime.

Miss Feakes returns from Scat's and unloads the sacks of feed herself, heaving them into the shed and leaving them amongst the tatty collection of rakes and forks and sickles. Miss Feakes always leaves the door of the shed open in summer so that the same family of swallows can breed in the top left hand corner, and today she goes up on tiptoe to see inside, because the chicks are chirping, but she feels a little dizzy and decides to go in for a cup of tea, well-deserved. Outside the kitchen her ancient car creaks as it cools down, and one of her cats wrests the last warmth from the engine by perching on the bonnet.

Miss Feakes is fortified by her tea and digestives, and in the company of her Labradors goes out into the hurst. She has established that if she collects one fallen branch every week and saws it up, she will accrue enough logs to see her through the winter. She has no other heating, and would not have been able to afford it even if she had. The oaks and beeches are kind to her, and she seldom has to wander far, but she likes birch logs best because they split so well. Miss Feakes likes to watch the flames of her fire because sometimes one sees a turquoise flame of unearthly beauty, so one can even look forward to winter.

On the way to the hurst she meets a neighbour. 'Hello Aggy, how are you?' asks Joan, and Miss Feakes replies, 'Orfy ell', because she had not expected to meet anyone and has not inserted her teeth. Her favourite qualifier is 'awfully' and so Joan knows that Agatha is awfully well. 'Lovely day,' says Joan, and Agatha agrees, 'Orfy ice.'

Now Agatha is in the hurst, the twigs breaking beneath her feet, and the pigeons calling. Her dogs put up an iridescent cock-pheasant, who cries petulantly and whirrs away across the field. From the distance comes the sound of tennis games, the hollow clonk of croquet balls. A boy somewhere is shooting a tin can with an airgun, and the pellets zip as the can skips and clatters along a gravel path. Overhead the whoosh of a hot air balloon from the club in Godalming sets her dogs barking, and

Fred, the hippy-haired mechanic from Alfold Crossways, putters towards Hascombe in his home-made motorized hang-glider, which one day he will fly illegally to Ireland, where he will fall in love, never to return.

Miss Feakes finds a newly fallen limb of beech, but it is caught up in brambles, and she hacks at its twigs to disentangle it. She has a billhook that she uses for this, which she also uses to split kindling. In the 1960s she used to imagine that the kindling was Harold Wilson, who was an 'awfully horrid little man'. In this village only one person votes Labour, and only one person votes Liberal. The Liberal is considered a madman, and the Labourite a potential traitor. He owns the pub, however, and therefore has to be put up with. Miss Feakes has voted Conservative ever since 1945, out of gratitude and respect for Winston Churchill.

Miss Feakes huffs and puffs as she drags the limb home. The dogs prance and growl, darting at the other end of it with their jaws, tugging at it, indulging some heroic doggy fantasy comprehensible only in their own misty imaginations. The wood scrapes and bounces on the stones of the track, and Miss Feakes feels an unaccustomed weariness. It is as if her legs are becoming churlish. 'Come on, old girl,' she thinks to herself. She believes that old people live longer if they make no concessions to age, and in any case she thinks of herself no differently now than she did when she was eighteen, and strong and striking.

At the gate Agatha hears the telephone ringing, drops the branch and runs for the back door. Without taking her muddy wellingtons off, she pushes the door open, darts into the kitchen to fetch her teeth, and dashes into the hall. Agatha is terribly excited, because nobody telephones her in the normal run of things. She is pleased that somebody wants to talk with her, she wonders who it is, she feels her heart jump in her chest with anticipation, and then she realizes that the telephone wasn't ringing. 'Oh fire and fiddlesticks,' she says, 'it's that bird again,' for there is a starling in the village that has learned to imitate the telephone, and it flies from oak to oak along with its flock, causing young girls to think that at last he's phoned, causing widows to think that a child has called, causing the rector to dread that it might be the rural dean.

Agatha plonks herself down on the second step of the stair. She feels disappointed and a little sick from all the rushing and hoping. She thinks that, since she's got her teeth in, she might as well phone someone herself. She tries to invent pretexts that she hasn't used before, and then she rings Joan. 'Oh hello Joan,' she says, her voice full of cheeriness, 'awfully nice to see you this morning. I just wanted to tell you that I saw some awfully cheap spades in Scat's this morning, and I thought "I must tell Joan". Didn't your son break yours? If I remember rightly . . . Oh you got another one . . . well never mind. Why don't you pop around later and we'll have tea? I've got some lovely digestives. It would be awfully nice.'

In the house next door, Joan's heart sinks into her shoes. She is making fudge for the Women's Institute, she is trying to listen to a soap opera on the radio, and she remembers all too vividly that Agatha's tea tastes of tomcat's water. She is sweating and uncomfortable, unsure whether or not it's because of the menopause or because of stirring the huge saucepan of boiling goo. 'Oh Aggy,' she says, 'you must come round here. I'm sure it's my turn. About five o'clock?' Joan is fond of Agatha, and even secretly admires her magnificent disregard for housework. Joan suspects that if she were to be widowed and live to a solitary old age, then she would end up just like Agatha too. Joan thinks it remarkable that Agatha's abundant halo of snowy hair is usually immaculate.

Agatha is thrilled to be popping next door later, and it is with renewed verve that she fetches two chairs from the kitchen and uses them to help her saw the log. Her new blade cuts sweetly, and she ensures that the sawdust falls on to newspaper so that she can use it as litter for the hamster. Waste not, want not. Thinking of the hamster inspires her to fetch it from its cage and let it run around her body, up one arm, across the backs of her shoulders and down the other arm. She puts it in the pocket of her cardigan and it falls asleep. Agatha fetches a deckchair and decides to have a doze in the garden, so that she will be feeling as fresh and normal as possible at teatime.

She catches the delicious pre-war smell of Joan's roses wafting in from the garden next door, and is lulled by the rattle and whine of a lawnmower in the middle distance. Her jackdaw flops out of the drawing room window and waddles portentously out into the middle of the lawn. It croaks from time to time, talking to itself about nothing in particular, peering between the blades of grass in the hope of interesting snacks, and then it menaces one of the cats, who regards it with aristocratic disdain and coolly parades away into the rhododendrons. A huge heron flaps slowly overhead, its belly laden with expensive goldfish from the big new pond constructed by the *nouveau-riche* couple who moved in recently because it was so convenient for London. A light aircraft crosses the sun, casting a fleeting shadow upon Agatha and her house and she is suddenly reminded of when the beautiful young men used to do victory rolls directly above, not a hundred feet in the air, teasing the tips of the oaks, and she could see them clearly in their cockpits, with their white silk scarves, and goggles, and leather headgear. She used to jump up and down and wave, and they would smile and wave with one hand as their wondrous and romantic machines swept them back to Dunsfold aerodrome after another successful defence of country and king, the exhausts at the sides of their engine nacelles spitting bravado and orange flame. And that was how she got to know some of the handsome airmen, because they all turned up one summer evening in a three-tonner, and, with the aid of a ukulele, serenaded her from the gate, and then vaulted over it and invited themselves to tea, saying that they simply couldn't resist coming to visit the beautiful girl who always waved to them when they were flying home from seeing off the hun. One day, on her birthday, two of them came over in a Gypsy Moth and dropped roses, and then landed in the field behind so that the cows panicked, and they came in and invited her to a dance at the mess. Agatha smiles in her sleep, remembering that she spent three days bullying the rector's daughter into teaching her how to waltz.

Agatha goes to tea with Joan at five o'clock precisely, and Joan notices that there is a little piece of bramble in Agatha's hair, but she doesn't say anything. They talk about how the village isn't what it was. There's no one to run the village shop, and week-enders and commuters are snapping up the houses so that local people, born and bred, can't afford to live in their own commu-nity. The cricket team is two men short, and Agatha says that she'd play in it herself if she were younger; 'I used to bowl an awfully good googly,' she confides, and Joan says that she didn't know that women used to play cricket. 'Still do,' asserts Agatha firmly, 'Polly Wantage used to play for England.'

'Gracious,' says Joan, 'did she?' Joan is surprised that one can live in a village for so many years and yet know others so slen-derly.

'She was quite the spin bowler,' says Agatha, 'wonderful leg-break.'

Joan tries to imagine Polly playing cricket, but she sees Polly only as she is now, apparelled like a man, in plus-fours, hairy tweed jacket and deer-stalker hat, prowling the woods in unrelenting pursuit of squirrels. Polly has a double-barrelled twelve bore shotgun, and her persecution of squirrels is just one of those quirks of character that no one has ever sought to explain. The children say that she eats them, but this has never been proved. Polly lives in a large house in the woods, at the end of a muddy track that is almost impassable in winter, and she shares it with her life-long companion, a secretive woman who is altogether mysterious. She wears fine dresses and lorgnettes, and is rumoured to be an artist, but hardly anyone has ever seen her. Everybody suspects that Polly and her companion might be more than friends, but nobody has said so openly. Polly has played cricket for England, she shoots squirrels, she is the kind of character who belongs to this soil and these people, in the same manner that the bracken belongs on Busses Common, and it is unwarranted for others to pry into details.

Agatha goes home and calls her menagerie; 'Chuffy chuffy chuffy chuffy chuffy.' She arranges the bowls about the floor, on top of the newspaper, and decides that she will spend the evening knitting another grey cardigan. Agatha is not fat, but she couldn't be bothered with brassieres, and has pendulous breasts. She knits vast and shapeless grey cardigans that she mistakenly thinks will disguise their fascinating motion, and she wears each one until it disintegrates. She sits in her armchair in the living room, with the windows open so that she can hear the linnets sing and her needles click together. 'Shoo shoo,' she says to the cats who come to tug at her wool.

Outside in the hurst, Polly Wantage is shooting squirrels. The twelve bore cracks, the dogs of the village are set to barking, and Agatha hears the little pellets pattering down through the leaves like the first drops of rain. Agatha deprecates this slaughter of innocent creatures, and she tuts about it to herself, but she pardons it because she thinks that Polly Wantage must be slightly dotty.

At eight o'clock she decides to have supper, and goes to make a pot of tea. She arranges four digestive biscuits on a plate, which she will eat slowly in order to make them last.

She feels a sharp ache in her left arm, and then a blow from a sledgehammer seems to strike her from within. She gasps and falls to her knees. She has never known such bone-breaking pain in her whole life, and she is bewildered, breathless, and astonished. She puts her hands to the floor and crawls a little way, but then lets herself collapse slowly sideways amongst the animals' dishes. She smells newsprint, mud, Kitekat and Chappie, and closes her eyes in agony and resignation.

Peace descends upon her like a mother's hand, and she has the feeling that she is flying away over the fields. Below is the stumpy tower of St Peter's Church on the hill, and, twenty miles away, the sparkling angel on the summit of Guildford Cathedral flashes a scintilla of golden light. She is higher than the rooks, and finds herself in a vast and empty space. She looks about expectantly, thinking that someone is coming to meet her, but there is no one at all. Not even her father, who spent his life behind a newspaper and a pall of pipe smoke, nor even her mother, who lived her life as if it were a penance.

There is no one to meet Miss Agatha Feakes. But then she looks down and realizes that there are hundreds of animals; there are cats and rabbits, goats and hens, guinea pigs and dogs. She is surprised to realize that she knows all their names, all their likes and dislikes, all their whimsies. It strikes her as won- drous that her life must have been so abundant in affection.

She is about to pick up the first rabbit that she had when she was six years old, but she becomes aware that someone is coa- lescing out of the light. He is tall and slim, he is dressed in RAF service dress, and he has his peaked cap under his right arm. On the left breast of his tunic he wears the purple and white diagonal stripes of the Distinguished Flying Cross, and the red and white diagonal stripes of the Air Force Cross. She is about to shake hands, but he leans forward and kisses her softly on the cheek. Surprised, she puts her hand to her cheek, and smells Sunlight Soap, brilliantine, and eau-de-cologne. Casually he removes the morning's brambles from her hair, and says 'Hello, old thing.'

'Alec?' she asks, incredulous; 'Alec?'

Flight-Lieutenant Alec Montrose raises a quizzical eyebrow and runs an elegant forefinger along his thin black moustache. He smiles, and Agatha's lips tremble at the memory. 'When I heard you'd been killed,' she says, 'I was most awfully upset. I cried buckets and buckets, for weeks and weeks.'

Alec bends down and puts his cap rakishly on the head of a sleeping Labrador. When he straightens up he puts his right hand on her left hip, and says, 'My dance, I think.' Out in the ether, Victor Sylvester's band strikes up their favourite tune. He draws her close and she lays her head on his shoulder. It is as if he is taking away all the accumulated weariness of life; it empties out of her like water from a jug.

In the arms of Alec Montrose, Agatha waltzes and whirls away on lightened feet, and, far off, the village in which she was born and nourished, and into whose soil her body will melt away, prepares itself for the night.

Notes on Contributors

Louis de Bernières is the author of the much-loved bestseller *Captain Corelli's Mandolin,* and a trilogy of novels set in South America: *The War of Don Emmanuel's Nether Parts, Señor Viva and the Coca Lord* and *The Troublesome Offspring of Cardinal Guzman.* He lives in London where he is currently working on a new novel set in Turkey.

Christopher Burns is the author of five novels, the most recent of which are *In the Houses of the West* and *Dust Raising.* He can often be seen walking in the Lake District with a large Old English sheepdog called Jake.

Peter Ho Davies was born in Britain and now lives in the United States where he teaches creative writing at the University of Oregon. His short stories have appeared in numerous journals including the *Paris Review, Story* and *Critical Quarterly.* He is the recipient of various awards including an O.Henry Prize and a Creative Writing Fellowship from the National Endowment for the Arts. His collection, *The Ugliest House in the World,* was published by Granta Books in 1998.

Leslie Dick is a writer who lives in Los Angeles and London. Her books include *Without Falling*, *Kicking* and *The Skull of Charlotte Corday*. She teaches in the Art Program at the California Institute of the Arts.

Romesh Gunesekera was born in Sri Lanka and now lives in London. His first novel, *Reef*, was shortlisted for the Booker Prize in 1994 and was awarded a Premio Mondello prize (Italy) in 1997. He is also the author of *Monkfish Moon*, a collection of short stories. His latest novel, *The Sandglass*, was published in 1998.

Tobias Hill was born and grew up in London. He has published two award-winning collections of poetry, *Year of the Dog* (NPF, 1995) and *Midnight in the City of Clocks* (OUP, 1996); his third collection, *Zoo* (OUP), comes out in November this year. Hill's first collection of short stories, *Skin* (Faber, 1997) won the PEN/Macmillan Prize for fiction. His first novel, *Underground*, will be published by Faber in January 1999.

Michelle Huneven's first novel *Round Rock* was published in 1997. She lives in Los Angeles.

Alan Isler was born in London in 1934 and went to America when still a young man. He taught Renaissance English literature at the City University of New York for twenty-five years. His first novel, *The Prince of West End Avenue*, was acclaimed on both sides of the Atlantic. In America it won the National Jewish Book Award and was one of the five fiction nominees for the 1994 National Book Critics Circle Award. In Britain it won the *Jewish Quarterly* Fiction Award. His second novel, *Kraven Images*, was pubished in 1996 and *Op. Non Cit.* (a.k.a. *The Bacon*

Fancier), a collection of four inter-related novellas, was published in 1997. He now lives in London.

Gish Jen's short work has appeared in the *Atlantic Monthly*, the *New Republic*, the *New York Times* and the *New Yorker*, as well as in numerous textbooks and anthologies, including *Best American Short Stories 1988* and *1995* and *The Heath Anthology of American Literature*. She has received grants from the Guggenheim Foundation, the Bunting Institute and the National Endowment for the Arts, among other sources. Her first book, *Typical American* (Granta Books, 1998) was a *New York Times* notable book of the year, as well as a finalist for the National Book Critics' Circle award. Her new novel, *Mona in the Promised Land* (Granta Books, 1997), was also a *New York Times* notable book, and was named one of the ten best books of 1996 by the *Los Angeles Times*.

Jen, a graduate of Harvard University and the Iowa Writers' Workshop, lives in Massachusetts with her husband and six-year-old son.

Alice Kavounas, a native New Yorker born to Greek parents, is a Vassar graduate and lives by the sea in Cornwall with novelist Fred Taylor. Her collection of poetry *The Invited* (Sinclair-Stevenson) speaks with 'clarity and force about family, inheritance, love and loss . . .' (Alan Jenkins, *TLS*). 'Avoiding Mrs Taraniuk' is from *Voluntary Exiles*, stories exploring innocence, age and the immigrant experience.

A.L. Kennedy was born in Dundee in 1965. Her first collection of stories, *Night Geometry and the Garscadden Trains*, won the Saltire Award for Best First Book and the *Mail on Sunday*/John Llewellyn Rhys Prize. This was followed by the novel, *Looking* *for the Possible Dance*, which won a Somerset Maugham Award, a second collection of stories, *Now That You're Back*, and a second novel, *So I Am Glad*, which won the Encore Award and was joint-winner of the Saltire Scottish Book of the Year Award. In 1993 she was chosen as one of the twenty Best of Young British Novelists. She wrote the script of the BFI/Channel Four film, *Stella Does Tricks*, and is working on a number of film and drama projects. Her most recent book, *Original Bliss*, a collection of short stories, was published in 1998. She lives in Glasgow.

Hanif Kureishi was born and brought up in Kent. He is the author of the screenplays *My Beautiful Laundrette*, *Sammy and Rosie Get Laid*, *London Kills Me*, which he also directed, and *My Son the Fanatic*. His novels include *The Buddha of Suburbia*, which won the Whitbread First Novel Award, *The Black Album*, the short story collection *Love in a Blue Time* and, most recently, *Intimacy*.

Philip MacCann's short stories have appeared in *New Writing*, *Winter's Tales* and the *New Yorker*. His first collection, *The Miracle Shed* (Faber, 1995) was awarded the Rooney Prize for Irish Literature. He lives with his family in Finland.

Livi Michael is the author of three novels: *Under a Thin Moon*, which won the Athur Welton Award in 1992; *Their Angel Reach*, which won the Faber Prize and a Society of Authors award in 1995, and was shortlisted for the John Steinbeck and John Llewellyn Rhys awards; and *All the Dark Air*, which was short-listed for the Mind Awards in 1997. She lives in Lancashire with the poet Ian Pople and their two sons.

Emily Perkins was born in New Zealand in 1970 and has lived in London since 1994. Her first collection of stories, *Not Her Real*

Name, won the Geoffrey Faber Memorial Prize in 1997. *Leave Before You Go*, her first novel, is published by Picador in 1998.

David Rabe's drama has been honoured by the Obie Awards, *Variety*, the Drama Desk Awards, the New York Critics' Society, and the Outer Critics' Circle. He has won a Tony Award and has received the Hull Wariner Award for playwriting three times. Sir Peter Hall's company recently staged an acclaimed production of *Hurlyburly* at the Old Vic, which later transferred to London's West End. He began his writing career as a journalist and has also written several screenplays, including *I'm Dancing As Fast As I Can* and *Casualties of War*. His first novel, *Recital of the Dog*, was published in 1993. He lives in Connecticut, where he is currently working on a collection of short stories for publication by Grove Atlantic.

Kamila Shamsie was born in Karachi, Pakistan, in 1973. She received a B.A. from Hamilton College, Clinton, New York, and an M.F.A. from the University of Massachusetts at Amherst. Her first novel, *In the City by the Sea*, is published by Granta Books in 1998.

Ali Smith was born in Inverness in 1962 and lives in Cambridge. Her novel, *Like*, was published by Virago in 1997, and her first collection of stories, *Free Love* (Virago, 1995), won the Saltire First Book Award and a Scottish Arts Council award. A new collection, *Other stories and other stories*, will be published by Granta Books in 1999.

Matthew Sweeney was born Donegal, Ireland in 1952. He has published several books of poetry, most recently, *The Bridal Suite* (Cape, 1997), and, for children, *Fatso in the Red Suit* (Faber,

1995). A selection of his work appears in *Penguin Modern Poets 12* (1997). Co-edited two anthologies: *Emergency Kit: Poems for Strange Times* (Faber, 1996) and *Beyond Bedlam: Poems Written Out of Mental Distress* (Anvil, 1997) and co-wrote *Writing Poetry* (Hodder & Stoughton, 1997). Does frequent readings and workshops, up and down Britain and elsewhere, and works regularly in schools. Was Writer in Residence at London's South Bank Centre in 1994/5.

David Treuer is Ojibwe. He grew up in the Leech Lake Reservation in northern Minnesota. His first novel, *Little*, was published by Granta Books in 1997. He is currently working on his second novel, *The Hiawatha*.

Erica Wagner was born and raised in New York City and now lives in London, where she is the literary editor of *The Times*. Her first collection of short stories, *Gravity*, was published by Granta Books in November, 1997; her work has appeared in several anthologies, including *The Ex-Files*, edited by Nicholas Royle and published by Quartet in June (1998). She is working on a book of stories based on traditional music.